James Irvine Robertson is an author and broadcaster living in Highland, Perthshire. He is a descendant of the Stewarts of Kynachan and inherited a chest of family papers in which he discovered this story.

D0971090

James Irvine Robertson

Castle Menzies

10 June 2003

The Lady of Kynachan

A Novel of the '45

James Irvine Robertson

CORGI BOOKS

THE LADY OF KYNACHAN
A Novel of the '45
A CORGI BOOK: 0 552 14298 0

First publication in Great Britain

PRINTING HISTORY
Corgi edition published 1995

Set in 10/11pt Monotype Ehrhardt by
Phoenix Typesetting, Ilkley, West Yorkshire.

Corgi Books are published by Transworld Publishers Ltd,
61–63 Uxbridge Road, Ealing, London W5 5SA,
in Australia by Transworld Publishers (Australia) Pty Ltd,
15–25 Helles Avenue, Moorebank, NSW 2170,
and in New Zealand by Transworld Publishers (NZ) Ltd,
3 William Pickering Drive, Albany, Auckland.

Reproduced, printed and bound in Great Britain by
Cox & Wyman Ltd, Reading, Berks.

To Carolle

CONTENTS

Author's Note	9
Foreword	11
Maps: Kynachan	14
Highland Perthshire	15

Part I
JEAN'S TALE

1	In the Valley of the Shadow	19
2	The Heir's Progress	24
3	A Farewell	29
4	Spectre	33
5	A Proposal	39
6	The Marriage Game	43
7	The Ball	48
8	*Tamhasg*	54
9	Courting	59
10	To Castle Menzies	66
11	Journey's End	73
12	Under Craig Kynachan	78
13	Kynachan	82
14	The Wedding	90
15	In the Bothy	95

Part II
THE RISING

16	Halcyon Days	105
17	The Black Bull	108
18	Interrupted Harvest	115
19	The Menzies Makes Ready	123
20	The Muster	127
21	The Chief Betrayed	133
22	Divided Duty	139
23	Drill	145

24 An Army Passes   150
25 Alang Wi' Royal Charlie   155
26 Edinburgh   164
27 A Thief Taken   168
28 Struan's Trophy   175
29 Soldier's Return   182
30 Waiting   188
31 Meg Enters the Fray   192
32 By Stirling   198
33 The Battle of Falkirk   204
34 Back to the Highlands   209
35 Interlude   216
36 Invaders from the Snow   223
37 Entertaining the Enemy   230
38 Occupation   234
39 The Atholl Raid   240
40 A Funeral and a Siege   246
41 Drummossie Moor   253

Part III

THE AFTERMATH

42 Naught but Whispers   263
43 Fugitives   270
44 In Shackles   274
45 Bissett Advises   279
46 On the Hill   284
47 The Raiders   287
48 A Visit From Kinnaird   293
49 A Proposition   299
50 A Woman's Weapon   304
51 Bohally Takes the Plunge   309
52 A Visit to Perth   317
53 Horse Thieves   323
54 The Road to Blair   329
55 Strike   337
56 Counterstrike   341

Envoy   346

Author's Note

With minor exceptions, the characters in this novel were real. They, and the events in which they took part, are based on history, the contemporary letters and papers of the Stewarts of Kynachan, or tales collected in the eighteenth and nineteenth centuries.

Foreword

The lands of Kynachan lie in Highland Perthshire, at the geographic heart of the mainland of Scotland. The northern boundary of the estate, which was triangular in shape, stretched three miles along the river Tummel, some dozen miles east of its source in Loch Rannoch. The west boundary marched south, up the burn of Shian, and across the long high ridge of Craig Kynachan to the rocky peak of the isolated quartzite mountain, Schiehallion – in Gaelic, *Sith-hallion*, or seat of the Caledonian fairies. From there the line went down the south side of the glen, squeezed between Craig Kynachan and the rising mountain, and ran back to the Tummel.

The old estate of Kynachan lies high in the hills but is open to the sun. Today the property's bottom lands have been drowned by the dammed waters of Loch Tummel; the scattering of houses across the estate's rough and whiskery expanse are holiday homes, save for a single farmstead whose inhabitants make a subsidized living from sheep. On the site of the old mansion of Kynachan stands a nineteenth-century farmhouse that looks across the tranquil waters of the loch towards the house of Bohally. Now much of the landscape is moorland and forestry plantations, interspersed with a few pasture fields – the home of red deer, meadow pipits, grouse, black game, and mountain hares.

Should one climb the rocky slope across the heather and peat bog of Craig Kynachan to the bluff at the east end of the ridge, one can see nestling in hollows among the conifers ruins of some of the old farm settlements, each a cluster of tiny cottages – testimony that this high land once carried a considerable human population. In the time of this story, three hundred people lived on the produce of the estate. After the Rising of 1745, led by Prince Charles Edward Stuart, the society of which the folk of Kynachan were a part was for ever broken.

*   *   *

The geography of the Highlands has always created enormous communication problems. In the past, people farming those glens whose soil could support a crop formed close ties of kinship within what they called their country, where they lived in semi-isolation. To defend themselves against cattle raiders from other glens, they banded together under an elected – later hereditary chief and often established federations with adjacent clans. The Scottish king, using this structure to further his own power, gave charters of land to the most powerful chiefs, which implied that their authority stemmed from him, and he exploited the natural rivalry between them to ensure that none of these subjects became over-mighty.

In such a culture, which has been described as Europe's last tribal society, a chief's status and power depended upon the number of fighting men he could raise. To keep his peace, the king granted vice-regal authority to the magnates and great chiefs within their territories. By the early eighteenth century, when in Edinburgh the modern structure of the law – its advocates, courts, and judges – had already taken shape, in the Highlands a chief could still hang people at his whim.

The Regality of Atholl, the setting of this story, began at Dunkeld, a dozen miles north of Perth, and stretched into the heart of the Highlands. The male line of the old Stewart earls had failed, and a Murray from the Lowlands, the Earl of Tullibardine, had married the Atholl heiress, thereby acquiring her lands. In 1703, the head of the family became the Duke of Atholl. The second tier of power under him – men such as the laird of Kynachan – were the duke's vassals, who, owing him allegiance, were sworn to attend his courts, uphold his law, and mobilize their armed tenants on his behalf and on his request. But the Stewarts and the Robertsons of Clan Donnachaidh, who made up most of the duke's vassals, did not regard him as their blood chief and upon occasion, if it suited them and they thought they could escape the consequences, his voice was ignored.

To most other Scots, and virtually to all Englishmen, the Highlands remained a remote, unknown land, peopled by armed savages who wore outlandish clothes and spoke a barbarous tongue. To such outsiders, little good came from the Highlands, save the herds of scrubby cattle that in the autumn swarmed through the mountain passes on their way south to markets at Crieff and Falkirk and onwards to England. Their drovers were the only Highlanders most southerners would ever see.

The Stuart king, James VI of Scotland, inherited the crown of England, in 1603, to become James I of the United Kingdom. The royal line spelled their name Stuart since Mary, James's mother, had been Queen of France. The French language has no 'w'. In 1688, the Roman Catholic James II abandoned the throne to the Protestant William of Orange. Despite strong opposition by many Scots and a widespread sense of betrayal, the Scottish Parliament was united with that of England in 1707. Eight years later, after the crown passed to George of Hanover, Jacobites, the partisans of James (Lat. *Jacobus*), rose in an attempt to restore the deposed Stuart line. John Stewart of Kynachan raised his tenants and was appointed a lieutenant-colonel in the Atholl Brigade, which went on to capture the citadel of Leith, outside Edinburgh. To demand the rebels' surrender, a government army led by the Duke of Argyll advanced from the capital. From the citadel's walls, John Stewart gave the response in the name of the rebels that is recorded in *The Annals of King George*: 'as to surrendering, they laughed at it; and as to bringing cannon and assaulting them, they were ready for him; that they would neither take nor give any quarter with him; and that if he thought he was able to force them, he might try his hand'.

Argyll withdrew. The rebel army marched on to England to join the southern Jacobites. The Atholl Brigade surrendered after a siege at Preston. On the following day was fought the battle of Sheriffmuir, which was the death-knell of the rebellion. Along with many of the officers, John Stewart was tried in London for treason and had his estate confiscated. For two years, Kynachan reverted to the Duke of Atholl, who had supported the government. But the duke's need for funds led him to sell back the estate, when once more John Stewart became its laird.

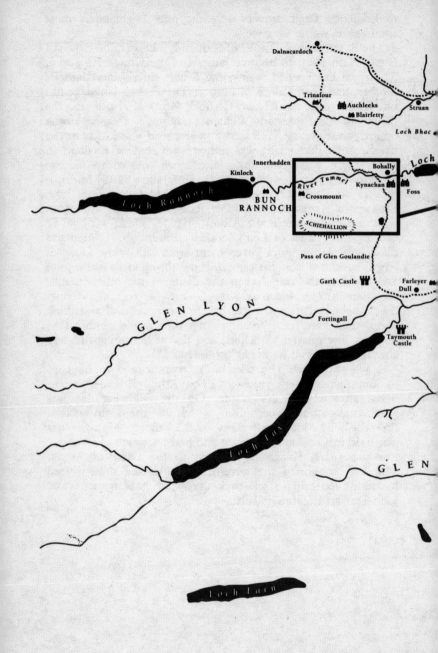

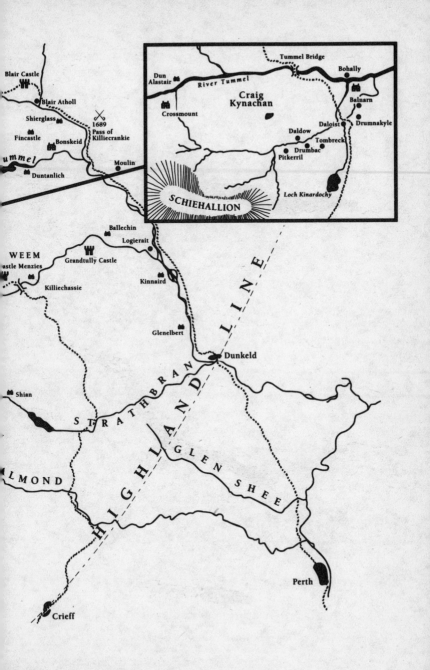

Part I

JEAN'S TALE

1

In the Valley of the Shadow

On the ridge above the meadows bordering the river Tummel sat a grey, single-storey house surrounded by little sheds and outbuildings. The place was built from the stones and boulders that littered the fields and moors around; its roof was a thick layer of heather thatch. Inside, John Stewart, the Laird of Kynachan, lay on his death-bed.

The room was cool. The walls were mud-plastered, and the floor of crude, rush-strewn flagstones sank into the dusty earth. In the wardrobe-like box-bed, the dying man breathed slowly, his eyes shut. His close-cropped hair, normally covered by a wig, was hidden by a linen night-cap. Beneath a small window, a sleeping deerhound stretched out in a patch of summer sunlight.

At the sound of a footstep the man stirred, and his eyes opened. He smiled to find his wife hovering over him.

'How do you feel, my dear?' she said.

'Peaceful, Janet. The Lord is being good to me.'

The laird was in his sixties; his cheeks were plump and unwrinkled and showed little sign of the consumption that had ravaged his body. His wife's hand moved to his forehead. Janet studied the small cupid's mouth that anchored the great keel of his nose to his face. It took all her courage to hide from him the anguish that she felt at the sudden deterioration in his condition, knowing that to show her distress would embarrass him. Although not one to question the ways of the Lord, she found it hard to believe that her husband's time had come. She prayed their son, David, would return before the end.

'The tenants and the country folk're beginning to gather in the yard. Word has gone round the strath that you're not long for this world.'

'Is there news of Davie?' the laird asked.

'No.'

The dying man gave a sigh.

'Don't fret. The Lord will have you, but not just yet,' his wife said, stroking his cheek. 'I'll make sure you live to bid Davie farewell.'

He gave her a small smile and touched her hand. 'A man couldn't have asked for a better wife than you.'

Janet gave a deprecating shake of her head. About her shoulders was a pale woollen shawl with red and blue stripes, and a curch, the white linen cap worn by a married woman, covered her grey hair. She was a plump, busy person.

On a table by the bed were a pewter water pitcher, a stoppered bottle of brandy, a wooden snuff mull, a silver quaich, and a small horn beaker.

'George Cairney's outside and would like to pay his respects. Do you feel up to it?'

'Show him in,' said the laird, his eyes once more closed.

'And when he's gone I'll send Donald in with some broth for you.'

As the woman left the room, the hound's shaggy head dropped back to the flagstones, raising a puff of dust.

'It comes to us all, Kynachan.' The words were in Gaelic. 'But are you sure your time is near?'

John Stewart looked up. George Cairney, tenant of Pitkerril, high in the shadow of Schiehallion, stood by the bed, twisting a blue bonnet in his horny hands. He was near fifty, and his hair and beard were unkempt. The laird gestured for him to take a chair.

'Aye, I'm sure,' the dying man said. 'The strength is fast ebbing from me. Help yourself to a drop of brandy.'

Cairney poured himself a generous measure and tossed it down his throat. 'I'm right sorry to see this day, Laird.'

Pulling a chair to the side of the bed, the tenant sat down, easing his dirk away from a spreading belly. His round shield, the target, was slung over the back of his short deerskin jerkin, and his plaid, the twelve-yard swath of homespun wool woven in muted vegetable-dyed tartan, was gathered at the waist by a broad oxhide belt from which the cloth fell in pleats to mid-thigh. Cairney's hairy legs were bare, and he was shod in crude brogues. On the floor by his side he placed his sword and target.

The tenant cleared his throat. 'I was wondering if you remember Jamie McDougall. He used to help me look after your beasts on the hill. A bit simple.'

'Daft Jamie? I remember Daft Jamie. He was the only one of my lads who didn't come home after the Rising.'

'That's right. He died at Preston. Would you take him my best wishes?'

'I'll do that.'

'And would you tell him the wee brown calf he rescued from the burn when it was in spate sired the three best cows on the hill? He'll be right pleased.'

'I'll tell him.'

'Aye, for sure Jamie'll be one of the warriors there to greet you on the other side, eager to escort the Laird of Kynachan in heaven.' Cairney gave his master a reminiscent smile. 'We would all have followed you into battle against the fairy warriors of Fingal himself. And the rest of the men of this country would have been at our elbows.'

'Do the bards still tell the tale?' the dying man asked, a gleam of animation on his face.

'It will be told so long as there's a single fire alight in Atholl. Even I find it hard now to sift the truth from the legend.'

'We made legends, you and I.'

Cairney shifted in his chair. 'Might there be a drop more brandy, Kynachan?'

The laird nodded towards the bottle. 'I'd rather you drank with me now than at my funeral.'

The tenant needed no further invitation. He drank and said, 'It'll be a grand funeral. Beggars'll flock in from all over the southern Highlands. No greater man than you has died hereabouts for years. I wouldn't be surprised if the duke himself didn't attend.'

John Stewart grimaced. 'The duke. He's a man without honour, fawning over the German lairdie in London.' At this, a fit of coughing overwhelmed him, and the old deerhound raised itself from the floor and came to lay an anxious head on the bed.

Cairney clicked his tongue in reproof, seizing the chance to take a pinch of snuff from the mull on the table. 'You shouldn't upset yourself, Kynachan. You can be assured of one thing. Daibhidh Og will never bring shame on his ancestors.'

'Aye. I thank God for Davie. I only regret I won't see my grandchildren before I die.'

Cairney chuckled. 'Where do you think young Willie Gow got those blue eyes? His mother was a pretty lass, and her belly was swelling long before that husband of hers got her before the minister.'

'I don't mean his bastards. Every lad sires a bastard or

two. I mean heirs.' The laird glanced towards the door to confirm that they were not overheard. 'George, I want you to go and see the wise woman.'

'Granny Dewar?'

'I must make sure Davie finds a woman worthy to be wife of Kynachan and mother to his sons. I want you to tell Granny Dewar to cast a great spell to make this so.'

A look of uncertainty crossed Cairney's face. 'I don't much like going to see Granny Dewar.'

'Like! I don't give a damn whether you like it or not!' The laird's voice was raised in anger. 'I order it. When—' Once more coughing interrupted him, and he raised his head. This time the linen kerchief that he held to his lips turned crimson with blood.

Cairney looked on with alarm. 'Are you all right, Laird?'

'Of course I'm not all right, you fool! But I'll not be dying until I've seen Davie. You go straight from here to Granny Dewar.'

'I shall do as you command, Kynachan.'

The sick man's head fell back to the pillow. 'Now, tell me, are the beasts coping well with the heat?'

'I've never seen them better. Plump and glossy, producing milk faster than the women can turn it into cheese. God willing, the harvest will be good, and folk in this country will have an easy winter – though you won't be here to see it.'

'I'll be in a better world than this.'

'God willing, Laird, God willing.'

Cairney drank the last of his brandy and rose as Janet came into the room. She was followed by Donald, the household steward, who carried a bowl of broth on a tray.

'That's enough, George,' said Janet, shooing Cairney towards the door. 'You'll be tiring him.'

'Aye,' said Cairney. 'I'll tell his people that Kynachan is submitting right cheerfully to the Lord's summons. Farewell, Laird, God speed, and mind me to all the folk I knew.'

'I will. Find a good calf on the hill and give it to Granny – and serve my son as faithfully as you've served me.'

'I shall always be Kynachan's man.' Cairney ducked his head beneath the stone lintel.

'What's this about Granny Dewar?' asked Janet, tucking a napkin beneath her husband's chin.

'Just a charm for Davie, dear.'

Donald spooned broth to his master's lips.

'It must be quite a charm to be worth a calf, Kynachan,' the steward said. 'The minister won't like that. And I'm told he's coming to see you a bit later.'

'You keep that canting black monkey away from me,' the laird grunted.

'John!' exclaimed his wife. 'You can't face your Maker with a curse against a minister on your lips.'

'My soul can survive without the attention of one who's sworn allegiance to King George.'

Donald shook his head. 'It's better to be safe, Laird. You—'

'And you hold your tongue, Donald.' In sudden anger the laird dashed the spoon away from his lips. 'Fuss and nothing but fuss! Thank God a man can die but once.'

2

The Heir's Progress

Although not yet six o'clock in the morning, the heir to Kynachan and his gillie were already an hour from Edinburgh on their way home.

The day was fine, and the high road was busy. Carts loaded with grain and coals creaked past them towards the city. Amongst the traffic were occasional Highlanders, driving cattle or leading ponies laden with furs and skins. These mountain men, recognizing their own kind, called out respectful greetings and received David's jaunty salutes in return. The drovers, owing to the dangers of their profession, carried guns, swords, and pistols under special licence from the military authorities. Other Highlanders had supposedly been disarmed of their traditional weapons after the Rising of 1715, but nowadays the ban was seldom enforced, especially in the case of gentlemen such as David Stewart.

Emerging from a cloud of dust kicked up by the hooves of an oncoming herd of cattle, the two travellers were eyed by a pretty girl who sat on a wall presiding over half a dozen goats. She registered David's handsome face, the eagle feather in his bonnet, and the richness of his clothes and equipment. Then she flicked the hem of her skirts to display every inch of her shapely bare legs.

The young laird reined his horse and swept off his hat in an appreciative bow. Behind him, his gillie, who led a pack pony bearing their arms and baggage, let out a groan.

'For heaven's sake,' said Willie Kennedy, 'have you not had enough for the time being?'

During their week in Edinburgh, the gillie had trailed in his master's wake while the young laird called on lawyers and men of business. Afterwards, often late into the night, Willie Kennedy found himself seated in a kitchen waiting for David to finish more intimate business with the woman of the house. When the sojourn was particularly prolonged, some serving girl might take pity on the plaid-clothed stranger nodding over his

24

ale in a corner of the room. That very morning, David had rousted his tousled henchman from the shadows where each night the kitchen maid spread her bed.

'It's always worth pausing for a sniff of a wayside bloom as fine as this,' said David, ever willing.

'This bloom's too often plucked.'

'Sixpence, your honour,' called the girl. 'Behind yon haystack.'

She spoke the Scots dialect of English rather than Gaelic, the language the two Highlanders had been using. Her head nodded to the nearest of the small heaps of hay in the field behind her. A hundred yards away, a team of rustics was beginning the task of carting the crop towards the farmstead.

'No,' she added after further consideration of David and the gillie. 'You for nothing. A shilling for your man.'

'Your judgement matches your beauty, my dear,' said David.

'A shilling!' growled Willie Kennedy, indignant.

'Cheap for a great hairy heathen brute like you,' said the girl with a toss of her head.

'Hoy!' came a shout from a distant figure, who waved a pitchfork in the air.

'Who's that?' asked David.

'My brother.'

'Love and brothers don't mix,' said Willie Kennedy. 'Come on, Daibhidh Og. Your balls'll be the death of you.'

'No sweeter end, Willie. However,' – David gave another bow and flicked his reins – 'perhaps another day, my dear.'

The girl returned a pout.

Their last evening in the city had begun at a tavern in the bowels of a building in Parliament Close, opposite the equestrian statue of Charles II. There, where men of rank and influence of the Jacobite persuasion congregated, Willie had gossiped with the caddies – the corps of Highland messengers and guides, who knew every householder in the city – while in a private room David and his peers toasted the King over the Water and success to the cause.

Layers of undulating tobacco smoke eddied and swirled above the candles and conversation. The table had been strewn with oyster shells and claret bottles, which serving girls had emptied into tankards as quickly as the harassed landlord could bring them. James Hepburn of Keith, a veteran of the '15, leant across to David.

'How's your father? I was sorry to hear his health is failing,' he said.

'Aye, I fear he'll not be travelling to this city again. He asked me to bid you farewell.'

'Wish him God-speed from me,' said Keith, 'and apologize to him that I'll be unable to make the journey to his funeral.'

The Jacobite laird removed his full-bottomed wig and reversed it to mop the sweat from his brow and shaven head.

'I trust you'll be as strong for the cause as your sire,' continued the speaker, his bloodshot eye fixing on David. The Laird of Keith was known to believe that only one man's loyalty to the Jacobites was beyond question – his own.

'Of course.'

'Your father risked his life and lost his estate. Would you do the same?'

David caught the eye of a friend across the table, and they exchanged rueful smiles.

'For two and a half centuries my family has fought and sometimes died for the Stuart dynasty. As I value my honour, I would do no less.'

Keith considered the reply, shifting his ample bottom on the bench. It was a reasonable answer, but he knew only one man whose honour was beyond question.

'Aye, but times are changing. There's no denying that the country's become more prosperous since the Rising. For an ambitious young man to succeed he must be Whig nowadays. Are you not an ambitious man, Davie?'

'I shall be Kynachan, sir. My only further ambition is to be as fine a man as my father.'

Satisfied, Keith drained his glass, nodding appreciatively when David refilled it.

'Twenty-five years ago,' the older man said, 'your father sent Argyll's army straggling back from Leith with a flea in their ear.'

It was a tale David had heard many times before, when the name of Kynachan had been written into the nation's history books. But it turned out that the Laird of Keith had a fresh angle on the affair.

'My wee brother borrowed a cloak and hired it out to the Whig officers at a penny a time.' The old Jacobite chortled. 'They needed to cover themselves while they shat their fear into the gutters.'

'The drum's nigh,' came a call from the tavern keeper.

It was a warning to those who might want to get home before householders sent showering into the streets the day's accumulation of their chamber pots from windows up to a dozen storeys above. He stood holding the brown paper he would burn to counter the forthcoming stench.

'Are you going on to the assembly?' asked Keith, hurriedly draining his glass. He gave David a wink as subtle as a slamming portcullis. 'No, you'll have no need. It'd be a poor lookout for the natural order of the world if Davie Stewart hadn't found a lassie with a welcoming bed after a week in town. But it's time you got wed, Davie – especially as your sire'll soon join his ancestors. Kynachan must have an heir.'

Now, on a ferry across the river Forth, David was considering the old man's advice. If he were to die without issue and his young sister Clementina were to marry another laird, Kynachan would become a mere adjunct to her husband's estate.

'Is it time I got myself a bride, Willie?' David asked.

The boatman altered course to allow a coal barge right of way, and the ferry's sails flapped in the light breeze. The horses, tethered inboard, snorted uneasily at the oily slap of the waves on the hull.

'You should,' said Willie. 'It may not be long before you're laird, and it makes folk unsure of the future if a laird has no heir.'

The boatman butted in. 'It makes precious little difference to them who their laird is,' he scoffed.

'You silly Lowland man,' replied Willie. 'What do you know about the people of our country? Daibhidh Og is my foster brother. He was raised amongst us and knows our ways. Soon he will be father to his people.'

'Lairds are like winters. Some are worse than others but all must be endured,' said the boatman.

'Watch your tongue, man,' said David mildly. 'You stray dangerously close to insult.'

The boatman paused, considering his passengers, their weapons, and the scowl on Willie Kennedy's face. Then he pulled a jug of whisky from beneath his bench, took a swig, and passed it across.

'Perhaps I was hasty. You're young Kynachan, aren't you? I've carried you across before – and him.' The man nodded at Willie.

'Your manners are as bad as your whisky,' growled the gillie after sampling the jug. 'Get this tub under way. We don't want to be sitting here all day.'

'Would you shackle yourself just for a brat, Willie?' asked David.

'No, but it is not I who will be Kynachan.' Willie re-tried the whisky. 'Women change when they marry. I have seen it often. Beforehand they are beautiful, gentle, and pliant. Then, after a few years' work and a bairn or two, they lose their looks and become shrews. I thank God it's you who must marry and produce an heir. It's your duty.'

'Aye,' said the boatman. 'Who'd ever be a laird?'

3

A Farewell

The heir to Kynachan rode into the yard outside the old stone house to find a small crowd of country people sipping whisky in the warm evening as they waited for a chance to say goodbye to their laird.

The guards at Taybridge had passed on to David news of his father's sudden deterioration, and the young man and his gillie had hurried the last dozen miles home.

David dismounted and stretched his limbs. Willie took the bridle of his horse. The people of the estate rose to their feet and clustered round him, murmuring soft Gaelic greetings.

'Does Kynachan still live?' David asked. Not waiting for a reply, he pushed through the throng to the stone doorway that opened into the living room of the house, where he stopped for a moment to beat the dust from his tartan jacket and trews.

Donald hurried to him from the kitchen.

'Does Kynachan still live?' repeated David, taking from his belt his brace of steel pistols and omnipresent dirk and placing them into the steward's waiting hands.

'Aye, he hangs by a thread.'

'Tell my mother I have come.'

In the sick-room, the old hound padded over with a wagging tail. For a moment or two David looked down at the death-bed, the weariness on his face melting into sadness. He made an effort to compose himself.

'Father?'

The dying man awoke. A weak smile flitted across his face as he looked up at his son.

'I'm glad you're in time, lad,' he said. 'I still have things to tell you before I die.'

'Wait till you're a bit stronger.' David tried to return the smile.

John Stewart grimaced. 'I will not see the sun set tomorrow. But I am not complaining. The Lord has spared me to die in my bed like an old woman. Something I would never have believed.'

David's eyes moistened despite his Highland stoicism, which taught a man to submit gracefully to fate and to curb unseemly emotion. His father, Iain Mor Choinneachain – Big John of Kynachan – was as respected and welcome by the firesides of his tenants as he was in the castles of the mightiest in the land. David saw the vibrant spirit shackled inside a failing body and the will confined to the struggle for each breath. Yet his father's eye remained fearless and alert.

'All went well in Edinburgh?'

'Aye, and folk there pass on their regards to you.'

Old Kynachan waved his hand dismissively. 'I'm past being shriven by the regard of others. Tell me, boy. Is it not time you chose a wife?'

'I must confess the thought had crossed my mind,' said David.

'Good. Kynachan must have an heir. But you need not worry. I have made arrangements for you.'

'What arrangements?'

'To make happen what will happen.'

David thought for a moment. 'I fear that is too subtle for me.'

'No matter. Your son will inherit Kynachan. Then your future will be secure – and mine.'

David sat down by the bedside.

'Take care of your mother,' his father continued. 'She's been a good wife to me and a good mother to you and Clemmie.'

'Of course I will, but you must conserve your strength now.'

The old laird's eyes held a sardonic gleam. 'What in God's name for? I'll not be climbing Schiehallion again. The Lord has pressing business with me.' Seeing the distress these words caused, he reached out and touched his son's hand in a caress. 'Don't fret, lad. It's your turn to be Kynachan. Then it will be your son's. I want my mortal remains to lie in the churchyard at Foss, beside your wee brothers and sisters. Raise a wall round our graves and let that be the burial ground for future generations of our family. Our dust shall mingle until the Day of Judgement.'

'It will be done.'

'And then tear down this hovel. We've silver enough for you to build a mansion house fit for the Laird of Kynachan. You'll have it ready for your bride.'

John Stewart's head fell back against the pillow, eyes closing. Thinking his father had dozed off, David began to rise, but the thin white hand stretched out, detaining him.

'Wait, boy. I'm not done with you yet.' The voice was a whisper, but the grip was strong.

David sat back in his chair. The evening was drawing in, and Donald tiptoed into the room to light the candles. Minutes passed. In the silence, David missed the sounds of everyday life that usually filled the house – the clang of iron pots, the squeal of the roasting spit, snatches of song and laughter. The door to the sick-room had been muffled by a heavy curtain. All he could hear was the lilting murmur of Gaelic from beyond the window, the whimpers of the sleeping hound, and the laboured breathing as his father's life ebbed away.

'Talk to me, boy.'

For a few moments, David was silent, marshalling his thoughts.

'A child I was, maybe eleven. I barely knew you. I was . . . not afraid of you, because you were my father and I loved you – but I was certainly in awe of you. You came to fetch me from my bed while the house still slept, and we climbed together to the top of Craig Kynachan to watch the sun rise. The strath was blanketed in mist. Only the peak of Schiehallion and the other mountains shared the blue sky with us. It was as if we stood on the roof of the world.'

'Aye,' came the dying man's voice over an exhaling breath.

'We saw a dove flying low over the mist, like a gull skimming the surface of the sea. You released your falcon, and it climbed into the sun, then fell from the heavens to smash the dove from our sight into the mist. Only a puff of grey feathers was left hanging in the air.'

His father nodded. 'I remember. It was a fine stoop.'

'You told me tales that day. The mist cleared, and columns of smoke rose from the glen as women banked the morning fires. You talked of our forefathers, of our people, and of the responsibilities that would fall to me when I became laird. You made me see what it was to be a man, what it was to be Kynachan.'

'Take your own son on such a morning to the top of Craig Kynachan.'

'I shall hold his hand, as you did mine, and we shall leap across the peat hags, startling the deer and the muir fowl. I shall tell him tales of his ancestors. How his grandfather made the name of Kynachan ring across Scotland to bring glory to our race. How he tempered strength with gentleness, and how the children of his blood and his people loved him.'

'Swear to me, son, that you will never betray the cause of the true king.'

'You need not ask, Father, but I shall swear it.'

'Aye. You're a good lad.' The old laird's hand fell back on the bed. 'It is finished. Have your mother come to me.'

Janet was soon by the bedside, tears on her cheeks. Her husband opened his eyes, smiling up at her.

'Underneath . . .'

She completed the quotation. 'The eternal God is thy refuge. Underneath are the everlasting arms.'

And with a peaceful countenance, the Laird of Kynachan closed his eyes, ready for his Maker's summons.

4

Spectre

The weather being hot, the body was laid in a sealed coffin
that was rimmed with scented ointments and placed on trestles
in the living room. Beneath the corpse, the grizzled deerhound
took up vigil. People filed past to pay their last respects. In
black flannel, the widow sat silent in an adjoining room,
where she received mourners.

Hundreds came. Janet nodded gravely as they passed and
spoke condolences in Gaelic or English that became more
emotional as the day wore on and the levels of ale and whisky
diminished in the several barrels provided. In mid-afternoon,
David led an all-male procession behind a piper to the burial
ground a mile across the heather in the shade of the ruined
church at Foss. Reading the service, the Episcopalian priest
sweated beneath his full-bottomed wig, cocked hat, black coat,
and gown.

An hour later, back at the house, women wailed the *corranach*
– a lament and eulogy of the deceased – after which fiddlers
struck up a plaintive melody that was accompanied by the
deerhound's dismal howls. By now, with the widow and chief
mourners joining hands in a solemn dance, tears streamed
down the faces of the normally phlegmatic Highlanders. Later,
Janet and fifteen-year-old Clementina led the withdrawal of the
womenfolk to another room. There, drinking claret, the talk
was of the trials and tribulations of widowhood and whether
they were an improvement on those of marriage.

Outdoors, mourners mingled in the meadow, feasting and
exchanging news. Passing on condolences to David, a tipsy
James Stewart, from Drumnakyle, the largest township on
the estate, suddenly frowned.

Their conversation broken, David turned to see what had
caught the tenant's eye. Hobbling through the crowd on the
arm of a pretty but sour-faced girl was a startlingly ugly
woman. It was Granny Dewar.

'What does that witch want?'

'You're not afraid of old Granny, are you, James?' David said with a smile. He knew that the giants in the hills, the kelpies that pounced from lochs to snatch unwary maidens, and the fairies that dwelt on Schiehallion held more significance to his people than Sunday sermons and prayers. The minister might save their souls, but a spell from Granny Dewar was of more immediate concern. It could make them sick, blight crops, ensure a son rather than a daughter, or prevent milk turning sour.

'I'd rather that one kept away from me, Kynachan.'

'Shame on you! She brought your children into the world.'

James Stewart made a sign to ward off evil. 'It's not her midwifery I'm feart of,' he said, hurrying off.

The old woman scowled after him. 'Was that Drumnakyle?'

'It was,' said David.

'Huh! His wife's a better man than he.' Granny Dewar looked scornfully after the tenant's retreating back.

'You're not being fair, Granny,' David said.

She squinted up at him. Granny Dewar had known David Stewart from his birth, when he had been given over to the charge of a wet-nurse and grew from babyhood in a cottage not fifty yards from her own. As small boys, David and his foster brother, Willie Kennedy, had often been on the receiving end of her sharp tongue.

'You've turned mealy-mouthed, Davie Stewart.'

'I'm laird now, Granny.'

'Aye, that's right enough, and I'm sorry about your father. He was a just laird. His yoke lay light on the necks of the people.'

'Thank you.'

'I hope they'll say the same at your own funeral.'

'So do I.'

'Then you'll have to stop your hunting and gaming and gadding about with yon Willie Kennedy and spend more time here with your folk.'

David's smile became a little fixed. 'Have you eaten and had some whisky, Granny?'

'There's time enough for that. I've got something for you.'

The old woman's head and shoulders, in spite of the warm sun, were covered in a heavy tartan shawl. Fishing beneath, she proffered a looped thong, to which was attached a tiny bundle tightly bound in scarlet thread.

'It's from your father,' she said.

David looked puzzled.

'It was his last command. Wear it round your neck for a week and keep away from the lassies. It's to bring you luck and happiness.'

He hefted the bundle in his hands. 'What's inside?'

'I'm not telling you my secrets,' she said indignantly, wagging a finger at him. 'Put it on and make sure you leave it on for seven days and nights.'

She watched as David tied the thong round his neck. 'Mind, no lassies!'

'I'll do my best.'

'You'd better, Davie Stewart.' The old crone parted her lips in a gummy smile. 'You'd better, else your balls'll drop off.'

She and her granddaughter disappeared into the crowd.

'Did I hear that old hag right, Davie?' asked James Robertson of Blairfetty, who was staring, startled, after the old woman. Blairfetty, another vassal of the Duke of Atholl, had an estate a few miles up Glen Errochty to the north. He had been an officer with John Stewart during the Rising and, like David, was one of the leading Jacobites in Atholl.

'She spoke in jest. That's Granny Dewar. She's given me this charm that I'm to wear for a week.'

'Your local witch, eh?' said Blairfetty. He prodded the little bundle doubtfully. 'If you've any sense, you'll wear an armoured codpiece, too.'

The feasting lasted a week. Each day a couple of hundred people expected to be fed and supplied with drink. The country folk came for a few hours, then departed to tend to their chores, but beggars and lairds stayed throughout. The former slept in barns, filling their bellies with oatmeal and whisky and their heads with songs and tales of the late Iain Mor. The latter discussed crops, prices, and politics. They drank bottles of claret at a long oak table in the living room of the house, sleeping off the effects where they sat. As a man slipped into unconsciousness, Donald would see that a lad checked that the mourner's cravat was not too tight. Upon awakening, a new bottle would be before him.

Every social and business transaction in the Highlands was sealed with drink, but drunkenness was scarcely known except at weddings and funerals, when – as David well knew – the importance of a dead man was reflected in the lavishness of the celebrations. To this end, the new Laird of Kynachan had spent heavily to provide his father with a fitting departure.

On the fourth day David took a hunting party to stalk roe deer in the wood of Kynachan, a relic of the ancient Caledonian forest now carefully preserved for its timber. And that night, going to bed sober, he had a dream.

He was scrambling over rocks on the summit ridge of Schiehallion. They were slick with the rain that fell from the sagging clouds. Ahead of him, as grey and blurred as the sky, a cloaked and hooded figure seemed to float over the sharp-edged boulders, never extending the distance between them, never allowing him to close it. Then he was in sunshine, part of the multitude of dancing mourners. Seated on top of the knoll by the house, his father vigorously played his viola da gamba. Suddenly David noticed that his partner was the anonymous grey wraith, but, just as he stretched out his arm to pull back the hood, the dream faded.

'The figure was probably Death,' his mother told him the following morning. 'Was it holding a scythe?'

'No, nothing. And I don't think it was Death. Granny Dewar's charm was meant to bring me luck. Father wouldn't have asked her to show me Death.'

'I'll say a prayer tonight to bless any visions you see, but I wouldn't fret about it. At a time like this we're bound to have strange dreams. For me at night your father is still alive. It's as if the days are bad dreams and the nights are real.'

The following night David was restless and he took off the amulet, placing it inside the upturned wig by his bed. The floor of his room – the room in which his father had died – was still cluttered with bedrolls, on which mourners lay head-to-toe like herrings in a barrel, snuffling in alcoholic sleep. He had barely closed his eyes before the figure of Granny Dewar appeared to him. She was naked, her skinny legs bowed, her empty dugs hanging to her waist, and her mouth split in a toothless grin. In one hand she held a bloody dirk, in the other she brandished, like a hunting trophy dripping gore . . .

David started awake, his chest wet with perspiration. The room was loud with the snores of the sleeping men. He stretched out his hand to the amulet and put it round his neck. After the heat of the day the night air was cool, and he closed the doors of the box-bed, his heart still thumping.

He slept. He was on a pony, climbing a narrow track on a dark winter afternoon. Gritty snow whipped against his face and plaid-wrapped body. On one side rose a sheer cliff; on the other, a bottomless chasm waited to swallow him and his mount. The wind howled, buffeting against him. Rounding a corner, he found that the path was blocked. Before him stood the grey, hooded spectre. The pony snorted its alarm and danced sideways towards the edge of the chasm. Desperately he tried to control it. Eventually the beast settled, but its nostrils remained flared and it rolled its eyes at the still, grey wraith, whose face was hidden by the deep shadow of the hood.

David dismounted and tied the reins to a stunted bush seeded in a crevice in the cliff. Somehow he knew he was dreaming, but he felt the sleet on his cheek, smelt the nervously sweating pony, and was almost deafened by the wind that moaned over the bare rocks. Stretching a fearful hand towards the motionless figure, he muttered a prayer.

Suddenly he could hear the gale roaring away down the chasm, leaving him in complete stillness, broken only by the harsh croak of a raven from somewhere in the crags above and the murmur from a burn far below. Between his fingers as he touched the hood, he felt material finer than silk. He pushed it back. He was looking at the face of a girl, a beautiful girl with wide-spaced, deep blue eyes and thick glossy-black hair. Her hand went to loosen the clasp at the neck of the cloak, and he saw that she wore a gold wedding band. The garment fell away from her shoulders, floating to the ground. She was naked.

A sudden shaft of sunlight turned the fine down on her skin to a golden aura. Her limbs were long and well shaped, and the nipples of her firm breasts were scarlet. She stood motionless, her face expressionless. He was spellbound. Only his eyes could move to feast on her beauty. His gaze was drawn to a small birthmark by her navel. It was shaped like a lion rampant, the crest of the Stewarts of Kynachan.

Then the slim curves of girlhood vanished, and in seconds her belly swelled through the months of pregnancy. She stooped to gather the clean, pink child that emerged from between her thighs, putting it to suckle at her breast. Part of his mind recognized the supernature of what he saw; part recognized that the child was a boy, and David was glad. The baby vanished, and again the girl's belly swelled. The grace of her movements when she stooped to gather the new child rendered the extraordinary sight beautiful. This time it was a girl, and in turn she was followed by another.

The babes disappeared, and the girl-mother was alone once more, her expression serene, her face and body achingly lovely to him. Desire rose within him, thick and choking, and he reached out to her. Then he was awake, his arms raised to the wooden ceiling of the bed. Head swimming with the dream, he pushed open the doors of the sleeping compartment. Streaming through a small window, the moonlight silhouetted a dim figure holding a lighted candle.

'Who's there?'

There came a throaty chuckle.

'Granny said Kynachan would see the *tamhasg* of his future wife this night, and he would have need of me. I'm Mary Dewar.'

Bending as if to kiss him, she snatched the amulet from his neck and held it over the candle. The flame leapt up, and the scarlet bundle was consumed. Her hand slipped beneath his nightshirt.

'Just you lie back, Kynachan.' Hitching her skirts, she climbed into the bed and straddled him. She drew the door closed behind her.

'Aye,' she whispered, 'Granny said you'd be as hard as the barrel of a pistol.'

5

A Proposal

Muffled in a cloak, a tall, thin figure stalked down the cobbles of a narrow Edinburgh wynd, carefully avoiding the snow-covered lumps of rubbish and ordure that he prodded with a suspicious cane.

In the darkening afternoon, ragged, blue-limbed urchins slid down the sinister ice chutes of the gutters, which in other seasons channelled slimy rivulets. The man frowned and swiped his cane at one of the boys, who nearly knocked him down. He was glad to escape their high keening cries, which echoed off the grey masonry of the tenements, when he turned down a pend that plunged into the bowels of one of the buildings. Twenty yards farther on, he mounted the staircase he sought.

On the fourth floor, fixed to the door in front of him was a risp. He forcibly rubbed up and down the ring attached to the serrated bar, which sent a harsh rasp round the landing. Mercifully the barrel – the dirty luggie – containing that floor's slops and excrement was frozen, thereby locking in the city's characteristic stench.

'It's yourself, sir.' Bella, the young housemaid, opened the door and bent her knee in a half-sketched curtsy.

'Is your mistress in the parlour?' The caller handed her his cane, cloak, and hat, a dewdrop trembling at the end of his long nose. He was around thirty years old, and his splayed feet made him walk with a duck-like waddle.

'She's her sister-in-law with her.'

'Announce me.'

He adjusted the tight, powdered curls of his wig and in a mirror smoothed the creases from his well-tailored blue broadcloth coat. He smiled at the result. The mirror returned a glint of gold from his embroidered cuffs.

The girl cocked a quizzical eyebrow at him. 'She'll've heard you at the door. And Miss Jean is waiting for you in the music room.'

'Announce me to Mrs Mercer just the same.'

With a shrug, Bella knocked on one of the hallway's three doors and put her head round. 'It's yon music master, Mr Stewart.'

'Jeannie's expecting him,' came Mrs Mercer's reply.

'I told him, but he wants to see you.'

From inside came an irritated click of Mrs Mercer's tongue. She had given the man five pound Scots only the other day, bringing nearly up to date the bill for his weekly lessons to her three daughters. It would have to do him until she and her family moved to Perth in the spring.

The music master spoke up over Bella's shoulder. 'I have good news, Mrs Mercer.'

'News?' came her voice again. 'Och, I suppose you'd better come in.'

Sitting by the fire with Mrs Mercer was her late husband's sister Meg, a peach-skinned, voluptuous woman, whose blue velvet gown, supported by hoops as large as fashion would ever permit, billowed out from her chair. Anna Mercer, some dozen years older than Meg, wore widow's black.

'Mrs Mercer, Miss Mercer.' Stewart bowed elaborately to each woman in turn. 'I trust I find you both in good health despite our inclement weather.'

His courtesies were a little ostentatious, and neither woman looked on him with much favour.

'Good news, Mr Stewart?' asked Anna Mercer.

'I have purchased a Highland property from His Grace of Atholl. I am now Alexander Stewart of Kinnaird.'

'Oh, yes,' said the younger woman. 'I heard that. And for twenty thousand merks.'

'How did you know I paid so much?'

'I hear most of the news of the town, and I have friends in legal circles.'

The widow sniffed at her sister-in-law. 'And from what I hear many of them are in your bed as well.'

Meg laughed. 'They come just for conversation and good claret. But, Alexander, what on earth does Edinburgh's foremost music teacher want with an estate in Atholl?'

'Until my grandfather lost his lands, for generations my forebears had been the Lairds of Kynachan.'

'Kynachan? Davie Stewart's Kynachan?' Meg said.

'You know him?' asked the music master.

'Who doesn't? Those delicious eyes! Alas, he doesn't come

to Edinburgh much, but he's not a man to forget.'

'He holds the land of my ancestors,' said the music master bitterly. 'His father was the first of his line on Kynachan.'

'Och well, Mr Stewart. I'm glad you're a laird again,' said Anna Mercer, conciliatory. 'Kinnaird, you say? Where's that?'

'North of Dunkeld, near where the Tummel joins the Tay. It's actually East Kinnaird.'

'Very nice for you, Mr Stewart.'

'Of course, I am to be known henceforth as Kinnaird.'

'Kinnaird?' snorted Anna. 'You'll not now be too grand to teach music?'

'Certainly not.'

'And your new-found station won't lift your fees?'

'I shall still tutor the sons and daughters of my peers at my usual rates. I consider it a privilege to introduce young hands and hearts to the muse of Orpheus.'

'Good. And I hope we're not taking up paid time at the moment. Jeannie needs all the teaching she can get.'

'On the contrary, your eldest shows considerable accomplishment in the musical art. I consider her among the most able and charming pupils to have benefited from my instruction over the past few years.'

'Well said, Kinnaird,' said Meg, rising to her feet. 'I'll just look in on the girls for a minute before I go. I shall expect them round at my levee tomorrow, Anna. My mantua maker is calling and he will bring some marvellous fabrics fresh landed in Leith.'

'They can only look, mind,' said Anna Mercer.

'Surely a maiden aunt can spoil her nieces. Would you not agree, Alexander?' Meg put her fan to her mouth in a contrite gesture. 'Forgive me. I must not call you that. You have metamorphosed into the Laird of Kinnaird.'

'I am honoured to be called by my Christian name by a lady of your beauty, Miss Mercer.'

'La, what gallantry. You must call round and dine some time.'

'I should be privileged, madam.'

'I shall send a caddy round to your chambers with an invitation.'

When Anna and Kinnaird were alone, the music master rubbed his hands together in glee. 'An invitation to the table of Meg Mercer! The most influential men in Scotland meet there.'

'Perhaps she asked you because you're a laird now. On the other hand, she may want a fiddler she doesn't have to pay.'

He smiled. 'A fine jest, madam. But I have a personal matter of importance to discuss with you.'

'Oh, aye? And what does the gallant Laird of Kinnaird want with an old widow woman like me?'

'I have made my way in the world, Mrs Mercer. I am now a man of land and fortune, respected by society. Dukes and earls employ me. I have decided the time has come to seek a spouse worthy to bear the sons that will carry my name.'

Anna Mercer laughed. 'By God, Mr Stewart, you flatter me. I am nearly forty; I have three daughters, two grown up. Surely I'm too old for you.'

'No, no, no.' To cover his consternation, Kinnaird pulled a silver box from his coat pocket and took a pinch of snuff. He blew his nose into a handkerchief. 'My dear Mrs Mercer, I could never presume myself worthy to ask for your own hand. I was thinking of the girls.'

'The girls? Thank Heaven for that. I must say, the prospect of marriage to you gave me a nasty jolt.'

'I can't think why,' the music master said, somewhat surprised.

Mrs Mercer gave him a sardonic look. 'No, I don't suppose you could. The girls, you say? Any one of them in particular?'

He waggled his hand. 'Abigail is, perhaps, still too young. Barbara and Jean, though, are both of marriageable age. Neither has experience of the Highland people, but they would soon learn the responsibilities as well as the privileges of being the Lady of Kinnaird.'

'Aye, I'm sure they would.' Anna took a sip from the claret by her side. 'You know, sir, I cannot help but feel you are a little indiscriminate. Is it not usual to settle upon one wife?'

'Oh, I shall – most certainly. But you approve of my suit in principle?'

'Let me put it this way. If one of my girls agrees to become your wife, I shall give her all the support she needs. But beforehand I suggest you make up your mind which of them to ask.'

6

The Marriage Game

Meg Mercer pushed open the door of the music room. Her two older nieces, Jean and Barbara, were sitting at a spinet. Both were dark-haired and wore simple gowns of red wool, with shawls round their shoulders.

'Are you leaving now, Aunt Meg?' said Barbara.

'Is Mr Stewart coming or not?' asked Jean, looking up from the little tune she was tinkling out on the keys.

'No longer Mr Stewart, Jean. He has acquired a Highland estate in Atholl and calls himself Kinnaird. He claims his family once held Kynachan.'

'Davie Stewart's lands?' asked Barbara. She was a tall girl, plump and well-shaped, with warm brown eyes.

'That's right,' Meg said, surprised. 'How do you know a man like him?'

'I don't, but I'd like to,' Barbara said. 'I believe he's very handsome.'

'That's neither here nor there,' said Jean stiffly. 'They say he has scant regard for a lady's reputation.'

'I don't mind that,' said Barbara.

'Well, you should,' her older sister said. After her father's death, Jean had taken it upon herself to be responsible for her sisters and even at times, her mother, who was unused to handling financial affairs. Where both Barbara and Abigail tended to be light-minded, Jean, who was small and slim, was of a more serious nature. This made her fine-featured face seem solemn.

'Anyway,' Jean continued, 'what does Mr Stewart want with mother?'

'Simply to announce that he is now a laird,' Meg said. 'You're coming to my rooms tomorrow. Some new French silks are in town, and, as the beauty and elegance of Mercer girls has dazzled Perth society for generations, I'm planning to have a gown made for each of you. It will be my farewell gift from Edinburgh.'

'How wonderful!' cried Barbara.

'Thank you, Aunt Meg,' said Jean. 'You are most generous.'

The moment Meg had gone, Kinnaird appeared at the door.

'My dear pupils.'

'Good afternoon, Mr Stewart, I hear you have purchased an estate. I am pleased for you,' Jean said.

'And I hope to make you pleased for yourself. Barbara, I wonder if you would be kind enough to leave us alone for a minute or two.'

Barbara raised an enquiring eyebrow at her sister. Jean gave a shrug.

'I was just going out to the kitchen, anyway,' Barbara said.

Kinnaird settled himself in an elbow chair by the tiny fire that struggled in the grate. Jean turned her back to the keyboard but remained seated on her stool and waited. Darkness had fallen. The yellow candlelight reflected off the polished floor and oak-panelled walls, making her face more gentle.

'Jean,' he began and immediately halted. 'I hope you don't mind my calling you by your Christian name.'

'You have done so these five years, Mr Stewart. Or should I now call you Kinnaird?'

'You may call me Alexander, my dear . . .'

The look of surprise in her cool blue eyes made him momentarily lose his thread.

'Mmm . . . I have been talking to your mother. I have some good news for you. You see, I am now established in the world as a person of substance, and it is time I took myself a wife.'

Again he paused. Jean's expression had turned wary. She had caught the drift of his conversation. Oblivious, the music master continued his speech.

'I know that yours is an honourable family, long established in Perth, and that your father was a respected man of the law in this city. You and your sisters have been brought up to be hardworking and virtuous and to understand household economy. In short, I have decided that one of you would make an excellent mother to my children. As you are the eldest, I should like to ask if you would accept my hand in marriage.'

Jean kept her head bowed and her expression hidden. 'I am sensible of the honour you do me, sir,' she began. Now she raised her eyes, and her tone changed. 'You say you have spoken to Mother of this?'

'Yes. She agreed to my suit. She said she would give you the support you would need.'

'Nicely put, Mama,' murmured Jean.

'I beg your pardon?'

'I wonder, Mr Stewart, did Mama explain our circumstances to you? Did you know that we girls have no tochers to bring into our marriages?'

'What?' Kinnaird's smug smile disappeared and he sat up in his chair. 'No dowry? But you must have. Your family has long been one of wealth, and your father a successful man.'

'He was, Mr Stewart, but when he died he left only debts. He lost his fortune in an unsuccessful merchant venture.'

'This is dreadful. I am most distressed by this information,' Kinnaird said, plunged into confusion. He extended a hand to indicate the room around them. 'But how can this be? These chambers cannot be cheap. This is a fashionable part of the city.'

'We depend upon the charity of my uncle, sir. My father's brother. He lives in Perth, which is why we must move there.'

'Your uncle. Ah, yes! He is a wealthy man – and a bachelor. You are his heirs. Is he not providing you with a proper tocher?'

'He has not said so, and, as to being his heirs, that is for him to decide. He may very well leave his wealth to Aunt Meg.'

'Nonsense! From what I hear he is zealous in his piety. He would not condone the . . . the eccentricity of her conduct.'

'Nevertheless, it is quite possible that our family will remain penniless and that we girls will depend entirely upon our future husbands for our support.'

Kinnaird was obviously embarrassed. 'This puts me in an awkward predicament, Miss Mercer. Since your father had no male heir, I was under the impression that you would inherit his estate as heir portioner with your sisters.'

'And, of course, a laird needs a rich wife.'

'Precisely,' he said. 'I am glad that you show such sensibility.' Then he seemed to remember something. 'Ah, but I have heard that your uncle is unwell.'

'This is so,' said Jean.

'Then he might soon be gathered to Abraham's bosom. And you will probably be his heirs.'

'A might and a probably. Coupled, they may produce a mere possibility.'

Kinnaird nodded. 'I fear you are right. I cannot tell you how distressed I am.'

'Under the circumstances I shall permit you to withdraw your proposal.'

'Thank you,' he said. From his broad sleeve he produced the snuff-dappled handkerchief and mopped his brow. 'It is most provoking. I have made no alternative plans to find a wife. I had assumed that you would be most suitable. You even have a certain facility for music.'

'Plenty of young heiresses would be proud to be wife of the Laird of Kinnaird. And some may be more musical than I.'

'Yes, but you are so sensible, too. It is such a pity you have no dowry.'

'Ah, well, it seems clear that our fates are not to be conjoined,' said Jean, and she briskly changed the subject. 'Now, since you will soon be losing me as a pupil, let us return to the study of musicianship.'

'Mother, you might have warned me!'

'I couldn't, but you turned him down, did you?'

Anna Mercer looked up from her embroidery. At her side, Abigail and Barbara were eager for their sister's report.

'Turned him down!' Jean exclaimed. 'He turned me down when I told him I had no tocher.'

'He asked me if I'd approve of him as a son-in-law,' Anna said.

Abigail screwed up her pretty face. 'Him? But he's so old.'

'Maybe so, but he has an estate,' Jean said. 'Besides, he's never been embroiled in scandal and he's gentle. That's more than can be said of many husbands.'

'I wish someone would propose to me,' said Barbara wistfully. 'Even him.'

'How can you!' cried Abigail. 'He looks like a heron and walks like a duck.'

'He was only interested in our money,' said Jean. 'Or lack of it.'

'There's no denying he's a canny man,' said Mrs Mercer.

'I could only marry a man who worshipped the ground I trod on,' said Abigail. 'And I'd probably have to love him back.'

46

'Don't be silly,' replied Jean. 'Reason, not emotion, should dictate one's choice of husband.'

'Still, it must be nice to be asked,' said Barbara dreamily.

Abigail stuck her tongue out. 'You have as much romance in you as a kipper, Jeannie Mercer.'

7

The Ball

'Mother, why should Barbara wear the blue sash?' said Abigail. 'Why can't I have it?'

'Because I'm older than you,' Barbara said, cocking her head to examine her reflection in the long, narrow mirror.

The Mercers had been in Perth for eight months. Their uncle had died soon after their arrival, leaving his considerable fortune to his three nieces. This allowed them to maintain a fine set of rooms in the third floor of a tenement near the centre of the city. Here, as in Edinburgh, rich and poor shared the same building, with the better-off sandwiched between tradesmen on the ground floors and poorer folk on upper floors, with perhaps a beggar family in the garret. On this particular early autumn evening the three sisters were dressing for the Perth Ball.

Barbara sighed. Even the firelight, flickering and dancing on the cream silk of her gown, could not turn her into the creature of mysterious allure she longed to be.

'Do you think I should pull the lacing of my stays a bit tighter?' she wondered aloud.

'As well as looking like a pair of linked sausages, you'd probably suffocate,' said Abigail. 'Mother, it's not fair.'

'Oh, stuff, child!' Anna Mercer was working on Jean's hair. 'You look lovely, Barbara. And they don't need to be tighter, do they?'

'Of course not,' said Jean. 'Mother, should I wear another patch?'

Jean was wearing a hooped gown of yellow silk, woven with purple flowers. Through her hair, in ringlets down to her shoulders, was laced a purple ribbon. She wore an amethyst necklace.

'No, dear,' said her mother. 'People might think you're hiding pox marks.'

'I've cut one of my patches into a heart to put by my dimple,' said Abigail.

'I didn't know you had a dimple, child,' Mrs Mercer said.

'Don't forget, this is Perth, not Edinburgh. They may not be ready for heart-shaped patches here. You won't find a husband if people think you frivolous.'

'Men prefer their wives demure,' Jean put in.

'Nonsense,' said Abigail. 'If men wanted their wives demure you would've found a husband before you were out of the cradle.'

'Abigail, that's extremely ill-mannered,' said her mother.

'I'm sorry,' said Abigail, dancing round the pile of gloves, fans, and ribbons on the table. 'I'm ready. How soon can we go?'

To anyone's eye – in white satin, with seed-pearls decorating the black velvet ribbons in her hair – Abigail would have been a delight. What girl of fifteen, dressed for her first ball, would not?

'Anyway,' she continued, 'we're all bound to find husbands now that we're rich. For our fortune, they'll even put up with frivolity.'

'Don't be so sure,' said Jean. 'Remember, the lawyers still stir the pot.'

She referred to the negotiations between their legal agents and their father's creditors, who believed that the girls were now responsible for his debts. Whether or not the creditors' claims were upheld, the lawyers would doubtless spin the matter out for a decade or more and wax fat on their fees.

'A mere formality,' said Abigail, resuming her dance. 'I shall catch the eye of a beautiful young Highland chieftain with two hundred pounds sterling a year and a finely turned calf. When he sweeps me off to his castle, I shall bear him wonderful sons, who will worship at my feet and fight for the Chevalier.'

'I hope such a thing never happens,' said Mrs Mercer. 'When men fight, the real sufferers are their widows and children.'

'Come, mother,' said Abigail. 'Everyone knows Scotland must have its own king and parliament again.'

'Not those who favour peace and stability.'

'But father supported King James,' Jean said.

'Yes,' said Mrs Mercer, 'but those were turbulent times. It's different now.'

'Your views have changed, have they?' asked Jean.

'Child, in 1715 I was too busy being a wife and mother to have views about anything. To me, the Rising was no more than drunken argument across the dinner table. The more claret your father drank, the more vociferous he became. I

49

know people who suffered for being Jacobites, while those who supported King George and the Whigs have prospered. But I'm just an old widow whose opinion counts for nothing.'

'Your opinion counts to us, Mother. But as you said, things are different now. Anyway, it's time we left for the ball.'

The Perth races, followed by a ball, were annual events that marked the traditional end of the Highland travelling season. Lairds who wished to winter away from their estates announced their arrival in town by coming to the races and ball, and those leaving after a brief season in society made it their farewell and gave their young a last chance to court their social peers.

As they came into the High Street, the Mercers saw that the stone staircase rising to the main entrance of the assembly rooms seethed with an excited throng. Women had replaced their everyday homespun, tartan shawls, and mob caps to don jewels and silks and to powder their hair.

The men outdid them. Lowland gentlemen in silk breeches and satin coats, encrusted with gold embroidery, mixed with Highlanders in plaids and tight-fitting tartan trews. Silver buttons and buckles gleamed, and gorgeous, barbaric jewelled brooches pinned tartans as rich in colour and complex in pattern as dye and artifice could create. Sedan chairs wove through the citizens and servants who lounged in the street, gawking and exchanging gossip. Plaid-wrapped Highland gillies kept to themselves, squatting by a wall, where they told tallish stories and sipped whisky. Over the hubbub came a cacophony of strings and woodwinds being tuned.

Eyes bright with eagerness, the Mercer girls handed their cloaks to a powdered flunkey in darned silk breeches. In the receiving room, candlelight shimmered from the mirrors and girandoles, and the air smelled of wax, rose perfumes, and lavender water. Fine walnut tables stood beneath pier glasses. The walls were lined by broad-seated chairs, their curved cabriole legs making them seem ready to spring out to dance the minuets and reels.

Anna Mercer joined a rookery of black-gowned older women in a side room. Many of them sat playing cards, lax in their chaperoning, not through indifference but because they did not begrudge the young some joy, for they knew that old age would bring bleakness enough to even the score.

The dancing began promptly, and soon the faces of the dozen fiddlers in the orchestra shone with exertion as they swirled the revellers through their paces. After half a dozen numbers the musicians rested, and dancers streamed through to the receiving room for refreshment – claret, tea, ale, or lemonade. There, blue pipe smoke writhed above fluttering fans and the babble of conversation of those too stiff or too married to enjoy the wilder reels.

Her fan whirring like a kestrel's wing, Abigail hovered by her sisters. 'Do you see that man over there?' she said. 'I heard him say he had an audience with Prince Charles in Rome last year.' She caught sight of her face in a mirror and gave a gasp of horror. 'Look at me, I'm all red! How do you manage to look so cool, Jean?'

'You must learn to glide and not let yourself be whirled round like a shuttlecock. Miss Murray used to say she could go through a reel with a copy of *Good Rules of Deportment* on her head.'

'She didn't dance with the clumsy ox who was throwing me around just now. Look, he stood on the edge of my gown and tore it.'

Her sisters gravely examined the small damage to the hem.

'You could sew that in half a minute,' said Barbara.

'Nonsense, it's ruined.' Abigail's fan abruptly ceased movement. 'Heavens!'

On the opposite side of the room an altercation was in progress. One of the guests had drunk too much and was arguing fiercely with his neighbour.

Barbara turned to look. She clicked her tongue in disapproval. 'That's Thomas Moncreiffe. I'm told he's just out of gaol for debt. It's his brother he's shouting at.'

A scandalized buzz ran round the room. A Highlander pushed his way between the two men, but Moncreiffe lifted his gold-topped cane and struck his brother on the head, knocking him to the ground. Then the assailant, his face livid with rage, strode into the throng and disappeared through a door leading to the street.

'How disgraceful!' said Jean. 'Look away, Abigail. We should ignore it.'

'I hope the poor man is not hurt,' said Barbara, who, like the rest of the guests, was craning her neck to see.

Reluctantly Jean looked back. The fallen man was now surrounded by a knot of people. The Highlander had wrested the cane from Moncreiffe and was standing slightly apart from the others, ignoring them. He seemed to be staring across at the Mercers. Jean felt a jolt run through her body as his eye caught hers and she averted her gaze, confused by a feeling she did not recognize.

'Do you see that Highlander?' asked Abigail. 'He's looking right at us. He's really quite handsome.'

'Don't be silly,' said Barbara. 'It won't be us. His eyes will be on someone else.'

'Do you think we can get ourselves introduced?'

'Don't fret,' said Jean, recovering her composure. 'If there is anyone suitable for us to meet, Mother will be scheming away next door, checking the whos and the whys.'

The injured man was helped through to a side chamber, and the music re-started.

'Barbara!' Abigail's shriek drew glances from those immediately round her. 'He's here, your music master – Stewart of Kinnaird.'

Barbara brought up her fan but failed to hide the colour that instantly irradiated her cheeks. 'What's it to me? He's not mine. Jean, what shall we do?'

'Absolutely nothing,' Jean advised. 'In this situation it is up to him to show his manners.'

'He's seen us. He's coming over,' said Abigail excitedly.

'Stop making such a fuss,' said Barbara. 'This could be most embarrassing.'

'Don't be such a goose,' said Jean. 'You liked him. Anyway, if one of us is embarrassed, it should be me. I'm the one he proposed to, not you.'

Kinnaird waddled across the floor towards them. Powder from his full-bottomed wig frosted his shoulders, and his red tartan plaid hung in swags over a bejewelled dirk. His kilt was predominantly blue, and the diced stockings that clothed his shanks were clearly padded to produce a manly calf.

'Ladies, how delightful to see you again after so many months.'

Placing one hand above his otter-skin sporran, Kinnaird flung the other in the general direction of the ceiling, thrust a foot forward, and swayed down in a deep bow. An overpowering scent of jasmine wafted from him.

'Miss Abigail, you were just a little girl,' he said.

'A phenomenon not unusual in our sex,' said Jean. 'And you, sir? I assume the damsels of Edinburgh are still privileged to be taught their scales under your tutelage?'

Kinnaird straightened with an easy, deprecating laugh. 'Ah,

yes, Miss Mercer. I am now often on my estate, but I am still a humble pedagogue of the art of Apollo.'

'Your pupils are fortunate indeed, Mr Stewart,' said Barbara.

'Kinnaird,' he corrected. 'I may say you are to be congratulated on having myself as a friend, Miss Barbara. I shall give you all introductions to my Highland cousins, the only families of note in this part of Scotland.'

'You are very kind,' said Jean.

'Yes,' said Kinnaird complacently. 'Miss Mercer, might I have the honour of the next dance with you?'

'Alas,' said Jean, thinking fast, 'I have to help Abigail repair her gown.'

'Oh,' said Kinnaird, looking Abigail up and down. 'Then you, Miss Barbara?'

'Go on,' Jean told her sister. 'I can manage.'

'My dear Barbara,' gushed Kinnaird, 'you are even more of a jewel than I remembered.'

He strutted off through the throng with the blushing Barbara on his arm. Abigail giggled.

8

Tamhasg

Anna Mercer was established by a window of the ante-room, talking to a black-clad dowager when Jean approached. Without interrupting the conversation, her mother pulled herself along the bench to make room.

'With me it's these pains I get in my belly. I'm regularly bled, but only laudanum makes any difference.'

'You poor soul,' said her listener, a skinny woman in her fifties, who suddenly hauled up her skirt – a concertina of hoops covered in black bombasine – and slipped off her shoe. She wiggled her toes. 'I'm a martyr to my feet, myself. When I do this, I can hardly bear it.'

'You shouldn't do it, then,' said Anna.

'Well, I don't very often, as it happens.' The woman wormed her foot back inside her shoe. 'And how are you, Jean? Are you having a lovely time?'

'Very nice, thank you, Mrs Smyth.'

Next door, the fiddlers dragged their bows in a single chord to announce that another reel was about to begin.

'There's the music, Jeannie,' said Mrs Smyth, 'and here's Sandy come to ferret you out. I'm sure he'll be wanting to dance with you.'

Sandy Wood, a stocky young man and something of a dandy, had smiled and nodded his way across the room to them. The queue of his wig was tied with a small scarlet silk bow.

'My dear Mistress Smyth, I swear you seem younger every time I clap eyes on you.' Sandy stepped back, cocking his head. 'And Mrs Mercer. Again I am struck by the good fortune of this fair city in being blessed with the presence of—'

'Stop your blethers, Sandy,' said Anna. 'You've not come here to flatter me.'

'Madam!' He feigned hurt. 'You doubt that I am true?'

'I know you're not, but you're honest about it, which is more than most.'

He turned to Jean, pretending outrage. 'They doubt me, Jean! Say something to protect my good name.'

'Take me off to dance with you,' said Jean, rising to her feet. 'Your good name is quite beyond my saving.'

He shot Jean a conspiratorial smile as he led her towards the doorway.

'A friend of mine wants to meet you.'

Jean returned a cool glance, although she had a suspicion who the friend might be. To her annoyance she felt her face colour, and she raised her fan until it subsided. 'Indeed. A she or a he?'

Sandy laughed. 'A he.'

'You astonish me, Sandy, and why does this he need you to be an intermediary?'

'He doesn't, but I wanted to make the introduction. I want you both for ever in my debt.'

'My, my,' said Jean. 'I hope I'm able to play my part. Who is he?'

'Davie Stewart of Kynachan.'

She stopped. 'I'm not sure I want to meet such a man. It was he who was involved in that lamentable scene with the Moncreiffes just now, wasn't it? And I've heard talk of him – little good.'

Again he laughed. 'What they say about Davie is not true.'

'Are you sure you're being careful of my reputation, Sandy Wood?'

'You are its own capable mistress.'

They had passed into the crowded reception room. Jean was unaware of the figure who had detached himself from a group of Highlanders by the fire and crossed to intercept them.

'Ah, Davie.'

'Thank you, Sandy. You can leave us now.'

'But—'

Before Jean could collect herself, she found her arm gripped gently but firmly. The rest of Sandy Wood's complaint was lost as she was whisked through to an alcove in the dance hall at the very moment a reel had begun.

'Well?' she demanded, freeing her arm. 'Why have you dragged me here? I am not a Sabine woman.'

In spite of her indignation, her heart was beating faster and she noted that her abductor had a strong, humorous face as well as the vivid blue eyes that had impaled her from across the room. His jacket and trews were tailored from red and black tartan, and his plaid was pinned at the shoulder by a jewelled brooch.

'I should like the honour of paying my addresses to you, Miss Mercer,' he said.

'What?' Jean felt a blush of catastrophic dimensions climb her cheeks. Disappearing rapidly behind her fan, she intercepted a quizzical glance from Abigail, who waited her turn to set to her partner in the reel. 'Do you mean you wish to pay court to me?'

'That's right. I want to marry you.'

'But we've never met before!'

'Sandy tells me your name is Jean.'

Suddenly she lost her temper. 'You astonish me, Mr Stewart. You wish to pay court to me and you did not even know my Christian name? Are you sure you would not prefer one of my sisters? Barbara has a larger frame than I and might well prove a better breeder. Abigail, perhaps, has more vivacity. I am the eldest, it's true, but you needn't worry. We are all equal heiresses to my uncle's fortune.'

He grinned. 'You're one of those Mercer girls, are you? That's most useful.'

'Mr Stewart, I am accustomed to the company of gentlemen. I find your conversation outrageous. Do not toy with me. I am not one of your doxies.'

The humour left his face. 'You're right, Miss Mercer. I apologize, but listen to me for a minute and then, if you wish, I'll escort you back to your mother. Please?'

Still angry, Jean was also flattered and undeniably curious. 'Granted.'

He hesitated, seeming lost for words, and rested one of his hands against the wall. She saw that it was slim with long, strong fingers and almond-shaped nails. A sudden picture of that hand stroking her body came to her mind and she blinked at the pang that shot through her heart.

'I suppose society would wish me to cluck and coo for a week, a month, or a year, or whatever is the usual period for these matters. It seems such a waste of time. You see, shortly after the death of my father, I saw the *tamhasg* of a young woman.'

'The what?' she interrupted, seizing on the word to engage her intellect and dampen her immodest sensations. The Gaelic term, which he pronounced 'tavask', was strange to her.

He frowned, seeking an explanation in English. 'It's a sort

of spectre of the living that can appear without the knowledge of the person whose it is.'

To make himself heard above the music he had moved close to her. Almost uniquely, she noticed, he wore no perfume, and his plaid released a faint earthy smell, like the land after summer rain.

'All right,' said Jean. 'You saw a *tamhasg*.'

He ducked her a shy glance before continuing. 'I knew that the woman it represented was to be my wife. You and I are going to be married, Miss Mercer. It was your *tamhasg* that came to me. I recognized you immediately I saw you across the room.'

Jean was dumbfounded. He was unsmiling.

'There's something else, too,' he said. 'As soon as I saw you this evening, I knew I loved you.'

Her anger and confusion melted away, to be replaced by pity. 'You poor man, you're serious. Five minutes ago I had never seen you and knew almost nothing of you. This is witchcraft.' Making a dismissive gesture, she turned back to the dance.

'Look at me,' he demanded.

Her eyes snapped back to his face, and she gasped at the burning intensity shown there.

'What I know is not witchcraft. Love is a gift of God, not Satan. I love you and want you, and it is your destiny that you shall be mine. Soon we shall have children, and they will bring honour to our name.'

His voice was low, but she could hear every word above the wild music of the fiddles.

'You bear my mark, Jeannie Mercer, and I know my love for you will endure until Schiehallion becomes dust.'

She stared at him for another moment or two, her face now death-white. Then she blinked, slowly, as if waking from a trance. 'I ... I don't know what to say. I have never imagined a situation like this.'

'Shall I return you to your mother?'

Her response was instinctive. Before she had time to think, her hand flew to his arm. 'Don't you dare!'

David's shout of delight and laughter caught the attention of the nearby dancers, who exchanged smiles – or knowing winks – at seeing Kynachan in intimate conversation with a beautiful girl.

He offered Jean his hand. 'Come outside. We must talk where we are not the object of so many speculative glances.'

For a fragment of time, Jean paused. Then she nodded. 'I shall just tell my sister.'

Swaying to avoid the candles in their sconces, she moved gracefully off behind the row of dancers.

'He's the Highlander who was staring at us. Who is he?' demanded Barbara.

Opposite her, a foolish grin on his face, the sweating Kinnaird clapped his hands in time to the music.

'Never you mind. We're only going out for some air.'

With a squeak of glee, Barbara hugged her sister. 'He's beautiful. If you decide you don't want him, can I have him?'

'Of course. Keep an eye on Abigail, would you?'

'I can do that all right,' said Barbara, 'but who's going to keep an eye on you?'

9

Courting

Light glowed from the doorways of the inns and house windows. The evening was mild, but Jean pulled up her cloak to cover her head. As she and David started down the street, a couple of Highlanders rose to their feet and fell in some twenty yards behind them. They carried swords and targes.

'Who're they?' asked Jean.

'My gillies. The taller is my foster-brother, Willie Kennedy.'

In the warm evening people were still about, and here and there householders leaned on the window sills of the projecting first floors of the buildings, chatting to their neighbours opposite as they watched the world go by. Half naked and filthy, a small child herded a black sow and a farrow of piglets across their path.

'Tell me about yourself, Miss Mercer.'

'No, I know all about me. Tell me about you.'

'What would you know?'

She laughed. 'I have seen you involved in an undignified fracas and I know your name. More than that is required before I could agree to marry you.'

They crossed the street by the Skinner's Gate, which led north out of the city. Here Perth's Highlanders congregated, and one reeled out of an alehouse into their path, hurling a few words of Gaelic back over his shoulder.

David muttered a sharp word. The man turned in drunken belligerence, his hand diving for his dirk. He focused on David's face, and his posture crumbled to cringing apology.

'What did you say to him?' Jean asked.

'You don't have the Gaelic?'

'My family have lived in Edinburgh since I was five.'

'You'll soon learn. In our country, few folk speak English.'

They entered a wynd by the Tolbooth, and ahead they could see the fast-flowing, swirling water of the Tay. By the wooden quay were tied a couple of empty barges, their furled sails blackened by dust from cargoes of coal. A salmon fisherman, his nets draped across the barges to dry, sat with his legs dangling over the river and chatted to a ferryman, who lounged by his oars. He looked up when David and Jean appeared but lost interest when he realised they were lovers, not potential passengers.

'Tell me why you're worth marrying,' said Jean. She was conscious of every movement he made, of the grace of his gestures as he removed his plaid, of the play of muscles in his leg as he bent to spread it on a low wall for them to sit.

'You're very direct.'

'The cheek of the man! You're the one who proposes marriage to women you've never met.'

'Not women. Just one woman.'

'Will you stop using that tone of voice and looking at me like that? I find it distractingly flirtatious.'

'Forgive me,' said David, an impish glint in his eye.

'You could say that with a bit more conviction – which doesn't mean I want you to kneel.'

Jean's embarrassment was compounded by the amused glances cast by the two rivermen, who had been joined by David's gillies.

'Stop playing the fool and tell me about yourself, David Stewart of Kynachan. Start there – Kynachan. I don't even know where it is.'

Rising from his knees, David settled on the wall alongside her. He gestured at the river. 'Some of that water fell on Kynachan. If you follow the Tay back into Atholl, it is joined by the Tummel, which flows past the mansion house I have built for you. We march from the river to the peak of the fairy mountain, Schiehallion. It's the most beautiful place in the world.'

'And how far away is it?'

'About a dozen hours' hard ride, much of it on the military road from Crieff.'

'They say you are a breaker of ladies' hearts.'

'There is only one lady's heart I'm interested in, and that I'll never break.'

She lifted her eyebrows, scornfully. 'Davie Stewart – words as smooth as molasses.'

'Is that what they say?'

'If they don't they ought to. I'm not sure I should trust you. The kind of illogical passion you declare is dangerous and not at all a suitable basis for wedlock.'

Rising, Jean strolled to the edge of the quay. In the dying light a late hatch of swallows skimmed low over the water.

'You have a fine woman there, Kynachan,' called the ferryman, speaking in Gaelic.

'She is small but her breasts are excellent,' agreed the fisherman. 'In spite of her rich gown she appears strong and capable of much work.'

'I thank you,' replied David. 'She is to be my wife.'

'I am pleased for you,' said the ferryman. 'Is she with child?'

'No, not yet.'

'A pity, but I am sure you will do something about that before the night is out.'

'Is she the one of your dream, Kynachan?' asked Willie Kennedy. 'She has the look of the one you described. Has she your mark?' Like the others, he was speaking Gaelic.

'She is the one. Note her well, Willie. This woman is to be guarded with your life. And pass the word round the people of all Atholl that Jean Mercer is to be the wife of Kynachan. A slight to her honour is a slight to our own.'

The gillie nodded his head in approval. 'This lass seems worthy of you. Even the fairies in the mountain will protect her.'

'It is time I took her back to the ball,' said Davie. 'I would not want to upset the rest of her family. She has sisters who would twitter and cluck like kain hens.' He looked towards the rivermen. 'May the river be generous to you both.'

'Long life and happiness to you and your lady, Kynachan,' said the fishermen. 'And may the Stuarts return to the throne of Scotland.'

'Amen to that,' said David. Taking a coin from a pouch at his side, he flicked it to the ferryman, who deftly caught it. 'A dram for the two of you.'

'My blessings upon you, Kynachan.'

David turned to Jean. 'Shall we return to the ball?'

'Yes. Otherwise the kain hens may be upset.'

Once they were back in the High street, the gillies again dogging their footsteps, David spoke. 'I thought you said you did not have the Gaelic.'

'All I said was that I had lived in Edinburgh since I was a small child. Our nurse was from the Highlands, and we spoke the Gaelic with her.'

'I apologize if the conversation offended you.'

'You assumed much.'

'It was the ferryman who made the assumption you'd be with child by morning, not myself. I am quite content to wait until we're wed – provided that shall be soon.'

She gave a peal of laughter. 'And what is this about your mark? You mentioned it earlier as well.'

'I'll tell you on our wedding night.'

'Don't be silly, you'll tell me now.'

'It is my crest.'

'So?'

'You bear it. At least your *tamhasg* does, so I know you do.'

'What is this crest?'

'The lion rampant.'

'I still don't understand. I have no lion sprouting from my head.'

David gently touched her gown over the spot where he had seen the birthmark on the spectre. 'That mark.'

Jean's face turned white, and her hand flew down to cover the place. 'But this is madness! Only my sisters and mother know. You can't have been gossiping with them.'

'No, until this evening I did not even know your name. I have certainly talked about the *tamhasg*, but I did not know it was yours.'

'Anyway, my mark is nothing like a lion.'

'Perhaps not upside down, the way you would usually see it.'

This time Jean's hands came up to cover her stricken face. 'You mean in this vision of yours I was unclothed?'

'Yes.'

'You have seen me naked!' She turned away from him, and when she spoke again her voice was cold. 'I think it best that I return to my mother. I wish no further truck with you.'

'Jean!'

'Damn you! I am no heifer carrying your brand!'

He grasped her shoulders. 'You don't understand. It is I who carry your brand on my heart, where it has been burning for fifteen months.'

'Let me alone!'

'Marry me, Jean. You must marry me. Our first child is to be a son – the heir to Kynachan.'

She looked sideways at him, her lips tight. 'I suppose you saw that too?'

'Yes.'

'God in heaven! I dare not ask what you did to me in this dream of yours.'

'Do to you?' He spread his arms, a picture of hurt innocence. 'I could do nothing. It was a dream. When I felt my love grow . . . and I reached out for you, you vanished. I woke up.'

'This is ridiculous! And whatever you say, the mark bears no resemblance to a lion, rampant or otherwise.'

'Yes, it does. You know, at the top, where the raised claws—'

'Stop it!'

David hung his head, looking contrite.

'You should be ashamed of yourself. I have never in my entire life been inflicted with so indelicate a conversation.'

'Marry me, Jean.'

She stamped her foot.

'Please?'

She looked at his woebegone face and bit back a smile.

'Must I go down on one knee again?'

'No! People will stare.'

'Next week. We can marry next week.'

By the time Jean and David got back to the assembly rooms the ball was virtually over. Anna Mercer, who was playing a last hand of cards, told her daughter that Barbara and Abigail had invited some folk round to their rooms for supper and more dancing. The girls had gone ahead to roust the servants and she would follow later.

David escorted Jean home through the dark wynds. At the Mercer residence, Kinnaird was in the parlour tuning a fiddle and talking to Sandy Wood. Jean left David with them and went through to the kitchen, where her sisters were being helped by a yawning scullery maid, turfed from her bed in the bottom drawer of the dresser.

'Jeannie, have you heard?' said Abigail, breathless. 'Kinnaird danced with Barbara all evening!'

Barbara's eyes were shining. 'And he lingered behind and asked if he might kiss me as we came into the close.'

'Ugh, kissed by him,' said Abigail. She spread her feet in imitation and put on a hollow voice. 'Call me Kinnaird, my dear Miss Barbara.'

'Ooh, Miss Abigail!' said the scullery maid, with a squeak of laughter.

'Don't be so horrid,' said Barbara. 'I think he's a kind and gentle man. But what about you, Jean? Where did you get to?'

'Yes,' said Abigail, 'the last time I saw you, you were being swept off by that glorious Highlander with the hungry look on his face. I believe his friend Thomas Moncreiffe is lucky not to have killed his brother. I'm told the man will drink himself to death inside a year. Who was your Highlander?'

'David Stewart of Kynachan.'

'Kynachan! So that's the famous Davie Stewart. You're wasting your time there.' Pulling herself onto the table, Abigail leaned across to take a plum from a bowl. 'He's only interested in hunting, cock-fighting, and strumpets.'

'How on earth do you know that?' asked Barbara.

Abigail gave an airy wave of her hand. 'Talk about the stairheads. Anyway, he's not for the likes of you.'

'Is that right?' said Jean casually. 'Do you think you could move yourself and take some wine through?'

'Kinnaird talked about him,' said Barbara, picking up a cloth to mop up some spilled ale. 'Davie Stewart was very helpful over his purchase of the estate of Kinnaird. It was David's father who mocked the Duke of Argyll in the Rising, you know.'

'Oh, yes, I know that,' said Abigail, sucking on her plum and rolling her eyes. 'Everybody knows that.'

'Don't speak with your mouth full,' said Jean.

Abigail accurately spat her plum stone into the fire. 'I can't think what Davie Stewart wants from you. He can't possibly believe he can seduce anyone so prim.'

'You are a vulgar child, Abigail,' said Jean. 'It's perfectly straightforward. He's next door, and he's asked me to marry him.'

Abigail's spluttered shriek degenerated into a ferocious coughing fit over the remnants of a second plum. Barbara managed a few desultory thumps on her back but was staring saucer-eyed at her elder sister.

'*Jean*, what on earth do you mean?' Barbara said. 'We've never even met him. And every heiress within a hundred miles of Perth has been trying to land him for years.'

'Is that so?' said Jean. 'He wants to marry me next week.'

'*Next week!*,' squealed Abigail. Then her face fell. 'You're making this up.'

'I'm not,' said Jean. 'And he's not concerned about my dowry, because he proposed to me before he even knew my name.'

'How wonderful!' said Barbara, with a sigh.

Abigail snorted. 'I don't believe you. You're pretty enough, I suppose, but you've never before had such a devastating effect on strange men.'

'He wants me' – here Jean's composure cracked for the first time, and she could not hide her smile – 'because he dreamed of the girl he would marry. When he saw me this evening, he recognized me as that girl. He says his heart is mine until mountains become dust.'

Great sobs came from Barbara. 'That's so beautiful.' She pulled out a handkerchief to dab her eyes.

'Why couldn't it have been me in his dream?' wailed Abigail.

Anna Mercer suddenly flew into the kitchen. 'Jean! What's this I hear from Kynachan?' She stopped, looking with amazement at her weeping daughters. 'What's the matter with all of you?'

'David Stewart proposed marriage to me,' said Jean, tears spilling down her cheeks.

'So it's true. But why are you all crying?'

'I haven't accepted,' said Jean, provoking an outburst of wails from her siblings.

Mrs Mercer flapped her hands and shooed Jean ahead of her. 'Ye daft lassie, hurry up next door before he changes his mind. He may be a mite impulsive, but I doubt you'll do better than the likes of the Laird of Kynachan.'

10

To Castle Menzies

Six months after the momentous ball, the four Mercer women left Perth, bound for Kynachan and Jean's wedding. Huddled in cloaks against the boisterous wind, they rode side-saddle on small horses, each led by a Highland gillie. Behind them, a string of a dozen pack ponies bore gifts and household furnishings as well as barrels of wine, fruits, and spices for the marriage feast.

The leader of the caravan, Charles Stewart, was a close friend of David's. Six feet tall, black-haired, and proud of bearing, he was descended from the Stewarts of Appin, in the west of Scotland. Growing up on the shores of Loch Tay, he had undergone the customary training in the use of weaponry and become famous as an expert swordsman. In his younger days, he had roamed the countryside in search of adventure, meeting and duelling with young men like himself. To settle him down, his father had obtained for him the little estate of Bohally, on the opposite bank of the Tummel from Kynachan.

The Laird of Bohally had known and admired David Stewart for most of his life, just as Bohally himself had been known and admired by David's sixteen-year-old sister Clementina for most of hers. Charles Stewart was now a gentleman-soldier in the Black Watch, a regiment formed to police the Highlands – particularly to control cattle theft, which was so prevalent as to be hardly considered a crime. Since the animals were made by God and ate on God's pastures, Highlanders held that cattle were surely the common property of mankind. As for the Lowlands, since the land was occupied by Highland folk in olden times, anything there was fair game.

In his trews and tartan jacket, a feather in his bonnet and a dirk stuck in his belt, Bohally was the model of a Highland laird. Behind him, his gillie led a pony that bore his master's dark military tartans, his musket, pistols, sword, and targe.

By late morning, the party had crossed the Highland line,

and Jean noted that the people were now dressed in plaids rather than the breeches worn just to the south. The grain of the landscape ran east-west, and they were travelling north, so their route led across hill passes from glen to glen. The small band had left Perth and ridden up the river Almond, crossing Glen Shee on drovers' tracks to Strathbran.

Wisps of mist hung above the valley bottoms. The winter had been mild, but leprous patches of snow broken by black boulders and crags still chequered the hillsides. Rocky, treeless slopes lay either side of the way, which ran alongside the small spate river. Where the boulders were sufficiently spaced to allow the use of a plough, clusters of crude, rubble-built cottages sat amid the furrows and ridges of their single, weedy field. Goats and sheep picked over the muddy stubble, and half-wild ponies dotted the hillsides beyond the head dyke, a stone wall separating cultivable land from the rough moors.

Being used to the rich farmlands of Fife and the Lothians, Jean found it difficult to find much to give her cheer in the inhospitable landscape and the dire poverty evident in the sporadic settlements. By one of these clachans, a plough gang, made up of three men and four ponies, dragged their cumbersome wooden implement along a raised strip in a field corrugated with other plough rigs. In some of the small patches of soil between the boulders men were wielding the *cas-chrom*, a clumsy combination of a spade and a plough, but people were sparse, and other travellers few.

They met a column of a dozen women, barefoot and barelegged, their heads bowed beneath the weight of loaded baskets, led by an old woman who chanted a dirge-like song to mark the step. A mile or two farther, a runner, his naked limbs splashed with mud, trotted past the Mercers' party, shouting a greeting. In answer to Jean's enquiry, Bohally said the man had come from Taymouth Castle, Lord Breadalbane's seat at the east end of Loch Tay. He would be carrying messages to Perth and Edinburgh.

The track joined the military high road from Crieff at the bottom of Glen Cochil, and there the party stopped to rest their ponies. A gillie produced oatcakes, cheese, and ale from a wicker pannier basket, and they ate, giving scraps of food to a trio of solemn little boys with tangled hair, runny noses, and sores on their skin. They materialized from behind a jumble of rocks to suck their thumbs and stare at the exotic wayfarers. When Jean tried to talk to them, her Gaelic convulsed them with laughter, and a gillie shook his fist, which sent them scurrying back to the rocks.

Anna Mercer was disapproving. 'Little savages,' she said. 'It's like another country up here. I hope you'll be able to cope, Jeannie.'

'Of course I will,' said Jean, sounding more resolute than she felt.

The travellers paused again on the edge of the escarpment at the other end of the glen, where the highway plunged down into the great glacial valley of the Tay. Ahead of them, the horizon was rimmed by snow-covered mountains. Since crossing the Highland line, Bohally had been giving the attentive Jean a running commentary on the landscape and its inhabitants. Now he stood in his stirrups to point north-west. Beyond the first ridge of mountains reared a great lazy triangle of snow, silhouetted against a patch of blue sky.

'That's Schiehallion, the edge of our country, the loveliest in Scotland. Here in Strathtay, Menzies country is bordered by the Campbells of Breadalbane, who hold Loch Tay and some of Glen Lyon.' The stirrups creaked as he turned east. 'Over there are the Stewarts of Grandtully. Sir Robert Menzies' lands extend into our own country and march with those of the Duke of Atholl and Struan Robertson.'

The hillside declined gently towards the flat, fertile flood-plain of the Tay, which they were rejoining for the first time since Perth. The clachans were now numerous, each with its complement of yapping curs, and the little cottages were the colours of the surrounding rocks, soil, and vegetation. Each sat at the centre of a web of muddy paths that linked it to its neighbours. The road was steep and rough, and Jean had to clutch tight to the pommel on her saddle as her pony scrabbled for a foothold on the slick stones. The clatter and slither of the hooves of the travellers' horses and the barking of the dogs brought tartan-muffled figures to their doors to stare at the ponies as they passed. Some called a greeting to Bohally or exchanged ribald remarks with the gillies.

The highway passed over the five-arch stone bridge completed by General Wade a few years earlier, the only span across the river from its outpouring at Loch Tay to the sea. On the far side, half a dozen soldiers of the Black Watch, kilted in the dark green government tartan, lined up in a half-serious guard of honour for Bohally and the ladies. Again they paused to exchange gossip of the neighbourhood for news from Perth and the world beyond.

Half a mile from the bridge, nestling beneath wooded crags, lay the settlement of Weem, whose little church and inn lay at the gates of Castle Menzies, the party's destination for the night. With its four floors, the castle dominated the strath, and Jean felt some relief. So far the Highlands had shown her nothing but rude huts and barren moorland, but this, although old-fashioned, was the equal in grandeur to the mansions round Perth and Edinburgh.

The castle sat amid rich farmland. Gunports pierced its thick stone walls. Bohally told them that the weakness of the castle's defences lay in its proximity to Weem. Twice the stronghold had been taken, he said, when its defenders had been absent, supping ale at the inn.

'Is there still a garrison?' asked Jean, as she stared up at the great building.

'No. But the Redcoats were here for a year or two after the Rising, when folk were disarmed.'

'Disarmed?' Jean looked at the two men who were quarrying a depleted but still enormous bank of peats adjacent to the castle. One had laid his weapons on the ground, but the other was hampered by his broadsword and targe. Both had stopped work to stare at the little column of ponies.

'The country's peaceful,' said Bohally, 'so nobody minds, and a Highlander without his arms feels as naked as a gentleman without his wig.'

Along with the master of his household, Sir Robert Menzies himself came forward to greet his guests. The unkempt curls askew on the head of the taller of the two men proclaimed the Laird of Weem. He was a big man, running to fat, and his green coat was spattered with mildew. In Highland society, where it was not unusual for a gentleman to be bilingual in English and Gaelic, able to hold a conversation in Latin or French, and even have a good smattering of Greek and Italian, the Menzies chief was known as a learned man. He owned one of the best libraries in Perthshire. Unlike many of the local gentry, he was a Presbyterian and a keen supporter of the government, but, as a result of a childhood injury, he was unable to excel at the martial arts, which clansmen expected of their leader.

'Bohally. Ladies. You must be exhausted. Ho! Ho!'

Sir Robert's hooting summoned half a dozen retainers from

the dank passage leading into the bowels of the building. They took the travellers' horses and cloaks. With a couple of deerhounds capering round his heels, the laird ushered his guests up two flights of clattering wooden stairs into a large, low-ceilinged reception room. Its tall windows overlooked formal gardens and the flat, treeless plain of the Tay.

A woman played on a spinet by one of the windows. In wing-backed chairs sat an elderly, black-garbed parson of gloomy mien and a young man, with a dark, thin, clever face.

'My dear,' said Sir Robert. 'Look what Bohally has brought for us.'

The hounds danced over to arrange themselves elegantly either side of the hearth as Lady Mary Menzies broke off her music to greet the Mercers. The elderly man was introduced as the Reverend Duncan McLea, incumbent of the parish of Dull, which included Kynachan. The young man, wearing a well-tailored blue coat and breeches, was James Bissett. His uncle, Thomas Bissett of Glenelbert, was one of the most powerful men in Atholl, Commissary of Dunkeld, Clerk to the Regality Court of Atholl, and Chamberlain to the duke.

While the minister glowered, Bissett had Edinburgh manners and gave a bow. 'Four beautiful sisters!' he exclaimed. 'Bohally, you bring treasures indeed to our country.'

Anna Mercer demurred. 'I know the Highland reputation for gallantry, Mr Bissett. But it's not the equal of the Highland reputation for blethers. These are my daughters. This one is Jean.'

'My dear,' said Sir Robert, clasping Jean's hand between his own and blinking short-sightedly into her face. 'This house will always be open to you and your family. I count your Davie among my closest friends.'

'You are very kind, Sir Robert,' said Jean, touched by the sincerity in his voice.

'Let the poor girl go, Rob,' said Lady Mary, giving Jean a warm smile. 'You must all be exhausted.' And she whisked the travellers off to rest and change.

Entering the dining hall an hour later, Jean was disconcerted to find fifty Highlanders already seated, waiting for the laird and his family. She was placed between Sir Robert and James Bissett. In deference to his host, Bohally, next to Lady Mary, wore the tartans of the Black Watch. Sir Robert had been enthusiastic in promoting the old militia into the first Highland regiment of the British army.

'Do you always entertain on this scale?' asked Jean, once a grinning, gap-toothed attendant had ladled some sheep's head broth into the bowl in front of her.

Crude trestle tables and benches stretched the length of the room. The farther from the chief's table, the more simply dressed and villainous appeared the diners.

'It's tradition, my dear. The chief is expected to have his house and his board open to his children.' The laird translated the Gaelic word *clann* directly into English to emphasize the relationship. 'If they're expected to fight for me, I suppose it's only fair I should feed them sometimes.' Inclining his head towards her, he lowered his voice. 'Mind you, the tradition doesn't mean I have to give them beef and my best claret. Their porridge, ale, and whisky is made from the oats and barley they pay in rent.'

To Jean's embarrassment, all the diners were examining her, some more openly than others. At the far end of the hall, one old man, his plaid torn, his hair and beard filthy and tangled, even stood on his bench to see her more clearly.

'Do they always stare so?'

'Stare?' Sir Robert looked around at his clansfolk. 'I see what you mean.' He delicately pulled a fibre of wool, a hazard of sheep's head broth, from his mouth. 'The whole country's heard about Davie's dream, you see, and they've all come to see what you look like.'

'But surely the estate of Kynachan lies in the next glen, still some hours' ride from here?'

'That's not far, not in the Highlands. Besides, we're all related round here. Davie's cousin married Commissary Bissett, Jamie's uncle' – Sir Robert nodded towards Bissett, who, Jean noted, was in animated conversation with Abigail – 'and Davie's some sort of kin to me and everyone else. His father was born a son of Ballechin, an hour down the Tay from here, and the Ballechin Stewarts stem from a bastard of James II, who was originally granted Stix, half an hour upriver. Very local. And of course James II was great grandson of Robert II, who sired the Wolf from whom half this country is descended and thus linked to Ballechin.'

As Jean did her best to maintain interest in this sudden cascade of cousins, a commotion at the far end of the chamber caught their attention. The old man was now declaiming to those round him.

'Hail to Jean, the woman of dreams! Hail the wife of Kynachan, the slayer of the enemies of the Men of Atholl, the son of Big John, the brother of Charles, the son of Patrick of the Battles, the son of . . .'

Sir Robert inclined his head towards Jean. 'Davie hasn't really done much slaying; there's not a lot of need for it these days,' he said. 'Mind you, it's an interesting pedigree, few like it in Atholl. My wife is a Stuart, daughter of Lord Bute, but most of the other Stewarts round here are from the west, like Bohally there, or descended from the Wolf. Do you know about the Wolf?'

'No, but I would like to.'

Sir Robert nodded approvingly. 'It's important that the new Lady of Kynachan know such things. When the Highlander isn't talking about his cattle, he's talking about his ancestors. They define his place in our society. The Wolf of Badenoch was a dreadful cutthroat, a great-grandson of Robert Bruce. His son, who built the castle at Garth you'll see tomorrow, was even worse. He was a regicide, but people prefer to forget that now. And a few generations later his descendant burnt out my own ancestor here.' Sir Robert gave a grunt of laughter. 'We're all very proud of being sired by such lines of scallywags.'

A goose, venison, and salmon followed the broth, while a few scraggy boiled chickens were spread amongst Sir Robert's clansmen. By now the roar of conversation, interspersed with songs growing bawdy as the whisky circulated, filled the hall.

The bearded ancient was helped onto the table and handed a harp, which he proceeded to tune. Lady Mary leaned across to Jean, interrupting a dissertation from Sir Robert on the differing qualities of the pastoral poetry of Greece and Rome.

'You must be exhausted, my dear. If Sir Robert will excuse us . . .'

Along with the men at the table, Sir Robert rose to his feet as the women made ready to withdraw.

'Of course, of course, my dear.' The laird gestured ruefully towards the bard. 'I must wait for a while, but I bid you good night, Miss Mercer.'

From the doorway, Jean looked back. Around the harpist a pool of silence had slowly begun to spread. Sir Robert had filled his glass and allowed an expression of glazed benevolence to settle over his face.

11

Journey's End

A fine drizzle hung in the air the following morning. The little column of ponies left the policies of the castle to travel across the plain towards the pass of Glen Goulandie. The landscape was pleasingly trim, and an old tower castle, with smoke pouring from its chimney, stood on the bank of the river Lyon beneath the oak woods on the flanks of Drummond Hill.

Jean eagerly examined the countryside as the high road began to climb the pass through the ridge of hills between Strathtay and Strathtummel. Mist hung above the trees and gullies like wisps of frozen smoke. To the left of the road, the land fell sharply into a ravine softened and screened by birch trees. From the bottom rose the roar of a foaming torrent, occasionally glimpsed as it crashed over jagged rocks. Beyond the ravine, the gentle slope of the hills was bisected horizontally by a head dyke.

Kicking his horse, Bohally trotted up alongside the sisters. 'See over there' – he pointed across the ravine to the ruins of a square keep that wore a diagonal garland of mist – 'that's Garth Castle. You can't see it from here, but the castle's on the point of a crag, and the ground drops sixty feet sheer into the burn.'

Jean shuddered. Even on a sunny day, the place would seem sinister. 'Who has it now?'

'Stewarts, of course. There are three Stewart estates to the west of here – Garth, Inchgarth, and Drumcharry. The families are very closely interlinked. Both my mother and grandmother were daughters of Drumcharry. I was born by Loch Tay, but I knew this country and your Davie long before I obtained Bohally.' He smiled across at Jean. 'I am proud to be his neighbour and friend.' Bohally's smile became a grin. 'It doesn't hurt that Clemmie is his sister, of course.'

'We had a sister called Clementina,' said Barbara. 'She was between Jean and me.'

'Your father must've been a good Jacobite,' said Bohally.

'Why?' asked Barbara.

Jean answered. 'Clementina Sobieska was the wife of the Pretender.'

'Of the king,' corrected Bohally. 'She was the rightful queen. Many good Jacobites named their daughters after her.'

'Sir Robert supports King George doesn't he?' said Jean.

Bohally waved a dismissive hand. 'The Menzies of Weem was e'er a Hanoverian. He's in pretty miserable company round here.'

'I believe Mr Bissett is a Whig as well.'

'That's right,' acknowledged Bohally. 'But he's in a special situation. He and his family owe their position to the duke and look after his affairs. They must share his politics.'

'I thought Jamie Bissett rather handsome,' said Abigail. 'I think I might wed him.'

'Don't be silly,' said Jean. 'You've only just met him.'

Barbara gave a whoop of laughter. 'Jeannie Mercer, you should be ashamed of yourself! Talk about the pot calling the kettle black.'

Jean had the grace to look discomfited.

'We'll be on Kynachan land soon,' said Bohally. 'Up here it's still Sir Robert's.'

At the top of the pass, the highway crossed a wasteland of bog cotton, marsh, and moor. Ahead, the cloud had cleared to reveal successive ridges of the Grampian mountains rolling into the distance. To the west, across the moor and a small loch, the great isolated massif of Schiehallion dominated the sky.

A little further on, Bohally reined his horse. The hillside fell away, and before them lay the valley of the Tummel. Like a doll's house, on the floor of the strath, sat a slate-roofed two-storey white house surrounded by stables and barns. Beyond it, across the river, lay a cluster of muddy cottages. A mile downriver, the grey water of a loch spread across the bottom of the narrowing glen.

'Is that the house of Kynachan?' asked Jean. 'And Bohally opposite?'

He nodded.

Anna Mercer's gillie led her pony alongside, where she took a large pinch of snuff and trumpeted into her handkerchief. 'It could be a lot worse, Jeannie,' she said. 'If that's Kynachan, it doesn't look a bad mansion house. I'd heard that some of these Highland lairds lived in hovels like those over the river.'

'Mother,' exclaimed Jean. 'That's Bohally across the river.'

Bohally waved away the insult. 'Kynachan had no better until last summer. It's a new house you're looking at, Mrs Mercer, built by Davie for his bride. I'll have one as good by the time I wed Clemmie.'

'You won't if you keep gallivanting round the Highlands fighting with cattle reivers,' said Mrs Mercer. Her sniff was not entirely due to the snuff.

'It's a lovely place,' said Jean, who had been feeling some trepidation, for the closer they came to their destination the more the settled farmsteads lining Strathtay had given way to wild slopes.

Her mother was unconvinced. 'Just you wait till a few winter gales have rattled round yon mountain. It'll not be so lovely under three feet of snow.'

'The mountain gives us shelter, Mrs Mercer,' said Bohally. He pointed to a long, high ridge which rose west of the house, hiding the river from their view. 'That's Craig Kynachan. Between us and the Craig is the glen of the Kynachan burn, where folk grow fine bere-barley and oats. And down by the river the land's as fertile as anything over by the Tay.'

The high road ran down through a screen of trees and round a sharp bend, where a well-used track struck off towards Loch Tummel. Half a mile on, they crossed the burn of Kynachan by a bridge where stood a watermill and a cluster of little cottages. From one came the metallic pounding of hammer on anvil.

In response to a shout, the hammering ceased. Men, women, and children emerged from the hovels to stare at the riders and call comments to each other.

'There's Bohally!'

'It's them. One must be the betrothed.'

'She's too old.'

'She's too tall.'

'That's a bonny one.'

Barbara leaned over to Jean. 'I suppose I'm the one that's too tall, but do you reckon it's you or Abigail that's the bonny one?'

Jean giggled. 'Neither of us. It'll be Bohally's horse.' She sat self-consciously upright in the saddle, slightly flushed, knowing that she was under the eyes of David's people.

Through the settlement – Daloist, according to Bohally – the land on their left, heather and tussocks, rose towards the slope of Craig Kynachan. On their right, a well-built stone wall protected cultivated land from the herds of cattle from the north and west Highlands that were driven down the high road, across Tummel bridge, and through the estate each autumn on their way to the great markets at Crieff and Falkirk.

A mile short of the bridge a track branched off the highway. Bohally dismounted and handed the reins of his horse to one of the escorting gillies.

'There's a ferry between Kynachan and Bohally,' he told the Mercers, 'but only for foot passengers. Angus'll take my horse round by the bridge.'

Over a rise in the ground, the track ran alongside the birch-lined burn. Round a corner the little cottages of Bohally came into sight once more, across a meadow and river, hard by the water's edge. The track now crossed the burn by a ford paved with well-packed cobblestones and curved between a field wall and a hillock. In front of them the cottages of the mains – the home farm – nestled into the slope, and, quite suddenly, the house of Kynachan lay a hundred yards ahead.

Bohally sensed Jean's excitement and gave her an encouraging nod. Returning a dazzling smile, she threw back her hood, eagerly nudging her weary horse up the final slope. No sooner had the party entered the courtyard than the heavy, nail-studded oak door – clearly saved from the former house – creaked open, and the face of the steward appeared. As they dismounted, Jean noticed the crest of the lion rampant carved on the lintel above his head. She caught her breath, touching the site of her birthmark.

'It's yourself, Bohally,' Donald called. 'And you have the betrothed.'

'Good day, Donald,' said Bohally. 'This is Miss Mercer, her mother, and her sisters.' He turned to Jean. 'Donald runs the household. He's another Stewart, like half the folk round here.'

'Aye, descended from the Wolf,' said Donald. He examined her from head to toe, and his face broke into a roguish grin.

'Heh, heh,' he chortled, bobbing his head half-way between a nod of greeting and a bow. 'I can see why yon *tamhasg* gave the laird such an itch in his loins.'

'Don't be coarse, Donald.' Janet bustled out of the front door. 'Hallo, Charlie. You brought them safely, then?'

'Aye, Lady Kynachan,' replied Bohally.

'And you'll be Jeannie,' said Janet, picking Jean out from her sisters at once. 'I'm Davie's mother.'

For a moment each woman searched the other's face, then they threw their arms round each other in a hug.

'Oh, dear,' said Janet, pulling away. 'You've got me weeping now.' Taking a handkerchief from the sleeve of her gown she blew her nose. 'Davie wanted to be here to greet you, but he's had to go up to Pitkerril. Och, you're a lovely girl right enough. Davie's a lucky man.'

'Thank you, madam,' said Jean. 'May I introduce my mother, Mistress Mercer? And my sisters, Barbara and Abigail.'

A barefoot youth held the head of Mrs Mercer's pony as she stepped carefully down to the mounting stone.

'Oh,' she groaned. 'It's good to get something under my feet again. Lady Kynachan, I'm delighted to meet you. Thank the Lord that Jeannie didn't fall for a McKay from the north. I'd never have survived the journey.'

'You poor thing, so long on a horse at your age,' said Janet, supporting Anna's arm before she could take umbrage at the aspersion cast upon her years. 'I could never have done it. And you have such lovely girls. Come in and have a dram. Davie should be back by dinner time. Clemmie's over the river waiting for you,' she said to Bohally.

'In that case, I'd best get home,' he said. Saluting the women, he ran off down the track, leaping easily over the wall at the bottom.

'Come in,' Janet said, herding the Mercers. 'Donald'll get folk to unload the ponies.'

'Lady Kynachan,' said Jean, 'I would like to ride to meet Davie.'

'You'll be seeing him soon enough, my dear. Come out of the cold.'

'Madam.' Jean had not moved.

Her mother frowned at Jean's lapse of manners, but Abigail giggled, earning herself a poisonous glance from her sister.

Catching Abigail's eye, Janet winked.

'Andrew,' she said, addressing the barefoot youth, 'saddle the wee grey for Miss Mercer.' Then she turned back to Jean. 'Return to the smithy and take the track up the burn. You can't get lost. He'll be coming that way.'

Janet smiled at Anna. 'Davie's father had that effect on me once.'

12

Under Craig Kynachan

Mounted on the stubby grey mare, Jean trotted back to the smithy and followed the path along the south flank of Craig Kynachan. On the other side of a chasm formed by the burn, the gently rising land carried the cottages of several settlements. With brief interruptions for bogs and rocks, the cultivated land stretched for a mile across the face of the slope towards Schiehallion.

She was not interested in the view of the mountain, nor in the hares, which froze as she passed, nor in the red kites rising from the skinned carcass of a fox by the track. She kept an eye ahead of her until she saw a horseman, a quarter of a mile away, cantering towards her, with a couple of setters at his heels.

Reining her mount, she waited until the rider drew near.

'Good day, Kynachan,' she called, wheeling her mare as he drew level.

'Good day to you, Miss Mercer,' responded David, who fell in alongside her.

'Under the circumstances, I would not think you forward if you called me Jean.'

'Thank you. Would you think me forward if I invited you behind that rock over there, spread my plaid, and covered you with kisses?'

'From head to toe?'

David gave the matter some thought. 'I think I would prefer to start at your toe and work up. Where I finished would depend.'

'I see,' said Jean with gravity. 'Yes, I fear I would think you forward. Like so much in life, timing is all important. However, in a couple of weeks, provided the weather was clement, I would think you backward if you did not invite me behind the rock.'

'I look forward to the occasion. In fact, I shall have Donald set up a love bower there for our future use. Meantime, would a simple kiss be permitted?'

She reined her beast, pretending to consider. 'A kiss, yes. Simple, no.'

David leaned over, and his arm encircled her waist. Before Jean was aware of his intention, he had swung her easily from her mare to the withers of his own horse.

'My love,' he said. He sealed her lips with his own and brought up his hand to cup her cheek. Jean's arm went round his neck.

For a long minute they kissed, the horse patient beneath them. At the warning growl of one of the setters, David drew back his head. From behind the boulder an old man had appeared.

'Long life, Kynachan. It is always a fine day for the kissing of pretty girls.'

'This pretty girl will be my wife in a fortnight, Alastair.'

'Is that so? Is she the one whose *tamhasg* came to you?'

'It is she.'

The old man examined Jean carefully before passing judgement. 'Aye, she has a fair countenance right enough, but she's a wee thing. Is she strong? Will she work hard? Is she showing pleasing enthusiasm when you couple with her?'

'Only time will tell,' said David, earning himself an elbow in the ribs.

Alastair shook his head. 'A wise man should learn these things before he takes a lass to the minister. But does she bring a worthy tocher?'

'The lawyers say so, Alastair.'

'That is something, at least. I wish you both many sons, a race of mighty warriors worthy of your forefathers.' He pulled a rusty broadsword from its scabbard at his belt and flourished it in salute.

Davie pushed his horse into a walk so that they drew away from the old man. Jean's riderless beast followed behind the setters.

'I can see we shall have to reconnoitre our love bowers carefully,' said Jean. 'Aren't you going to put me back on my horse?'

'No,' said David. 'You know, I wasn't expecting to see you until I got home.'

'Huh! I wager you would have given me a polite bow, a peck on the hand, and spent the following few hours talking to Bohally. I wanted to see whether you felt the same now as you did in Perth.'

'Jeannie Mercer,' said David. 'I have thought of little else but you since I saw you last. May I kiss you again?'

'You may,' said Jean. Lifting her face towards him, she parted her lips. After some moments, she drew a shuddering breath. 'Enough, Davie,' she said, but her hand traced the shape of his chest beneath his shirt.

'I think it's as well we're on a horse, my girl. Otherwise Alastair would have to report us for ante-nuptial fornication, and we'd be summoned before the minister in Dull.'

He flicked the reins, his left arm held tight round her waist. She nestled back into his chest and gave a little purr of pleasure.

'We met the minister at Castle Menzies. Full of righteous gloom, certainly. Gloomier still when I told him I was an Episcopalian. But he surely wouldn't dare summon Kynachan?'

'He might well. His Kirk Session have charged other lairds with immorality.'

'What were you doing at Pitkerril?'

'Settling a dispute over the ownership of a calf. They're a hard lot up there, too quick to sort their quarrels with a dirk. I won't have my people threatening each other.'

'I'm pleased to hear it,' said Jean. 'Some of Barbara's friends from Edinburgh believed the Highlandmen would cut our throats, and they wept and wailed when they bade her farewell.'

David laughed. 'There's another reason to keep the peace at Pitkerril. The largest landholder, George Cairney, is a decent fiddler. It would not do for him to have his fingers taken off by some lout's broadsword just before our wedding. How was your journey?'

'The road was fair enough. Bohally kept away both the rain and the brigands. As easy a journey as one could wish for.'

'Sir Robert?'

'Sir Robert was very hospitable and sang your praises. I had a little room off the main stair, and the wind wailed up the garderobe all night. I am most glad that you do not live in a castle.'

One of the setters, ranging ahead of the horses, checked by a clump of heather. At a whistle from David it put up a covey of grouse, and the birds skimmed across the track ahead, curving out of sight over a shoulder of the hillside.

'There might easily be four hundred people coming to our wedding,' he said.

'Four hundred!'

'Two hundred of our own people on Kynachan and many of the neighbours will attend. The end of winter's a good time for celebration. For the night of the wedding, the house will have to sleep fifty.'

'But what of us?' Her eyes were wide with consternation. 'I hope there is no horrid Highland custom whereby all these neighbours sit by our bed, take snuff, and pass comment upon our actions?'

'The horrid Highland custom is that we must spend our nuptial night in a bothy.'

'Alone?'

'Quite by ourselves. A gunshot east of the house lies the driest and stoutest little bothy on the estate. On my return from Perth last autumn I had it rebuilt and filled with soft, sweet hay from the flower meadow by the river. Clementina has laced the hay with lavender, and the goose girl's bare bottom has certified there's not a thistle amongst it. We withdraw there, and Bohally will mount guard on the door. By the time the rising sun strikes the top of Schiehallion, we will truly be man and wife.'

'With rainy weather it could be several days before there is sunshine on the mountain.'

'This is certainly to be hoped.'

For a minute or two, they jogged along, content.

'My mother has seen you?'

'Yes. I thought I would ask her to take me round the estate to meet the people before we are wed.'

'There's always a new baby to welcome or an old person to bid farewell. My mother knows the estate and the people better than I. She ran it during my father's absence in England during the Rising.'

'It must be hard for her after so many years as the Lady of Kynachan. To her I must feel like a usurper.'

David shook his head. 'Not so, she has longed to abdicate. You are the mother of her grandchildren.'

'I pray we do not disappoint her.'

'We won't.'

Jean moved her head away with a smile as he nuzzled the back of her neck. 'Stop it, Davie Stewart. You'll wait until our union has been blessed by the priest.'

13

Kynachan

Two days later, as dawn broke, Jean crawled from the bed she shared with her sisters. Across the landing the door to the parlour was open, and Anna Mercer's snores reverberated through the house.

Leaving Barbara and Abigail asleep, Jean came down the wooden stairs in search of breakfast. In the chilly dining-room a couple of crumpled linen napkins and crumbs on the cloth-covered table showed that other members of the household were already about.

Jean ate a bowl of porridge and drank some ale before leaving in search of her mother-in-law. Today she would tour the estate and meet the tenants of the townships. A young housemaid, sweeping the hall with a heather broom, directed her to the garden behind the stables.

Outside, under the assault of the rising sun, the mist was in full retreat up the sides of the strath. The garden was protected from marauding livestock by a stone wall, and the bare vegetable patch was bordered by raspberry canes and fruit trees. In it, the little round figure of Janet was talking to an old gardener.

'Good morning, my dear,' she called. 'Did you sleep well?'

'Very well, thank you, Mrs Stewart,' replied Jean.

'Did you find yourself some breakfast all right?'

'Yes.'

'Davie's over at Crossmount.' Janet waved her hand vaguely to the west. 'Some of their tenants have been letting their cattle stray into Kynachan Wood, and Davie's gone to sort it out.'

'Is that where we are going?'

'No, we go the other way, first to Balnarn. The principal tenant there is Hugh Reid, and Colin tells me his newest bairn's poorly' – here the gardener nodded sagely – 'so we'll take some medicines over.'

The head of Andrew, the young gillie, appeared above the wall, and Janet told him to fetch a jug of whisky from Donald.

'A full jug?'

'Aye, of course a full jug. If there's any left we can bring it back.'

'There'll no be any left.'

'And put in a few cheeses – twenty, say. Then saddle the ponies.'

A quarter of an hour later, Janet led the way south from the house across half a mile of rock-strewn heather. A few goats and sheep foraged for the first shoots of spring amid the mosses and lichens. Behind Jean, Andrew led a pony with loaded baskets hooked onto the pack-saddle.

Splashing across a little burn on their approach to the township, they could hear women's song, accompanied by a rhythmic scrape of hand mills and the knock of stone on stone. The spring sunshine had brought folk outside their cottages to grind oats and bere for the porridge and bannocks.

The song broke off as the ponies skirted a midden and arrived in the midst of the cluster of cottages. Stiff-legged dogs strutted out to greet the visitors, and young children hid behind their mothers or darted into the low doorways to peep shyly at the strangers. By each heather-thatched dwelling lay a depleted stack of peat, a midden, and a small patch of land surrounded by low turf walls, where the cottagers grew kale to supplement a diet of meal, milk, and blood tapped from the veins of the living cattle.

Christina Reid, a tall, fair-haired woman in late pregnancy, came out to greet them. She wore the close-fitting linen cap that denoted a married woman and the ubiquitous tartan shawl.

'Good day, Lady Kynachan.'

'Good day, Christina,' replied Janet, grasping Andrew's helping hand and sliding awkwardly from the pony. 'It has the promise of a fine morning.'

'Aye. We need it. The land needs drying out before it's put to the plough.'

'I've brought Miss Mercer with me, Christina. She is the betrothed of Kynachan. Jean, this is Mistress Reid, wife of Hugh Reid, the first tenant here.'

Christina Reid appraised Jean frankly. 'You are welcome here, Miss Mercer. May you and Kynachan have many fine sons, who will bring honour to his name.'

'Good day to you, Mistress Reid,' replied Jean. 'I shall pray the child you carry will have good health and come easily into this world.'

83

'God willing,' said Christina. 'Would you honour me by coming to my hearth?'

'Thank you,' said Janet. 'I've brought yarrow and meadow-sweet, as I hear you've a sick bairn. Andrew, bring in my bundle and the whisky.'

Jean ducked through the low doorway, and her eyes took a moment or two to adjust to the smoke-filled gloom. The roof, a tight lattice of blackened willow wands covered by turf and heather, was carried on three pairs of crucks, each pair split from the curving limb of a tree. Wicker baskets in various sizes hung from the rafters. By the smouldering fire in the centre of the earth floor, an old woman rocked a fretful baby. After a few moments Jean could make out a couple of hens cocking their heads in a beady stare, invisible chicks stirring the feathers of their breasts. A black iron pot of simmering water was suspended from a chain.

Jean looked at the child. 'Poor little scrap!'

The stench of the sick baby mingled with the peat-reek and the smell of dung from the three cows tethered beyond a chest-high wicker partition. In one corner, a pile of dry heather rustled with other children and puppies. The furniture consisted of two meal kists, a clothes chest, a couple of rude chairs, and a box-bed enclosed by curtains. Wooden bowls and pots, most of which Jean presumed were concerned with milk and cheese production, were stacked against the wall.

Pulling her plaid over the child's pinched face, the old woman closed her fist over her thumb in a gesture to ward off the evil eye.

'It's all right, mother,' said Christina Reid. 'She is the one who will wed Kynachan.' Then she apologized to her guests. 'Mother's a bit addled these days. She suspects the fairies whisked away my bairn and left a changeling. But it's not true. It's my own babe right enough.'

For a moment it looked as though the old lady would take refuge in senile aggression, but her frown relaxed and she bowed her head, muttering a greeting to Jean as she sat down on a bench beside her.

'The bairn is her grandson,' explained their hostess. 'He is named William after my father.'

'He lost an arm at Preston,' said Janet.

'Fighting with Kynachan for the Chevalier,' said the old lady, spitting accurately into the fire. 'Good for nothing after that. Didn't last more'n a couple of summers.'

Janet sighed. 'He was a brave man who brought honour to his family.'

The old woman spat once more.

Moving from the doorway, Janet gently lifted the covering plaid from the baby's naked body. 'Och, the wee mite. I brought something to stop him scouring. Andrew!'

Whisky jug in hand, the young gillie pushed his way through the curious women who crowded the doorway. Christina Reid produced a shallow wooden cup – a quaich – and offered the spirit first to her guests, then to the other women, all silent as they stared at Jean.

'They say you're from Edinburgh, Miss Mercer,' said Mrs Reid. 'But you have the Gaelic.'

'My family have lived round Perth for many generations,' replied Jean. 'But it is true that much of my childhood was passed in Edinburgh.'

'Is that so? My brother went to Edinburgh when he was in the Lowlands for the shearing three summers ago. He told us everybody lives in houses that are bigger even than Castle Menzies.'

'Well . . . yes. But in each building live many families. Some have to share a single room. My own family had but three rooms.'

'Your mother bore many children?'

'Four. But where are your menfolk?' asked Jean.

'On the hill.' Mrs Reid gestured to the hearth. 'This morning the fire burned unusually hot, and the porridge boiled more quickly than normal – a sign that we should begin cutting the peat this day.'

'That's a fine drop of whisky, Lady Kynachan,' said the old lady, dipping a corner of her shawl into the quaich and giving it to the child to suck.

'Aye. It's from Rannoch. The laird has it in for the wedding.'

'Tell me, Miss Mercer. I have heard that fine ladies in Edinburgh wear gowns with hoops so large they could shelter a calf beneath. Why?' asked Christina Reid.

'It's just the fashion of the moment,' said Jean.

'And how many of these gowns could a body buy for the price of a cow, would you say?'

'I fear I would not be knowing the price of a cow,' confessed Jean.

By the time they left the township, Jean had been given

exhaustive details of the genealogy of each family, their degree of kinship to each other and to the laird. Kings' bastards had married the daughters of prominent lairds, whose daughters married lesser landowners in the district, and so on down to the tenants' younger sons' daughters, who married landless labourers. Thus almost every family in Atholl could trace a link through to their laird and the royal house. Many on the estate were named Stewart, but there were also Reids, Gows, Robertsons, Dewars, Camerons, McDougalls, McDiarmids, and even a family of Campbells.

Through the course of the day, the two ladies of Kynachan travelled from hamlet to hamlet, until Jean's head began to reel with the effort of remembering the names of the women, the details of their families, and their position in each little society – whether wife of tenant, subtenant, or poorest labourer.

At one settlement, the women, bent under the weight of great wicker baskets strapped to their backs, were carrying dung from the middens to spread on the infield. One of the cottages was having its thatch removed, and that, too, was being spread on the land for the fertilizing value of the soot that impregnated the straw and bent grass. At another clachan Jean and Janet encountered a packman selling fish hooks, needles, ribbons, and combs. Other than those guiding a single plough team, he was the only able-bodied man they saw all day.

Between townships, Janet continued to feed her future daughter-in-law with information.

'There're fifteen families on Drumnakyle.'

'Mr Stewart's the leading tenant?' asked Jean, determined to fix as many names as possible in her mind.

'That's right. James Stewart. Not close kin, though. Not all Stewarts are sibs of the king. We're going next to Daloist. There's a township over the ridge, but that's Kinardochy and belongs to the Menzies. Even though they are so close, our people don't have to do with them. They prefer their own Kynachan folk. John Forbes is tenant of Daloist. He runs the mill, to which our folk are thurled, and the smithy – a big man on Kynachan. He's also an elder of the kirk over at Dull. Forbes is a widower, and his sister keeps house for him.'

'Davie says the minister is very strict.'

'He is that. Folk go over the pass to Dull on Sunday, and he puts the fear of God into them. He believes the fiddle to be the instrument of the Devil, though, and they won't have that. Given a chance he is inclined to try to extend his authority over the spiritual welfare of the people into matters that are the concern of the lairds, and we're all Piskies of course. Our priest, Duncan Cameron, has a chapel in Fortingall and gets on fine with the minister there. Duncan holds a service for us in one of the houses twice a month. Usually Kynachan or Foss. Sometimes Portnellan, by the loch.'

By the end of the afternoon, Jean had learned that the people of the townships worked the land in common, drawing lots each season to determine which strips of land in the infield would yield the harvest that would be theirs. The main tenant might have half a dozen ridges of the infield and the right to graze half a dozen units of livestock on the outfield – the less accessible land within the head dyke, which was fertilized only by grazing animals. A unit of stock was a cow and her calves of one, two, and three years, or the grazing equivalent in sheep, goats, ponies, or geese. The humblest labourer in the crudest bothy might have to rear his family on the produce from less than a single lot.

All held their lands from the laird, in exchange for cash, produce, and labour. The fires of the mansion house consumed large quantities of peat, and the tenants had to keep it supplied. In times of trouble, they must answer the laird's summons. Every boy was taught by his father to handle the broadsword and dirk, and was given the theory of musketry. The laird held regular musters of his fighting men, when they practised the skills of warfare.

The ladies visited the township of Tombreck and called at Drumbac and Daldow, the latter the only settlement north of the burn of Kynachan, where the poor boggy land on the edge of Craig Kynachan had the compensation of facing south to the warming sun. By mid-afternoon, they were approaching the last township, and Janet was still feeding the weary Jean with facts.

'Pitkerril now. George Cairney's been principal tenant for twenty-five years. He's no farmer, but he's the best cattle-man in Strathtummel. He looks after our own beasts when they're on the hill in summer. He was fined by the baron court for taking timber from the Wood of Kynachan for years without permission, and it bankrupted him. Davie took over George's debts and let him stay.'

'Was there not some trouble here a day or two ago?'

'Aye. George persuaded Davie to let onto Pitkerril a couple of families from Rannoch, who had lost their lands. They're a rowdy lot, but Pitkerril's the last clachan on the estate, and having some tough lads on our boundary is no bad thing. It helps keep the cattle thieves away.'

'According to Bohally, that's the job of the Black Watch.'

'It is, and the thieving's not nearly as bad as it used to be. Although Struan Robertson is as good a friend and Jacobite as one could wish for, some of his clansfolk have no respect for other people's cows, and Struan does little to discourage them.'

'You'd think there'd be little danger of theft since most of the cattle seem to live in the cottages.'

'The danger's in summer. All the livestock and most of the people on the estate go up to the shielings round the back of the mountain in Glen Mor for the grazing. That time is a couple of months away yet, and man and beast are on short commons until the summer growth takes off. Folk're always grateful for a cheese, but never more so than now. You wait to see how much food they'll get through at the wedding.'

'I think after the wedding I shall leave the running of the estate to Davie. There is too much to learn.'

Janet reined her pony. 'Jean, my dear. You must try to know as much about the estate and its people as he does.'

'My duty is to be a loving wife to Davie and a good mother to his children, and to manage his household. Surely that is enough.'

'That's what I thought when I married Davie's father. I was the daughter of a minister and knew little of the Highlands or its people. But when Kynachan was away during the Rising, and later in prison, I had to run this estate.'

'But that was more than twenty years ago. Such times of turmoil are past.'

'I'm sure you're right, but being wife of Kynachan is not the same as wife to a merchant, a man of the law, or even a lowland laird. You are the link between the wives of the country folk and Davie. You must know them and earn their respect. Sometimes Davie will rely on you for advice so that his rule over the people is just. And life is uncertain. You can never tell what the future may bring. It may be many years before there is an heir who could run the estate.'

'I refuse to consider widowhood before I am even wed.'

'When circumstances required it, I found that I was strong.'

'If circumstances require it of me, I shall be as steel,' said Jean. 'But until then I shall keep my blade in its scabbard.'

'Fair enough,' said Janet, and she kicked her pony back into motion.

14

The Wedding

The Highlands can deliver a blizzard in June, but they can also give days in spring when it seems incongruous that trees are without leaves and fields are bare instead of blowsy green with summer ripeness. Jean and David were wed on such a day.

In the preceding week, the house had been rich with the scent of roasting meat and fowls. The ovens had baked tarts, cakes, and pies. Chains of pack animals had carried supplies from Perth and brought extra fodder for the forthcoming influx of ponies.

Jean and her sisters had spent the night before the wedding with the neighbouring Laird of Foss. Wearing an ivory silk gown embroidered with silver and a matching cloak trimmed with ermine, the bride set out at noon, carrying in her hand a posy of violets. Set in her hair was a band of silk patterned with the Stewart chequer of blue and white. Under a cloudless sky, she settled herself on the side-saddle of a white charger, supplied with an armed escort by Struan Robertson.

The animal was placid – it had to be. Along the track to Kynachan, her attendants kept up a continual roll of musketry from their assortment of illegal weapons. The flat bangs echoed off the hillsides, keeping the rooks, kites, and buzzards wheeling nervously high above the strath. Every settlement they passed answered the gunfire with shouts, streamers, and pipe music, so that the procession began to resemble an army on the march through hostile country.

By the time they splashed through the ford, Jean's retinue had been augmented along the way by many of the country people, and the final few yards were thronged by cheering tenants and neighbours. Putting aside their arms, the escort moved towards the whisky and ale that had been laid out on trestle tables in the meadow, while Jean and her sisterly maids-of-honour entered the house.

David was waiting for her in the parlour. All his laces and buttons had been undone by his friends, led by Bohally, who stood by him to ensure that no ties bound him, symbolizing his freedom to accept the one that would be indissoluble until death. If his stockings fell to his ankles, his cravat hung loose, or the flap on the front of his breeches needed his hand to preserve decency, so be it.

The ceremony was short, the minimum from the Book of Common Prayer, and then the wedding feast was served. The crowd spilled out of the yard and up the mound west of the house, their soft Gaelic painting pictures to each other of the beauty of the bride, the virtue and courage of the groom, the honour of his family, and the memory of David's father.

Mingling easily with the people were the local lairds. They came from all Atholl, Rannoch, Glen Lyon, and Strathtay – Stewarts of Ballechin, Innerhadden, Garth, Crossmount, Tempar, Fincastle, Bonskeid. Robertsons of Lude, of Fascally, Auchleeks, Bohespick, Woodsheal, Kindrochit, Trinafour, Blairfetty. Menzies lairds from Fortingall and Glen Quaich. Fat, thin, old, young, stupid, clever; drunkards, braggarts, and saints. In their tartan trews, they and their red-faced wives had ridden over on shaggy ponies with their gillies and unfledged children swarming round them.

United by blood and common interest, the wedding of one of their number was an occasion when they could meet, celebrate, and politic. At the same time, their wives tried to prevent their daughters giving too much to their neighbours' sons as whisky and music flowed beside barns – warm, dark, and fragrant with heather and hay.

From an armchair in the parlour, an old man in a red cloak, a gold-topped cane by his side, called out to David when the bridal pair passed by.

'About time you were wed, Kynachan,' he said.

'I could say the same to you, Struan.'

'Pray God I never get that drunk.'

David laughed. 'Let me present you to my wife. Jean, this is Alexander Robertson of Struan, the mighty puissant chief of the Clan Donnachaidh.'

Struan bent forward in his chair to kiss her hand.

'I thank you for my steed and my noisy escort, sir,' said Jean.

'A treat for the lads, my dear.' He lifted a quizzing glass to examine her. 'Thank Christ your *tamhasg* didn't visit me. Otherwise I'd've wed you myself, drunk or sober.'

Jean wrinkled her nose. 'A poet of your distinction should do better than that.'

Struan chortled. 'A poet of my distinction. You didn't read my work at maid school.'

'I believe you are a poet in many languages, sir.'

'Nothing to be proud of, my dear. Merely the legacy of a lifetime of foreign exile in the service of the true king.'

'They say King Louis of France described you as the first gentleman of his court,' said Jean.

Pleased, Struan took a pinch of snuff. 'The kindness of kings is nothing, my dear, compared with that of a lass as pretty as you.'

Jean flicked her posy in mock flirtation. 'La, sir! And they say Struan has no time for those of my sex.'

'Be reasonable, child. How could I feel anything but warmth for your sex before so fair a representative on a day such as this?'

From the throng of guests, Commissary Thomas Bissett, a small man in middle age and one of the few in breeches and silk stockings rather than Highland dress, came hurrying across. His pearl-buttoned waistcoat stretching tight across his neat pot belly, he bowed to David.

'Cousin, allow me to give you and your lady my best felicitations on this most propitious of days.'

With his eye on the waistcoat buttons, Struan gave a grunt of laughter. 'Pearls before swine, I do believe, Bissett.'

Bissett returned a glacial smile. 'I don't follow you, Struan. But there again, I never would.'

The old chief smiled his appreciation of the retort, and Bissett turned back to David.

'As well as myself,' he continued, 'I am here to represent His Grace, who is in London, but would otherwise, of course, be here. His Grace charged me to pass on his good wishes.'

'Thank His Grace for me, Thomas.'

'My nephew seems to find the company of your sister congenial, Lady Kynachan,' said Bissett, now addressing Jean.

Along with Kinnaird, who was still carrying through a stilted mating ritual with Barbara, Bissett's nephew, James, had volunteered to join the bride's party at Foss. He had made himself extremely agreeable to Abigail, further bolstering the impression made upon her at Castle Menzies.

'You can't blame the new Lady of Kynachan for the company her sister keeps, Bissett,' Struan taunted.

The commissary pursed his lips in annoyance. 'I'm surprised you dare venture from your own country, Struan, for fear the duns get you.'

'You don't have to worry yourself about me,' replied Struan. 'I've thirty lads outside with my interests at heart, and, should one of his guests be threatened, Davie'll turn out a few more.'

'Gentlemen, please,' said Jean. 'No disagreements. Not today.'

'Nor any day, my dear,' said Bissett. 'Eh, Struan?'

'If Justice and Honour prevail, there is never a reason for men to quarrel, Mr Bissett,' said Jean.

Struan snorted with laughter. 'We can't argue with that, Bissett.'

Heaving himself to his feet, Struan removed his cloak with a flourish, handing it and his gold-topped cane to an attendant. 'Madam, if Thomas would excuse us, would you do this old man the honour of a dance?'

In the courtyard the enthusiasm of the musicians was being reinforced by whisky, and the revellers – Aunt Meg amongst them – were in the midst of a rowdy reel.

Struan led Jean to a quiet corner. 'You've a fine man there,' he said.

'In Davie? I know.'

The old chief honked a pinch of snuff into the warm March afternoon. 'Even here in Atholl, there are plenty who've taken the oath to German Geordie and mean to keep it.'

'Like Mr Bissett?'

'No, I don't mind Bissett, although he's a bit of an old woman. Of course, his master's elder brother – still exiled in Rome with King James – is the real duke. William's devotion to the Jacobites cost him his dukedom.'

'You too have suffered over the years for the cause.'

'I first was privileged to take arms for the Stuarts forty years ago, along with Davie's father and grandfather. Thirty of those subsequent years I spent in exile.'

'I hope you can pass the rest of your days in peace.'

'In peace, girl? My wish is that I live until the Stuarts are kings again. That won't be done with peace. Our politicians are a rabble of rogues intent on lining their own pockets and oppressing the people. The English are not interested in us. They are thieves and men without honour.'

'Enough of this,' said Jean. 'I am not going to be harangued about politics today.'

'Aye,' said Struan. 'I'm sorry.'

She felt the dry warmth of his thin fingers as he touched her arm.

'One thing though, Jeannie Mercer; your Davie is an important man for the cause. Many of the younger lairds listen to his words. If the time should ever come again, do not try to dissuade him from his duty.'

Jean leaned over and kissed the old man on his cheek, inhaling the odour of claret, snuff, and peat smoke that impregnated his coat. 'Davie will always do what he believes right. I could not influence him against his conscience. Nor would I want to.'

He squeezed her hand. 'Davie's a lucky man.'

15

In the Bothy

The newlyweds retired soon after dark.

In the parlour, Anna Mercer and some of the more soporific guests had been listening to a bard who was enough of an entertainer to know when he was about to lose his audience. Hearing excited steps on the stairs outside, he had managed to draw his tale to a hurried close before the door burst open.

'They're ready!' shouted a red-faced laird, his wig askew.

The bride and groom were in the hall. Hand in hand, jostled by the inebriated throng, they pushed their way through the front door. There, two grim-faced Highlanders, fully armed and holding flaming torches above their heads, stood waiting either side to escort the newlyweds solemnly across the courtyard. Guests streamed from the house and barns in their wake.

At the edge of the yard waited two more torchbearers, and beyond them, at intervals, Jean could make out a double line of torches marching across the garden to the wood, where, flickering between the bare trees, they lit the path to the wedding bothy. At the head of the column, a piper worked his complaining instrument into life. As the bridal couple passed each pair of torches, the bearers fell in behind.

Jean looked back. A three-quarter moon was floating between the clouds, its austere light on the silent mass of Craig Kynachan contrasting with the dancing torchlight and bubbling pibroch of the bagpipes.

'What's the piper playing?' asked Jean.

One of the torchbearers just behind them, a bearded ancient, with a rusty sword banging against his knees, spoke up. 'It's his own composition, lady. A lament. He learned his art from a man of Skye.'

'It is very fine. But a lament is hardly appropriate.'

'He composed it for this very occasion, lady. It's "The Lassies' Lament for Kynachan". It expresses the sadness of all the young girls in Atholl on this happy occasion of the laird's wedding.'

'I see,' said Jean, digging her nails into David's palm. ' "The Lassies' Lament", indeed.'

'Pibrochs are composed to celebrate memorable or heroic events,' said David. 'It's a very good indication of my quality.'

'That's right,' broke in the ancient, who had a disconcerting habit of falling back, when David and Jean thought themselves out of earshot, and then of closing in again for fear he might miss something. 'If I were a lassie like you, I would think myself very fortunate. Kynachan's a very fine lover.'

'Davie,' exclaimed Jean.

'Och, it's not Kynachan who told me,' continued the old warrior. 'The bard has some excellent verses on the subject and he recites them most movingly – most movingly indeed. I expect he shall be composing a few more by the morning.'

Ahead of them, by the door of the bothy, stood the last two torchbearers and a grinning Bohally, a naked broadsword in one hand and horn whisky flask in the other. The little building had been freshly lime-washed and looked snug beneath its new heather thatch. Leaving David there, Barbara and Abigail led the bride inside.

A deep bed of hay, covered with sheets and fur rugs, half filled a good portion of the single bay. Lining a shelf between the top of the rough stone wall and the roof, hundreds of freshly picked primroses, their petals still damp from the woods, reflected the soft light of a couple of oil-filled cruisie lamps. Glowing peats in the hearth warmed the air.

Outside, as the pipes continued to play, David was raucously disrobed by his peers. Within, Jean's sisters helped remove her wedding finery, which they exchanged for a lace-edged, embroidered linen night-gown.

Barbara put her head through the door to announce that the bride was ready. Jean stood demurely by the fire as Bohally entered. Leaning forward, he kissed her on the cheek, stammered a blessing, and dived out. He was the first of many. By the time David was thrust into the bothy, Jean had been kissed by the lairds and closer male kin and had endured more than one drunken caress.

The couple suddenly found themselves alone. Jean retreated to the large white rug made from the winter skins of mountain hares. David barred the door on the crackle of torches and babble of whiskied voices.

'They'll be away back to the house now?' she asked.

Her eyes were large over the top of the sheet that she had pulled to her nose. David still wore his linen shirt, its drawstring loose, and his breeches.

'Yes. Charlie'll make sure of that. He'll chase off the piper too, once he's finished his lament.' David looked at his bride and smiled, his face full of love and tenderness. He stretched himself the length of the rug, propping himself on his elbow. The scent of crushed lavender in the hay momentarily mastered the peat-reek.

'I was proud of you today,' he said, keeping his tone conversational.

'Proud of me?' Jean's head came round to look up to his face. 'Why?'

'You have already gained the respect of the people of this country. Some never do.'

'If they have any regard for me, it is because I am the wife of Kynachan.'

'No. It is because you show interest in their lives and customs, and because you have a cantankerous old dog like Struan lauding you to any who will listen.'

'Don't you be rude about him. He's a great man.'

'That's true.' David seemed content to lie chatting by his bride. 'I didn't get much to eat. I asked for some food to be put in here in case we got hungry. Have you seen it?'

He looked round the confines of their chamber. Jean lifted her head. With flowers filling the shelf on all four walls, the only possible hiding place was their bed.

'Ah!' She sat up, her shining black hair sliding down her back like the fast glide of dark water. 'That's what this lump must be.'

Lifting a corner of the rug, she thrust her arm into the soft hay and pulled out a basket, its contents protected by a napkin, and a jug of whisky.

'That was an excellent idea, Davie. I didn't eat either. I was too nervous.'

She darted him a swift glance, but he was looking into the basket.

'So was I.'

'You! What've you got to be nervous about?' She took a handful of raisins.

'You're young. You can take things like this in your stride, but I'm set in my ways. I haven't been married before – any more than you – or had a wedding night.'

His face seemed innocent; she laughed. 'Poor little Davie. Have something to eat and you'll feel better.'

He tasted a pot of jam with his finger, spooned some onto an oatcake, and handed it to her. He spread one for himself, and they leaned back companionably on the bed, chewing and looking up to the rafters.

With the door secured against the wind, the little flames from the oil lamps never wavered but cast still, soft shadows on the walls and the woven twigs above them.

'Barbara told me Kinnaird proposed marriage to her this afternoon,' Jean said.

'I'm glad. Would you like a sip of whisky?'

'No, thank you. I suspect Kinnaird is simply after Barbara's fortune.'

'He is certainly a careful man.'

She looked shyly at him over the sheet. 'I used to believe that such deliberation was the surest foundation for marriage.'

'And now?'

'And now I feel pity for my sister, although she professes a fine sensibility towards him.'

David removed the stopper of the whisky jug. He filled a shallow quaich and looked round for somewhere level to put it while he replaced the stopper. He smiled and set it carefully down on the sheet, which covered Jean's breastbone. She drew in her breath and the quaich tilted.

'Don't talk or you'll spill it,' he warned.

Placing the jug on the floor, he leant over her. 'Careful,' he murmured, his lips gently caressing hers, 'you don't want whisky all over you.'

She closed her eyes as his hand gently traced the line of her cheek and throat.

'You are so beautiful,' he whispered. 'You are more than I ever dreamed of.'

He kissed her again. This time her lips responded, and the hay beneath them rustled. Her hand made tentative contact with his shoulder. Then suddenly her body went rigid, and she gave a stifled squeak.

David pulled back. 'Don't be afraid, my love. It's all right.'

'It isn't! The whisky!'

'Damnation,' said David, as the quaich slid down between them.

Jean sat up, plucking the top of her nightdress away from her skin. 'It feels horrible.'

'Take it off. I'll help you.'

'Yes – no!' She bit her lip to half conceal a smile and twirled her hand. 'You must turn round.'

'But we're man and wife.'

'Not until the marriage has been consummated. And I'm bashful, so hide your eyes, Kynachan.'

'You're a tyrannical wee thing,' said David with equanimity.

'Comes with the position of eldest sister.' Her voice was muffled by the nightdress she was drawing over her head. 'Right, you can turn back.'

She had pulled up the sheet, but now any apprehension in her eyes had been replaced by something more akin to anticipation. David lay flat on his stomach, his face within inches of her ear. He blew softly.

'That tickles.'

'But it feels good.' He lifted a thick coil of her hair and laid it across the white fur. With the tip of his tongue he touched her ear lobe. 'So does that.'

'Mm.' As he kissed her neck, her hands fell away from the protecting coverlet. Her eyes were shut, but her long black lashes fluttered, and she drew in her breath.

Slipping his hand beneath the sheet, he trailed a finger over the swell of her breasts and cupped her chin. Their lips met for a few seconds, and his tongue slipped between her lips, withdrawing before she could react. Momentarily she tensed but then relaxed, and her lips parted.

This time the tips of their tongues touched. He pushed his arm beneath her head, so that it nestled in the crook of his arm, and his other hand stroked a path down from her chin, between her breasts, to her stomach. Her muscles flinched at his feather-light caress. Then, responding to the most ancient of instincts, her hips stirred.

'Your skin is so soft I can scarcely tell where my finger tips end and you begin,' he said. 'You feel like smoke.'

Outside, the rising wind soughed through the trees, but within the warm womb of the bothy the flames held steady, and the only sounds were their breathing and the rustle of hay. Carefully, David drew back the sheet, catching his breath at the beauty of her body. He kissed the peak of her breast and felt her nipple rise between his lips.

She gasped, clasping his head, pressing him to her. She ran her hands through his hair and across the width of his shoulders. Drawing away, he slipped off his breeches and rose to his knees to remove his shirt. When she thought the garment covered his face, she opened her eyes to steal a glance at his nakedness.

His torso was slim and golden in the lamplight, with no spare flesh and little hair on his chest or stomach to conceal the supple play of muscle beneath the skin. The arch of his body as he pulled the shirt over his head emphasized his triangular shape from shoulder to loin and drew her eye down to his erection.

Her eyes widened. 'Don't hurt me.'

'Why would I hurt something as lovely as you, Jeannie Mercer?' he murmured, his eyes feasting on the delicate strength of her shoulders, the firm swell of her breasts, the deep red of her nipples against her milk-white skin. 'Don't forget, I have been dreaming about you and loving you for months.'

'You can see now it isn't,' she said.

'What isn't?'

'Like a lion rampant.'

'It is a bit.'

Again his head dipped, and his tongue drew a lazy line across the valley between her breasts, from one nipple to the other. Her arms came up round his back, her fingers pressing into the grooves between his ribs and sliding hesitantly over his shoulders. He trailed his hand, as gentle as the kiss of a butterfly's wing, across her stomach, across the springy tuft of hair above the cleft of her thighs, down the side of her leg. He drew arabesques on her satin skin and thrilling sensation followed his touch, like catspaws of wind across a cornfield.

Her body turned towards him. Her lips sought his, her arms pressed him to her, and her hips ground against his loins.

Then she pulled away. 'Davie,' she gasped. 'Oh, my Davie.'

His fingers stroked low over her stomach, and her legs parted to his touch. He shifted to kneel between her thighs, his hands now stroking the curves at the side of her slender body and moving across her breasts, her belly, her thighs, and between her legs – squeezing, caressing, moulding – and all the while he marvelled at his possession of her and the implacable intensity of his love.

She clenched her fist against her forehead and trembled as waves of sensation surged through her. Still on his knees, he placed his hands beneath her, raising her body into his lap. And carefully he entered her.

Slowly he rocked, inch in, inch out, gently, easily. Her hands clutched at his back, her fingers digging deep into his flesh.

Once more his mouth sought hers, and his tongue thrust into her. Her hands moved to the compact muscle of his buttocks, and she pulled him deep inside her, flinching at the sudden shaft of pain when he broke through her maidenhead.

Then her consciousness was swamped by the beauty of what she felt. Both her heart and her body had opened to him like a flower. Slowly he moved. She felt no pain, or, if she did, it was overwhelmed by the intensity of the fever coursing through her, and she responded, unbidden, in natural concert with him.

In the darkness outside, the wind had risen to a near gale, hurling squalls of rain against the thatch. Bohally had long since given up his vigil.

Within, a sheen of perspiration reflected the lamplight from the two entwined bodies moving slickly against each other. Their breathing grew faster, their movements more urgent, as the collision of their loins drove shock waves through their flesh. Each pressed at the other, demanding fulfilment and release. Inside each swelled the hurricane of sexual orgasm.

'Oh, Jeannie, my love, my darling,' he groaned, violent thrusts of his loins driving his seed deep into the rippling waves in her womb.

Her face contorted. Her hips arched to receive his final lunge. A single short cry broke through her lips, and their bodies collapsed, hearts bumping, hair damp with sweat.

After a few moments he drew away, raising a shiver in her as he touched her erect nipple with his lips, and they lay spreadeagled, side by side, regaining their breath. She looked at him, cheeks flushed, lips swollen, eyes misty with the aftermath of passion.

'Is . . . is it always like that?' She almost sounded afraid. 'I mean . . . I didn't mean to . . . I don't know what came over me.'

He rolled over onto his elbow and gazed down at the slim, now passive, body of his wife. He touched her lips. 'Hush, Jeannie.' His voice was tender. 'Never have I felt anything so beautiful. I knew I loved you to the depths of my soul but I never knew that love could make itself so concrete.'

'But I was wanton. It was as if a beast I could not control had taken me over. And look at me.' Lifting her arms, she made a graceful gesture down the length of her naked body, her legs akimbo. 'I'm shameless.'

'So am I,' said David.

Her eye went to where his flesh once more jutted rampant, and she gave a little cry of surprise. 'What an astonishing thing it is! Will it hurt you if I touch it?'

'No.'

Her long fingers gently stroked his shaft. 'It's so soft. The skin's like satin.' She squeezed and laughed with delight. 'And so hard, too. I can't believe all that went into me. It's like magic. Do you want to put it inside me again? I want to do what will please you.'

Caressing, his hand moved up her side and cupped her breast. 'Put it in yourself.'

'What do you mean?'

'Kneel over me on your hands and knees.'

'Heavens! I never imagined my vows would lead to this.'

Rising, she slipped across his hips and rested on her knees, her hands on either side of his head. Her hair, cascading down round his face, created a dark tunnel between them. His hands moved slowly over her buttocks and up her back. Her eyelids fluttered. He gripped her, spreading her, and once more eased into her. She sighed, snuggling down on him, making small adjustments of her hips so that she could feel him inside her.

For a while, she lay on his chest as he caressed her back, whispering words of love into her ear. Then she rose so that her body was erect over his, her hair falling to shield her face and breasts. She moved her hips in a slow circle, pressing herself against the hardness of his groin. She threw her head back, and he ran his hands across her buttocks, round her slim waist, and up to her breasts. She moved her hips faster until she climaxed once more, and her cry of fulfilment was lost in the roar of the wind in the trees.

Part II

THE RISING

16

Halcyon Days

Summer was the time of plenty. After the peats had been cut and stacked to dry until autumn, after the land had been ploughed and planted, came the Beltane celebrations on the first of May. Every hearth was extinguished, and a great bonfire lit on the top of Craig Kynachan, from which the fires in the townships were re-kindled for the baking of the Beltane bannock. At dawn, the girls would gather at the Fairy Well on the east flank of Schiehallion, dance round it, and drink, for the first water taken from the well on Beltane day would bring luck throughout the following year. Later in the morning, the townships migrated to the shielings high on the upland pastures round the mountain.

Led by a piper, the chattering women left their cottages, baskets strapped to their backs, their fingers busy on spindles. Children scampered through the heather alongside the track. Behind them, menfolk led ponies that bore precious timbers to repair winter damage to the simple shieling huts or that dragged sledges piled with pots, pans, spinning wheels, and topped by the occasional granny. At the rear of the procession came the bellowing livestock, reluctant to leave the growing crops, now to be unmolested by their hungry mouths.

Some of the shielings were on Craig Kynachan, but most were in Glen Mor, between the great curtain wall of Schiehallion and the hills that rose sharply to Carn Marg to the south. As the summer bothies were rebuilt and re-thatched, cattle, ponies, sheep, and goats would spread out over the hillsides, tearing at the patches of sweet soft grass.

Young animals and young people would doze in the heather, or play along the burn that tumbled through the glen. Women sang songs as they spun wool and flax in front of their huts or made butter and cheese from the abundant milk to pay their rents and help sustain their families through the winter.

When the sun went down, fiddles, Jew's-harps, and whisky would appear, and folk sat round the fires by the burn, telling tales of the heroic days of Fingal. His warriors lay in a loch on Craig Kynachan, resting on their elbows, swords and shields by their sides, waiting for the third and final blast of the horn before springing back to life to rescue Scotland from her enemies. As their elders talked, young lovers found privacy in the accommodating depths of the heather beneath the northern lights – the Merry Dancers – which rippled across the star-bright sky,

With few surnames in any locality, most Highlanders had nicknames to tell them apart. Often these were based upon a physical characteristic. Bohally, for example was known as Tearlach Mor – Big Charles. Lairds' wives were usually adjuncts of the estates, as in Bean an Foss – wife of Foss – or Bean an Blairfetty. Jean became known to the country people of Atholl as Bean Daibhidh Choimeachdan – wife of Davie who is always in attendance, or Doting Davie.

The months following her marriage were the happiest Jean had ever known. She and David delighted in each other's company, and their joy infected those around them. Bonnie Jeannie and Doting Davie became celebrated in songs, not a few of them indelicate.

That summer they travelled throughout Atholl and beyond, meeting kinsfolk and staying with other lairds. Unaccompanied except for Willie Kennedy, they crossed remote and lonely passes. David knew each peak and gully across Atholl and Rannoch. A boulder could trigger a tale about an ancient skirmish against a raiding party of Campbells, or a loch the story of the monstrous kelpie who dwelt in its depths, snatching maidens who came too close.

'I am no maiden. It won't want me,' Jean had said on that occasion.

In the woods and hills west towards Rannoch, on the fringes of Struan Robertson's lands, were men who lived by cattle reiving, banditry, and by the receipt of blackmail paid by lairds and tenants to protect their stock. In a remote glen or glade, David and Jean would occasionally encounter a few shaggy men, who were immediately drawn by the wealth exhibited by the couple's clothes and ponies. But most, recognizing David, greeted him with an enthusiasm that raised Jean's eyebrows. The few who did not know him kept their distance, wary of the quality of the arms carried by the tiny party and the chieftain's eagle feathers in David's bonnet.

In late summer, David was appointed a commissioner in

a lawsuit over the shielings above Glen Lyon. For centuries the Campbells of Breadalbane had been spreading eastward, acquiring land by force, threats, and marriages. Now the earl had fixed his predatory eye on the shieling grounds traditionally used by the Glen Lyon townships, and the Court of Session in Edinburgh had appointed David to inspect the disputed lands and estimate the number of cattle, horses, sheep, and goats the hills could carry.

For a fortnight, between Loch Tay and Loch Rannoch, David and Jean ranged the high mountain plateaux, springy with moss and heather and broken by black peat hags. At Kynachan the horizon was the hills on either side of Strathtummel, but up here the sky stretched a hundred miles between distant mountain peaks. In the remote corries, where the shielings lay, the Glen Lyon folk made them welcome, delighted to have their lonely firesides graced by the presence of the celebrated Daibhidh Choimeachdan and his bride.

In the evenings, by some gently babbling burn, Jean would sit beneath the stars, snuggle into David's arms, and listen to the stories, songs, and legends of the Highlands. The best of the simple shieling huts would have been vacated for the honoured guests, and, later, the silence of the hills would be augmented by the snores of Willie Kennedy, wrapped in his plaid outside, and the uninhibited joy of the visitors' love-making.

When she bathed in the burn in the morning, Jean would be surrounded by the women, whose mixture of envy, admiration, and bawdy humour made her both laugh and blush. Once she was shyly approached by a newly married girl who begged a fragment of Jean's clothing or ribbon, with which to make a charm to enrich her own marriage bed. David preened.

17

The Black Bull

On their way back home from Glen Lyon, half a mile from the house of Kynachan, Jean and David were attracted by a commotion in a field. Beyond a wall stood a small solitary rowan, in whose lower branches Clementina was comfortably perched. Dodging round the trunk, a stringy black bull tore up the ground in hot pursuit of a terrified, pox-faced Highlander. Occasionally the man made a leap at the tree, only to be vigorously fended off by Clementina's bare foot.

'Rescue me, Davie,' she called to them.

'Don't you dare,' ordered Jean. 'Clemmie's perfectly safe up there, and that beast looks vicious.'

'Who is the fellow, Willie?' asked David.

'I have seen him at the goat fair at Kinloch Rannoch,' replied the gillie. 'I do not know his name or his family.'

A few feet of the dry-stone wall had collapsed, leaving a gap. On the ground lay a stout stick with the bull's ring tied to its end, from which the animal had broken free. It was nimble on its feet, sharp of horn, and looked angry enough to continue its pursuit indefinitely.

Dismounting, David went to the wall. 'Do you need rescuing, Clemmie?'

'I suppose so. I was peacefully minding my own affairs when these two God-forsaken creatures came crashing through the wall at me. I thought it wise to take myself from harm's way, and I would be quite content if this miscreant' – she waved a threatening foot – 'would not insist upon trying to join me. It is quite evident there is not room for both of us.'

'Help! Help!' shouted the Highlander.

The bull had paused, the trunk between itself and its intended victim. Clementina threw a stick, and the animal snorted, tossing its head and pawing at the ground.

'Who are you?' demanded David. 'And where are you taking that animal?'

'I am servant to Struan, sir. The bull is his. Shoot the brute, else I perish.'

'I'd sooner have it dead than let such a scrawny creature near any Kynachan cow, but I can't go around damaging neighbours' property. However, I know a sure-fire way of taming a beast like that.' David turned to Willie. 'When I have it, put the ring back in its snout.'

'David,' exclaimed Jean. 'What are you going to do?'

Her pony, made curious by the alarm in her voice, swung its head to look at her.

'Don't worry, my dear, I know exactly what I'm about.' He patted her leg and handed over his plaid.

'Stop him, Willie!'

'I couldn't do that.' Willie leaned forward in his saddle, his craggy face alive with interest. 'I wager he's going to twist its tail.'

Davie had stepped through the wall into the field, walked a dozen yards, and stopped. His arms hung by his sides.

'What do you mean?' Jean wailed. 'He's going to be killed!'

'Och, no. I've never heard of anyone being killed twisting a bull's tail. Mind you, I've never actually met anyone who has tried it.'

'What!'

'But Fingal did. He bound his beast in chains of mist.' Willie came down from his pony and picked up the staff and ring.

'What are you doing, Davie?' asked Clementina, standing up on her bough.

'Come on, your honour,' shouted the animal's keeper. 'You distract it, and I shall run for safety.'

The bull took exception to this counsel. Accelerating with astonishing speed, it galloped about the tree, forcing the little man to scuttle round the trunk. The animal circled, and its rolling eye chanced upon David. Lowering its head, it charged, crossing the ground as swift as a deer.

At the last second, David sprang to one side and as the animal pounded past he grabbed tight hold of its tail and somersaulted. The bull stumbled, its back legs went to one side, and it fell, burying a horn in the soil. Leaping forward, Willie Kennedy grabbed its other horn and threaded the ring back through the helpless animal's nose.

Willie took hold of the staff, and both he and the bull rose to their feet. David released the tail, and the beast shook its head tentatively and then stood quiet, realizing it had been captured.

'Wonderful, Davie!' Clementina jumped down from the tree.

'Oh, thank you, sir,' said the Highlander. 'You've saved me a beating.'

'What is your name?'

The man hesitated. 'Alister Breck.'

'I should have you up before the baron court for negligence in the care of a dangerous animal. Take that beast to the smith and get him to close the ring more tightly.'

'Yes, sir. I'm sorry.'

'You were also willing to put my sister in jeopardy in order to preserve your own skin. Tell Struan to choose another to do his business. If I come across you on Kynachan land again, I'll crop your ears.'

Alister Breck paled. 'Yes, sir. Sorry, sir.'

'Be off with you!' David picked up his wig and bonnet. Turning towards the road, he saw that Jean had trotted off down the track.

He called after her but she did not acknowledge him. Clementina giggled.

'I'm afraid you're in trouble, brother dear. Jeannie didn't appreciate that, but I did.'

'So did I, Kynachan,' said Willie Kennedy. 'I'd've done it myself had I thought of it.'

'You're daft enough to be telling the truth, Willie,' said Clementina.

Jean and her mother-in-law were waiting in the parlour when David and Clementina returned.

'Davie was marvellous,' said the excited Clementina. 'You should've seen him, Mother. He flipped the bull over on its back and saved me from being trampled and gored to a bloodied pulp.'

'Don't you ever dare do something as stupid as that again!' said Jean, her eyes blazing.

'I'm sorry, my dear.'

'Aye,' agreed his mother. 'You should be more responsible. You're a married man and Laird of Kynachan, not some giddy gamecock like Bohally. You haven't even got an heir yet.'

'It's not through want of trying,' said Clementina.

Just then the door to the parlour opened, and Donald appeared carrying a letter on a silver salver.

'What's this?' asked David, slitting the seal.

Donald jerked his thumb over his shoulder. 'The Perth carrier brought it, Laird. He's having a dram at the back door while he waits for the reply. It's Kinnaird wanting you to march boundaries with him and his neighbour Gilbert Stewart.'

'We can go on our way to visit my family at Perth,' said Jean.

'Why not let me open the missive first?'

'The carrier says Foss has sent for the Watch,' continued Donald. 'He's lost a beast, taken in broad daylight.'

David clicked his tongue. 'If people were alert, that sort of thing could not happen.'

'Aye. Foss's vowed to hang the thief and anyone who gives him aid. The times we live in,' said Donald, with a shake of his head. 'You'd think anyone with an ounce of sense would be suspicious of a black bull being led by a stranger.'

The following week, Jean and David stayed two days at Castle Menzies, then travelled along the north side of the Tay to Ballechin, where they spent the night with David's cousin, Charles Stewart. The next afternoon they crossed the ferry behind the regality court-house at Logierait for the final mile to Kinnaird.

There, the laird greeted them in front of the mansion house, which was still in the process of construction. The gorgeousness of his Highland garb contrasted with the dusty practicality of David's tartans. When Kinnaird bowed, the afternoon sun flashed from the yellow rock crystals set in the hilts of his sword and dirk and in the brooch securing his plaid.

'My, you're a pretty Highland man, Alexander,' said Jean, humour dancing in her eye at the sight of him.

'When in Rome,' said Kinnaird. 'And I see no need to allow my sartorial standards to slip when I enter the land of the Gael.'

'Quite right,' said David. 'You shame the rest of us.'

'My valet is an Edinburgh man. He can press a coat or powder a wig like an angel, but he considers Highland dress barbaric. I wear it to please the country people.'

He led them into the three-room cottage he was using until his house was complete. 'Your family is well? Was your journey easy?'

'Aye,' said David.

'Accosted by no black bulls?'

David smiled ruefully. 'That tale'll've reached Perth by now.'

'So modest, Kynachan. I'd wager it's the talk of Edinburgh. If not, it will be when I return there next week.'

For the rest of the afternoon, while the men climbed the hill to clear the marches between Easter and Wester Kinnaird, Jean was left to her own devices. They returned in the evening, when David extracted his wife from a group of old women in a nearby clachan.

'They call him the Waddling Laird,' said Jean, as they strolled back to Kinnaird's house.

David laughed. 'You'd think he'd be called the Bard or the Music Master. Folk usually have great respect for musicians.'

'Not for Alexander, I fear. Did you have a successful afternoon?'

David grimaced. 'Not too bad. On the top of the hill is a stretch of ground that's considered unlucky, and neither of them wanted it. It's the first time I've ever seen lairds trying to give each other land.'

Although the living room of the cottage was small, Kinnaird had brought his comforts from the capital. The table was mahogany, the spoons silver, the drinking vessels glass, but the Edinburgh cook could not disguise the toughness of the old kain hen – supplied as part of some tenant's rent – that was the foundation of their supper. Their host had changed to Lowland dress and wore a silk coat and breeches. Also present was Kinnaird's brother, John, a sullen, silent man, who managed the estate when the laird was away.

They avoided politics. Although David's enthusiasm for the Jacobite cause was well known, Kinnaird, a Whig by inclination, was too cautious to venture an opinion. Two bottles of claret into the evening, their host was emboldened to broach a subject that concerned him.

'Jean, you know that James Bissett is considering offering for the hand of your sister Abigail?'

'I knew they had formed a mutual affection. I am so glad.'

'Considering, I said, merely considering. Unfortunately there is a difficulty, which may threaten my own suit with Barbara.'

'That would break her heart,' said Jean in dismay.

'May threaten, I said, merely may.'

'You'd better explain yourself,' said David.

Kinnaird felt for the claret, changed his mind, and took some brandy instead. His hand trembled slightly as he drank. He had no wish to rouse David's ire.

'I'm sure it is just a hiccup,' he said. 'I have been advised by my lawyers that the draft marriage contract is unsatisfactory. Problems with her tocher, you know.'

'Barbara's tocher is just the same as Jean's,' said David. 'And that suited me fine.'

'But the greater part of their inheritance is still enmeshed in the courts.'

'True. However, there's sufficient aside from that for any reasonable man.'

'According to my advisers, much of the problem stems from the fact that each sister's affairs are dealt with separately. If their interest in the residue of their uncle's lands were to be handled in common, there would be a greater chance of a speedy conclusion.'

'And on this depends your marriage to Barbara?' asked Jean, scorn in her voice.

Kinnaird looked surprised by her tone. 'As you know, I consider marriage a serious affair. It behoves a sensible man to venture cautiously towards the state of wedded bliss. The knot once tied is not easily loosed, save by the Lord. I am naturally most fond of your sister, and such a matter left undone might affect our future happiness together.'

'Do I understand the position correctly?' asked David. 'If I don't let you take care of Jean's interest in her fortune, neither you nor young Bissett will wed her sisters?'

'Well . . .'

David turned away from Kinnaird to his wife. 'Is that what you want, Jeannie? Or would you rather I challenged him for belittling the honour of your sisters?'

'Barbara wants to marry him. He's not going to be much good as a husband if you kill him in a duel.'

Kinnaird smiled, the brandy making him reckless. 'Quite right, Jean. Of course, Kynachan, you will have to pay your share of the costs of our action. Twenty-five pounds sterling ought to cover it. I'll take your paper – oh, and one other thing. Since my own forebears long preceded yours at Kynachan, many of them lie in the burial ground at Foss. I would like you to ensure that the inclosure where they lie is kept in good repair. It is hard for me to maintain this responsibility from here.'

Leaning back in his chair, Kinnaird swirled the brandy in his glass. For a moment or two, David looked at him quizzically and then shook his head in disbelief.

'First you want money from me, Kinnaird. Then you suggest

I would dishonour your dead by neglecting their graves. Jeannie, are you sure you want this fellow as a brother-in-law? I think it would be better if I called him out.'

Kinnaird examined David, realized that he was not speaking in jest, and choked – brandy spilling on his waistcoat. His suddenly pleading eyes turned to Jean.

For a wicked few seconds she did not answer. Then her compassion came to his rescue. 'No, Davie. Do not fight him,' she said.

'Oh, thank God!' exclaimed Kinnaird, mopping his brow. 'I . . . I would have hated to have run you through, Kynachan.'

18

Interrupted Harvest

Kinnaird and Barbara were married in Edinburgh the following spring. By then, Abigail was already the spouse of James Bissett. Their wedding had taken place in the autumn of the previous year at Glenelbert, the Bissett family's estate, north of Dunkeld.

Jean bore her first child, John, in the summer of 1740. Seventeen-year-old Abigail died in childbirth that December, her daughter, christened Charlotte, living for just a week longer than her mother.

The early 1740s were hard years in the Highlands. Harvests were poor, and the government, conscious of its neglect of Scottish interests, was uneasily aware of the undercurrent of discontent that was always liable to manifest itself in support for the Jacobite cause.

In 1743, after Charles Stewart of Bohally had left the regiment, the Black Watch was ordered south, supposedly to be reviewed by King George, who had expressed a wish to see his kilted soldiers. Reluctantly, the regiment marched to England. Whilst they had sworn an oath of allegiance to the king, they had enlisted on the understanding that they would serve only in Scotland.

The regiment camped outside London, but there was no sign of the king. Rumours spread amongst the men that the review had merely been a ruse to bring them south, with the intention of despatching them to the West Indies, where they would be wiped out by fever. In spite of the hurried arrival of the aged General Wade, who inspected them on Finchley Common, the Highlanders had lost faith in their officers and in the word of the government. Striking camp in the middle of the night, many set off back to Scotland.

The government sent an army after them, which caught up a hundred miles north of London. The Highlanders surrendered their arms without a struggle. Three of their number were made examples, court-martialled, and shot in front of their comrades at the Tower of London. The regiment was then shipped smartly to the Continent to join the rest of the British army, who were fighting the French.

Throughout the Highlands, but particularly in Atholl, where many of the soldiers had been recruited, there was outrage at this treatment of their people. The three executed men became martyrs, and the government in London shrank still further in popularity.

The Jacobites drank their toasts to the King over the Water, plotting and dreaming of the time that would come again. But the court of King James in Rome was riddled with British agents, who reported little threat. James was openly Roman Catholic, unacceptable to the people of Britain, and his eldest son, Prince Charles, frittered away his days on arduous hunting trips, testing himself as well as the shadowing spies.

Since William of Orange had taken the British throne in 1688, it had suited Louis XIV and his successors to use the Stuarts as weapons in their rivalry with Britain. By religion, blood, and conviction, the French kings were supporters of the Stuart claim to the British throne, but they were unwilling to commit themselves to so speculative a venture as an armed invasion across the Channel. The French would support insurrection with arms and gold, perhaps, but the Continental powers were locked into the Wars of the Austrian Succession, and no armies could be spared to help the Jacobites. Even the most enthusiastic supporter of the Stuarts knew that to have any chance of overthrowing the House of Hanover their cause needed the support of a French army.

In February 1744, Atholl society gathered to celebrate the christening of a great-great-niece of Struan Robertson at the Hermitage, his much-loved house a few miles up the Tummel from Kynachan. Government spies mingled with Jacobite lairds but heard nothing save gossip, rumour, and discontented talk.

The harvest was good that autumn, yet the following winter was bitter. An iron frost fringed the burns with icicles, and early snows blanketed Schiehallion. Sheltered from the prevailing south-west wind by the bulk of the mountain, Craig Kynachan remained relatively free from snow, and the people of the townships foraged on its flanks for fodder to supplement the meagre supplies of hay for the snugly housed cattle. Almost as compensation for the winter, spring came early in 1745.

*   *   *

In the house of Kynachan the main meal of the day was at six in the evening. Round the dining-room table sat David, his mother and sister, and Jean. John, above in the nursery, had been joined by Jessie and newly-born Euphemia.

'I want a proper walled garden this year,' said Jean. 'We should be growing much more fruit than at present. Against a south-facing wall we could have apricots and even peaches.'

'Peaches?' said Janet, disbelief in her voice.

'I don't see why not,' responded Jean. 'I'm told the duke is even growing pineapples.'

Three children and half a dozen years had, if anything, added to the beauty of the woman David had married. Her smile was easy and serene, and within her figure-hugging bodice she was still as slim as a girl.

David had aged. His short-cropped hair was beginning to recede, but his body was still supple and firmly muscled.

'What's a pineapple, Mother?' asked Clementina, who was still waiting patiently for Bohally to name their wedding day.

'I'm not sure. A kind of apple, I suppose.'

Janet appeared unchanged, still small, round, and grey. Since David seemed unable to take his eyes – or his hands – off his wife, she hoped to see the day when the nursery at Kynachan would ring with a dozen young voices.

'It's not like an apple at all. If anything it is like an enormous spiky pine-cone, and it grows from the ground,' said Jean.

'Oh, aye?' said Janet, doubting. 'And what do you do with a thing like that?'

'You eat it, of course. It's a rare and exotic fruit from tropical climes. I shouldn't think half a dozen people in Scotland have ever tasted one.'

'Pineapples are very good,' said Donald, picking up the tail of the conversation.

Jean looked at him with scepticism. 'How on earth would you know, Donald?'

The steward had brought in boiling water to make tea, which in fashionable circles was replacing claret and whisky as the correct drink at dinner. In Edinburgh, so rumour had it, at breakfast some preferred tea to ale.

'I've tasted it, my lady,' he said.

Rummaging in his sporran, Donald fished out a small key, using it to unlock the tea caddy on a shelf of the alcove where glasses and plates were stored. Under the gaze of a portrait of David's father, wearing a full-bottomed wig and armour, he put three pinches of black tea into a clay bowl, added some salt, a dollop of cream, and stirred. He then added hot water, tasted it, and, with a flourish, poured some of the lukewarm mixture, first for Jean, then for Clementina. David and his mother held out for tradition with a firm refusal.

'When have you tasted pineapple?' asked Jean.

'Last year, my lady. His Grace's head fruit-gardener is kin to me, married to my mother's cousin's husband's niece, who came from Tummelside. He grew a few in a forcing house but wasn't sure if they were good enough for His Grace. I told him they'd do fine.'

'I see.'

'Mind you, I wouldn't want to eat it that often. Two were quite sufficient.'

David gave a snort of laughter.

'I'll tell you what, Kynachan,' Donald continued. 'If you do a decent job of building a walled garden and put in a warm house, I'll see if I can get some seeds from Douglas. Of course, you need a cultivated palate like mine to appreciate pineapples. They're not for everybody.'

'Thank you, Donald,' said Jean. 'You can leave the tea on the table.'

'Right, madam.'

Jean waited until Donald had gone. 'Do you think the laird might be able to build a walled garden to Donald's satisfaction?'

'I think it's a grand notion,' said Janet. 'They're building one at Crossmount.'

'Then there must be one at Kynachan too – if you think our palates are sufficiently discerning,' said David, spooning a large helping of syllabub onto his plate. 'I'll try to fit it in before the hay harvest.'

As the golden days of a fine summer slipped by at Kynachan, on the Continent the Duke of Cumberland, King George's fat son, lost the battle of Fontenoy to the French. Atholl, however, rang with pride when he singled out the Black Watch for their distinguished conduct in the action. The battle had cost both sides dear. As a result, the likelihood of French adventuring in support of the Stuarts shrank still further. Both Whigs and Jacobites relaxed, sure there could be no rebellion in the Highlands that year.

Assisted by four men and three ponies, David dug out foundations, selected, cut, and fitted stone to stone to enclose over an acre of ground for the garden. The west wall was largely composed of the gable end of the house, together with the kitchen behind and the backs of the sheds and cattle byres, which straggled down the hill to the mains. Unable to resist demonstrating his expertise, learned when his father and he had been given the contract by General Wade to build the bridge over the Tummel a decade earlier, David constructed a couple of low, arched entrances. Proud of his skill, he showed them off to Jean, who regularly brought the three children from the house to inspect their father's progress.

Euphemia was in the arms of her nurse, Mary Dewar, but Jessie could toddle, and John was now five. He was already scrambling over the rocks and hiding in the heather to ambush other small boys, representing the Redcoats, or the Campbells, or the French.

Stripped of their plaids, the men worked on their wall in the warm sun, while the breeze rippled across the growing crops on the river meadow below them. The chirr of grass-hoppers filled the air. Butterflies and bees jousted over the wild flowers, and swallows and martins darted round the low, thatched roofs of the steadings.

With the young people up at the shielings, the townships had become the territory of old women. Their spinning wheels clattering, or their fingers busy knitting or basket-making, they gossiped in the sunshine and looked out over the fertile strath and its sparkling river. At night, when daylight scarcely faded from the northern sky, David and Jean would lie naked on their bed in the parlour, hearts pounding after their love-making, while the scent of honeysuckle, together with the grating cry of the corncrake, drifted through their open window.

The fine weather continued to hold into the second half of July. David suspended wall building and moved his little team to make hay in the meadow below the house.

Within a few weeks it would be time to begin harvesting the grain, which was maturing early. Later, when the year's crop of cattle was sold, David and Jean planned a trip to Edinburgh, where Anna Mercer now lodged with Barbara and Kinnaird.

In the midst of haymaking, the Duke of Perth and his entourage stopped at Kynachan on his way to visit Struan at the Hermitage. The duke was head of the small group of chiefs and nobles that constituted the Jacobite Association, leading proponents in Scotland for the restoration of the Stuarts. After the discovery of letters implicating him in Jacobite plottings, the authorities had issued a warrant for his arrest. For a while, the duke had deemed it wise to spend time visiting less accessible parts of the realm, where government writs were difficult to enforce.

In the cockpit in a barn, the duke wagered and lost the price of a fine stallion but took a brace of Kynachan fighting cocks to the Hermitage, where he hoped to recoup his losses. David forbore to tell him that Struan Robertson was amongst the least promising sources of gold in the Highlands. For years, weary and frightened debt collectors had passed back through Kynachan after being bounced out of Rannoch by Struan's clansmen, who were outraged at the temerity of duns to demand money from their chief.

Turned and turned again, the grass was bound in sheaves and cocked into stooks on top of the ridges. The household servants and Clementina joined David and his co-workers to load ponies with the dry, sweet-smelling crop. The animals were led to the mains, their tails swishing against the flies, where the hay was piled into little stacks and thatched with heather.

On the last day of haymaking, when the sun rode high in the sky, Jean and her mother-in-law brought out jugs of ale. Doting Davie lay with his head in his wife's lap watching an eagle soar in the sky overhead. After the women returned to the house, he and his fellow haymakers went on dozing in the sunshine.

After some time, their peace was broken by a sudden shout. 'Look there!'

David lifted his head and quickly rose to his feet. Coming down the track was the figure of a runner, who moved with an economical, shuffling stride. Splashing through the ford and responding to David's cry of 'Kynachan!', he jumped the wall and trotted to them across the field.

'David Stewart of Kynachan?'

The messenger carried his plaid in a great roll round his middle, leaving his legs and chest bare. Dried spittle flecked the side of his mouth and sweat oiled his wiry torso.

'I am Kynachan,' said David.

'Greetings! I am Donald Cameron, messenger to Lochiel. Prince Charles has landed at Borrodale. He is gathering an army to take his father's throne. I am come from the Hermitage. Struan and His Grace of Perth request your company forthwith.'

David stood silent, absorbing the implications of what he had heard. A murmur of excited Gaelic washed round him. After a moment, he snapped himself back to life.

'Do you wish refreshment? Some food? Some whisky?'

'I thank you, Kynachan, but I have still far to go.'

'God-speed and safe journey, Donald Cameron.'

'God save the King's Grace,' said the runner. He turned and loped off across the field, disappearing into the trees that lined the track.

'Finish off the hay,' David told Willie Kennedy. 'Then send word to Bohally and the leaders of the clachans – Balnarn, Drumnakyle, Pitkerril. And John Forbes. I want them to meet me at the house tomorrow afternoon.'

'Shall I bring the men down from the shielings?'

'No, do nothing more until I give you word. The position should be clearer when I return from the Hermitage.'

David strode swiftly up the track. He crossed the yard, calling for the stable boy to saddle his horse, and entered the house, where he bounded up the stairs and burst into the cool peace of the parlour.

Jean sat at her writing desk, checking the inventory of the larder before its stone shelves began to refill with the summer's harvest. The walnut long-case clock had only just chimed three. She had not been expecting him back so soon.

'Is there something wrong, Davie?'

'The prince has landed. I am ordered to the Hermitage for instruction.'

The quill pen dropped from Jean's fingers, splattering ink across the paper. She rose, gripping the bureau, the colour ebbing from her face until it matched the snow-white of her linen apron.

'Davie,' she whispered.

David was by her side, his arms around her, uncaring that the dust of the afternoon's work clung to his bare chest.

'It's happening, my love. Scotland will regain its rightful king – a king of our own race of Stewart, what my grandfather and father fought for all their lives. God has given it to us to restore King James.'

'Oh, my darling.' She inhaled the odour of his warm body. 'We were too happy.' She whispered it, and he did not hear.

'I must be going.' He stood back from her, his eyes bright. 'I'll be back as soon as possible. I've sent for Bohally and the tenants to meet me here. I need a shirt.' He looked wildly round the room.

'There's water in the jug. Rinse yourself down, and I'll find you one.' Jean moved towards a chest of drawers.

'My boots! My new boots!'

'Your new boots have not yet come from Perth. Your old ones'll be fine.'

'My trews!'

'Here are your trews – and try not to spray too much water on my desk.'

'Think what it would be like if I were too late, if it were all over before I could get there.'

'The Stuarts have been waiting more than fifty years. They won't do anything till you've got your trews on.'

'I'll be back,' David flung over his shoulder as he ran for the door, snatching his pistols and powder horn from a shelf as he passed.

From the window, she watched him throw his leg astride the horse and gallop out of the courtyard. She stood there for a few seconds as the swirl of dust kicked up by the animal's hooves slowly settled. She saw the old hound, its tail between its legs, climb stiffly up the hillock by the house to watch for its master's return.

'Where has Davie gone?' asked Clementina, rushing into the room.

'Prince Charles has landed and is raising an army,' said Jean, turning slowly from the window to see Janet behind her daughter.

Clementina clapped her hands. 'The prince! He's landed. Our prayers are answered.'

'Not all of them. Not yet,' Janet said grimly. 'And Davie?'

'He was called to the Hermitage.' Jean's voice was dull.

Clementina paused in her exultation, puzzled.

'What's wrong, Jean?' she said. 'Was there bad news as well?'

19

The Menzies Makes Ready

As Lochiel's runner trotted over the pass and along Strathtay, the news he carried spread ripples of disturbance through the townships.

He paused briefly at the alehouse in Weem and took on board a few mouthfuls of oatmeal and some whisky before continuing on his way. The soldiers lounging against the parapet of the bridge had challenged him but then waved him past on hearing that he was on Lochiel's business. Had they suspected the nature of that business, the messenger would have been detained. Their loyalty was to King George, whose interests would not be served should his enemies be roused before the forces of the state had time to nip a putative rebellion in the bud.

Cameron had told the news to James Menzies, the innkeeper, who left his wife in charge of the establishment and hurried through the gateway leading to the wooded policies of Castle Menzies. Before the castle, the formal knot garden wilted in the sunshine, and the innkeeper was grateful to escape the heat when he plunged into the cool darkness of the castle itself.

The hall porter, dozing in his chair, opened a bleary eye at the sound of James Menzies's feet on the stone flags.

'Is the laird about?' demanded the innkeeper.

The porter jerked his thumb. 'He's outside somewhere but he'll be back for his dinner.'

The smell of roasting meat drifted tantalizingly down a stone passage.

'I must see him. I have news.'

'Well, you'll have to find him yourself.' The porter paused. 'What news?'

But he was talking to himself, as the innkeeper had already left. The porter thought for a moment, then closed his eyes again. If the news was worth hearing, he would hear it soon enough.

At the back of the castle, a scullion was tipping waste onto the midden, disturbing a swarm of flies. In response to the innkeeper's query, he waved his hand towards the hill. James Menzies hurried up the path to the walled garden, which lay on the slope facing south and was as big as many of the estate's farms.

Gardeners, busy tending fruit trees or weeding amongst the ranks of vegetables and bushes, straightened their backs to watch the innkeeper climb towards the terrace, where the laird seemed to be sleeping peacefully in a hammock, his wife and daughter chatting quietly beside him as they sewed. The terrace was higher than the castle roof, and the view encompassed the strath, stretching as far as the peak of Ben Lawers, fifteen miles away, where patches of snow still skulked in the corries. Across Sir Robert's unbuttoned waistcoat lay an open book.

'Laird!' called the innkeeper as he approached.

Jerked from his slumbers, Sir Robert grabbed for his book and looked wildly about him. His eyes settled on the messenger.

'Oh, hallo, James,' he said. 'It's a bit hot to be running around. Will you have some lemonade?'

The innkeeper was tempted. Sir Robert was the only man for a dozen miles with an underground ice-house capable of preserving its harvest from the winter loch through the hottest summer. And the cost of a single lemon would pay the wages of one of the gardeners for three days. Struggling to regain his breath, James Menzies shook his head.

'A runner from Lochiel has just been through, Sir Robert. He carries word that Prince Charles is in Scotland and is raising the flag of rebellion.'

Sir Robert sat up. The book finally left his chest and knocked over a beaker of lemonade on the table alongside him. Swaying, the hammock nearly tipped its occupant to the ground.

'What? What?'

'Rebellion, Sir Robert. The Highlands are rising.'

'At last!' exclaimed his wife. Lady Mary, born Lady Mary Stuart, was a daughter of the Earl of Bute and a descendant of Robert II, founder of the deposed royal house of Scotland.

Sir Robert waved his wife to silence. 'Where is this runner? Where is the prince?'

'The runner's run on, as runners do, Sir Robert. He gave no further information than what I have told you.'

'It'll be no more than another rumour,' said Sir Robert. 'It's too late in the year to begin a campaign. Besides, the French have no troops to spare.'

'Don't be such a killjoy, Robert,' said his wife.

'Killjoy, my dear? There is no joy in rebellion. Brother pitted against brother. The country laid waste by warring troops. Decent men dying in ditches or decorating gibbets. Joy comes from peace and stability.'

'How can you say that, Father?' demanded his daughter. 'Scotland is oppressed by the German usurper.'

Sir Robert glared at the girl, his eyes popping. 'What nonsense has your mother been feeding you? Look round you, child. Are we oppressed? Can you feel the tyrant's boot upon your neck?' He turned his attention to the innkeeper. 'What do you say, James. Are you oppressed?'

'Should we not be doing something, Laird?'

'And think what would happen if the bloody man really has come to Scotland.'

'Robert! Your language!'

'I'm sorry, my dear. But the first thing that always happens when there's trouble is the invasion of our home by soldiers.'

'If they're the soldiers of King James, they will be welcome,' said Lady Mary.'

'Not by me,' said Sir Robert grimly. 'My father and my grandfather supported the Protestant settlement. I've no time for some flashy young papist on a fool's errand from Italy. James, go to the bridge. Alert the sergeant to what you've heard. It's the Watch's job to sniff out tales of rebellion.'

'So you won't be calling out the clan for the prince, Sir Robert?' spoke up one of the gardeners, a dozen of whom had sidled over to be within earshot.

'Absolutely not! If there's any troop-raising to be done, it'll be for the government.'

'But Robert—' began Lady Mary.

'But me no buts, my dear. It is my duty and my desire to keep my people from becoming embroiled in a madcap escapade.'

The innkeeper was now answering questions from the huddle of garden workers. Sir Robert shot him a malevolent look.

'To the bridge, James Menzies, this instant. The rest of you, back to work.'

'Robert—' began Lady Mary again, a dangerous glint in her eye.

'Peter!' interrupted her husband.

One of the gardeners looked back.

'Find the factor,' Sir Robert said. 'Tell him I'd be obliged if he'd meet me in the castle as soon as convenient.'

'Shian?'

'Of course Shian, you blockhead!'

'Mind yourself, Laird,' said Peter. 'You don't want to have a seizure.' The gardener was concerned, never having seen his sunny-natured chief so angry.

'Do not be insolent, man.'

'Och, it's not that I'm being insolent, Sir Robert,' said the gardener. 'It's that Shian is in Rannoch, as you well know, and not expected back for a while.'

'Well, send a messenger to hurry him here.'

'As you wish, but I doubt he'll be back any sooner.'

Lady Mary's warning look instantly silenced her daughter's giggle as, with an air of injured innocence, Peter clumped down the steps towards the castle. The Laird of Weem cleared his throat noisily and picked up his book, but the calm of his summer afternoon had been irrevocably shattered.

20

The Muster

On the following afternoon, the leaders of the Kynachan townships were gathered in the dining-room of the mansion house. For the best part of an hour, while they waited for David's return from the Hermitage, the whisky jug had been under pressure.

'Well?' demanded Bohally, the moment the laird arrived. 'What news?'

Donald handed David a tankard of ale and withdrew to the wall, where he lingered, his ears well pricked.

'Not much from Struan or His Grace of Perth, I'm afraid,' David said, taking a long draught, 'but Lochiel's men were there, waiting for the two of them to sober up. So were Blairfetty and Woodsheal. The prince is on the west coast. The clans are rising for him – the Camerons, the Macdonalds, the Stewarts of Appin so far. The Redcoats at Edinburgh and Stirling are expected to march into the Highlands to do battle.'

'It could be a very difficult situation,' said John Forbes, shaking his head doubtfully. An elder of the kirk, Forbes was inclined to agree with the minister that the nation was better served by King George than it would ever be by King James. 'The Redcoats'll probably be marching by Crieff and passing our own doors in a day or two. The duke is a firm supporter of the government. We'll—'

David interrupted. 'Times are changed. William, the rightful Duke of Atholl, has returned from exile with the prince. He has commissioned me major to raise a battalion from Strathtummel but to do nothing until further orders.'

'Prince Charles has a French army with him?' Bohally asked, his face bright and eager.

'No, his ships had to beat off an attack from the English navy during the passage across. All vessels but his own had to return to port for repairs. The French are coming later.'

'Two Dukes of Atholl!' With some courage, John Forbes was

still trying to make his point. 'A man cannot tell which way his loyalty lies.'

David knew that Forbes was usually wise enough to keep his politics to himself. The laird also knew that the miller was thinking of the fat cattle up at the shielings, which belonged to the people of Kynachan. The animals would fetch a good price from the drovers – so long as they were not diverted to feed a hungry army, whatever its political complexion.

'A man who cannot tell which way his loyalty lies' – David's voice was mild – 'may have his throat cut by either side. But on Kynachan we have no doubts. We are for King James. Any who would be otherwise should creep away at dead of night with their families and never expect to see this country again.'

'A man would as well die!' said George Cairney, who knew that no Highlander would ever voluntarily quit his home glen. Cairney, a bear of a man now in his fifties, was as fierce and unquestioning in his loyalty to David as he had been to David's father when, with James Stewart in Drumnakyle, he had fought alongside the old laird in the Rising.

'He has that option,' agreed David.

'And I would help any traitor on his way!' said Bohally, glaring at Forbes. Bohally's dirk, fifteen inches of well-oiled steel, slipped from the scabbard at his waist to lie on the table in front of them.

'Charles, for heaven's sake put that away. You're my men, at my table.' David waited until Bohally, shame-faced, re-sheathed his dirk and mumbled an apology. 'Hugh, how many men can you field from Balnarn?'

'Eight, Kynachan,' Hugh Reid reported resolutely. Like his brother Alexander, ten miles east in Drumchaldane, Reid – although still merely a tenant holding Balnarn at the laird's pleasure – was considered a *duin'-uasal*, – a gentleman of Atholl.

'George? What from Pitkerril and towards the mountain?'

'Six good men you could take to hell and back. And another half-dozen I doubt would survive to make the return journey.'

Next David turned to James Stewart, whom he also knew to be influenced by the minister's Whig opinions, but this tenant would never oppose the laird's will.

'Drumnakyle has fifteen men who bear arms. But I must tell you that the harvest is only a week or two away, and they will be needed then.'

'The harvest will be safely gathered,' David assured him.

'I will not let my people starve. And you, John, you have three men?'

'I have, Kynachan.' Having said as much as he dared, Forbes's tone was carefully neutral. He himself had a club foot, which precluded him from being numbered amongst the fighting men of the estate.

'Bring the men down from the shielings,' David told them. 'Make careful inventory of all weapons and check their condition. Take swords to the smith to be sharpened. Report on what is needed to Hugh, who will see to it that each man is armed and carries enough meal for a week.'

He paused, gauging the mood of his lieutenants. 'It'll soon be our turn, lads, to fight for the king. Our fathers and forefathers fought with honour, but this time the outcome will be different. Come, gentlemen, let us drink. Success to the prince and the men of Atholl!'

Upstairs in the parlour, Donald was giving the women a report of the meeting, but he broke off when David and Bohally came into the room.

'I would not trust Forbes,' Bohally was saying.

'He has no option. He will do as I command,' replied David.

'Well, Kynachan? It's just the same as last time, is it?' said Janet.

'No,' said David. 'This time we are led by the prince.'

'And you've got me,' said Bohally.

'Aye, Charlie, I've got you. You'll be my captain and adjutant.'

David sat down to sip the glass of claret that Donald had put beside him.

'And what about you, Davie?' asked Jean.

'I must go politicking. Bissett'll be trying to persuade the lairds to support Duke James and the government. I have to convince them otherwise.'

'Treacherous dog!' exclaimed Clementina.

'No,' said David. 'Cousin Thomas serves the family of Atholl. He will be as diligent for Duke William once he is established at Blair.'

'And don't forget that Jamie Bissett's my brother-in-law,' said Jean. 'And we're partners in the matter of the Mercer inheritance. There will be few families in this affair without members on both sides.'

'Pooh!' said Clementina. 'I shall speak to no Whig until the last one has surrendered.'

'It's as well you weren't in my shoes last time,' said Janet. 'otherwise we'd've lost Kynachan for good.' She heaved herself from her chair and headed towards the door. 'I don't know whether I'm glad or sorry that this day has come, but I pray that you are all kept safe from harm. And Clementina, I'll expect you up before too long. Charlie's not a hero yet.'

'Mother!'

'Don't play the innocent with me, my girl.' Janet sniffed. 'Sometimes I think men fight just to excite feelings of tenderness in the female breast.'

By early August, the countryside seethed with talk of war and revolution. The prince circulated a pamphlet offering amnesty to all who had served the Hanoverians, provided they now acknowledge King James as their rightful sovereign. From the farther end of Rannoch came news of the first probing runs by Camerons and Macdonalds recruiting along the shores of the loch amongst their clan members.

On the nineteenth, William, Duke of Atholl, raised the prince's standard at Glenfinnan, at the head of Loch Shiel. A few days later his brother, Duke James, deciding he could no longer count on the loyalty of his vassals and tenantry, withdrew from the castle at Blair to his more southerly seat at Dunkeld. From there, should the situation look like becoming a threat to his own safety, he could easily slip to the Lowlands. For a hundred years, each generation of the men of Atholl had taken arms in favour of the Stuarts. Duke James had few illusions as to the strength of his own support compared to that of his elder brother.

The people began coming down from the hills. Although plenty of grass still lay on the shieling grounds – where every extra week that the stock could put on flesh was a week snatched back from winter – this was no time to sit singing songs on a hill before an inattentive audience of sheep and midges.

When the inhabitants of Balnarn returned to their township, Bohally was waiting for them alongside Hugh Reid. Leaning on his broadsword, his bonnet carrying a single eagle feather, a sprig of oak – the clan badge of the Stewarts – and the white cockade of the Jacobites, Bohally stood in front of Reid's cottage. Cacophonous livestock, herded by the children, streamed over the ridge from beyond Drumnakyle and the hills above. Behind trudged the people, some bowed under baskets of cheeses and butter, some leading ponies that dragged the sledges.

The summer had been kind to them. Two children had been born and survived the traditional first mouthful of earth and whisky. The cattle had been augmented by fifteen calves. Only one had since died – and that because a cross-eyed Campbell had been passing through the mountain glen when the animal was born, and he must have cast a malevolent spell.

Ignoring the milling mass of animals behind them, Balnarn's eight men of fighting age gathered on the track in front of the cottages. Bohally appraised them. This was the last of the settlements he had visited over the past two days. He had been to each township in turn, testing the quality of the men who could bear arms and checking on their weapons.

'You know what's going on,' he told the little band. 'The prince is here at last. He's relying on the men of Atholl to put his father on the throne. All along the Tummel, the Tay, and the Garry, swords are being sharpened. With us are the Camerons, the Macdonalds, the Appin Stewarts and the rest of the great fighting clans. Against us' – he gave a savage grin – 'are the Campbells.'

His mention of the ancient enemy of the clans of Atholl raised a gleeful roar of derision from his listeners.

'The prince has sent word for us to wait, to be patient, and not rise till he has come – not to give warning to the government spies, who infest the country, of the mighty size of our army. The men of Kynachan are the best warriors in Atholl. And that means the best warriors in the Highlands.'

The men cheered. The rest of the people had gathered round to listen, and Bohally raised his voice to reach them above the bleating sheep and goats and the lowing cattle.

'The laird has decided we're not going to lose that edge, so he's found the best fighter in Scotland to sharpen you up.' The orator paused just long enough to make his audience wonder whether one of them was expected to ask the identity of this mighty warrior.

'Who else but me!'

The laughter greeting his claim was not scornful. Bohally's prowess, particularly with the broadsword, was legendary. He had once bested a son of Rob Roy in a duel, wounding him in the arm and forcing him to yield. Besides, it was wise to boast of one's skill. The greater a man's reputation, the greater his enemy's fear when facing him.

Bohally raised his sword with a flourish and let out a mighty roar: 'God save King James!'

21

The Chief Betrayed

The day after Lochiel's runner came through, Commissary
Thomas Bissett arrived at Castle Menzies. Sir Robert was with
his master of works, going round the new wing, which consisted
of private apartments and offices that had been completed the
previous year. When word was brought of the commissary's
presence, the Laird of Weem hurried through to the library to
greet him.

'Have you heard the rumour, Thomas?' asked Sir Robert.

Bissett was looking out of the window, his hands clasped
behind his back.

'I have.'

'It'll be nothing but wishful thinking by some disaffected
element or other. I heard the runner came from Cameron
country. Some damned seer will have been having visions in
his cups, and the local peasants will have passed the word
round.'

'Not so, Robert. His Grace's elder brother, William, has
landed with the Pretender's son. Many of the Macdonalds
and Camerons are joining him.'

'How do you know?'

'Word has also come from the Isles. It is clear that Charles
Stuart was hoping to raise the Highlands against His Majesty,
but we have heard from gentlemen loyal to the throne that the
Pretender's son is without an army and has only a handful of
supporters.'

'We'll have a tinchel to hunt him.'

'Hmm,' said Bissett, recalling that in 1715 the excuse of a
tinchel, or great stag hunt, had been given by the Earl of
Mar to gather together the Jacobite opposition prior to the
Rising. 'It's certainly an idea, Robert. However, I consider
it more important to ensure that our own country avoids
becoming involved in trouble.'

'Ha! I'm with you there, Thomas. You'll have a glass of
claret?' Sir Robert limped over to a sideboard and poured

a couple of glasses, handing one to his guest. 'I suggest we muster our people and station them at the passes to keep the rebels away until the army can deal with them.'

Bissett did not seem greatly enthused by the notion.

'His Grace is concerned by the arrival of his brother,' he said. 'As I'm sure you realize, some of the vassals may make mischief, claiming that their loyalty lies with His Grace's brother rather than with His Grace himself.'

'Do you think they'd be so rash as to attach themselves to such a speculative enterprise?'

'Twice in the time of men still living the Stuarts have gained adherents from Atholl to fight against their lawful king,' said Bissett. 'On this occasion I would like to think it otherwise, but we would be fools to count on it.'

'You are too gloomy, sir.'

'You believe so? Blairfetty fought in the last Rising. He is still a Jacobite. And my dear wife's cousins, Ballechin and Kynachan—'

'Surely not. Ballechin is too cautious and Davie is still wrapped up with that pretty little wife of his.'

Bissett gave a short laugh. 'Aye. He and Jean are a rare sight. But she won't keep him from Prince Charlie. I tell you, Kynachan was supping Jacobitism from his mother's tit, and I fear many of the younger vassals will be swayed by him. And look at Struan. He'll turn traitor. He always does.'

'He's too old to fight.'

'Struan'll make trouble until they nail his coffin shut. Have you thought of your Rannoch tenants? Who do you think they'll fight for?'

'They are peaceable, law-abiding folk.'

Bissett gave Sir Robert a sardonic look. 'The last time Rannoch was peaceful and law-abiding was one Wednesday afternoon, during the reign of King Robert Bruce, when a blizzard was raging. Your tenants there will be rebels. They are twixt Struan's lands and Lochiel's.'

As well as lord of the great tract of land from beyond Taybridge to the gates of the Earl of Breadalbane's castle at the end of Loch Tay, the Menzies held sway over the Slios Min lands on the north shore of Loch Rannoch and much of the bleak moor that stretched towards Glencoe. Scratching a living there amongst the great peat mosses were broken men – MacGregors, Camerons, and Macdonalds – who could not find land to rear their families in their own clan territories.

'Nonsense,' said Sir Robert, 'Shian is there now. He'll make sure Rannoch stays loyal. He should be with us in a day or two, when I'll instruct him to bring out my people for the king. But what are you going to do?'

Bissett grimaced. 'I go from here to Blair. His Grace is moving to Dunkeld, where he will wait to see how the situation develops. I must pack up the castle's valuables and ship them to Edinburgh.'

Sir Robert looked concerned. 'I don't much like the sound of that. It would surely be better if His Grace remained at Blair to rally support.'

'It is not my place to dictate to His Grace on such a matter,' said Bissett.

'Who's to raise the Atholl clans for the king, then?'

'I,' said Bissett.

'You?' Sir Robert looked at the figure before him. He laughed. Bissett was small, plump, and wore a worried frown. 'We're a sorry pair, Thomas. I, a cripple, raising Strathtay, and you, hardly a martial figure, Atholl. The sooner we have some regular troops in the district to sort this business out the better.'

'Aye, Rob. With that in mind, I have sent despatches to General Cope in Edinburgh. If he acts quickly, this rebellion will be quelled before it starts, and the Pretender's son will soon scurry back to Rome.'

At the moment when Bohally was being cheered by the men of Balnarn, Archibald Menzies of Shian presented himself before his chief in the library of the castle. The factor had been just old enough to be involved on the side of the Jacobites in the 1715 Rising, a fact that his chief may have preferred to forget. The estate of Shian lay by Loch Freuchie, in Glen Quaich, high amongst the hills south of Strathtay, but for much of the year the laird and his family lived at Farleyer, the dower house of Castle Menzies, from where his chief's lands could be more easily administered.

The Laird of Weem was in his usual green coat, while Shian was decked out in the tartan trews and jacket of a Highland gentleman. He also bristled with sword, dirk, and pistols. Rising from his chair, Sir Robert clapped his factor affectionately on the back.

'By God, Archie, I'm glad to see you safe returned,' he said. 'No sword slashes or bullet holes in your plaid, eh? If Bissett would be believed, you must have fought your way past the Hermitage and beaten off Davie Stewart's attack as you journeyed through Kynachan.'

'The country is completely peaceful, Sir Robert.'

'I knew it! This tale of the landing of Prince Charles is nothing more than rumour.'

Shian pulled a sheet of paper from his sporran and handed it across to his chief.

'It is no rumour. These are circulating through Rannoch and Tummelside.'

Sir Robert skimmed the document, which was the prince's appeal to Highlanders to join his army.

'The cheek!' snorted the laird. 'He offers pardon for all who have served King George, provided they join him. I suppose I'd better send this south to the authorities. We're in about the best position to hear what's happening in the Highlands.' He spun the paper contemptuously onto his writing table. 'What do you think, Archie? Is anything going to come of this? Has Prince Charles brought an army of Frenchmen with him?'

'The prince will be relying on the clans.'

'Curse the man! He'll bring chaos and destruction to all who associate with him. Did you see Kynachan or Struan? Bissett believes they will bring their people out against the government. Struan might, but I can't believe Davie would. Will our tenants in Rannoch remain loyal?'

Before Shian could answer, the library door opened and Lady Mary swept into the room. She smiled.

'Archie! Wonderful news, isn't it? Has all Rannoch risen for the prince?'

'Not yet, my lady, but—'

'My dear' – Sir Robert was flushed with unaccustomed annoyance – 'I wish you would not come barging in like that. Shian and I are discussing matters of business, and I would be grateful if you would leave us alone. If you wish to talk to him, let it be over dinner.' He turned to Shian. 'May I send word to Farleyer to ask Lady Shian to join us?'

'Shian's news concerns us all, Robert. It is right that I should be here,' said Lady Mary.

'Mary!' exclaimed Sir Robert, outraged at her undermining of his authority.

'Oh, do stop fussing, Rob. I promise I shall remain as quiet as a mouse.'

'I agree with her ladyship, Sir Robert,' said Shian. 'I believe she should stay.'

'I won't have it!' said the Laird of Weem, as he gave in. 'Rebellion is springing up even in my own house.' He went to look out of the window over the fields towards the Tay. 'I'm afraid we must accept the possibility that many of the lairds on Tummelside may join this rebellion.'

Turning from the view, Sir Robert looked at his wife. 'I'm sorry, my dear. I know you have a regard for Prince Charles and I know many of our friends are of the same opinion. But I am the Menzies, and our country prospers because my family have always supported the government. I am not going to squander what my forebears have fought for. It is not impossible that the nation depends upon us as the first line of defence for law and liberty against chaos. We must all do our duty.'

He faced his factor. 'Archie, I want you to raise the clan. Press any man in the castle to send word and post guards on all tracks and paths leading north from here so as to prevent any rebels from moving against us.'

Sir Robert picked up his Bible. 'I shall pray for the success of the forces of King George and further pray that any of our friends so misguided as to join the rebellion do not suffer too greatly as a consequence of their actions.'

There was silence when he finished. Lady Mary had found a chair by a great wall of books and was looking at Shian, her expression unfathomable. Red in the face, Shian fiddled with the eagle's feather in his bonnet.

'Well?' said the Menzies. 'Don't delay, Archie. The sooner you send word, the better.'

'Sir Robert,' said Shian. 'You are the Laird of Weem, chief of the Clan Menzies, respected and beloved by all your people.'

The chief shook his head in deprecation, reddening in his turn. 'There's no call for sweet words, Archie.'

'Listen to him, my love,' said Lady Mary. 'Archie has not finished.'

'Aye,' said Shian. 'Sir Robert, you yourself have many times proclaimed that you are not qualified to lead our clan in battle.'

'Yes, yes.' The chief, who often thought his injury a blessing in disguise, slapped his stiff leg. To him the Highland warrior culture was outdated, and he was only too happy to abandon his martial duties to Shian. 'This is why I am leaving it to you to raise the clan.'

'Aye, sir. And it is my duty to consider all aspects of military strategy.'

'I agree totally,' said Sir Robert, nodding vigorously. 'I hope you don't think I was usurping your function by advising you to guard the passes. If so, I apologize, but it seemed the obvious move.' He looked at Lady Mary with a smile. 'Perhaps I should have been a soldier after all. I have studied the campaigns of Hannibal, Scipio Africanus, and Caesar. None of them would leave a pass unguarded.'

'The part our clan will play in this crisis has not been my decision alone, Sir Robert. I have discussed it with our other chieftains – old Culdares, Bolfracks, Woodend.'

'And with me, Archibald,' said Lady Mary. 'Robert, I am at one with Shian and the others.'

'I don't understand,' said Sir Robert.

'I should have thought you'd have caught the drift, my dear,' said his wife. 'Clan Menzies is coming out for King James and the Stuart succession.'

22

Divided Duty

Sir Robert Menzies lifted his head from his book in answer
to the knock. The high-ceilinged library was cool and quiet
and, on a day when no wind whistled through the chinks and
crannies, the musty smell of old leather filled the air. The
door opened, and the gloomy features of the minister of Dull,
Duncan McLea, appeared.

'Duncan,' said the Laird of Weem, 'join me in a glass of
claret.' He waved his hand to a bottle by his elbow.

The minister came into the room and gave a sniff. 'This is
not the time to be drinking claret, Sir Robert.'

'You think not, eh? Since nobody takes a blind bit of notice
of anything I say, it seemed the most sensible thing to do.'

'It's a disgrace. We are commanders of the souls and the
bodies of the people, both of us supporters of the established
church and the lawful government of this realm. And without let or hindrance that treacherous dog, Shian, goes round
fomenting rebellion.'

Sir Robert's mouth tightened. 'You're not in your pulpit,
minister. And I'm in no mood to listen to a rant. The tide of
events has left you and me stranded.'

'But you're the Menzies. You can banish from this country
whom you please.'

'Starting off with my good wife, I suppose.'

'I'd heard,' said the minister. Hitching up his black coat-
tails, he sat down and placed his hat on his knee. 'Aye, they're
strange times that we live in. I've been in this parish many
years and I never thought that the embers of Jacobitism could
be fanned to a flame once again. Och, over the pass, yes.'
He flapped his arm towards the north. 'You'd never get the
likes of Kynachan missing a chance like this to make trouble,
but among the Menzies . . .'

A stray curl on his white wig bobbed as he shook his head.

Sir Robert smiled ruefully. 'Like me, you're out of touch,
Duncan. I suppose everyone knew our views and because of

it didn't talk about theirs. It seems that only you and I are surprised.'

'Surprised, perhaps. But I hear the talk now. Folk are frightened. Most don't want to be involved, but they fear the fanatics. You could do something, Sir Robert. If you put word out that those who refuse to have truck with the rebels need fear no reprisals, a lot of people would sleep safer in their beds.'

Sir Robert said nothing for a few moments as he considered the minister's words. 'I had decided it best to remain silent, Duncan. It was the agreement in our clan that Shian should lead in times of war.'

'But not that he should be free to decide which wars to fight.'

'Perhaps not. But he has the support of the other Menzies lairds.'

'But—'

'If I became involved now, it would just lead to strife and dissension.'

'I'm disappointed in you, Sir Robert.'

The laird flushed with annoyance. 'Be careful, sirrah! Remember who nominated you to your charge. It would not be difficult, particularly now, to have you lose it.'

'We must do our duty, Sir Robert.'

'Agreed. But the path of duty is not always clear.'

The minister moderated his snort of contempt into a cough.

'I see my prime duty to the clan,' continued Sir Robert. 'I do not believe the outcome of this affair can be influenced by you or me. Yet when it is over, we may be able to mitigate the effects of this folly.'

'You intend to sit supine?'

'Yes. You too, I hope. When the rebellion fails, the government will seek revenge. Then we must fight for our people.'

'I imperil my immortal soul if I do not denounce this unnatural uprising,' said the minister.

'I doubt it. Three times St Peter denied our Lord, yet he was forgiven. He feared for his own life; we fear for others, many of them fools or innocents.'

The minister leant forward and helped himself from the thick green-glass bottle marked with the initials CM.

'This is a good drop of wine,' he said, smacking his lips.

'I've only three casks left. I've ordered more, but if there's trouble, who knows?'

'I've heard Shian's men are going round all the clachans telling folk to prepare but not yet to muster.'

'Is that so?'

'You know why? They're frightened of the Redcoat army that General Cope'll be bringing from the Lowlands to hunt down Charles Stuart. They'll camp at Taybridge. The officers will quarter here. They'll want to know if there're rebels about. What are you going to say to them?'

'What do you suggest?' asked Sir Robert.

'I—' the minister hesitated. 'I wouldn't presume to influence you, Sir Robert.'

'Ha!' said the Laird of Weem. 'Indeed the times are out of joint when Duncan McLea reserves his advice.'

The minister scowled. 'You've been telling me to keep my own counsel for the last ten minutes. If you really want my opinion, you should tell the general that every manjack he sees will be pressed into service against him by the likes of Shian and Kynachan. Then the Redcoats'd pick them up. It wouldn't surprise me if that nipped treachery in the bud in these parts.'

'I couldn't do that. I'd be betraying my friends and my own people.'

'If you don't, I shall. And no man can stop me.'

Sir Robert stared thoughtfully at the minister, then pushed back his chair and walked to the window. Below, in the neatly patterned box-lined beds of the knot garden, a gardener was raking the gravel, his bare legs tanned by the days of sunshine.

'All right, Duncan. When the general comes, I shall have a word with him. But I insist you keep your own mouth shut. I shall have to face considerable opprobrium. There is no need for you to share it.'

Over the next fortnight, General Sir John Cope gathered His Majesty's Forces in North Britain. Leaving the cavalry to cover the Lowlands, he marched north from Stirling on the twentieth of August, hoping before he did battle with the rebels to augment his army from clans who supported the government. At Crieff, he met a few dignitaries, amongst them James, Duke of Atholl, his younger brother Lord George Murray, and Cluny, chief of the Macphersons, but the general failed to obtain more than a handful of Highland recruits.

The Redcoats continued their march at first light, and Castle Menzies prepared to receive them. Well before the first army scouts had appeared on the hillside at the north end of Glen

Cochil, Shian Menzies trotted into the courtyard behind the castle with a couple of gillies. He was accompanied by David Stewart and Willie Kennedy.

The castle bustled with preparations. Valuables were being locked away, and the great room at the top of the building was being prepared for the English officers.

Lady Mary greeted David with a kiss and told him that her husband had left early that morning to go fishing. While Shian stayed at the castle, David rode to meet Sir Robert at the burn of Camserney, which tumbled down from the moorland above.

Leaving his horse in Willie's care, David climbed through the trees that bordered the burn. He found the Laird of Weem standing impatiently by a pool at the base of a small waterfall, while a ragged small boy fixed a worm to the end of his line.

'Any luck?' asked David.

'Of course not' – Sir Robert nodded at the boy – 'but Hamish here tells me there's a monster trout beneath the falls that once ate a goat that fell in.'

'That's right, Kynachan,' confirmed the young gillie, 'but the fish is protected by an *uraisg*.'

David sat down on a rock beside the stream. 'You know Cope will be at Taybridge tonight, Rob?'

'Aye. No doubt he and his officers will dine and sleep with us. You, too?'

David smiled. 'I'll be with Shian at Farleyer, but I'd be interested to meet the general.'

'If his intelligence is up to snuff, he'll be equally interested to meet you.'

The small boy had finished baiting the hook. 'Try it now, Laird. Let the worm fall so that it is carried near yon boulder across the pool.'

Sir Robert dangled his eight-foot hazel rod across the base of the little falls and flicked the worm, on a line of waxed linen, towards the designated spot.

'We're on the verge of events that will shape the future of Scotland, Rob,' said David. 'It saddens me that you and I are on opposing sides.'

'We have no choice. The Menzies of Weem is Whig, Stewarts of Kynachan and Ballechin Jacobite. It's always so.'

'You've got'im!' shouted Hamish.

Sir Robert had not been watching his line; now he jerked it, and the rod bowed.

'It's enormous!' he cried.

'It's the boulder,' said David. 'I hope Cope's not too well informed – and no better informed when he leaves Castle Menzies.'

'I fear it is indeed the rock, Hamish.' Sir Robert was jerking ineffectually at his rod. 'That *uraisg* must have been protecting the fish once again.'

'You'll be right, Laird,' said the lad, 'but I didn't see it. It must've been hiding beneath the falls.'

Keeping a wary eye on the supposed lair of the *uraisg*, the boy lifted his shirt and waded into the pool to release the hook.

'Well?' said David.

Sir Robert laid his rod against a boulder. 'What are you, Davie?'

'I don't understand.'

'I would say you're Kynachan first of all. Then you're a Jacobite.'

'I've never thought like that, but you're probably right.'

'I shall do as you would do. I am the Menzies, father of my clan, before I am a Whig.'

David rose to his feet and clapped his friend on the back. 'May the trout bite as fiercely as the midges, Rob. If I don't see you back at the castle, God be with you.'

'And you.' Sir Robert turned his attention back to the burn. 'The great fish will have taken fright, Hamish. We'll go upstream and come back to it in an hour.'

'What I was going to suggest myself, Sir Robert,' shouted the boy.

Sir Robert had scarcely picked his way a dozen yards through the undergrowth when a black-clad figure stepped from behind a birch tree. The Laird of Weem started in surprise.

'Good heavens! It's you, Duncan.'

The minister jerked his head in the direction that David had taken. 'I hear that he and Shian're staying at Farleyer tonight. The Lord has delivered them to the Redcoats.'

McLea had spoken in English, which was incomprehensible to Hamish, who, with downcast head, stood behind his chief.

'I told you to keep out of the way,' said Sir Robert.

'I was just making sure you knew where the king's enemies lay.'

'Well, I do. So be gone – and keep low until the Redcoats have marched.'

'The Lord's business is in your hands,' said the minister. And he crashed away through the saplings.

A movement beneath an oak some yards away caught Sir Robert's eye. A Highlander was flitting through the dappled sunlight.

'Hamish, look,' said Sir Robert, pointing. 'Someone's skulking over there. Go and summon him. I wish him to follow the minister to ensure he stays away from the soldiers.'

'It's all right, Sir Robert,' replied Hamish. 'That's Donal Mor, one of Shian's men from Glen Quaich. He'll knock the minister on the head if he goes near a Redcoat. The same as I'm to do to you.'

23

Drill

The midday sun chased cloud shadows across the strath and the forty-five men who had mustered by the river Tummel. Six came from Bohally, the rest from the townships of Kynachan. The youngest was fifteen and the oldest, his great-grandfather, seventy-two. Ten had been out in 1715 with David's father.

The little army was draped in dirty plaids, the muted tartans helping their wearers blend into the trees, rocks, and heather of their country. Each man carried a targe and dirk. Most had broadswords, many of them rusty. The others carried the long-handled Lochaber-axe – the Highland equivalent of the pike – or sickle blades carefully dovetailed into stout poles. There were also a dozen muskets and fowling pieces.

Congregated on the track were the rest of the estate's population. Amongst them were twenty or so spectators from the Menzies township of Kinardochy, whose tenants had still to hear what was expected of them during the emergency.

All were engrossed in the progress of a mock duel between Bohally and Hugh Reid, the speed of whose movements was underscored by the short interval between the metronomic clash of sword against sword. Bohally leaned back as Reid lunged forward, his blade sliding down his opponent's to be caught momentarily by the twin iron lugs at the top of the basket hilt. A murmur of approval rose from the critical crowd. Bohally, with a powerful twist of his wrist, had forced Reid to relinquish his grasp or be left with a broken sword.

'It's not like that in a real fight,' said George Cairney, spitting contemptuously on the ground.

He stood in front of the fighters from Pitkerril, the only man on the field armed with the old-fashioned claymore, the great sword that had been superseded by the more manageable broadsword.

'There isn't time for fancy thrusts and delicate footwork,' he said. 'I'd've smashed through Bohally's sword and had his arm off quicker than an adder's bite.'

'You're right on some of that, George,' called Bohally, running his blade between finger and thumb to check for nicks that might have dulled its cutting edge. 'Fighting's about speed and aggression. If you are defending yourself, the battle is probably lost.'

'It's strength, not speed,' corrected Cairney.

'Try me,' said Bohally.

Cairney needed no second bidding. He grinned and stepped forward, reaching behind his head to grasp the hilt of his great sword in both hands and sweep it out of its sheath. The blade hissed through the air in a wide, glittering arc, straight towards Bohally's head.

The latter scarcely moved his body. His sword came up, kissed the blade of the claymore, and diverted it so that it grazed past his shoulder to smash uselessly into the ground. A flicker of Bohally's wrist drew a stream of blood from each of his attacker's naked forearms.

'Damn you,' growled Cairney, lifting his sword to prevent blood running down the blade.

'You silly old fool!' shouted his wife from the midst of the laughing spectators. 'He could take your balls off without disturbing your plaid!'

'Shut your face, woman!'

Under the bonnet and tangle of greying beard and hair, Cairney's face was red with rage and humiliation. He bent to pluck a tuft of grass, using it to wipe the blood from his arms.

'A good man with a broadsword', said Bohally, now carving diagonal slices through the air, 'will always beat a good man with a claymore – even one as good as George – through his speed.' As he demonstrated, the blade seemed to take on a life of its own.

'Once you commit yourself to a stroke with the claymore, that's it. But your broadsword can change direction.' In the air round his body the big man made the sword dance in a blur of motion. A supple roll of his wrists would send it shimmering off in another direction.

'When you leap from the heather at your enemy, he'll try to block your stroke with his target and bring his own sword in from the right.' Bohally showed them. 'But change the direction of your blow and catch him in the small of his shoulder. If you don't kill him, then you certainly put his right arm out of action.'

The onlookers murmured their appreciation. Amongst them, complete with children and hounds, was the laird's family.

'The lad could pluck a running chicken with his sword,' said Janet, full of admiration. 'And let it live to tell everyone how good he was.'

'That's all very well,' said Jean, 'but he won't be facing chickens. They'll be Redcoats with cannon.'

She carried Euphemia on her hip. Jessie, at the stage when small blonde children look like angels, was in the charge of Mary Dewar, now twenty-five, unmarried and uncertain in temper.

'If Father was here he could easily chop Uncle Charlie into bits,' said John.

'Johnnie, that's not nice,' said Clementina, pink with pride as Bohally showed his skills.

'Well, he could. He's Kynachan. Pah! Pah!' The boy mimed a couple of mortal blows with an invisible sword and fell upon the neck of his victim, a long-suffering setter. The dog braced itself against the impact, refusing to roll over and play dead.

Bohally sheathed his sword. 'Would you like a wee bit of a battle?' he shouted to his troops.

'Aye!' yelled the men.

John jumped up and down in excitement.

Bohally split them into two groups, mollifying George Cairney by appointing him leader of the men from the settlements west of the high road. Hugh Reid led those from the east.

'I want to see a charge,' ordered Bohally. 'Balnarn's men attack first. Then back the other way. Don't press home, for God's sake. We don't want any broken heads.'

Amid the spectators, an old man produced a set of bagpipes. He squeezed a preliminary groan from his instrument, then burst into the clan rant, 'The Stewarts' White Banner'. Down came Bohally's sword and with berserker screams the twenty-two men from the east split themselves into two wedges and bounded across the grass stubble towards the resolute twenty-three from the west.

'Pitkerril!' roared Cairney, waving his claymore over his head as he waited to receive the charge. His cry was enthusiastically taken up by the other defenders. In the absence of an alien enemy the inhabitants of the clachans held each other in fairly cheerful rivalry and contempt.

'Drumnakyle!' yelled a fair proportion of the watching women, whose menfolk piled into their opponents, smashing swords into targets.

In spite of Bohally's assurances of the comparative merits of types of sword, the attackers gave Cairney – swirling his claymore round his head – a wide berth. There seemed no way to go within the curtilage of his mighty blade without either killing him or being killed.

'Pitkerril!' bellowed Cairney once again. Since nobody was attacking him, he decided to go to the assistance of the adjacent warrior, a grey-bearded ancient, whose blue bonnet was scrunched down to his ears to warm his egg-bald head. The man was on his knees, his target held over his head, patiently enduring the unenthusiastic assault of a weedy youth, who clumsily struck at him with a rusty Lochaber-axe.

At Cairney's approach, the youth dropped his weapon, hauled his opponent to his feet, and the two took off across the field towards the river. Cairney ran after them as fast as the unbalancing weight of his sword and his bow legs would allow, yelling curses and calling on them to stand still and fight.

Watching with his hands on his hips, Bohally caught the eyes of Clementina and the other women and shook his head in mock despair as the laughter of the spectators joined the laughter of the men. At the edge of the field the two reluctant warriors scampered over the dry-stone wall, but their pursuer was blown. Propping his sword against the wall, Cairney sat down on a convenient boulder and took a pull on a horn flask, which he produced from the greasy depths of his plaid.

Jean snorted. 'The man's a drunken buffoon.'

'Davie's father used to say there was no better man on the estate than George Cairney,' said Janet. 'He also said that men who laugh together will fight together. Charlie knows what he's doing.'

Replacing the flask, Cairney hauled himself to his feet. He raised his hairy, blood-streaked forearm to shade his eyes against the sun.

'Kynachan!' he bellowed, pointing beyond the onlookers.

David was trotting down the dusty track from the high road, Willie Kennedy behind him. They both showed signs of hard travelling. Reining in by the small crowd, the laird dismounted. Hungry for information, his people pressed in.

'What news, Davie?' asked his wife.

'Sir Robert's staying out of this business, but Shian Menzies will raise his clan.'

'Thank God,' said Bohally.

'The Redcoats camped at Taybridge last night. Shian and I visited General Cope this morning at Castle Menzies. He asked us for intelligence of the rebel mob.'

David now raised his voice so that his words could be heard by all.

'The Redcoats will be marching past us in a couple of hours.'

'Hooray!' whooped Cairney. 'We can set up an ambush at the bridge.'

'No,' their chieftain told them. 'We're not going to attack, not today. Carry no arms and keep all livestock out of sight. Be careful not to taunt the enemy, but it's a fine chance to take a look at them.'

24

An Army Passes

The day's showers had served to dampen the dust on the road.
By the time Bohally and the family of Kynachan had taken up
a vantage point on a hillock a hundred yards back from the
highway, harbingers of the Redcoat army had come into sight
– a small party of Highlanders wearing dark government tartan
over crimson tunics, splashing through the mud, their eyes
searching the moorland on either side.

'Scouts,' said David. 'From the top of the pass they'll've seen
there's no threat of ambush.'

The sounds of the army snaking down from the hill had been
audible for some time. First came the ear-piercing squeal of
wood on wood as grease dried out on the axles of carts and gun
carriages, then the penetrating crack of marching speed being
beaten out on the kettledrum, and finally the murmuration of
a multitude of human voices.

'If the general expected trouble, he'd have a skirmish line
preceding him,' said Bohally. 'He must know there isn't anyone
to oppose him this side of the Great Glen.'

'At the moment,' said David.

The vanguard of the main column, a single squadron of
dragoons, their harnesses jingling, came slowly into sight. Next
came a group of officers in three-corner hats, with scarlet
tunics, gold lace, powdered wigs, and glossy black boots to
their thighs.

'Sir John Cope is the neat little man on the grey horse,'
David pointed out.

The laird's wig and trews, the eagle feathers in his and
Bohally's bonnets, and the women's clothes made the small
party recognizable as gentry. An officer on a chestnut mare
left the column and picked his way across the heather towards
them. He wore riding breeches of skin-tight buckskin, and his
scarlet coat and yellow saddlecloth were thickly trimmed with
gold braid.

The Redcoat gave a negligent flick of his whip in salute.

'Captain Poyntz, 6th Regiment. Good day to you, sir,' he announced himself to David, his eyes briefly appraising the men before lingering on Jean and Clementina. He was about thirty, with dark hair, cold eyes, and skin pitted by old smallpox scars. 'The general requests you to call out your tenants in support of their king and country. We have arms and bread for each man.'

'Alas,' said David, 'whatever my own feelings in the matter, in this country we are pledged to follow His Grace of Atholl. The people will not come out until he commands it.'

'The Duke of Atholl? Quite so. His Grace is now in Edinburgh, I believe.'

'So I have heard it said,' replied David.

'His elder brother is with the Pretender's son,' the Redcoat said. 'We will have the two of them by the heels within the week.'

Clementina made a contemptuous grunt that attracted the officer's glance. He looked deliberately down from her face to her breasts, and his saddle creaked as he leaned forward to examine her bare ankles and feet. Her jaw clenched and cheeks flamed as he settled back with a small, dismissive sniff.

'The general would like to know your name, sir,' said the officer.

'I met Sir John at Castle Menzies. I am David Stewart of Kynachan. This is Charles Stewart of Bohally. I am sure we will meet again.'

'Not where we'd be introduced, I'll be bound.'

The captain jerked round his horse's head and walked it delicately back to the road, where he spurred the beast to a canter in order to catch up with the general.

'What did he mean by that last remark?' asked Jean.

David shrugged. 'That he does not consider me a gentleman, I suppose. Therefore he and I would never frequent the same circles. Either that or he expects our next meeting to be on the battlefield.'

'The dog, you can't let him get away with that!' growled Bohally. 'He was insulting your blood. You must challenge him.'

'You'd have me kill him in a duel with his whole army looking on?' said David. 'Do you think the prince would be best served by having a Redcoat army sack Kynachan and string you and me from Tummel bridge?'

'They wouldn't dare! We're living in the eighteenth century!' said Jean.

'It's what I would do if I were Cope. If I wanted my men to fight when I met the enemy.'

A scarlet and white caterpillar, the infantry undulated down the high road in front of them. The companies marched in columns, three men abreast. The different regiments wore either cocked or mitre hats, and the facings of their heavy scarlet coats were yellow, blue, or white. Bayonets and ammunition pouches for their muskets hung from white cross-belts.

At the head of each formation, alongside the colours, which were furled and encased in leather tubes, a boy tapped out the time on a kettledrum. Rain had fallen on the troops while crossing the pass; the tops of their knapsacks and the shoulders of their coats were darkened by water, and their white gaiters were splashed with mud.

As the vanguard passed, soldiers still rounded the corner across the burn, filling half a mile of road. They marched in step, small men most of them, many pink-faced boys, their heads turning to look at the Stewarts, their glance diffident. Others in the columns were older; their eyes stared boldly at the women from beneath the brims of their hats.

Towards the rear marched a couple of score Highland troops. They had expected to be shipped to the Continent to join the rest of the Black Watch. Instead, they were trailing through Atholl, their own country, part of an invading army, while their own people, their clansmen and kindred, watched them warily from a safe distance.

'Poor devils,' said Bohally, who had spent half a dozen years in the regiment.

'About fifty Highlanders joined the army at Crieff and another fifty deserted,' said David. 'Most of these men are from Atholl and Breadalbane. They may've taken an oath of allegiance to the German lairdie, but Cope's a fool if he expects them to wage war upon their own people.'

Behind the infantry, flanked by a small cavalry escort, came the artillery – teams of ponies harnessed to carts carrying four small cannon, each capable of firing a one-and-a-half-pound ball, and four mortars. Behind them followed ponies, four hundred of them, some bearing wicker baskets, others canvas-covered bundles strapped either side of their backs. Like the troops, they were in neat files, the leading rein of each animal attached to the pack-saddle of the one in front.

'What are they carrying?' asked Jean.

'I wouldn't mind getting my hands on a few of them,' said Bohally. 'The long bundles are arms – muskets, swords, bayonets. They would have been issued to anyone who joined. I don't know what's in the baskets. Ammunition?'

'Bread,' said David. 'Wheat bread. I saw it yesterday. It'll be mouldy and inedible in a day or two. Then they'll rely on the countryside and what the sutler has for sale.'

Behind the ponies, the sutler's wagons were covered by waxed sailcloth. The contents were his own property, and he was making sure that nothing deteriorated in the drizzle before it had been sold to the troops.

When the soldiers had passed, the people of Kynachan thought it safe to approach the high road more closely, particularly when a tempting herd of black cattle, in a tight, jostling bunch, filled the road behind the wagons. George Cairney broke from the cover of a gully and trotted across the heather towards them, but, attracted by drovers' cries of alarm, a mounted skirmisher spurred his way back down the column, and Cairney ran for safety across a patch of boggy ground.

Last but for a pack of scavenging dogs came the whores, wives, and children. The women, loaded with their possessions, trudged at the tail of the column, their skirts tied between their bare legs to keep clear of the mud. Catching sight of the gentry, they despatched a few children across the heather to beg. Bohally drove them off, barely comprehending the stream of curses they flung at him in piping, heavily accented Lowland Scots.

'What do you think will happen now?' asked Jean on their way back down the lane towards the house.

'I don't know,' said David. 'There'll be a battle, I suppose, but I doubt if we'll be involved. Our task remains the same – to make sure that the country comes out for the prince when he arrives in Atholl.'

'After the battle, we could be ordered to cut the road to prevent the Redcoats' retreat,' said Bohally.

'No,' said David. 'We won't see that army again. Even if Cope returns, it will be through Blair and Dunkeld, with the prince hard on his heels.'

'So we do nothing,' said Bohally, frustration in his voice.

David grinned. 'An awful weight of soldiers crossed over Tummel bridge. Since we maintain it, it seems only fair that we charge a small toll.'

'Ah, yes, what a marvellous idea,' said Bohally. 'It would be a shame not to free some of those spare muskets from the Redcoats' yoke and put them to good use.'

'You be careful, Davie Stewart,' warned Jean in alarm. 'I don't want you doing anything stupid.'

That night the government army camped at Trinafour, a few miles north of the Tummel. By morning, they were a dozen ponies the poorer. Four had been liberated by Bohally and David, the rest by a band of Struan's experienced raiders.

Cope continued his march. The prince's little army lay in wait for him in an impregnable position at the Pass of Corryarrack. If Cope attacked here, his regiments would be destroyed. The Redcoats feinted towards Corryarrack but declined battle. The sensible course would now have been for them to retreat the way they had come, thus protecting the Lowlands. But the general followed his orders to continue north. There, it was hoped, some of the loyal clans would join the government army. Save for a few dragoons and garrisons at the castles of Stirling and Edinburgh, this left the Jacobites unopposed as far south as Newcastle, where the aged Marshal Wade was commander in northern England.

The prince began his advance to claim his father's kingdom.

25

Alang Wi' Royal Charlie

A week after the Redcoats had marched through Kynachan, word came that the prince had arrived with his army at Blair Castle. On the following day David and Bohally rode to a meeting, called by the Jacobite Duke William, at which the Atholl Brigade was reconstituted. The prince held a review of his army on the castle lawns and received chieftains and lairds of Atholl, who swore fealty.

That evening David rode home. No sooner was he through the door than the women came running down from the parlour and Donald rushed from the kitchen.

'Well?' demanded Clementina. 'Did you see the prince?'

'Yes,' David said. He handed Donald his sword and plaid amid a tangle of excited hounds.

'Oh, David! What was he like?' Clementina hopped from foot to foot.

David pursed his lips and sucked in his breath, groping for the appropriate words. 'He seemed an equable man.'

'Equable!' shrieked Clementina. 'You brute, is that the best you can do?'

'When I kissed his hand I thought him most equable.'

'You kissed his hand!' Clementina turned tear-filled eyes to her sister-in-law. 'Jean, he kissed the prince's hand.'

'Stop snivelling, you stupid girl,' her mother told her. 'And you stop this nonsense, David. Now tell us what happened at once.'

Settled in the parlour, a dram at his elbow, David began his tale.

'It's been the most remarkable day. There are two thousand Highlanders at Blair. I saw Keppoch, Lochiel, Ardshiel, Innernahyle, Glencoe, and a dozen others.'

'The prince,' implored Clementina.

'The prince,' repeated David, his eye momentarily on Donald, who was busying himself trimming the wicks of the tallow candles. He shot him a wink. 'The prince is tall, taller than me, but not quite as tall as Bohally. He is well made and he wore Highland dress – a kilt and a plum-coloured coat trimmed with silver. Oh, yes, and his bonnet had three eagle feathers. He seemed a jovial fellow.'

'What colour is his hair?'

'He wore a periwig,' said David. 'A white one, the same as mine.'

'His complexion?'

'His complexion.' David frowned. 'I don't know. He had skin, I suppose. Yes, he must have had, otherwise his eyes would have fallen out of his head, and they were undoubtedly present. Brown! He had brown eyes. And he speaks English with a foreign accent.'

'Why did you kiss him?'

'Lord Nairne, the duke's cousin, will be the colonel of our battalion. The prince has appointed His Grace a general. We kissed the prince's hand to show fealty.'

'Were there ladies round the prince?' asked Clementina.

'No ladies, but plenty of ancient warriors with long white beards and drawn swords peering round for government assassins. Thomas Bissett hovered in the background, wringing his hands as he tallied the cattle and meal His Grace distributed to the clans. I suspect Thomas remains Duke James's man.'

Jean had been keeping unnecessarily busy with the thread on her spinning wheel. When she finally spoke, she said, 'When must you go again?'

At David's chuckle, her head jerked up.

'Tomorrow,' he said. 'I am asked to go to a ball at Lady Lude's. The prince is to be present.'

'What!' shrieked Clementina.

'He has commanded me bring the three ladies of Kynachan.'

Later, when the candles were low and the rest of the household had retired, Jean sat with her prayer book in her lap. David was writing at the desk.

She said, 'It was wicked of you to tease Clementina so.'

'Such opportunities come too rarely to be squandered.'

'You should have seen your mother and Clemmie. The hullabaloo! I don't know which of them was worse, ransacking the cupboards and closets for fripperies that haven't been seen at every wedding in Atholl for the last ten years.'

'What about you?'

'I don't need to catch His Royal Highness's eye. I have my prince already.'

David smiled. 'A more modest gentleman than I would blush.'

'I could never have asked more of a husband than you have given me,' said Jean. 'That is simple truth.'

'We shall take rooms in Edinburgh for the winter,' he said.

'You think the fighting will be over by then?'

'There can be little doubt. Many of the Atholl lairds'll take persuading to come out, but thousands of soldiers from Spain will be in Scotch waters in a couple of days, and I heard the prince say that his supporters in England will field an army of twenty thousand for the cause.'

'So many,' said Jean. 'That's good.'

There was a few seconds' silence, save for the scratching of David's pen.

'I had news of Kinnaird.'

'You surprise me. I would have thought he'd stay in the music room until all the trouble was over.'

'I expect he will. When he heard word of the prince's landing, he went scuttling back to Edinburgh with your sister. His brother was at Blair, but there's little fire in his belly. He complains of his health and doubts he can raise more than half a dozen of Kinnaird's tenants. Since Alexander is already looking after our interests in the matter of your inheritance, I thought I'd ask him to be executor of my will – just as a precaution.'

'When do you expect to march?'

'In a few days,' said David.

'I see.' Jean's face was in shadow, her expression unreadable.

David put down his quill. 'Take care of Kynachan while I'm away. Look after Johnnie and my mother and the babies.'

Jean rose to her feet. The book slid down her long skirts to the floor. Standing by the desk, she caressed the back of his neck. 'Take care of yourself, for my sake.'

'Of course.' He turned to face her, slipping his hands under her gown to touch the soft bare skin at the back of her thighs. Drawing her towards him, he leaned his head against her belly.

She sighed. 'Come to bed, Davie.'

The proximity of war heightened sensibility, and the ball at Lude simmered with excited tension. The house was full. The women were beautiful, the fiddlers second to none in Scotland, and the candles shone on gorgeous tartans and shimmering silks. In high spirits, the prince requested the tune 'This is no my ane House' and led the widowed Lady Lude, almost swooning at the honour shown to her, onto the floor for the first reel.

Such was the crush of people determined to see Prince Charles that dancing was almost impossible. Jean was presented to him, making a deep curtsy, while Lady Lude, adoringly by his side, tapped her fan impatiently. Away from the bubble of glamour surrounding him the talk was of war.

Janet was content to sit out in an ante-room, chatting to those of her generation who had lived through the last Rising, but Clementina and her contempories could not get enough of the prince and followed him from room to room. David and Bohally spent much of the evening in urgent conversation with their commander, Lord Nairne, their hostess's brother.

Next morning the prince and his army departed for Perth, leaving the Atholl Brigade to follow when its recruits had been gathered. The best news over the following days was that Lord George Murray, younger brother to the duke and considered by many to be the most able soldier in Scotland, had accepted a lieutenant-general's commission in the Jacobite army.

The rebels needed this encouragement, for although the men of Atholl had flocked to Blair to greet the Jacobite duke and the prince, they had then returned to their townships. They had two dukes – one demanding they fight for the prince, the other supporting the government. And not all lairds were like David, not all were in their prime, willing to fight for the cause because they knew it just. Some lairds were boys or old men, some found the issues less than clear-cut, and more than a few believed the future might lie with the Hanoverian succession.

Furthermore, times were changing. A generation or two earlier, no tenant questioned his laird's authority. Only the un-hesitating obedience of the warrior to his chief down the years had maintained the clan's control over its country and repelled invaders. But the law was beginning to supersede the sword, and the Presbyterian church preached support for the government.

On Kynachan all were Jacobites, but their loyalty to the laird was coloured by the knowledge that he could evict them from their homes at the slightest hint of dissent. So it was along much of the Tummel and into Rannoch. Where the influence of David and Struan Robertson predominated, the lairds were all Jacobites, and tenants had little recourse but to fight.

Not a few potential warriors in Atholl, if they could keep out of the way of the ardent Jacobites, hoped they could sit out the rebellion safe at home. In Strathtay many determined to follow the example of the Menzies chief – in spite of pressure from their war-lord, Shian – and avoid the looming conflict.

On the twelfth of September, the first contingent of the Atholl Brigade left to join the prince's army. The problems of recruitment were evident. Only Lord Nairne's battalion, its warriors swept speedily under arms by the keenest of the Jacobite lairds, was ready. James Robertson of Blairfetty was having problems rousing Glen Errochty for the battalion to be commanded by Lord George Murray, and both he and Duke William stayed in Atholl to threaten and cajole men to join the cause.

David was at the head of the men of Kynachan. Behind, each with his tail of tenants, were Stewarts of Foss, Garth, Lassintulloch, Fincastle, Tempar, and Duntanlich. Even along the Tummel recruitment had not been without problems, and Bohally was left behind to gather the remaining and more recalcitrant men from the east end of the strath.

The night before their march south, the people of Kynachan had bidden farewell to their menfolk. The young men had crowded together in the largest of the cottages in the clachans, squatting round the central peat fire, drinking whisky, boasting of the deeds they would perform. In the smoky shadow, girls watched and listened, hands clasped between their knees, waiting to enfold their sweethearts in their arms and give them some special memory to console them in the hard times ahead.

In the homes of the married men, children had been bundled into the dried bracken and heather in the corners, where their grandmothers sang soft lullabies to keep them amused. By the fire, the cottager and his wife had made love, talked, or even quarrelled. The future might bring plunder, wealth, glory, or death for the menfolk. The consequences would be enjoyed or endured by their women and children.

Men had gathered in the grey pre-dawn at the edge of each township, stamping their new rawhide brogues, slapping their sides against the chill, until their captain had checked that all were present. Most of them now carried a firearm – a flintlock or older wheel-lock musket – as well as a broadsword, target, dirk, powder flask, and a meal pouch. Disturbing the sleepy beasts, the men had moved swiftly down the tracks, their thoughts still with their wives and mothers.

David and Bohally had already been waiting at the muster point in a field, Camp Haugh, alongside the river, when the men of Kynachan began to arrive. As the sun rose, so did their spirits. Bohally bantered and encouraged them. He told them that he would gather an army to join them, and that, at Corryarrack, faced only by a pack of Macdonalds and Camerons, the Redcoats had run away. A man of Atholl, he added, was worth three Macdonalds and at least a dozen Campbells from Argyll.

The lairds from Bunrannoch, arriving with their ill-armed followers, went to David for instruction and to establish lines of communication and responsibility. This was essential. A Highlander would follow and take orders from his own chieftain without hesitation, but the less well an officer was known to him the less willing was the warrior to accept his instructions. To be effective, the Highlander had to be commanded by his own laird.

One of the few who appeared oblivious to the conflict of interest in Atholl was old Alexander Robertson of Struan. Cocooned in a plaid and slumped on the back of a huge but docile horse, with two hundred and fifty of his clansmen clustered protectively round him, he arrived at Camp Haugh in the company of his piper, his runner, his bard, his herald, his arms bearer, and a large barrel of claret. With a grandiloquent sweep of his arm, he acknowledged the cries of his name that greeted him from the men of Tummelside, who had so often fought alongside his clan.

Two thousand government soldiers had marched through Kynachan under General Cope. Four hundred and fifty Highlanders went south along the same road, hoping to be joined by recruits from Fortingall, Glen Lyon, and the Menzies contingent from Strathtay. They were to rendezvous with Lord Nairne at Crieff before continuing to join the main rebel army outside Edinburgh. People from townships all along the Tummel lined the road, cheering and waving their menfolk to war.

'May God preserve them,' said Janet when the sound of the last piper had died away.

'Jean!'

The shout penetrated the thick stone wall of the storage barn. A single bar of dusty sunlight lit the cheeses and smoked mutton hams suspended from the rafters. Her gown protected by a linen apron, Jean was counting the sacks of grain that were raised on capped boulders to keep them from rats. As well as the harvest from the mains, produce was arriving as tenants settled their rents.

'Jean!'

'Just a minute.' She chalked the result of her tally on a slate, placed it on a neatly darned jute sack, and went outside. Under the malicious gaze of the resident flock, scrawny kain hens, brought in to pay rent, pecked miserably at the periphery of the midden.

'Oh, good, there you are,' said Clementina from the front door of the house. 'Do you know Grissel Macdonald? Her husband's a tenant on Portnellan.'

'A big woman with a dark complexion? I have heard she has a fine singing voice.'

'She's sobbing in the kitchen.'

Jean paled. 'She has news?'

'No, not about the army. At least I don't think so.'

Jean hurried through the hall to the kitchen.

'What's wrong?'

Watched by Janet, Donald was pouring a little whisky into a quaich for the distraught woman. She was slumped on a stool by the table, with a bundled baby on her knee.

'Lady Kynachan,' she said, turning a tear-streaked face towards Jean.

'She wants you to give her back her husband,' said Janet, her lips tight together.

The woman slipped from the stool and crabbed across the flagstone floor. She took Jean's hand, covering it in tears and kisses. 'Lady Kynachan,' she whimpered.

'I don't understand,' said Jean, freeing her hand. 'Pull yourself together, Mrs Macdonald. Explain to me how I can help you.'

'Oh, my lady. I can't cope without my man. I have six small children, none of them strong, one afflicted with the gravel stone. And my husband is not a well man, being subject to fits. And the harvest is poor and only half of it is in.' She broke down again into sobs. 'Oh, my lady. My children will starve.'

Bewildered, Jean looked over the woman's head to her mother-in-law. 'What has all this to do with me?'

'Ask Kynachan to let my man go, my lady, I beg you.'

'Bohally has recruited the men of her township,' explained Janet.

'What?' Jean addressed the woman at her feet. 'Is that it? Your husband has joined the prince's army?'

'Oh yes, my lady. And he's not a fighter. He just wants to live in peace, doing no harm to anybody.'

'But my husband hasn't the power to let him go, Mrs Macdonald. We're all in the same position. All our husbands have gone to fight for the prince. We may not like it, but we all have to make sacrifices. You should be proud of him for volunteering to fight for his king and country.'

'Volunteering!' Through her tears came a shaft of bitter anger. 'Bohally said join, or he'd hough the cattle and burn our cottage.'

The words hung in the air. Donald looked furtively at Jean and then at Janet, gauging their reactions.

'He wouldn't do that,' said Clementina. 'Never!'

'And why should he have to threaten it?' demanded Jean, her sympathy giving way to anger. 'If you and your husband had a scrap of loyalty and honour . . .'

'Loyalty and honour?' The kneeling woman's voice was filled with scorn. Her baby began a thin, undernourished wail as she brandished it. 'Laird's words! Honour won't fill the belly of a dead man's child.'

'Enough!' Her face white, Jean took a step back. 'We all have our duty. If you are not satisfied, petition the duke.'

'Petition the duke! Aye, but which duke? The duke in the castle or the duke who'll be back with the Redcoats?'

'Get out of this house! I'll not listen to treason. My husband risks all for his rightful king. Those who do not support him are his enemies. And mine.'

Grissel Macdonald was not finished. 'I lay my curse upon . . .'

'That's enough from you, woman,' interrupted Donald. 'You don't want to get yourself into more trouble.'

He took her by the arm, half dragging her towards the door. 'Go on, be off with you!'

'Wait, Donald,' called Jean. 'Give her some meal. Enough for her and her family for a week.'

Donald scowled. 'A waste of good food, if you ask me.'

'I won't,' snapped Jean.

'As you please, my lady. Come on, Grissel.'

'You did right to give her meal,' Janet said when they had left.

Jean sighed. 'She angered me, but I cannot blame her.'

'What do you mean?' said Clementina. 'She was hateful to tell lies about Charlie. And she's obviously a witch.'

'She was trying to do what she believes best for her husband and family. So am I. I want her man by Davie's side. She wants him by hers.'

'There was none of this sort of thing last time,' said Janet gloomily.

'That is as may be,' said Jean. 'Last time we lost. This time we won't.'

26

Edinburgh

Tummelside rejoiced when news was received that the Highland army had taken Edinburgh without a shot. The defending dragoons had fled before the Jacobite advance, and the Camerons had successfully rushed one of the city gates when it had been opened to allow entry to a coach. Only the castle garrison still held out for King George, lobbing the occasional cannon-ball whenever Highlanders showed themselves at the top of the High Street.

In Atholl, the continual buzz of rumour, fuelled by speculation, imagination, and prognostication, crystallized again a few days later. With their fighting men in the south, the folk in the clachans had been fearful of the possible return of Sir John Cope's army. Now came news that it had been shipped south from Inverness to a point east of Edinburgh, at Dunbar. The government troops had met the Highland army in battle on the twenty-first of September, at Prestonpans.

The Atholl Brigade had crossed the river Forth at the Fords of Frew, bypassed Stirling (where the garrison in the castle still defied the rebels), and joined the rest of the prince's army, camped at Duddingston, outside Edinburgh, on the nineteenth. The next day, they had marched out to meet Cope's army.

A general's success in the eighteenth century depended on how skilfully he used the three arms of warfare available to him – artillery, cavalry, and infantry. It was a precise art, each move by the enemy requiring its counter, and soldiers were trained accordingly. A Highland commander had but one weapon – the charge – and victory depended upon from how advantageous a position he could deliver it. Cope's army was the equal in number to the rebels, but its men had not been trained to face such a charge, and they had a healthy dread of it. Since avoiding combat with the prince at Corryarrack, government ranks had been augmented by the dragoon regiments left to guard Stirling and Edinburgh, but these had already fled in panic before the Highlanders' approach to the Scottish capital.

At Prestonpans, the government army was in a strong position, guarded by the sea to the north, rough morasses to the south, and the high park walls of Preston House to the west. It was from here that Cope expected the Highlanders, and he was confident of victory. But the Redcoats were unseasoned troops, and their morale was low.

Lord George Murray had been disappointed by the Atholl Brigade. Their armaments were poor and, aside from the men of Tummelside under their lairds' command, many were undisciplined and showed little martial enthusiasm. Along with the Robertsons and the McLauchlans, they were ordered to form the second line. The son of a local laird showed the rebels a way through the marshes, and when dawn broke the Highlanders were advancing onto the field from the east, to face the enemy with the sun in the Redcoats' eyes.

Even before their whole army had drawn up on the field of battle, the front ranks of the Highlanders had charged. Pausing within a hundred paces of the enemy, they discharged their muskets and dropped the empty weapons. Shielded by the smoke of their fire, they split into wedges of about a dozen men and pressed on, brandishing swords and dirks. When these screaming savages erupted from the powder-smoke, most of the Redcoats turned and fled.

A disorganized rabble, hampered by their constricting uniforms, the regular troops had little chance of outpacing their pursuers. Cope and four hundred of his dragoons found safety in England – Cope gaining the reputation as the first general in history to bring news of his own defeat. A hundred of the infantry took refuge in Edinburgh Castle and seventy more at Berwick. Eleven hundred unwounded soldiers were captured, but the broadsword was a terrible weapon, designed for hacking rather than stabbing, and the field became an abattoir. The ground was littered with severed limbs, heads, and bodies showing ghastly wounds. Reports of casualties varied, but Lord George estimated that for the loss of thirty-four Highlanders, six hundred Redcoats were killed and six hundred wounded. The rebels called their victory Gladsmuir.

Held in reserve, the Atholl Brigade took no part in the slaughter, but many of them joined the rest of the Highland army to loot the dead. Under the firm control of their lairds, the men of Strathtummel remained in their ranks and undertook the grim task of clearing the battlefield of wounded. The prince, considering the enemy misguided subjects of his father, joined Lord George in urging that humanity be shown. The Athollmen and the Camerons spent the night with the defeated enemy to ensure they were not molested by the drunken victors.

In general, the people of Edinburgh had supported the government. Knowing little of the Highlands or of Highlanders, the citizens had not been looking forward to the advent of those they considered barbarians, with their alien speech and dress. After the battle, while the prince and his council planned their next move at the Palace of Holyroodhouse, the city was full of awe-struck Highlanders, marvelling at the great cliffs of stone buildings, the wealth, and the metropolitan bustle. In stews and alehouses and in the dank, dark closes and wynds that branched off the High Street, the amused citizens, overcoming their fears, set about to relieve the victors of their booty. It was not hard. One Highlander gave away a looted watch because, when it stopped ticking, it had obviously died.

The first battalion of the Atholl Brigade was detailed to police the city. Lord Nairne was occupied with Lord George Murray and the other senior commanders who advised the prince, while Bohally was still putting together reinforcements in Atholl. So, as well as the maintenance of order in Edinburgh, the task of re-equipping the battalion with captured arms fell to David.

The Town Guard's headquarters were half-way down the High Street. Most of its members were Highlanders, who looked upon the position as a comfortable berth at sixpence a day, and they were quite willing to assist the Jacobites in keeping the peace.

The Athollmen set themselves up in the Lawnmarket, in the rooms of a minister who had fled before the prince's advance. There, the West Bow, leading from the Grassmarket, joined the great High Street, which stretched the length of the hill on which the city was built, from the castle to the palace.

Late in the afternoon of the fourth day after the battle, David had a visitor. He was at his papers in the minister's parlour when he heard a familiar voice outside the door brushing aside the attempts of his guard to stop her.

Meg Mercer's gown was purple, and her hat sported two immense purple plumes. One was pinned with the rebels' white cockade, the other with the government's black.

'Where's Willie Kennedy?' she demanded, as she burst through the door. Behind her, a shame-faced Highlander was still waving his musket.

'Good day, Meg,' said David, putting down his quill and rising to his feet. 'Willie's on an errand.'

'Your watchdogs have only the Gaelic – hopeless in this city.'

'They don't need English to keep people out.'

'I think they merely keep you in. Which is why I've come. You've been playing soldier long enough. Everyone else is strutting round Holyrood, lit by the prince's reflected glory. I want you to adorn my dinner table tomorrow. Make sure you wear your tartans.'

'I'm much too busy, Meg.'

'Nonsense. It's your duty to attend. I am filling the table with Whigs, and you can persuade them to fight for the prince.'

David shook his head, but it never occurred to Meg that she would not get her way.

'If you don't, I'll get an order from Johnnie Nairne or His Highness.'

David gave her a wry look. 'All right, I yield to superior forces. I shall come. Now please, Meg, I must work.' He picked up his pen and gestured to the papers strewn over the table. 'I find myself running half our army as well as this city.'

'You're in danger of becoming a bore, Davie Stewart.' Coming round the table, Meg linked her arm with his. 'I am taking you across the street to visit your sister-in-law. I was shocked to hear from Barbara that you have not yet called. Jean'd never forgive you, especially as your mother-in-law has a fever. A visit from you will be a tonic to her.'

'I suppose I could spare a few minutes now,' said David. 'I have been intending to pay respects to Jean's family. I have also some business with Kinnaird.'

'He'll be delighted to see you.'

'I have a guinea that says he won't.'

Meg laughed. 'Nonsense. You're just another of his wife's embarrassing relations – like me.'

27

A Thief Taken

Willie Kennedy, back at his post outside the door to the minister's parlour, fell in behind David and Meg as they left the house. A crowd of idlers and small boys were at the mouth of the close, watching the comings and goings of the rebel soldiers.

In Edinburgh, a Highland gentleman would normally have worn knee-breeches and a coat instead of his tartans, but the kilt and plaid had become the Jacobite uniform. The throng of merchants, lawyers, and fashionably dressed ladies in the Lawnmarket and round the Luckenbooths by St Giles were experiencing the novelty of their city under occupation. Many nodded and smiled greetings at Meg and her companions. Those unacquainted with them, noting the steel pistols at David's belt, the twin eagle feathers in his bonnet, and the watchful presence of Willie Kennedy alongside, gave the three-some respectful passage through their midst.

'Huh!' grunted Meg. 'It is quite provoking. Nobody has eyes for me at all.'

'Twas ever thus, Meg, when you were with me,' David teased.

'I see that military responsibilities haven't dented your vanity,' she countered.

In this part of town were concentrated the pewter and tinsmiths, and the clatter of their trade soon shut out the cries of the hucksters when David and his little entourage plunged into the base of the tenement opposite.

The door was opened by a servant girl, who started back, her hand to her mouth, when she saw the figures on the ill-lit landings.

'Rebels!' she gasped.

'Don't be stupid, Bella,' said Meg. 'Go tell your mistress her brother-in-law is here.'

'Yes, Miss Mercer,' said the girl. She curtsied to David and hurried off to do Meg's bidding.

A few seconds later, Kinnaird came rushing down the hall. 'Meg – and Kynachan!' he exclaimed. 'How dreadful! I was afraid you might turn up. I suppose you'd better come in.'

'A guinea, please, Meg,' called David with delight as she went on ahead towards the parlour.

Kinnaird pushed past David onto the landing and peered down the stairs. 'Did anybody see you? I would not like it thought I was a Jacobite. What are you doing here?'

'I came to visit my wife's relations and you.'

'No, what are you doing in this city?'

'My battalion is maintaining the law.'

'Ha! In that case you should arrest that crew in Holyrood.'

'You surprise me, Alexander. With the Redcoats beaten, I would have thought none would be stronger for the prince.'

Kinnaird snorted. 'Mayflies, dancing for a day.'

'Stand guard outside the door, Willie,' said David. As usual, he felt a touch of irritation when in the presence of his brother-in-law.

'No,' said Kinnaird. 'It will advertise our unfortunate connection to the whole city.'

David's jaw clenched. 'You may be husband to my wife's sister, Kinnaird, but take care what you say.'

The music master's face brightened. 'If anyone spotted you, I suppose I could always say you forced yourself into my apartments.'

Willie Kennedy had taken his post outside the door.

'Do you think that wee lassie could bring me a dram, Kynachan?' he asked, speaking in Gaelic.

'She'll give you a dram, man, but nothing else,' said Kinnaird. He turned to the girl and spoke in English. 'Get this man some whisky. If you dally with him, I'll thrash you.'

'I'd no dally with the prince himself on the common stair,' said Bella, giving her master an indignant look before going off to carry out his orders.

'I trust all is well on my estates?' said Kinnaird, as he led David through the hallway to the parlour. 'Reliable news from the north is difficult to obtain since order broke down.'

Seated by the fire, Barbara turned from conversation with her aunt, and her face broke into a smile of delight. 'David, I was worried you might have been wounded in the battle.'

'Hardly one of the rebels had a scratch,' said her husband, pouring Meg, then David, a glass of claret. 'The whole

169

performance was a national disgrace. I suppose you did your fair share of slaughter?'

'We were in the reserve.' David went across to Barbara, bending to kiss her cheek. 'I'm sorry to hear your mother is unwell.'

Barbara grimaced. 'She has had a fever for the last week. The physician visits but his medicines seem powerless to make an improvement. Even bleeding brings her little relief. How is my sister and the bairns?'

'Jean is concerned for the safety of so many of our tenants and friends, of course, but Atholl is peaceful, and most of the harvest safely in. She hopes you will all come and stay now that the danger seems over.'

'How can it be over while the rebellion continues?' asked Kinnaird.

'I am not privy to His Royal Highness's strategy, but we have no opposition in Scotland. Without an army against us, there can be no danger to Atholl. Particularly when men of your brother's mettle guard the country in our absence. He has been made lieutenant in Logierait by His Grace.'

'He has not made himself conspicuous in the Pretender's cause?' said Kinnaird with alarm.

From Meg came a hoot of derision. 'No doubt as conspicuous as a crouching ptarmigan in a blizzard.'

'He's his brother's brother,' said David. 'Don't fret. He has done no more than he must, and that with reluctance.'

Meg rose to her feet. 'I shall go to cheer up Anna and tell her of her dashing son-in-law.'

The gentlemen bowed as she left the room, and Kinnaird refilled David's glass.

'What times we live in,' the music master said. 'So many lives disrupted. I was fully hopeful that we might soon achieve a resolution of our court processes concerning the Mercer inheritance, but this rebellion is the excuse for yet more of the law's delays. I may be forced to ask you to cover the further costs.'

David waved a dismissive hand. 'There are more vital matters afoot. Anyway, I have pledged every penny I have towards His Highness's cause.'

Kinnaird was aghast. 'Risking your life is one thing, but to risk your fortune is simply irresponsible. Although I suppose you're bound to lose your estate anyway when the rebellion is over – even if you are not killed.'

'My husband is a careful man,' said Barbara defensively.

'He's that, all right,' agreed David. 'That's one reason, Alexander, why I should like you to be my executor. All Scotland may be laid waste, but you'd be safe, wringing your hands on top of the ruins.'

'It is as well that someone can keep his head, Kynachan. However, I will agree to your request, even though it may be construed as connivance with a notorious Jacobite.'

'I saw the prince arrive at Holyrood,' said Barbara. 'It was like a Roman triumph. He is prodigiously handsome. If the ladies of Edinburgh had their way, King George would come to pay homage at his feet.'

'And if men had theirs, my dear, your prince would vanish and allow business affairs to return to normal. You talk romantic foolishness. It is as well your sex is subject to mine,' sniffed Kinnaird.

At the sound of an altercation on the landing, he cocked his ear.

'What now?' he groaned.

The servant girl appeared in the doorway and bobbed a little curtsy to David. 'Your man wants you, your honour.'

David rose. 'If you'll excuse me for a moment, Barbara.'

'I suppose I'd better come too,' Kinnaird grumbled.

The two men went into the hallway. The front door was open, and on the landing a small knot of men argued with Willie. One was George Cairney, a wild figure, still with his claymore strapped to his back. Another, in dull red breeches and coat and carrying a Lochaber-axe, was a member of the Town Guard. The third figure was clasped firmly by the scruff of his neck. He was a pock-faced Highlander but he wore a blood-spattered dragoon's tunic, a sleeve of which was missing. His unclothed arm was supported in a broad, bloody sling.

'What's this, George?' asked David.

Cairney gestured to the guard. 'This man is Robert Stewart, kin of Bonskeid.'

'I am honoured to meet you, Robert Stewart,' said David. 'Bonskeid would be with us now if his tenants had not turned him back because of his youth.'

'God grant you long life and a successful campaign, Kynachan,' said the Town Guard. He nodded to the prisoner. 'I apprehended this man down the Cowgate. He was trying to pick a gentleman's purse. He claims to have fought with the Atholl Brigade at Gladsmuir.'

David looked at the scruffy figure. 'I don't remember you

on the march, man, though I don't deny your face is familiar. Whose company are you with? Are you a deserter? What's your name?'

'I am a wounded hero. I wasn't exactly with the Atholl Brigade. I was . . . with Shian Menzies.'

'You don't sound very sure.'

'No, perhaps it was Struan. My brain is addled with my wound. See how grievously I was hurt.' He lifted his injured arm, indicating the blood on the sling and his coat.

David was unimpressed. 'The blood will be that of the Redcoat who inhabited the tunic before you. Where have I seen you?'

'He looks a rogue to me,' said Kinnaird. 'Not much of a rogue either.'

'What happened to your arm?' asked David.

'A cannon-ball. The shot was so thick it blocked out the rising sun. It tore the earth around me to a tilth as fine as wheat flour. As I fell, my blood nourished a rose bush, and from it sprang a white bloom to honour our great prince.'

'By God,' said Kinnaird. 'He has a tongue in his head, though I doubt the wit to back it.'

'Cannon-fire, eh?' said David.

'Aye, even Fingal himself would have quailed before that storm of iron.'

'Cope's gunners fired but a single shot before they fled. I believe they even omitted to insert a ball. I think we'd better see his wound.'

'I'm not having the wretch bleed all over my landing,' said Kinnaird.

'I doubt he'll have much gore to offer.'

'I know him,' exclaimed Willie Kennedy, who had been racking his memory. 'Alister Breck. You remember, Kynachan? Yon black bull! You said you'd cut off his ear if you saw him again.'

'Only on Kynachan land, your honour. Oh, forgive me, sir. May my bones lie in foreign soil if I ever committed a dishonest act since that day.'

'By Heaven, you're right, Willie! Alexander Breck Stewart. Get that bandage off him.'

A slash of a dirk cut through the encrusted sling, and it fell, emitting a clink when it hit the floor.

'There's a curious thing,' said Willie Kennedy. He opened out the bloody linen with his foot and revealed two gold watches, a silver snuff-box, some silver buttons, and three gold rings.

'By God!' said Cairney with admiration.

'They're mine,' said Alister Breck, struggling in the Town Guard's grasp. 'They all belonged to dead Englishmen.'

David bent to pick up the snuff-box. On its lid was engraved a crest. He showed it to Kinnaird. 'This came from no Whig. It's a Cameron crest.'

'Two of Lochiel's officers were killed,' said Cairney. 'You wretch, you have been robbing our own dead!'

'Lock him up in the Tolbooth,' said David. 'Lord George can have him hanged in the morning. Any of his booty unclaimed by its owners can be sold for the cause.'

'You can't, your honour. I was never a soldier. I am a simple tenant of His Grace of Atholl. God save the prince!'

'You're either a deserter, man, or you're one of those carrion crows that follows the army in search of plunder,' said David. 'Either way you'd decorate a gibbet better than you would the hills of Atholl. Take him away, George.'

'If you hanged your army one by one, the country would soon get back to normal,' said Kinnaird, as he and his guest returned to the parlour. 'I confess, however, to a sneaking admiration for Alister Breck. I'm even grateful to him. Lord Lovat invited me to dine with him to hear the tale of the black bull and afterwards he requested me to instruct his daughter on the spinet.'

Back from the sick-room, Meg told David to go next door to his mother-in-law but to be careful not to tax her strength.

He found Anna Mercer in her bed, her eyes bright with fever. David was alarmed by her apparent weakness, but she managed a tired smile when he entered.

'I'm sorry to see you like this, madam.'

'It's good to see you, Davie.'

He moved to kiss her hand, but she waved him away.

'I strive to keep this contagion to myself,' she said. 'Tell me, are Jean and the children well?'

'They are, and looking forward to the time when you can visit Kynachan once more.'

'I'll wait till King James is on his throne and you're an earl.'

David laughed. 'To the victor the honour and the spoils! By Heaven, I never gave that side of things a single thought. Besides, there is nothing I want more than Kynachan and the love of your daughter. I am honoured to possess both.'

'You are a very precious man, Davie. Take care of those I love.' She paused a moment. 'I see shadows gathering.'

David, too, felt that this might be their final meeting and he took her hand to give comfort.

The dull boom of one of the castle cannon made her frail body start.

'Take care of yourself most of all, Davie.'

Only then did he realize that she feared for his life and not her own.

28

Struan's Trophy

Driven by an October gale, squalls of rain clattered on the dining-room window of the mansion house of Kynachan. Jean and Clementina had finished breakfast, and Jessie played on the rug by the fire. Jean was instructing Donald to organise repairs to the roof of the peat shed.

A horse trotted into the yard, prompting pandemonium upstairs in the parlour. Roused from the hearth, the baying setters scrambled across the floor and clattered down the stairs towards the front door. Jessie hauled herself upright and ran over to her mother's skirts for protection.

'I'll go,' said Clementina, rising from her chair.

'As I was about to say, Donald,' continued Jean, 'I know Margaret Gow at Drumnakyle thatched her own cottage last year, so you can ask her . . .' She stopped. 'Donald, are you listening to me?'

'No, I'm not. What's going on out there?'

Silence was the least likely outcome of a visitor's arrival. No murmur of greeting had been heard, and hardly a yelp, since Clementina had opened the front door.

'I'd better take a look,' the steward said.

He was forestalled by Clementina, pink in the face, returning to the room. Only one caller could explain her blush, the drops of rain on her hair, and the dark patch of damp on her apron.

'Guess who's here!'

'Bohally,' exclaimed Jean and Donald in unison.

'They can see through walls in this house,' grinned Bohally in the doorway, with the dogs gambolling round him. His plaid, heavy with rain, dripped on the floor. 'Lady Kynachan.' He gave a short bow in greeting.

'How good to see you, Charlie,' said Jean. 'Let Donald take your plaid. Can he get you some food? There's little more than oatcakes and cheese, perhaps some salmon. But we still have claret.'

'I'll see what I can find,' said Clementina, dashing out.

'Now, Miss Clementina,' Donald clucked, and he hurried out after her, saying, 'You be careful. There's little enough to spare . . .'

'You have news?' asked Jean.

Bohally put his hand in the pouch hooked onto his broad leather belt. 'I have a letter.'

'From David?' Without waiting for confirmation she snatched it from his hand. Breaking the seal, she unfolded the sheet and rapidly scanned its contents. 'He's well. He's coming home.'

'Home,' echoed Jessie.

Janet came in. 'What about home? Oh, it's Charlie. A very good day to you.'

'Madam.' Bohally gave another bow.

Janet snorted. 'Since when have you been bowing and scraping, Charlie Stewart?'

He smiled. 'Since I've been reporting to Duke William at Blair. I've just come from there. I'm on my way to Taybridge to fetch some reluctant recruits.'

'Yes, we've heard about that. We had Grissel Macdonald from over the river complaining.'

'Was she, now? She's the exception along the Tummel. It's along the Tay and up Glen Lyon that we're having to tickle folk out.'

'What's wrong with them?'

'They've been ruled by Whigs too long. Duke James and Commissary Bissett. Half the men have forgotten their clan loyalties, and the other half have forgotten how to use a broadsword. The lairds too. Still, we're getting an army together. We go round the country reminding folk of their responsibilities. If a tenant is rich enough, we let him pay to escape our net. We need silver almost as much as soldiers.'

'Reminding them of their responsibilities wasn't the way Grissel put it,' said Janet.

Again he grinned. 'Some of my keener lads can be a might upset at those who shirk their duty.'

'My mother has a fever, but my sister is well. He'll be here in a few days,' said Jean, still reading the letter.

'Davie?' said Janet with eagerness. 'You have news?'

'That's right,' said Bohally. 'He's bringing the officer prisoners taken at Gladsmuir to Perth. Then he comes here to join the duke, and we all march south.'

Clementina returned carrying a tray laden with wine, a

couple of roast woodcock, a few slices of beef, and some sweet biscuits. She laid it on the table by Bohally.

'That looks like our dinner,' said Janet gloomily.

'We can spare it,' scolded Clementina. 'Charlie's a soldier and doesn't know when he'll get his next meal.'

'I'm an old woman and now I don't know when I'll be getting mine.'

'Have some of this, Mrs Stewart.' Bohally had produced a little knife from its sheath by his dirk and offered Janet some beef.

'Don't be ridiculous. I've just had my breakfast.'

'He hopes to spend a night or two here,' said Jean, giving a précis of the letter. 'Lord George Murray shows him great favour. Davie marched out to Gladsmuir alongside the prince. He says he hopes Charlie has many more soldiers, as they have plenty of captured weapons, but the men are melting away.' She lifted her head from the page. 'Charlie, that doesn't sound very good.'

'The deserters? Sitting in camp outside Edinburgh they've got nothing to do. They'll've got a bit of booty, and so they decide to come home as if they'd been on a great cattle raid. As our country borders on the Lowlands, it's easy for the Atholl lads.' Bohally took a swig of claret. 'I'd probably do the same myself. We're picking them up in the alehouses by Taybridge and the ferry at Dunkeld. I'm going down to bring some of them back to Blair. With the deserters and the fresh recruits we'll have five hundred men to march south.'

'You'll be at Taybridge tonight?' asked Janet.

'No.' He jerked his head over his shoulder. 'I'll bring them as far as Bohally this evening.'

'You'll have to come across for supper,' said Jean.

'That's a good idea,' agreed Janet. 'We can listen to all your grand gossip about the duke, and Clementina can spend the day dreaming about the secret assignation she'll have with you tonight.'

'Mother!'

War or not, Sunday was still the Lord's Day. Most people walked over the pass to the parish church at Dull, where during his two-hour sermons the Reverend Duncan McLea breathed as much hell-fire as he dared against the Jacobites and those of his parishioners who had joined them.

But convinced Jacobites would not worship with a minister

who had sworn an oath of loyalty to the Hanoverian king. Usually their spiritual needs were supplied by Duncan Cameron, the Episcopalian clergyman at Fortingall, but he was now a chaplain in Lochiel's regiment. His ancient predecessor had taken advantage of the Jacobite ascendancy and turned a stable by the inn at Tummel bridge into a little thatched chapel where he had fifty in his congregation. Most were the families of the local lairds, but a few tenant and cottar folk joined them, particularly those from the clachans facing the longest walk to Dull.

After the service, the worshippers exchanged news at the chapel door before splitting up to walk home. The blustery, damp grey day was warmed by the birches on the face of Craig Kynachan, which flamed with autumn colour.

'Disgraceful sermon,' sniffed Janet once they were out of earshot of the priest. 'Though I suppose we should be grateful to have any preacher at all.'

'I thought it highly appropriate,' said Clementina with a giggle.

'Where did he say the text came from?'

'Joshua,' said Jean. 'Where God is fulfilling his covenant to King David.'

'And David slew seventy thousand Philistines,' quoted Janet. 'The man didn't mean King David. He gave us a great soupy smile when he read it.'

'He meant well,' said Jean.

Janet snorted. 'What sort of an excuse is that for a preacher of God's word? Anyway, I thought it most presumptuous of him to call David David.'

'You'd rather he called him Kynachan Kynachan?'

'You know very well what I mean.'

Ahead of them, a small party of homeward-bound chapel-goers began gesticulating excitedly.

Janet frowned. 'What's with those folk?'

'Hush,' said Clementina, stopping them. 'Is that the pipes?'

The rush of the wind against their ears made it hard to hear.

'There's someone coming down the road,' said Jean.

'Come on!' called Clementina, breaking into a clumsy run, hampered by the pattens she wore to protect her shoes from the muddy road.

'They're not diving into the heather, so it won't be the Philistines,' said Janet.

'And it won't be Davie,' said Jean. 'He'll be coming the other way, from Blair.'

Round the corner appeared the vanguard of a column of Highlanders, led by two pipers. In the stiff breeze, a long battle pennant, embroidered with three wolves' heads, snaked behind the standard.

'It's Struan!' said Janet. 'It's the Robertsons. That's Rob Ban of Invervack in the front. But what on earth have they got with them?'

The clansmen, proudly shouldering new muskets, marched briskly towards them. In their midst was a large four-wheeled carriage, half a dozen men on each of the shafts and another dozen hauling on ropes. One of the back wheels was missing, and a pole had been bound to the axle so that four men could bear its weight. The carriage, lacquered royal blue, had a graceful pagoda roof.

It rumbled to a halt alongside the women, and the door was suddenly flung open. Struan, a three-cornered hat upon his head, leaned out to bellow at his men. The pipes groaned to silence, the banner drooped, and the clansmen substituting for the missing wheel let go their pole. The coach rocked for a few moments but settled upright.

'Ladies,' said the old man. Standing in the doorway, he looked at the ground a couple of feet below and bellowed for his gillie.

One of the men came hurrying round. Struan frowned at him. 'Well, Angus? What did I tell you to do whenever we stopped?'

Angus looked baffled. Struan struck out at him with the cane in his left hand.

'The steps, you witless son of an ox and a donkey,' the chief roared. 'How many times do I have to tell you?'

'Oh, aye,' said Angus, dodging the blow amid laughter from the circle of surrounding Highlanders. He returned from the rear of the carriage carrying a set of three steps, which he fitted to a bracket beneath the open door.

Struan climbed carefully down to the ground. Doffing his hat, he gave a deep if shaky bow. He was wearing a gold chain and a rich cloak of wolf fur. Straightening, he swung an arm towards the carriage. 'Do you like it?'

'It's certainly impressive,' said Janet.

'It's General Cope's,' said Struan, indicating the coat of arms painted on the door. 'And this is his chain, this is his cloak, and this is his hat.' He had indicated each in turn. 'And there're a couple of barrels of his best brandy on the bench opposite.'

The women peered in through the door and admired the blue leather upholstery and matching padded silk panels.

'What do you want with it?' asked Janet.

'Want with it?' Struan seemed taken aback. 'We're taking it home as a trophy of war.'

'I've never heard of such a thing. You'll not get it beyond the bridge. You've already broken one of the wheels, and the track along Rannoch is difficult enough for a pony, let alone that monster.'

'You're a typical miserable woman, Janet Stewart,' growled Struan. 'We'll take off all the wheels, and my lads'll carry me home. Won't you, lads?'

This raised a cheer from his men, and the chief nodded his satisfaction.

'I've done with fighting, myself. I thought I could still wield a sword but I can't. I could do no more than watch at Gladsmuir.' Struan turned to Clementina. 'Did you know, young lady, I fought beside your grandfather?'

'Aye,' said Clementina.

'That'll be three generations of your family I've fought alongside. Probably four, if you assume some of the bastards Davie spawned are fighting by now.'

'You're a wicked old man, Struan,' said Janet.

He winked ostentatiously at Jean. 'I won't linger. I hear that Davie'll be here as soon as he has done business with the duke. I'll send over a bottle or two of this brandy for him. I'd like you to assure him that my lads will be ready to march when he is.'

'Were you near Davie in the battle?' asked Jean.

'Aye. He and his men were as brave as any of my own clansmen. Mind you, some of the men that came south were a disgrace to Atholl. Lord George didn't dare let them fight, and half of them still deserted.' He shook his head. 'The country's gone to the dogs. King James will be too good for them. Folk have lost all sense of honour.'

He gave another bow, replaced his hat, and struggled up the steps. His hat caught the top of the door and as he grabbed for it he overbalanced, tumbling forward into the coach. Angus stuck a brawny arm through the door and hauled his chief onto the bench before removing the steps.

'Carry on!' shouted the old man.

His voice being muffled, nothing happened. He poked his head out of the window. 'For the love of Jesus, will you get a move on!' he bawled.

Drones broke raggedly into life as the pipers filled their bags, and once more the carriage lurched into jarring motion across the stones and boulders, onward to the bridge and the Hermitage.

The women watched the column until it rounded a corner.

'Davie hasn't any bastards, has he?' asked Jean.

'Of course not, dear. Struan was just teasing you,' said Janet. 'It was Willie Kennedy who was chased by the minister. David always got away with it.'

29

Soldier's Return

Late that drizzly afternoon, David brought sixty men home across Tummel bridge. Fifteen of them continued on to Foss, led by the son of the laird. The rest dispersed across Kynachan.

The setters ambushed David on the track and they alerted the household to his approach by rushing up the stairs to the parlour.

'Davie!' said Jean, understanding at once why the dogs were excited. She abandoned her sewing, her son, and her seat by the fire to speed down to the front door.

They met in the yard, Jean plunging her arms into the folds of tartan that enveloped the bearded figure outlined against the darkening sky.

'Oh, my love, I have missed you,' she whispered.

David hugged her fiercely, and she felt the hard familiar body smelling of damp woods and the heather.

In the parlour, logs were piled on top of the sullen peat to make a blaze. David was soon installed in a chair, his feet resting in a bath of warm water, a glass of mulled claret by his side. The household was seated in a semi-circle, waiting for the warrior's news.

'We want a daily diary of what you've been doing since you were last here,' demanded Clementina, who held Euphemia on her lap.

'Have many of our lads been hurt?' asked Janet.

'No,' said David. 'No-one the entire length of the Tummel. We were in the second line and were hardly involved in the battle. The campaign could not be going better. The prince has set up his court at Holyrood house, and the army grows daily.'

'Have you been eating properly?' asked Jean.

The setters, staring doe-eyed at their master, had once again joined Jessie and John by the hearth.

'I saw Barbara and Kinnaird. He wasn't very pleased to see me. His brother is supposed to be the family Jacobite, and Kinnaird the Whig.'

Clementina tutted her disenchantment.

'Barbara sends her love to everyone, as does Mrs Mercer, but she was most unwell.'

'You said in your letter. She is no better?' asked Jean anxiously.

David grimaced. 'I fear not. I saw Kinnaird again just before we left Edinburgh, and he said that Barbara may be sickening too.'

'They'll be fine. The Lord'll look after them,' said Janet. 'There's always something going round Edinburgh.'

'Barbara is cheerful,' continued David in a lighter tone. 'Still a good Jacobite, which annoys her husband.'

'Tell us more about the battle,' ordered Clementina.

'We captured most of the Highlanders of Lord John Murray and Lord Loudon's companies. I escorted Pat Murray of Ochtertyre and young Straloch to Perth along with the Redcoat officers we took prisoner.'

'What were they like?' asked Clementina.

Her brother gave a shrug. 'You saw many of them march through Kynachan last month. That officer who came over to us, Captain Poyntz of Guise's regiment – he was wounded and taken. He recognized me and was most put out of joint.'

'He was a horrid man,' said Clementina.

'He's some mother's son,' said Janet. 'Was he sore hurt?'

'The poor fellow lost his hand but he's progressing well. We treated the prisoners like gentlemen. They are subjects of King James, just as we are, but merely misguided.'

Clementina made a face at her brother that he feigned not to notice.

'On the way here, we passed a night at Tullibardine, and Lady George Murray gave us dinner. Peter Halkett of Pitfirrane was the most senior officer captured. He and I dined at her table.'

'And what happens next?' asked Jean. 'Is the king to be crowned at Holyrood? Is the Union now dissolved?'

'That is for people more important than me to decide. Arms and troops are landing from France and Spain. The government army's away fighting on the Continent. Throughout all England men are poised to rise for the prince. He could consolidate his power in Scotland or he could march on London. There's no-one to oppose him.'

'But is not one kingdom enough?' said Janet.

'The prince is God's rightful heir to four countries –

Scotland, England, Wales, and Ireland. It is his duty to regain all of them, and ours to assist him.'

'It's funny,' said Clementina. 'Charlie's become a bit pompous as well. He puts it down to playing court to the duke at Blair.'

David gave a rueful smile. 'Perhaps I'm the same. I've been mixing with princes – one, anyway – and all those English gentlemen.'

Blissfully, he wriggled his toes in the basin.

'You must be tired,' said Jean.

'Not really, but it's a relief to know there aren't a dozen decisions to make and a dozen messages to send. Clemmie, is there another jug of hot water?'

Clementina, a not insensitive girl, rose to her feet and suggested to her mother that they went to the kitchen with the children.

'Oh, Donald can take care of the supper,' Janet said absently.

'Perhaps Jean and Davie would like to be by themselves for a bit, Mother.'

'Oh, I see,' said Janet, looking sheepish. 'How silly of me. Come on, John.'

Clementina scooped up the two girls and followed her mother out.

Jean moved the bath of hot water and knelt on the sheepskin at her husband's feet. Leaning forward between his thighs, she wrapped her arms round his waist.

'You feel wonderful! God alone knows how much I've missed you.'

'And I've missed you, my love,' he replied, holding her tightly to him. 'This has been the longest we've been apart since we were wed.'

'I know.'

'The lads tease me about it. They call me Doting Davie.'

'Quite right.' Her voice was muffled, buried in his chest.

He flinched.

'That's why it's called a nipple. It's for nipping. How long are you home for?'

'I am ordered to Castle Menzies tomorrow to organize recruiting in Strathtay and Glen Lyon.'

'Tomorrow!' Lifting her head, Jean gazed at him in dismay.

'It has to be. The prince is sweeping all before him, but we seem unable to raise and keep a regiment. The men of Atholl have been staunch for his family for two centuries, but . . .'

'Hush now!' Removing one arm from round his waist, she placed her finger across his lips. 'Start worrying about that tomorrow.'

He kissed the finger. 'What news is there from Kynachan?'

'Not much. The harvest is in. No rents are seriously outstanding. Margaret Robertson at Achmore has had a son. Oh, yes, and Struan passed by this morning on his way to the Hermitage. He said his men will be ready to march with you to Edinburgh.'

'Good. Woodsheal is to be their captain. They'll join with Shian's men and—'

'Hush again.' Her finger caressed his lips once more. 'We are done with the war for the night. Our time is too precious to waste.'

Her hand was moving under his kilt.

'Ah, it's Doting Davie. By the feel of him, he's been lonely.'

'You bawdy baggage, Jeannie Mercer.'

He leaned forward, his lips meeting hers. His hand slipped under her gown and up the naked skin of her thighs to grip the globes of her buttocks. She tore her mouth away from his and held him back. Crossing the room, she wedged a chair beneath the door handle.

She came to him, lifting the front of her petticoats to expose her naked body. She sat astride him, and his arms came round beneath her thighs to support her body as he entered her.

'Hallo, Jeannie,' he said tenderly, looking into her eyes.

He parted his own knees and began slowly to raise and lower her, her flesh linked to his. His movements grew faster, and her body strained to respond within the iron constraint of his arms. He lifted her to the sheepskin rug, her heels high in the air, and they came to a mutual, shuddering climax.

After a moment, still inside her, David sat back on his heels and pulled the rucked mass of her skirts from her head.

'Heavens,' she gasped when her face was once more exposed to view. 'Perhaps we should part more often.'

Alongside, the setters thumped their tails, soothed by the return to normality.

'My heart is yours until Schiehallion is dust,' he said softly.

Tears sprang into her eyes, and her hand flew up to caress his cheek. 'Oh, my love. My sweet, sweet love.'

'I find myself thinking of you at the oddest moments during the day,' he said. 'Sometimes when I am immersed in matters of business, men's lives perhaps dependent on my judgement, I will suddenly feel you with me and I wonder whether all the glory in the world is worth the price of being away from you for one moment.'

He leant forward and kissed her gently on the lips. 'I frown, I laugh, I talk matters of moment with the generals and colonels. I make jokes with the lads to keep them cheerful. But inside I am yearning for you.'

She said nothing but cupped his cheeks in her hands, as if she could hold his face above her for ever.

There was a knock on the door and an announcement.

'Supper in five minutes, my doves.'

'Thank you, Clemmie,' said Jean, without the trace of a tremor in her voice, her eyes still staring into those above her.

'Do you think she knows what we've been doing?' asked David.

'Of course. She's nineteen years old, and Charlie has long been a noted swordsman. It doesn't upset you, does it?'

'If they find a tithe of our joy, they have my blessing.'

She gave a little wriggle of her hips. 'I'm sure they'll bear that in mind, my sweet.'

The following morning, David marched once more to meet his men, this time at Daloist. It was a muggy, autumnal day. Mist hung between the yellowing trees, and the burns were brown and swollen.

Jean went with him. Bohally had marched in from Blair a few hours earlier, and now he and Clementina straggled behind.

At the muster point the atmosphere was akin to a games or a wedding. People milled, pipes skirled, and excited children wove through the throng. But louder even than the bray of the great warpipes was the scream of the grindstone in the smithy, where men queued for the final kiss to their broadswords.

Old age might have prevented Struan from joining the army, but his Robertsons were already there, exchanging banter with the girls from the townships of Kynachan. They clustered round the warriors, their proximity belying their modest down-cast eyes and shy giggles.

'These are the men to go to war with,' said Bohally, his eyes sparkling as he looked about him. 'No shirkers and cowards here. I shall bring you back glory, Clemmie.'

'Just yourself'll be enough, Charlie,' Clementina told him,

exchanging a complicitous glance with a woman whose husband was frenziedly waving his bonnet.

Somehow the density of the crowd allowed Jean and David a moment's privacy. 'I'll write whenever possible,' he said.

'And I you.'

Their eyes locked for a few moments, then he lifted his head.

'Bohally! Fall in the men!'

Bohally moved through the throng, bellowing out his commands. David touched his wife's cheek.

'Take care of yourself and what is ours, Jeannie.'

'Give her a kiss, Kynachan!'

The anonymous shout elicited a roar of approval.

'Go on, Doting Davie!' cried another voice. 'It'll bring us luck.'

The exuberant Highlanders lifted their bonnets, and a few fired their muskets, jetting boiling powder smoke into the air. The pipers struck up a rant.

Drawing his plaid round them, David kissed her. Children cheered, old men stood proud, and women wept. The men of Atholl marched once more to war.

30

Waiting

For three days, David remained at Castle Menzies helping Shian gather recruits. In daylight Sir Robert kept out of the way in his library while the Jacobites took over the great hall, distributing arms to the arriving new soldiers. Amongst their kinsfolk and acquaintances in Strathtay and Glen Lyon, the men from Strathtummel found it hard to employ the ruthlessness needed to press reluctant clansmen. To avoid future bitterness between neighbours, David obtained help from the Macphersons, a clan from Badenoch with few ties to the people of the surrounding clachans.

In the evenings, Sir Robert emerged from his seclusion and played host to his fellow chief, Cluny Macpherson, and to the other Jacobite lairds. When the rebel officers were gathered in the castle courtyard to march south, Sir Robert took David aside and pressed a copy of Pope's *Essays* into his hand.

'It will give you something to read in the evenings, David. He has some fine sentiments. I'd be interested in what you think.'

Then the Laird of Weem embraced his friend and stood glumly by Lady Mary as they watched the Highlanders depart to join their men camped by Taybridge.

In the hills beyond Strathtay they left the charred cottages of stubborn folk who had refused to join the men of Atholl. In the hearts of some of the marching Highlanders was horror and sadness at what they had been forced to do to their own people. Rumours even circulated of a few reluctant men who had misread the touchy pride of the wilder men of Badenoch and now lay in their graves, with musket balls in their chests, leaving their dazed families to depend on their neighbours' charity.

In Strathtummel, life went on as usual. Bonfires were lit on All-Hallows' Eve, when the spirits of the dead were abroad. The duty of the living was to make them welcome on their return to the mortal world to revisit their hearths and lands. Those born on this day would be cursed with the gift of second sight, the ability to foresee the future, usually the deaths of those about them. One such was the old wise woman, Granny Dewar, but she fell into a fit, and nobody on Kynachan could make sense of her ravings.

The prince's army left Edinburgh for England. As soon as it was out of sight, the garrison sallied forth from the castle, whereupon a thankful city reverted to the government. In Atholl, volunteers from the northern and western Highlands filtered across Tummel bridge to Perth to join a fresh army being gathered to reinforce the prince. At the same time, some of the men who had escaped recruitment came out of hiding and were joined in the townships by a trickle of deserters who, unwilling to fight on the alien soil of England, had evaded the guards posted on bridges and passes by Duncan Robertson of Drumachuine, the Jacobite governor of Atholl.

Jean found she missed David more with each day that passed but she had little time to brood. His absence meant that the folk on the estate expected her to fill his role as laird, and they brought her the everyday problems they had previously presented to him. She adjudicated on the boundary between two townships after one had taken advantage of a downpour to help a burn change its course. She reprimanded those who cut turf to thatch their cottages from within the head dyke. She set a price for the linen that the tenants had given as part of their Martinmas rents, even though the market was dead and she could do nothing but stack the yarn and cloth in a shed, hoping that the damp and rats kept away. She grew even closer to her mother-in-law, who had endured the same separation from her husband thirty years earlier and had also been expected to be laird as well as mother to tiny children.

A fortnight after David left Kynachan, a letter arrived from Meg in Edinburgh. The carrier had come via Castle Menzies and was grumbling to Donald over his dram in the kitchen when Jean and Clementina entered.

'You have to keep your mouth shut these days if you travel the country. One laird threatens to arrest me for spying for Prince Charles, the next for spying for King Geordie.'

At the table Donald was plucking an old gander, which had succumbed to wounds after driving off the fox that threatened its harem.

'There's a letter here from Edinburgh, my lady,' he said. 'It's from your aunt.'

'From Meg?' said Jean, taking it from the table. She addressed the carrier. 'Are they well at Castle Menzies?'

'Aye, my lady,' he replied. 'And they send their good wishes.'

'Is there news from the south?'

The carrier shrugged. 'Just rumour – the Redcoats have been issued with silver bullets, because the prince is the devil in disguise.'

Donald laughed. 'That'll cure desertion. Imagine the plunder after a battle!'

Jean had broken the seal and unfolded the letter. Her face went white, and Clementina put a supporting arm round her sister-in-law's waist.

'What is it?' she whispered.

'My mother and sister. The fever has killed them both.'

'Oh!' gasped Clementina, her hand flying to her mouth.

Jean went slowly to the back door, raising a flurry of goose feathers as she stepped outside. Clementina started after her, but Donald placed his hand on her arm.

'Let the Lord help carry her grief for a moment, Miss Clemmie.'

Jean wept in her mother-in-law's comforting arms, but, conscious of the number of people who depended on her now that David was away, for the most part she grieved in private. During the day she was about the estate with a brave face for all her people. Death's fickle despotism was familiar to everyone, and the folk of Kynachan admired the stoicism with which Bean Daibhidh Choimeachdan appeared to absorb her tragic blow.

As autumn moved towards winter, news and rumour came north with every pedlar, deserter, and messenger. Carlisle had fallen to the rebels with scarcely a casualty. Marshal Wade refused to fight. Separating tale from truth was impossible. Manchester had provided a regiment. The army was in Derby. King George had fled to Hanover. London prepared to receive the prince.

In the hills about Kynachan, the roar of rutting stags had ceased. The first great storm of the season raged in from Rannoch, plucking at thatch and turning the sky into a playground for the rooks, which twisted and tumbled in the aerial torrent. Rumours continued and grew gloomier. The main government army, under the Duke of Cumberland, had landed from the Continent. The Highlanders were in retreat. There had been a battle. The Jacobites were back in Scotland.

The first snows sugared the top of Schiehallion. Wispy skeins of geese and swans, like ribbons thrown across the sky, mellifluously chanted their way south. Mud on the road and tracks was frozen in the mornings. The cattle were back in the cottages, where they were waited on by the women, who brought them what greenery still survived the dying year.

Yule came but was inevitably subdued. Each household normally feasted to the limit of its means or its man's ability as a hunter or poacher. There might be haunches of deer, hares, moor fowl, perhaps a wild goose if a feeding flock came within range of the handful of scrap iron poured down the barrel of some ancient wheel-lock gun, or – when they came up from the Tummel and the sea to spawn – a salmon scooped from a shallow pool in the burn. Great shinty matches between the townships and the neighbouring estates were usually held, or bonspiels on frozen Loch Kinardochy, but, as the snow crept down the sides of the mountains, this year there were no men to hunt or play.

The retreating rebels, shadowed by government armies, came to rest for a few days in Glasgow. But, exhausted and dispirited after long months of marching, hundreds of Highlanders decamped and flooded north to the passes of Atholl and beyond. Drumachuine came through Kynachan to ensure that river crossings were well guarded and to try to persuade Struan to discourage deserters on their way home through Rannoch. The old chief had been offering them whisky and ferry rides across the Tummel.

As the old year ended and 1746 began, Atholl was gripped by frost, which turned the bogs and marshes to stone. Flurries of gritty snowflakes blew across the corries and heather, spreading a mean, ill-bleached sheet across the ridges and furrows of the fields. The Jacobite army left Glasgow and marched through the sullen countryside north towards Stirling, threatening once again to attack Edinburgh, whose citizens had become more stoutly Whig with every yard of the prince's withdrawal.

The government army in Newcastle, which had failed to intercept the Jacobites as they marched south to Derby, stayed inert as the rebels marched back. Now Cumberland replaced its commander, the septuagenarian Marshal Wade, with Lieutenant-General Henry Hawley and ordered him north to the Scottish capital, from where he should advance against the rebels and bring them to battle.

31

Meg Enters the Fray

The government army reached Edinburgh on the sixth of January, and Hawley's first action was to set gallows in the Grassmarket. A coarse and brutal professional soldier, the general was as quick to hang his own men in the name of discipline as he was to hang rebels.

Removing her white cockade, Meg Mercer began entertaining officers in her rooms in the High Street. One, an old friend, Sir Robert Munro, chief of his clan and colonel of the 37th Regiment, brought along his commander, Major-General Huske. That bluff old soldier, nicknamed Daddy by his men, was soon purring with contentment by Meg's side as she flirted with him.

During the evening, he told her that the rebels had marched from Glasgow to Stirling, where they were besieging the castle, and in a couple of days the army would march to confront them. Huske had no respect for the Jacobites and expected to give them a brisk lesson in the art of warfare before he returned to fight the professional armies of France on the Continent, where he had been engaged since the reign of Queen Anne.

'Do you expect there to be a battle soon, General?' Meg asked.

'I should damn well hope so. I haven't come all this way for the sake of my health. It shouldn't amount to much, though. A rabble of peasants is no match for seasoned troops.'

'They beat General Cope.'

'Shocking, weren't it? But I never thought much of the silly old fool. He was sound asleep at Prestonpans. We won't be surprised again. A little brisk work by our artillery, and the rebels'll scurry back to their hills.'

'I have never seen a battle,' said Meg, toying with an idea in the back of her mind.

'Really? Ain't much to see usually. Lots of bangs, smoke,

and shouting, and a bloody mess to clear up afterwards.'

Meg's handsome young footman, a coal haulier until he had caught her eye, topped up the general's glass.

'Nevertheless,' she crooned, 'I should greatly value an opportunity to witness your heroism.'

'Generals aren't heroic, my dear,' said Huske with a short laugh. He nodded across the table to Colonel Munro. 'We leave that to people like Sir Robert.'

'I don't believe you. I insist I have the chance to see a great general lead his army into battle,' said Meg. She leaned over to tap Huske on the nose with her fan.

He blinked happily.

'I cannot refuse you, my dear. I'd be honoured if you'd be my guest when we give the rebels a drubbing. I'll do my best to lay on some good sport. We'll be marching soon. If you hold yourself in readiness, I'll send an escort for you.'

'How exciting! I can find myself an escort but if I am not to be prevented from joining your column I shall need a safe-conduct.'

Then and there, on a sheet of paper provided by Meg, the general wrote that she was to be allowed freedom of passage by the forces of His Majesty. He signed it and pressed his signet ring into a blob of sealing wax that she herself melted onto the paper.

No sooner had her guests left than Meg summoned her footman and told him to hire a couple of horses and a chaise, which he was to provision.

'Claret, brandy, plum cake, sweetmeats – perhaps duck eggs or smoked beef,' she reeled off. 'Oh, and three dozen woollen scarves.'

She then sent for Bella, who had come into Meg's service when, following the death of his wife and mother-in-law, Kinnaird had abruptly dismissed the girl. It had angered Meg to learn from Bella that the music master had been attempting to ingratiate himself with the authorities by blackening David's name at every opportunity.

Bella entered the room and curtsied before her mistress.

'You remember when Mr Stewart of Kynachan visited my niece in the autumn?'

'Aye, Miss Mercer.' She darted a quick smile. 'I remember his man, too.'

'And that private in the Town Guard who brought round some malefactor or other – do you remember him?'

'Aye. Robert Stewart his name is.'

'Good. Find him and tell him I want to see him. Pack a bag, too. We shall be going to Stirling for a few days.'

Early next morning, Robert Stewart presented himself at Meg's door. Leaving his Lochaber-axe against the wall outside, he was shown into the parlour.

'You are Robert Stewart?'

'Aye, ma'am.'

'Good. Help yourself to whisky.'

The Town Guardsman poured himself a large dram and stood lifting the tails of his coat to warm his backside against the fire.

'Do you know who I am?' Meg continued.

'Aye, ma'am. All the town knows Margaret Mercer.'

'But who are you, Robert Stewart? Are you an Edinburgh Whig now? A servant of the magistrates?'

When the man shifted his feet unhappily, Meg felt hope. With King George's Redcoats in full control of the city no-one need fear to declare himself Whig.

'I am first a Highlander, ma'am, of the family of Bonskeid, descended from the Wolf and the king.'

'You sound the man for me, Robert Stewart. I need an escort. I wish to visit my niece's husband.'

'Indeed. Would that be Kinnaird?'

'No, he is my late niece's widower. I mean Kynachan.'

'Kynachan? A fine gentleman, to be sure. But he is major in Nairne's regiment. He is with the prince.'

'And at Stirling, I believe. In a day or two General Huske will be marching from here to do battle with the prince's army. The general has invited me along to watch the spectacle. I thought I might slip through the lines beforehand and am looking for an attendant.'

'I see,' said Stewart, then suddenly he grinned. 'I thank you, ma'am. I was fearful I would miss the making of history by my kindred. I should like to fight alongside the men of Atholl – once, at least – to add honour to my race.'

It was Meg's turn to smile.

'But, Miss Mercer, it would be remiss of me if I did not advise you that such a trip will have dangers. Is your business with your brother-in-law so important?'

'Aye, to me it is. My niece and my sister-in-law died a short while ago. I know Kynachan will not yet have heard. I would like to break the news to him myself and not leave the pain of it to his wife. Besides, the city is dull these days, full of canting ministers, and I need a little excitement.'

Accompanied by five regular battalions as well as dragoons and militia, Huske marched from Edinburgh on the thirteenth of January. Meg's chaise was waiting for the army beyond the city walls. Robert Stewart, in postilion's uniform, rode the nearside horse. With the hood of the carriage open, Meg had wrapped herself in a blue cloak against the dawn chill. The vehicle sat low on its springs, heavy with provisions. Beneath Bella's seat, opposite Meg, was hidden Robert Stewart's musket and powder horn, issued to him when he joined the Town Guard.

Mounted skirmishers led the column, then an advance guard of dragoons. Huske and his staff followed, and the general reined his horse by the chaise, removing his hat in a bow. He was in excellent spirits.

'Good morning to you, Miss Mercer. Nothing like it, is there? An army on the march.'

'They are indeed a fine body of troops.'

'D'y'mind if I join you, ma'am?'

'I would be honoured, General.'

Meg had not expected this. Huske dismounted, gave his horse to the charge of a young aide-de-camp, and settled himself on the seat beside her, giving an affable nod to the pink-cheeked Bella.

Robert Stewart looked about him with some alarm when he found himself under the supercilious scrutiny of officers of the general's escort, who fell in alongside. The Highlander smiled uneasily, but their gazes remained as chill as the morning.

Meg's ample supply of brandy kept the old soldier content as the vehicle rattled through the dormant landscape and small knots of country folk who gawped at them from the roadside. With the chaise becoming the focal point of the army, Huske's reminiscences about past campaigns on the Continent were constantly interrupted by gallopers bringing information to the commander and shuttling back down the long column bearing his orders.

On Meg's right hand, a corpulent major of Hamilton's Dragoons, on a large grey gelding, seized every opportunity to engage Meg in conversation. Eventually, with a few choice words, the possessive commander sent the man back to ride with his regiment.

For an hour in the middle of the day, the vanguard of

the army paused to allow those in the rear to catch up. The general conducted Meg to a farmhouse, where a meal had been prepared by an advance party of the commissariat. Robert Stewart and Bella remained by the chaise, discouraging the curiosity of the thronging military as best they could.

In the early afternoon, Huske halted for the day at Linlithgow. Advance pickets had reported that the army had been under observation by rebel cavalry since noon and that a substantial body of the enemy had been seen retreating west towards Falkirk. The general set up his headquarters in the semi-ruined palace, an old residence of Queen Mary. During the confusion, as the government army set up camp, Meg made her excuses to an aide, and the chaise continued west along the high road. Apart from a few scouts who shadowed the rebel force as it retreated, a small knot of dragoons guarding the bridge over the Avon, half a mile from the town, made up the last outpost of the government army.

The sergeant at the bridge stopped them, warning that they would be ill advised to travel further, for the rebels would surely loot their baggage. With acquisitive interest, he eyed the trunk lashed to the back of the chaise. Meg produced her safe-conduct, but still the sergeant hesitated, until the offside carriage horse saved the situation. It gave the sergeant's mount a vicious nip on the rump and, as the cursing soldier tried to control his plunging beast amid the laughter of his troopers, Robert Stewart urged the chaise across the bridge.

The horses were now tired, and the pace of the carriage had slowed to a gentle walk along the empty road, which – running as it did between the capital and the garrison town of Stirling – was normally one of the kingdom's busiest thoroughfares. A red-faced Presbyterian cleric, travelling in the opposite direction, reined his donkey and harangued Meg for venturing towards the papist insurgents, from whom he had thought it politic to flee. A view-halloo from Robert Stewart, who sighted a cavalry patrol trotting along the road towards them, made the minister dig his boots into his steed's belly and bounce off down the road in an undignified scramble, one hand on his hat and wig and the other holding his reins and bag.

'Ooh!' said Bella, as the horseman approached. 'These sodjers get prettier and prettier.'

The riders wore blue coats faced with red, scarlet and gold waistcoats, and gold-laced hats and belts.

'What kind are they, ours or theirs?' asked Meg.

'Ours,' said Stewart. 'Government horses have their tails cropped. And they'd be in better condition than these miserable beasts.'

'That's Johnnie Wedderburn of Blackness in the middle of them!' said Meg.

She and Bella stood up in the chaise and waved their excitement as the patrol thundered to a flashy, snorting halt.

'Meg Mercer, by God!' exclaimed one of their number.

The breath and sweat of the horses steamed in the cold, still air.

'You know her, Johnnie?' asked the commander.

'Heavens, yes. Meg and I have been friends for years. In fact—'

'Johnnie.' Meg's voice was amused but it cut off the flood of words about to pour from the cavalryman's lips.

Introductions were made. The soldiers were Lifeguards, they said, the cream of the prince's forces. Meg was told that the Atholl Brigade was at Bannockburn, guarding the prince, but that Lord George was at Falkirk, where she was sure to be welcome for the night. General Huske's pass was much admired.

'I hope you'll excuse my mentioning it, Miss Mercer,' said the patrol's captain, 'but I feel it might be wise if you removed that.' He pointed to her head.

'How silly of me,' said Meg, laughing. She took off her hat and unpinned its black cockade. 'One gets so used to wearing it in town that I quite forgot about it. Bella, did you bring the other one?'

Bella rummaged beneath her seat and extracted a portmanteau, but an extensive search failed to locate the appropriate emblem. Robert Stewart was rather better prepared. Retiring behind a dry-stone wall with the long bundle that contained his musket, he now re-emerged in a plaid, a broadsword and dirk stuck in his belt. He still wore his riding boots. Before remounting the chaise horse, he carefully arranged the folds of his plaid round his thighs and loins.

'I think it as well we provide an escort for you to Falkirk,' said the patrol commander. 'Johnnie, take a couple of troopers and see Miss Mercer safe.'

32

By Stirling

On hearing the news that the government army was marching to Falkirk, the prince had drawn up the Jacobite forces in line of battle on Plean Muir, a few miles west of the town. When the enemy declined to advance further, the rebels stood down, and the prince returned to Bannockburn House and the charms of his host's niece, Clementina Walkinshaw.

Elements of the Jacobite forces were mounting an ineffectual assault on nearby Stirling Castle, but otherwise the rebels appeared to have no clear objectives. The prince and his staff seemed content to wait until the government army made the first move. By now the best drilled and disciplined of the Highland contingent, the Atholl Brigade, had been chosen by the prince as his bodyguard, but morale was low. The men were frustrated by the inactivity of their role and by the indecision they sensed among the high command. Officers of the brigade sought permission to join Lord George Murray, who faced the enemy at Falkirk.

In a small ante-room off the entrance hall of Bannockburn House, Major David Stewart warmed his hands at a small coal fire. He was with Shian Menzies and James Robertson of Blairfetty, major of the Second Battalion. The latter was grumbling. The Jacobites had been reinforced at Stirling by a contingent from France as well as by volunteers gathered at Perth during the invasion of England. These newcomers had doubled the size of the army, but veterans of the march felt that the prince favoured these fresh soldiers above themselves.

'The lads think they should be parading up the Canongate this moment, not hanging around as His Highness's entourage.'

'Aye,' said David. Like all the Highlanders, he now sported a tangled beard, and his wig had long been discarded.

'Lord George couldn't wait to return to Falkirk,' said Shian. 'He said the more space between himself and the prince, the better for the good of the army.'

'It's these damned Irishmen,' exclaimed Blairfetty. 'They

poison the prince's mind against Lord George – and us. The lads feel they no longer have the prince's trust. And . . .'

Blairfetty broke off as the broad frame of Willie Kennedy filled the doorway. The prince had levied clothes from the city of Glasgow for his ragged army, and Willie wore a new shirt, coat, waistcoat, stockings, bonnet, and shoes but was still enveloped in his tattered plaid.

'Yon laddie's coming back,' Willie announced.

The laddie was Charles Corn, an exotically uniformed Irishman, who, like several others of his kind, hoped that his lack of lands and honours would be made good by the prince's success. The arrogant incompetence of these adventurers was intolerable to the Highlanders, who knew that the failure of the Rising could cost them their lives. If captured, Corn, on the other hand, a professional soldier in the service of France turned secretary to the adjutant-general, would be exchanged for a British soldier taken on the Continent and would still have a career in the army of King Louis.

'I'm sorry, gentlemen,' reported the young Irishman, 'but His Highness has a cold and is too fatigued to hear your petition today. He commands you to return to your men and to parade again tomorrow morning – after he has breakfasted.'

'God! This is too much,' exclaimed Blairfetty. 'A gentleman would not treat a beggar thus.'

'You spoke to the prince?' asked David, incredulous.

'You question me?' Corn's voice was haughty.

'If he doesn't, I do,' roared Blairfetty. 'I am a chieftain of Clan Donnachaidh. No papist popinjay orders me around.'

'You insult me, sir!'

'I'm amazed you have wit enough to observe it,' came the reply. 'Bullet or blade, the choice of how you die is your own.'

'I'll not brawl like a peasant,' retorted Corn.

David gripped Blairfetty's arm to prevent him from snatching his dirk from its sheath.

'You spoke to the prince?' repeated David.

'I spoke to Colonel O'Sullivan, who speaks for the prince.'

'Take us to O'Sullivan,' ordered David.

Corn hesitated, then bowed, and led the three men through the milling mob of attendants and aides who filled the large entrance hall of the mansion.

The prince's plump adjutant-general lay on his bed in his nightshirt beside a roaring fire. The room was hot and stuffy. A surgeon was bandaging his arm. With his free hand the officer waved a feeble greeting to the Highlanders.

'More than three heroic pints,' said O'Sullivan proudly, indicating a large basin filled with his blood. 'You see the cost to my health of this campaign.'

'Have you passed our message to the prince?' demanded Blairfetty.

'Yes, but His Highness orders your continued presence as his guard.'

'Did you tell him our men melt away? If we sit on our arses much longer he won't have a guard left.'

'If only your damned Highlanders would just do their duty,' moaned the adjutant-general. 'I sometimes think they're more of a handicap than a help to His Highness's cause. Thank God we have recruited some proper soldiers now.'

David drew his breath at the slight, but before any of the Highland officers could remonstrate O'Sullivan suddenly sat up in his bed, wild-eyed.

'Quickly, man!' he said, grasping the arm of the surgeon. 'Help me to the close stool. The purge is working.'

The surgeon steadied the adjutant-general and lifted his nightshirt as he crawled from the bed and settled himself on a chamber pot. Within a moment, both sound and smell indicated that he had found relief.

'Aah!' groaned O'Sullivan. 'His Highness little knows what I endure for his cause.'

'Come,' said David to his companions. 'We waste our time here.'

In gloomy silence, the three officers and their gillies left the house and ran the gauntlet of sentries, who challenged them every few yards as they strode down the carriage drive to the high road. Around them in the afternoon dusk, dozens of fires twinkled amongst the trees of the park land, where most of the Atholl Brigade was camped. No pipes played. An occasional voice was raised in anger or drunken arousal. Otherwise, save for a few snatches of melancholy fiddle music, so different from the stirring jigs that had been played on the march south, the cantonment was silent.

The officers separated. David and Willie continued on for another half mile to the roadside cottage that served as headquarters for the shrunken numbers of the Tummelside battalion. Outside the little building a vehicle was drawn up.

'We've visitors,' announced Willie.

'That's sure enough,' replied David.

In contrast to the dreariness of the rest of the camp, his headquarters had all the appearance of an inn during a cattle tryst. The door was open and sounds of merriment came forth. A fiddle was playing a reel. Clad in their Glasgow clothes, men squatted in front of the cottage, passing round whisky and brandy.

Pushing his way into the bothy, David took in the animated scene – the officers clustered round Meg at the fire and Bella, amid a tight circle of onlookers, her long chestnut hair floating round her head, was dancing with the venerable figure of George Cairney. Bohally looked up. David jerked his head in summons.

'I thought George was on sentry duty,' he said.

'He was relieved by a private in the Town Guard who came with Miss Mercer,' Bohally said. 'Were you successful? Can we join Lord George?'

'No, we parade again for the prince's inspection in the morning. There are no fresh orders – and I want no discussion of it amongst the men. Keep them busy tomorrow. Drill them. Organize contests between the companies. Then drill them and drill them again.'

Business attended to, David elbowed through the throng to Meg. Standing in front of her, he swept off his bonnet in a bow.

'Davie!' she cried. 'At last you've come!'

'That's what all the lassies say to him,' shouted one of the Tummelside men.

The wag was hushed by his comrades. The men of Kynachan had once been proud of their youthful laird's reputation as a gallant – some of it had rubbed off on them – but now the phenomenon of Doting Davie was almost sacred and not to be sullied by innuendo.

One of the young captains of the battalion, Henry Stewart of Fincastle, reluctantly made space by Meg for his major. Before sitting by her, David bent to kiss her cheek.

'I might have expected you, Meg.'

The noise in the room gave them privacy.

'Edinburgh was becoming dull, Davie – nothing but Whigs. If you won't come to my parties, I must bring one to you.'

'I thank you,' said David, looking round at the flushed, excited faces of his men. 'You have cheered us all up.'

'I thought you might need it.'

'Is our plight that obvious?' He kept his voice low.

'It is, Davie. General Huske says sixty thousand soldiers are in arms against you. If you hope to be alive and a laird this time next year, you'll have some humble pie to eat.'

'A dish I could never stomach,' said David with a grimace. 'I'd rather face an honourable death in battle. That way Kynachan may not be forfeit.'

Meg's voice suddenly flashed anger. 'Damn you, David Stewart, and damn your Highland honour. You are responsible for the lives of the men who follow you as well as for your own. There's no trick or glory to dying – but your infernal honour will leave my niece and her children unprotected. It's they who will face the consequences of your actions – they and the women and children of Kynachan, whose men you have taken away.'

David paled under the lash of her tongue. 'Sweet Jesus,' he whispered. 'The bullets of the enemy are kinder than your words. Have you come here to tell me that?'

Meg gave no quarter.

'No. There's more news – none of it good. Anna Mercer and Barbara both died of fever in November. I wanted to tell you before you saw Jean.'

'She knows?' There was acute distress in his voice. Meg nodded, and a terrible echo of his wife's pain touched him.

'Another thing – Kinnaird is no friend of yours. He plays some long game and misses no opportunity to keep your name before the authorities as an arch-rebel. But I believe you could still save yourself if you withdrew from the rebellion. Nor am I without influence. I have friends who might help wash your political sins away.'

The men crowding the bothy, noticing the tension between their commander and the visitor, shot them uneasy glances. Observing this, Meg gave a brilliant smile and called to Bella to open the last hamper.

'Well, Davie?' she asked, watching Bella pull out armfuls of red woollen scarves and pass them round the delighted men. 'Will you try to save your life and estate? Or will you squander all in a cause which is surely lost?'

David wearily rubbed his eyes.

'Come on, man,' urged Meg. 'You're not a savage, bound by outmoded custom. Use your wits.'

'Stop this. It serves nothing but tears my heart – and maybe yours. It's too late. Anyway, I could not betray my friends and my honour. To do as you suggest would bring the name Stewart of Kynachan into contempt throughout the Highlands.'

'I hoped you would show more courage, Davie.'

'Were you a man, I would kill you for that.'

Meg leaned to him and kissed his cheek.

'Let the Lord record that I tried,' she said.

Meg returned to Falkirk, where she was a guest of her friend Mrs Graham, a doctor's widow. The next day three thousand Highlanders from clans loyal to the government joined Hawley's army in its camp just west of the town. The general himself was staying to the east of Falkirk at Callendar House.

The closeness of the two armies forced the prince to draw up his troops on Plean Muir for the third successive day, but still the enemy did not attack. It was obvious that such a state of affairs could not continue, and in the early afternoon the prince called a council of war. There, Lord George proposed an immediate assault.

A feint by Jacobite cavalry to the north of the wood that lay between the two armies convinced government scouts that the rebels were retreating towards Stirling for the night. Meantime, Lord George led the bulk of the prince's army south for a surprise attack on Hawley's camp.

A thud of hooves brought Meg and her hostess rushing to the window to see General Hawley gallop past towards the government camp. He was hatless, his face frenzied, and his wig was askew. He still had a white dinner napkin tied round his neck. Suddenly, in the distance, could be heard the popping of musketry.

Quickly the women donned cloaks and crossed the road to the church, where they panted up the stone steps to the top of the steeple. Looking south-west, towards the moorland a mile away, they saw the distant flash of muskets in the darkening afternoon.

'It's the battle, all right. We're going to have a fine view,' said Meg, but as she spoke a curtain of rain swept down from the heights and the scene was blotted from their sight.

33

The Battle of Falkirk

The Atholl Brigade, amongst the first on the ridge, was drawn up on the right of the second line of the prince's army. All day it had been unusually clear, and at the head of the men of Kynachan, David could see north to the Ochil hills, which rose abruptly, a dozen miles away, from the plain of the river Forth.

Although the Jacobites commanded the heights above the government camp, David observed that the terrain would suit the enemy cavalry. The ground was barren – heather, reeds, and rough grass. On the other hand, it would be impossible for Hawley's artillery to be dragged up from the valley to play a part in the forthcoming battle.

For fifteen minutes the Athollmen waited as the rest of the rebel regiments formed up on the left. Then, at the moment the dragoons crested the ridge, the weather suddenly changed. A great black cloud rolled in from the south and swept across the moor, shrouding the armies in torrential rain, which drove into the faces of the government infantry as they scrambled up from the plain below.

The enemy cavalry opened the battle by feinting towards the Macdonald regiments, in the front line, trying to draw their fire. But the Highlanders refused the bait. The left was not yet in position, and Lord George did not want to launch his attack piecemeal. He ordered a slow movement forward, and the Macdonalds advanced, pace by pace, their faces resolute, their targes held in front of their bodies.

Then the government's three cavalry regiments launched their charge. Lord George, on foot in the front of the Macdonald regiments, waited until the dragoons were within ten yards before raising his musket as a signal to fire. The volley that followed emptied eighty saddles. Many of the surviving troopers turned and fled, but a few broke into the ranks of Clanranald's regiment. The Highlanders threw themselves to the ground, stabbing upwards with their dirks into the bellies of the horses, and grabbed the dragoons by their clothes to haul them from their mounts.

Two of the enemy cavalry regiments took flight, and, in spite of Lord George's commands to hold their positions, the three Macdonald formations charged in pursuit. The dragoons plunged down the hill, scattering some of their own infantry who still toiled up the moor. The remaining regiment, Cobham's dragoons, galloped helter-skelter between the two armies, attracting rolling musket-fire from the centre and left of the Jacobite line.

In the heavy rain, reloading was impossible. As the unbroken government infantry approached, the Highlanders dropped their firearms and charged. The Redcoats offered only weak resistance, many of their guns misfiring, before they turned tail, and – except for the disciplined Atholl Brigade – the Jacobite second line broke ranks to join the chase. Order vanished from most of the battlefield. Knots of Highlanders ran down their enemies as wolves would deer, dragging them to the ground to slit their throats and ransack their bodies at leisure.

Not all Hawley's army had disintegrated. On the government right wing, a ravine separated the combatants, and here the three regiments under General Huske, unseen by the Jacobite right, were still doggedly climbing towards the ridge where the rebel army had been drawn up.

Alone on the top of the moor, the six hundred Athollmen still stood in their ranks, lashed by the wind and rain. Considering the brigade the flower of the army, Lord George had been reluctant to waste them in minor skirmishes, and in spite of months of campaigning the men had yet to be blooded. Jittery, they longed for a chance of action, which would serve to wipe out their fear.

Down on the left, they now saw the Royal Scots, a regiment in the French Service recently landed to join Prince Charles, apparently take sudden fright and flee from the field. The rest of the Highlanders had disappeared, and nothing could be made of the state of the battle.

Grateful for an opportunity to move about, David and Bohally went amongst the Tummelsiders, steadying and encouraging them.

'What's happening, Kynachan?' yelled George Cairney above the wind.

'Some say a battle,' shouted David.

Like everyone else's, Cairney's face and clothes streamed with rain. 'For God's sake, let us join in before we drown,' he bellowed. 'This is weather for fish, not fighters.'

'Aye,' roared David in reply. 'Shove your hand up my kilt and you could tickle a salmon.'

'A tadpole more like,' bellowed Cairney, a great grin spreading across his face.

The ranks of the battalion buzzed as the banter passed from man to man. Bohally caught David's eye and winked his approval. Suddenly Lord George came hurrying out of the rain towards the waiting regiment and waved his sword for a general advance. In disciplined formation, the Athollmen began to march forward down the hill.

David and Shian joined Lord George and his two aides in front of the men.

'Thank God you held,' the general said, clapping David on the back. 'Otherwise the field would have been left to the enemy and the way open to our rear.'

Some of the fleeing dragoons had blundered into soft ground and now, stripped of their uniforms, they lay strewn across the tussocky bogs. In the gloom, their pale, mutilated bodies looked like scattered sheep. The rain had washed them clean. Alongside the riders were their horses, slaughtered by the Highlanders, who believed that these animals were trained to kill.

Led by wailing pipes, the Athollmen continued down the hill, along the way collecting parties of Keppoch Macdonalds engaged in plundering the dead. Well out of gunshot, isolated companies of Redcoats straggled from the battlefield.

The intermittent popping of musketry grew more concentrated. A reconnaissance party returned with the news that the three regiments of Redcoat infantry – twice the strength of the rump of the Highland army – were just beyond sight, still in their formations and retreating unopposed down the hill.

Lord George moved the brigade to confront them, but realized that the enemy's numbers were too great to attack. In a lane at the bottom, some of the government cannon had become bogged down and now lay abandoned by their artillerymen, who joined the foot regiments as they retreated past.

The Atholl Brigade halted at the base of the hill. Still harried by random groups of Highlanders, the surviving Redcoat army was in full retreat down the high road towards Falkirk. Darkness was rapidly drawing in, and the rain continued to pelt down from the inky sky. Accompanied by two columns of reserves, the prince caught up with the Athollmen.

A short conference took place. Some of Prince Charles's officers were reluctant to pursue the Redcoats into town, where the enemy could easily take up positions in the houses lining the road and force the Jacobites to run a gauntlet of musket-fire. Dismissing these fears, Lord George insisted that the army press forward. The Athollmen marched in to occupy Falkirk, which was lit up by the flames of tents burning in the government camp. At the other end of town, the Redcoat rearguard marched out.

Opposite the church, Mrs Graham's house was dark and shuttered, but David beat upon the door. Eventually it opened a crack, and a frightened old man looked out.

'Mercy!' he exclaimed. 'A rebel! Are the Redcoats beat?'

'Well beat,' said David. 'Is Miss Mercer still safe here?'

'She is that. Come in. You're like a drookit rat.'

David squelched into the small hall. Farther along, the old servant opened a door. Meg and her elderly hostess came bustling out.

'Have we won?' shouted Mrs Graham.

'Indeed, yes. Hallo, Meg,' said David. He felt somewhat awkward before her, recalling their conversation of the evening before.

Meg had no such inhibitions. 'Thank God you're alive,' she cried, and, ignoring his sodden condition, she hugged him fiercely. 'We were up in the kirk tower but couldn't see a blind thing.'

'We couldn't see much more on the field. As far as I know, we suffered few casualties. Our own lads didn't fire a shot.'

'You'll be wanting to spend the night?' asked Mrs Graham.

'There's a bed here for you and room in the barn at the back for the Kynachan men,' added Meg. 'Though not for the whole regiment.'

There was another knock at the door, and when the old man hurried back from answering it he was agitated.

'It's an Irishman saying Prince Charles himself needs a bed. I tried to tell him we have no room, but he's taking over the whole house.'

An hour later, Meg's chaise was parked just off the high road by a stable on the edge of the town. In the barn, her horses added to the steaming fug produced by the men of Kynachan, who snored inside their soaking plaids.

Inside the chaise, Meg lay on one bench, David on the other. Bella was on the floor, and underneath the coach bedded Willie Kennedy. He was chaperone, instructed by his comrades to make a hullabaloo should any lurch of the coach reveal that in the heat of the moment their Davie might forget to dote.

Through the sound of the rain drumming on the oiled canvas hood, Willie heard the springs creak just once – when Bella slipped from the coach to join him beneath.

34

Back to the Highlands

The battle achieved little. Four hundred government soldiers lost their lives in the fighting and General Hawley expressed his displeasure at being defeated by charging five of his officers with cowardice and executing some fifty of his men. Four dangled all day from the gibbet in the Grassmarket in Edinburgh. But the Jacobites found no way to exploit the victory. One clear beneficiary was the retired General Sir John Cope. In the London coffee houses, he had bet all comers that the first general to face the rebels would be given a drubbing. Now he became rich.

The castle at Stirling had been impregnable for centuries, and so again it proved. Twelve hundred of the prince's troops had been occupied in its siege and had laboriously set up cannon on an eminence below the fortress walls. This artillery was allowed one shot before the garrison guns opened fire and in less than an hour destroyed the battery.

For a week the Jacobites stayed round the town, their ranks thinning as more men deserted with the plunder acquired at Falkirk. Then another government army, commanded by the prince's cousin, the Duke of Cumberland, began its march from Edinburgh. The prince wished to attack, but the Highland commanders urged caution and recommended a retreat to Inverness, where, safe in the mountains, they could regroup, gather fresh soldiers, and launch a summer campaign.

Coherent orders were not issued, and the Jacobites straggled north from Stirling, little more than a disorganized rabble. At Crieff the army split into three to continue their retreat. The artillery and wheeled vehicles travelled towards Blair along the lower road through Dunkeld, where the weather was least likely to give them problems. The cavalry and the Lowland regiments, under Lord George Murray, took the longest route, up the east coast. Led by their royal commander, the Highlanders marched due north through the high passes.

All morning Castle Menzies had been in turmoil. In the small hours, a runner arrived, and Sir Robert and Lady Mary were wakened early with the news that the clan regiments would be marching from Crieff in a few hours' time and would camp that night at Taybridge. The prince would seek hospitality at the castle.

Lady Mary's excitement knew no bounds, but Sir Robert was horrified. At this stage of the proceedings, he explained to her, he was not about to risk everything by becoming identified with a lost cause. Having no intention of playing host, he retired to the topmost turret of the castle with his last bottle of claret and a pile of books. He left instructions that he would require a hot meal and whisky every seven hours, day and night, until the royal visitor had gone.

The turret commanded the south-west corner of the castle. Through an arrow-slit, Sir Robert had an excellent view of the road from Taybridge, although whenever he peered out the icy wind made his eyes water. With his spyglass he saw the advance guard of the Highland army stream down the road into Strathtay, and he was sourly thankful when the squeals of a pig being slaughtered below drowned out the faint bagpipes that preceded every company as it marched across the bridge.

Buried in his fur cloak, he had lost himself in Plutarch, until a rap at the door broke his concentration.

'Go away,' he shouted.

'I have a lantern, Sir Robert, some whisky, and a chamber pot.'

Realizing that all three items were necessities if he was to maintain his vigil, the Laird of Weem drew back the door bolt. At first he did not recognize the figure before him.

'Hiding out, Rob?'

'What the devil? By God, it's Davie Stewart.' The cloak fell to the floor as Sir Robert embraced his friend. 'I couldn't be more pleased to see you alive and well.'

'You've chosen a chilly roost up here.'

'Is your prince down below?'

'Aye. Lady Mary has placed him in one of the bedrooms off the main stair, where he can be easily guarded. He has seventy in his entourage. She has told him you have a fever and do not wish to infect his followers.'

'Wise woman, Mary. Is Shian here? Have we lost many of our men?'

'Aside from desertions, not one, and there's not a scratch to any man from Kynachan.'

'Thank God. I have prayed for the preservation of all our people. What of the campaign? By all accounts, you made a bold march to Derby for no good reason – then came marching back. I believe George Murray commands your army. Is he that poor a strategist?'

'Lord George ranks with Montrose and Dundee.'

'Oh, yes? You thrash Hawley at Falkirk, and then this inglorious rout north.'

'Lord George was not allowed to follow up the victory. This rout was brought about by contradictory orders. I will say this only to you. Lord George has worked miracles to preserve the prince from his own folly.'

'I thought you Jacobites believed Prince Charles would be an adornment to the throne.'

'He is not the man his father is. I do not deny his courage, and he has a fine touch with the common folk. Otherwise he is a vain, petulant, ignorant boy, swayed by the worthless sycophants who surround him.'

'Dearie me.'

'His every whim he believes will become reality. He invented ships filled with armies of Frenchmen and Spaniards to reinforce us and said the English would flock to his standard.'

'I did think that unlikely. The English peasant is an ox-like creature who hasn't handled arms for a century – nor has his master.'

'Apart from a regiment from Manchester – much of it the scum of the city, who joined for the rations and the chance of plunder – the recruits we picked up south of the border could be numbered on the fingers of one hand. The men are beginning to lose faith with him. We all keep a brave face to the world, but pessimism is a cancer eating its way into our ranks.'

'Are you going home?'

'As soon as His Highness releases me. Then we continue north.'

Sir Robert threw up his hands despairingly. 'Haven't you had enough? You must know you cannot win.'

David twisted his face in a grimace. 'You too, Rob? I had Meg Mercer urging me to turn traitor a few days ago.'

'She's right, Davie,' said Sir Robert. 'You have done all that you honourably should. Get out now. Get out before it's too late.'

'No, Rob. Life has never been as simple as you would wish it. We are all prisoners of fate.'

'God! The tragedy of this whole enterprise could make me weep.'

'Have a dram with me. Then I must chase our deserters before returning to Kynachan. My lads are already on their way. Time at home is too precious to squander.'

David and Shian searched out runaways in Strathtay over two days. The prince went hunting in the hills and visited the school for pipers at the mouth of Glen Lyon. In the evening, Lady Mary gave a reception for him and his principal officers.

While Prince Charles made merry, the surrounding country was in uproar. The Jacobite duke was back at Blair and had sent round Atholl the *crois-tàra*, a cross of two charred sticks dipped in blood, which demanded on pain of death the presence of clansmen to defend their country. The government soldiers were now at Dunkeld and Crieff, probing across the Highland line.

A day or two later, on his way to Blair, the prince rode past the entrance to Kynachan. The clans followed an hour behind, banners waving, pipes playing, and they camped at Trinafour, just as Cope's army had done a few months earlier. The men of Kynachan were granted a few precious days and nights near their families while they recruited amongst the townships. For once they could thank their neighbours for being reluctant to fight.

In the house of Kynachan, Jean was at work in the kitchen alongside a new maid, fourteen-year-old Morag, who was fresh from the mains.

Hearing the distant bark of a dog, the girl broke off her song and listened.

'D'y'think they'll be here soon, mistress?'

'That's the third time you've asked me, and I still don't know. They may not come at all.'

'I've a new ribbon for my hair,' said Morag, tossing scraps of meat into a simmering pot. 'It's red. D'y'think my Andrew'll notice?'

'I'm sure he will.'

Morag's song began again.

'They're here!' yelled Clementina, crashing down the stairs from her vigil upstairs at the window of the little room between the parlour and the nursery. Skirts and petticoats flying, she tore through the kitchen, dogs at her heels, and flew out of the back door.

'They're here, they're here, my lady,' cried Morag.

'Have you put in the onions?' demanded Jean.

'The onions? Yes, yes.' Morag was hopping up and down in her excitement.

'Then I'll see you in the morning.'

Drawing a ladle of water from the tub, Jean rinsed meal from her hands and dried them on a scrap of linen. On her way through to the hall, she checked in the mirror to see that her hair had not strayed from beneath her white cap. When she reached the front door her husband was marching into the yard.

For a moment she stood looking at him, at the remembered grace of his movements, at the broad shoulders, at the way the smile played across his lips, and at his eagerness and the admiration of her that she saw in his eyes. Then she ran to meet him.

'You're thinner,' Jean said, pulling back from his embrace. 'You're skin and bone.' Tears welled in her eyes.

He said nothing.

'I'm sorry.' She blotted her cheeks with a handkerchief. 'Clementina's off in pursuit of Charlie. Your mother and Donald have taken the children to Drumnakyle. They should be back soon. No-one will see me shaming you like this.'

'You don't shame me, my love.'

She too was thinner, drawn by sorrow and worry. He knew he was responsible for this and had taken her support for granted, without considering the misery it would inevitably bring her.

'Yes, I do. I should be brave like you. I usually am.'

'I know you are, my darling.'

She gave herself a little shake and then faced him with a brilliant smile. 'How long?'

She saw the flicker across his face.

'Not long,' she said, but her smile did not fade.

He dumped his sword and pistols on the hall chest and, arms round each other, they climbed the stairs to the parlour.

'I saw Meg. She told me the news of your mother and sister. I am so sorry.'

'I have done most of my grieving,' said Jean. 'It was the Lord's will, though sometimes his will can break a body's heart. Is the fighting nearly over?'

David sat down wearily in his usual chair by the fire.

'I don't know,' he said.

She pulled off his muddy boots, noting the signs of strain

about his eyes and each scratch on his skin. Jean knew she could plead with him to stay for ever, but, if he did, he would not be the man she loved.

'What happened? We win the battles and yet we retreat.'

He shrugged. 'Edinburgh, Stirling, Perth. They all support the Whigs. In England, the country people were indifferent to us, if not hostile.'

He drained the glass of claret by his side. She poured him another.

To his own ears, such news was inconsequential. He wanted to obliterate the present in her arms, to find once more that place of love and joy where all that mattered was each other. There the past and the future held no fears, and each moment was complete.

'And what now?' she asked.

'Tomorrow the lads are recruiting all over our country. His Grace expects us to join him at Dalnacardoch in a few days with a thousand men.'

'If the men refused to fight when the prince was winning, why should they join now we are in retreat?'

'When our army moves out, the enemy moves in. They will punish any man who has served with us, deserter or not.'

'Then you are to abandon Atholl?'

'Only until we march south again in the spring.'

'But what of us meanwhile?' whispered Jean.

He had no ready answer. He did not know, and he dreaded what he could not know.

'I doubt if any soldiers will come this way. If they do, accept no promissory notes for what they buy. Demand silver or gold – and plenty of it. The English took enough from us.'

He put his hand into his money pouch and handed Jean a small wooden box. 'I brought you something from the south.'

She opened the box. A sapphire ring nestled on a bed of black velvet.

'It's beautiful, Davie.' She savoured his name as she spoke it.

'It's from Derby. On our last night there, Shian, Blairfetty and I were summoned to Lord George's lodgings in the market place. Before we went in, I purchased the ring from a merchant.

The next day we began our retreat. This ring was bought at the high moment of the campaign.'

He held out a hand to her, and she came into his arms. For long seconds he held her close, his arms trembling as he felt her heart beat within her slender body. Then the moment was lost.

'Kynachan!' came a fierce voice from the hall. 'I have a message from Blair.'

35

Interlude

That night, in households across Kynachan, the returned soldiers were telling stories of the hardships, high points, and humour of the campaign and catching up on gossip and local affairs. As best they could, their women cosseted and feasted them.

In the dining-room of the mansion house, silver and snowy napkins had been laid by each place, and a line of steaming dishes filled the centre of the table.

Bohally and David were kilted and be-wigged. Jean was still in mourning and Janet in her usual widow's black, but Clementina was in white, the blue ribbon of maidenhood in her hair. Even Donald was in knee-breeches. It was the first real festivity at Kynachan since the previous summer.

David said grace. The steward had filled the glasses with claret and was shuttling back and forth from the kitchen.

'Most of the time we slept under the stars,' Bohally was saying, 'but one night in the north of England we found lodgings in a farmhouse. My bed was a heap of bracken, and it was moving.'

'Moving?' echoed Clementina, tears of laughter reflecting the candlelight in her eyes. 'You mean with vermin? How dreadful.'

'Good heavens, no,' said Bohally. 'Any English louse that dared scuttle up our kilts would have been torn limb from limb by those already in residence. Our lice were Jacobites, the match for any three of theirs.'

'Och, Charlie.' Janet was hooting with mirth.

'I poked round beneath the sheet and found a little boy, no more than three or four years old. The good wife then fell on her knees, sobbing, "Oh, your honour, your honour. I've only the one son but look, I've three fine plump daughters. Will one of them do instead?" At first I had no idea what she was talking about. Then I realized she thought I would eat the brat. She believed we were all cannibals.'

'That can't be true,' said Clementina.

'I assure you it is. The one she eventually roasted for us was a bit overdone. I prefer my lassies pink.'

'You're disgusting, Charlie,' laughed Janet.

'You nearly had horsemeat this evening,' said Jean. 'An elm in the wood of Kynachan shed a limb three weeks ago, killing a pony.'

'It was witchcraft,' said Clementina.

'I think it was just the cold,' said Jean. 'Anyway, I gave a haunch to Catherine Stewart in Drumnakyle after the damp spoiled some of their stored grain and left them short.'

'Isobel Forbes had a baby,' said Clementina. 'The father's away with you – young Angus Ferguson.'

'Angus? He's a good lad,' said David. 'Not much in the way of wits, but he always does his best and never croaks. John Forbes's daughter?'

'Yes,' said Clementina, a ghost of a smile on her lips. 'The minister'll be after Angus as soon as things get back to normal.'

Just then Donald shouldered the door open, a bottle in either hand.

'I've an announcement to make,' said Bohally. 'Clemmie and I'll be wanting our own priest when the fighting is over. Davie has given me permission to pay court to her.'

He looked round at the others, surprised at their silence.

'Well, haven't you anything to say?'

David faltered and began to offer his congratulations.

'No, not you. You know about it already,' said Bohally.

'You can't expect me to be bowled over, Charlie,' said Janet. 'Clemmie told me you two were to be wed years ago.'

'Me, neither,' said Jean. 'In fact, I thought you were betrothed before Davie and me. But of course I congratulate you.'

'Donald,' said Bohally, crestfallen, 'it's news to you, surely?'

'Och, no. It was myself who suggested the match to the old laird, fifteen years since.'

At Drumnakyle, half a mile across the heather, James Stewart was frowning at the contents of his wooden platter.

'It's certainly very tasty.'

'The beast hadn't been dead long, and the kites and buzzards hadn't spotted it,' said his wife.

'I think it's delicious, Mother,' said their son Ian, gulping his food. 'When I'm finished, I'll be going down to a ceilidh at the Macdonalds.'

Mrs Stewart looked up from her needle. She was repairing her husband's plaid. In the dim light her face was gaunt, etched by the strain of providing for her family without the labour of her menfolk. 'You mind yourself though, Ian. You don't want to be caught like Angus Ferguson.'

It seemed to her that her son had gone away a boy and now here he was, a man, as tough and sinewy as his father. Ian's skin was burned and chapped by days of marching.

'Young Angus?' said her husband, sawing at a rubbery chunk of meat with his dirk. 'What's he been up to here while he's been away?'

'The minister's after him. Isobel Forbes has named him father of her baby.'

Her husband chuckled. 'Isobel, eh? I'm not surprised. For a year or two that one's been a mantrap waiting to snap shut on some unwary lad. A man as publicly righteous as John Forbes often has bairns that stray.'

At Daloist the atmosphere was different.

'What have you got to say for yourself, Angus?' roared the righteous man.

'I'm sorry, Mr Forbes, but . . .'

'I'm an elder of the kirk, I'm responsible for the moral and spiritual well-being of the people. It's up to me and my family to set an example, and what do you do?'

'But . . .'

'Fornicate with my own daughter! Conceive a child in God-less lust.'

The bastard under discussion lay in its mother's arms. She lounged on the heather couch by her aunt, who acted as housekeeper to her widowed brother.

'I'm sorry, Mr Forbes. It only happened once, though.'

'It only takes once, you fool. I suppose you sneaked in when I was out on kirk business? Debauched my daughter in my own house?'

'Oh, no, Mr Forbes.' The unfortunate Angus stood before his interrogator, twisting his bonnet in his hands, head down-cast. 'It was at the shielings in the summer.'

'What! The shielings, you say?'

'That's right, Mr Forbes. When the whisky and the music had taken away my senses, and I thought I was in fairyland. I believed Isobel was an angel.'

Behind Angus's back Forbes saw his sister going through

some feverish arithmetic on her fingers. The child had arrived in December, only seven months after the people had emigrated to the shielings. Such a large and healthy baby could only have been conceived before Angus's angelic experience.

'An angel? A harlot, more like,' said her aunt, throwing a dagger-like glance at her niece.

Angus was no mathematician. ''Tis my child,' he said, 'and I'll do what's right, Mr Forbes.'

Under the circumstances, Forbes realized, it would be politic not to go too far in castigating either sinner.

'I should hope so too, lad,' he grunted. 'Ante-nuptial fornication is a much lesser sin than pure fornication. But how do you propose to support a family? You have no land.'

'I'll ask Kynachan. He'll see me right.'

Back at Drumnakyle, Catherine Stewart whispered, 'Take care of Ian.'

'Don't you worry about Ian,' her husband replied. 'Tell him to look after me.'

Their box bed formed part of the partition between the living room of their cottage and the cattle. The crunch of their cudding was as soothing as the tick of a long-case clock.

'He's a grand lad, Cath. You'd've been proud of him. He was always cheerful on the march and kept our spirits up. When things looked dangerous, he never flinched.'

She turned her head to muffle a thin cough.

'How has your health been?' he asked.

'Och, it's just a wee bark.'

'You must keep your strength up. I don't want to worry about you.'

'It's your strength I'm worried about.'

In her voice was a seductive softness. He grunted. After twenty years of marriage he knew the meaning of that tone.

'You don't have to worry about that, wife.' The heather mattress rustled as he moved to cover her.

On the writing desk in the parlour of the mansion house a single candle flickered in the draught. The laird and his wife lay in bed, Jean resting her head on her husband's shoulder as his hand gently stroked the small of her back.

'I'll give Angus a bit of land on Pitkerril,' he said.

'Why there?'

219

'He's good with cattle. If George Cairney keeps an eye on him, he could take over the hill for us when George gets too old. It would also be a kindness to put as much room as possible between him and Daloist.'

Her loins felt bruised by the passion of their recent love-making, and she touched his salty skin with the tip of her tongue.

'I love you, my husband.'

'And I you, Jeannie Mercer. A day will never pass that is not diminished without you at its beginning and its end.'

The room was silent for a moment, save for the snuffle of a hound sleeping in front of the fire.

'I am Kynachan. That was the rock on which my life was founded. But now I know that only one thing is sure. Compared to our love, everything is insubstantial, shifting like cloud shadows on Schiehallion.'

Events moved swiftly over the next few days. Government forces were scouting north of Crieff, posing a direct threat to Menzies country. Shian abandoned Strathtay and withdrew across the pass to Kynachan, where he joined David to prepare for the next stage of the retreat.

On Saturday, the eighth of February, a letter came from Duke William at Blair saying that five hundred Campbells had occupied Dunkeld and that the Tummel battalion should march immediately to join him for an attack. But the men were recruiting over fifty miles of country and were not due back until the following afternoon.

David sent word to Rannoch, to Colonel Robertson of Drumachuine, who commanded Clan Donnachaidh, asking him to send his regiment. Before further action could be taken, another message arrived, countermanding the first. Now David was ordered to muster the men and march to Blair to join the retreat north.

On Sunday, the ninth, it was drizzling.

Donald came into the dining-room, yet another set of orders in his hand for David. Papers concerning supplies of powder, ball, and meal were strewn across the table. Down at the mains, a herd of half-broken ponies waited to be loaded with supplies for the next phase of the march.

Shian Menzies was being briefed by one of his officers, who had just arrived from Strathtay. Jean sat quietly at the end of the table and calculated how much meal could be spared for the army without too great a risk of starvation for those left behind at Kynachan.

David opened the orders and uttered an exclamation. Both Shian and Jean looked up.

'What now?' asked Shian.

'Read for yourself.' David tossed the paper across to the commander of the Menzies Regiment.

Shian gave a snort of disgust. 'Damn the man.'

'Damn who?' asked Jean.

'Colonel O'Sullivan, one of the prince's Irishmen. Lord George says he's worth two regiments – to the enemy. Unfortunately he's high in the royal favour.'

'Bless me,' said Jean. 'And what does he want with you, Davie?'

'He orders me to cut Tummel bridge,' said David.

'But why?' asked Jean, dismayed.

Shian indicated his officer. 'Douglas says Redcoats have been seen at Weem, that's why. Cut the bridge and it'll hinder their advance.'

'And ours,' said Jean. 'Our army has used the bridge and will use it again.'

'That's true,' said David.

'I know it's true,' said Shian. 'But O'Sullivan orders it cut.'

'He doesn't have to live here when this affair is over,' said David. 'It would cost him nothing to ravage every estate and town in Scotland. If we begin laying waste to our own country, it can only encourage the enemy to do the same.'

'There's another factor,' said Jean. 'Whatever the outcome of the Rising, the authorities will shake their heads sadly at the cost of repairing the bridge. Then they'll find the contract, signed by General Wade, stating that Davie Stewart of Kynachan has been paid fifty pounds sterling to keep the bridge in repair until 1750. That'll lift their spirits, particularly when it was Davie Stewart himself who cut the bridge in the first place.'

'We'd need to break the main arch. Rebuilding it would cost a great deal more than fifty pounds,' said David.

'And money is going to be hard to come by in Atholl after this,' said Shian. 'You'd have to become a courtier at Whitehall and be appointed Comptroller of Customs at Leith, or some such, and never let your fighting cocks beat the king's.'

'Enough,' said David. 'We cannot possibly cut the bridge. It requires masons, men experienced in stonework.'

'Of course it does,' agreed Shian. 'In spite of the fact that you built it, you haven't wit enough to prise one stone from another. Nor have I. However, I would send a messenger to Blair to explain that the bridge cannot be cut for lack of skilled men.'

'Wise advice,' said Jean.

On Monday morning, for the third time in five months, Jean bade her husband farewell. Shian's regiment, the ponies, and most of the men of Kynachan had gone ahead the evening before. Willie Kennedy and the three other fighting men from the mains joined their laird in the yard of the mansion house and soon they were marching swiftly along the highway and in sight of the inn by the bridge.

The day was cold, and the country would have seemed deserted but for the smoke that seeped through the roof of the inn. David heard the ring of hammer on chisel and he cursed.

Three stonemasons plodded their way back over the hill towards Blair, their pony laden with the tools of their trade.

'Who did he say he was?' said the fat one.

'Major Viz,' said the tall one. 'Funny name, but there're some funny folk about. He'll be one of these foreigners gadding after Prince Charlie.'

'He didn't sound foreign to me,' said the thin mason.

'I'm glad he stopped us, though,' said the fat one. 'It seemed a shame to destroy a bridge like that.'

'Not if you get the job of rebuilding it,' replied the tall one.

'True,' replied the fat one. There was a short pause. 'I suppose Mr O'Sullivan will want us to go north with Prince Charlie.'

'I suppose,' said the thin one.

'Do you want to go north?' asked the fat one.

'No,' said the tall one. 'But I want what Mr O'Sullivan owes us for cutting Stirling bridge. Once we get that, we're back down there to rebuild it properly for the Redcoats at five times the money.'

They walked in silence for a few minutes.

The thin mason squinted at his companions. 'Major . . . what was it again?'

36

Invaders from the Snow

Two days after the prince left, both snow and the forces of the government occupied Strathtay. Although Lady Mary had seen the wisdom of her husband's instructions to clear up all traces of the celebrations held in honour of Prince Charles, Sir Robert was under no illusion about the difficulties he would face in explaining the activities of his clansmen to the authorities. But he had little chance to make his case.

The two servants he had posted at the bridge to assure the Redcoats that the rebels had abandoned Strathtay had been frogmarched back to the castle by the sergeant in charge of the scouting party. Sir Robert, who had been fussing all morning about how to greet them, had his piper strike up a welcome when the soldiers approached.

The sergeant, ignoring the request from the steward to wait until summoned to Sir Robert's presence, had followed the servitor, rudely bursting into the drawing-room, where the laird and his wife were waiting.

'In the name of His Majesty, this castle is commandeered,' the sergeant announced. 'You have an hour to clear the premises. Any civilian remaining when the colonel arrives will be arrested and imprisoned.'

'Do you know who I am?' Sir Robert demanded, gaping. This was one scenario he had not imagined.

'No,' said the sergeant.

'Let me see your orders.'

'No.' The sergeant grinned, tapping his head. 'They're in here.'

'You have no authority to take over this house. I am Sir Robert Menzies. I am a known supporter of the government.'

'Good for you.' The sergeant hefted his musket. 'I follow orders. If you don't get out, I'll kick you out. You can petition the colonel afterwards.'

An hour later, as the two hundred-strong detachment of Redcoats marched across the bridge, the Laird of Weem and his family, accompanied by a couple of retainers, struggled through the snow with a cartload of their possessions to the dower-house of Farleyer, where they would take up long residence.

By the next day, the townships had disappeared under the white blanket, and only the leak of grey smoke revealed that they were other than a scattering of large boulders. Inside the cottages, old men, women, and children waited for the snow and the Redcoats to go away.

The movement of pedlars and messengers had ceased even before drifts blocked the pass across to Strathtummel. Although the footpaths connecting the clachans showed signs of traffic, on the highway itself the snow lay untrodden, and Kynachan lay in an eerie limbo between opposing armies.

A week after the Atholl Brigade had marched north, as dusk was gathering on the flurries that hunted along the flanks of Craig Kynachan, three sharp raps on the front door echoed through the mansion house.

Jean was in the parlour, reading aloud from Aesop's *Fables* to the three children, the youngest in her nurse's lap. Clementina dropped her sewing and went over to the window to peer round the curtain.

She gasped. 'Redcoats!'

Twenty or so soldiers were spread across the yard in rough columns of four. Some stamped their feet, others beat their arms round their scarlet coats. One opened the door to a stable, but his attempt to see inside seemed defeated by the windowless gloom. Clementina drew back when, suspicious of the movement at the window, one of the soldiers unslung his musket.

A bellowed curse from Donald silenced the dogs, and he opened the door. Jean and Clementina heard a murmur of voices, then the steward's footsteps on the stairs.

'The Redcoats say they're snowbound and want to spend the night.'

'But there are dozens of them,' said Clementina.

'What do you think, Donald?' asked Jean, searching his face.

He shrugged. 'They're not Campbells, my lady. For what it's worth, the officer mannie at the door seemed civil enough. His men can sleep in the barns, and we can put him in the bed in the dining-room.'

'They are already searching the barns,' said Clementina from the window.

'All right,' said Jean briskly, 'show the officer where to bed his men, Donald. I suggest the threshing shed, and give them a few peats so that they can cook.'

Donald gave a grunt, most of it approval. 'Do I offer them meal, my lady?'

'Let them starve,' said Clementina.

'They're not going to do that, Miss Clementina,' replied Donald. 'I said the mannie seemed civil. I didn't say he'd run away if you said boo. What we don't give, they'll take.'

'The men'll have their own rations,' said Jean. 'We'll entertain their commander to dinner. My mother-in-law is in the kitchen?'

'Aye, and I think she'll want to stay there.'

'That's fine. Clementina and I will receive him.'

'I will not!'

'Because they are at war with their rightful king, Clemmie, does not release us from the obligations of civilized behaviour. Besides, when our men go back to England, they may find themselves asking the wives of those outside for shelter.'

Donald withdrew. Mary Dewar took the children across the landing to the nursery. Clementina checked her appearance in the mirror.

'Sit down, Clemmie. We must look completely calm.'

Jean sat at the spinning wheel by the fire. Clementina lifted a book from a shelf and took a chair.

'Are you frightened?' she asked.

'No, not at all,' replied Jean after a moment's consideration. 'I think I'm rather excited. I feel this in some way lets me share what Davie is doing.'

'My father would have been horrified to know we were about to entertain a Redcoat at our table.'

'We must make of this what we can and keep our wits about us.'

Save for the tick of the clock and the rhythmic rattle of the spinning wheel, the room was silent.

'I wonder if the Redcoat's handsome?'

Jean smiled in spite of her tension. 'If you're nice to me, I'll promise never to tell Charlie you said that.'

'You monster.'

Clementina rose to shut the door behind the returning dogs. Spotted by tiny snowflakes, their coats were chill against Jean's hand as they came to be greeted.

No sooner had Clementina taken up her book than Donald knocked. 'Captain Webster, my lady.'

The Redcoat entered the room and gave a deep bow. 'Ladies, I apologize for this most unwarranted intrusion. James Webster, 27th Regiment.'

The officer's eyes flicked round the room before they focused first on Clementina, then on Jean. He was tall, in his late thirties, and had a long face, with cavernous black-stubbled cheeks.

'You are welcome to share our house and eat at our table, Captain Webster,' said Jean. 'In the Highlands, we would never turn a traveller from the door, especially in weather like this. I am Mrs Stewart and this is my sister-in-law.'

'Most hospitable, ma'am. Lots of Stewarts about these parts, I'm told. Not a name to forget, either – not these days.' He unhooked his cloak and sword belt and tossed them to Donald. 'Forgive me, ma'am, but one of my men must make a quick search of the house.'

'May I ask why?' Jean's voice was cold.

'Orders, ma'am.' His tone was flat and uninterested. 'Sar'nt!' he barked.

'Sir.' The sergeant appeared in the doorway, his musket held across his body.

'Quick look round. Be careful.'

'Careful, sir?'

'If you don't want the skin off your back. We don't want anything belonging to such lovely ladies damaged or lost.' The captain's lips writhed in a smile.

'Accompany the sergeant, Donald,' said Jean. 'When you have shown him round, bring us brandy.'

'Brandy, eh?'

'Yes, Captain. I'm told it's excellent,' said Jean. 'It was a gift. General Cope marched by here last summer. It was his.'

'Was it, by jove!'

'Do sit down, Captain.'

'Thank you, ma'am.' Taking the chair opposite Jean – the one normally occupied by David – he pulled a snuff-box from his coat pocket and took a liberal pinch. 'Most kind, most kind.'

'You have come far?'

He let out a short bray of laughter. 'Flanders, ma'am. We were busy fighting the Froggies until this business came up. But today, from some godforsaken spot down the road.' He waved a negligent hand towards the window. 'I took out a patrol a couple of days ago to look for rebels, but the rascals have all run away.'

Again his laugh brayed out.

'Can't say I blame them. I'd run myself if I heard I was coming.'

'And where is your headquarters, Captain?'

One of the setters padded across the floor and sniffed round the captain's boots. He put his hand down to scratch its ear.

'Castle Menzies, ma'am. The colonel took the bed just vacated by the Pretender's son. He said the bedbugs were uncommon ferocious. Accustomed to bluer blood than his, I dare say.' He whinnied laughter. 'Is your husband not here, ma'am?'

'He is not.'

'Not likely to be, I suppose. Not with a name like Stewart. And this estate?'

'You're on Kynachan, Captain Webster.'

'Stewart of Kynachan? Heard the name, I do believe.'

'We are friends to Sir Robert Menzies. My husband is a friend and colleague of Marshal Wade. We are kin to Commissary Bissett, who administers the country of Atholl. It is not surprising you have heard our name.'

'All loyal subjects of His Majesty, to be sure,' said Webster.

'As are we, sir,' said Jean.

Appreciating the ambiguity of her reply, he laughed again.

The sergeant appeared in the doorway, Donald at his heels.

'No men in the house, sir,' the soldier reported.

'And what am I, then, you nasty wee man?' muttered Donald in safe Gaelic.

The soldier was dismissed. Donald came in with a bottle and a single glass. Captain Webster smiled affably at Jean.

'So kind of you, ma'am. I must say, I am rather concerned about you ladies being alone and unprotected in times like these.'

'We're not alone and unprotected.'

'Oh? I thought you said your husband was away.'

'He is, sir. However, there are still a couple of hundred folk on this estate, and a thousand more between here and Castle Menzies to whom we could turn for help.'

'Ha! And I wager not one of them would raise a spark of interest in the breast of a recruiting sergeant!'

Jean gave him a frigid smile. 'Perhaps, but this is not a standard against which I am accustomed to measure my friends.'

'Quite so,' said Webster, watching Donald pour a small measure of brandy into the glass. The officer took a sip and smacked his lips appreciatively. 'Your kinsman, Mr Bissett, tells us every man capable of wielding a broadsword in this valley has been traduced by your husband.'

'Neither I nor my husband can be held responsible for the beliefs of Commissary Bissett, Captain Webster.'

'Nicely put, ma'am. However, we shall shortly be continuing north in pursuit of the rebels. I cannot guarantee the conduct of the troops that will follow us.'

'I am not sure I understand you, Captain.'

'Not all His Majesty's troops are commanded by gentlemen like myself. There're some dreadful ruffians in the army – officers who may cast a blind eye upon theft by their men. Aye, and even brutality against innocent civilians. If they thought it concealed wealth, many would tear the very thatch from your roof.'

'How appalling. It is fortunate our roof is slate,' said Jean. 'What do you suggest we do?'

The captain smiled reassuringly. 'Don't worry, ma'am. I can offer you the king's protection.'

'Fill the captain's glass, Donald,' said Jean, overriding Clementina's hoot of disbelief.'

'Most generous, ma'am.'

Donald did as he was bade, but without grace.

'The king's protection?' prompted Jean.

'Yes. We can take charge of your valuables and issue you a receipt on behalf of His Majesty. Your property will then be lodged in the vaults of the Bank of Scotland in Edinburgh until you judge conditions safe for its return.'

The captain took a sip of brandy.

'Mercy!' gasped Donald, his mouth slightly ajar. 'He must think you're a havering idiot.'

'Donald,' snapped Jean, in English. 'Don't drop the brandy.'

'Oh, no,' said the captain, leaning forward to take the bottle from Donald's hand. 'Give it to me.'

'Perhaps you could offer the captain's men some refreshment, Donald. They must've had a long, cold day, poor things.'

Webster laughed. 'The King's 27th Foot consists of illiterate peasants and scoundrels, not poor things – and certainly better off without strong drink. Kind of you to offer just the same, ma'am.'

'Please, Captain. Such hospitality is one of the pretty customs of the Highlands.'

'D'y'know what you're doing, my lady?' muttered Donald.

'Yes,' hissed Jean from the corner of her mouth.

'I'm sorry' – the captain waved an impatient hand – 'no drink for my men.' He picked up his glass and swirled the brandy in front of the candle flame.

Behind him, Donald waggled an imaginary drink in the air and jerked his thumb towards the barn. Jean nodded.

The captain looked at her. 'Even this glass, ma'am, has a value and is worth placing within the king's protection.'

'Shall I leave the brandy bottle in the gentleman's hands, my lady. Or would it be safer under the king's protection?' Donald spoke in English.

'It is remarkably fine brandy,' said Webster, smacking his lips.

'Leave it, Donald. I'm sure the captain is hungry, so we'll eat as soon as supper's ready.'

37

Entertaining the Enemy

Half an hour later, supper was announced. By then Webster had sown appreciative comments about Clementina's beauty, but his words had fallen on stony ground. He had also consumed a third glass of brandy.

Picking up the bottle now, the Redcoat offered his arm to Clementina. Reluctantly she placed her fingers upon it and allowed herself to be escorted down to the dining-room.

Jean lingered behind with Donald.

'Have you given the soldiers whisky?' she whispered.

'Certainly not. They'd've been sure I was poisoning them. But I sold them a jug – and it wasn't dear.'

'Good, I want them drunk. All of them. Have Morag take whisky round their sentries. Then get her to hold the ferry this side of the river.'

'Whatever scheme you're brewing, I hope it works, woman.'

'So do I, Donald.'

In the dining-room, Webster was exercising his charm on Clementina.

'A pretty girl is wasted round here. Like savages the world over, all the natives want is a set of child-bearing hips and a face that'll frighten away the lecher next door.' He leered. 'A girl such as yourself is a fine wine, needing a sophisticated palate to be appreciated. You should be rolled round the tongue and sucked through the lips of a man who knows what he's about.'

If the captain believed the way to a girl's heart was through such words, accompanied by a few bubbles of spittle, the disgust on Clementina's face should have disillusioned him. But it was not her heart that interested him. Pouring himself another brandy, he leaned forward to peer down at the few fashionable square inches of skin, well above the swell of her breasts, at the neckline of her gown.

'You should be decked with jewels – emeralds, I think, with your colouring. Have you an emerald necklace?'

At that moment Clementina's colouring best matched ruby. 'No, sir. I have no necklace.'

'Pity.' He surveyed the room, dismissing the wooden candlesticks and the portraits of John Stewart and William Mercer, but his eye tarried on the silver cutlery.

'Sit down, Captain,' said Jean, entering the room. 'At the head of the table, of course.'

'Thank you.'

He slumped down in the chair and picked up a spoon, hefting the weight of it in his hand. He turned it over to examine the hallmark.

'Edinburgh,' said Clementina.

'I beg your pardon?'

'The castle mark on the spoon.'

'I see. Part of a set of a dozen or so, I suppose?'

'No,' said Clementina.

'Yes,' said Jean. 'I have decided to take up your offer of the king's protection. I shall have all the valuables in the house packed up, ready for you to take away in the morning.'

'Jean,' exclaimed Clementina. 'Do you think that wise?'

'Why ever not, Miss Stewart?' asked the captain.

'Well, as you say yourself, sir, the country is full of rebels, deserters, and bandits. A military patrol might well expect to be attacked, but a household of women is a threat to nobody.'

'Tush! The rebels are miles away.'

'In which case we hardly need your king's protection.'

'Fortunately, Lady Kynachan has a wiser head than yours, missy, and just as pretty.'

At that moment, Donald came through the door carrying a steaming ragout of beef.

'Excellent,' beamed Webster. 'You know what they say about a soldier's appetite, eh?'

'I can imagine,' said Jean. 'Bring the captain some more of that brandy.'

During the meal, the captain's intake of brandy almost halted as he packed his belly. Jean and Clementina sat in virtual silence, picking at their plates, but their guest did not notice their abstinence.

The dogs had come down from the parlour and were at the officer's knees. He amused himself by tossing titbits for them to snatch out of the air, something the master of the house would never have tolerated. Both dogs shot the occasional guilty glance at Jean.

Afterwards the party returned to the parlour, where a fresh brandy bottle suffered deep inroads. Realizing Jean's intentions at last, Clementina picked up her harp and sang a Gaelic lullaby. Soon the captain's head began to nod, his eyes closed, and a reverberating snore came from his mouth. The brandy glass toppled from his lap and smashed on the floor.

'That's enough,' said Jean, getting to her feet to inspect the sleeper from close range. 'He won't wake up for hours.'

'What do we do now?' said Clementina.

'Pack up our valuables and leave. This man is an obvious thief and probably a good deal worse.'

'Did you never trust him?'

'Did you? He's an enemy officer. Help Mary get the children ready and send your mother here.'

Clementina hovered by the sleeping Redcoat. 'You could get Donald to slit his throat.'

Jean looked at her with surprise. 'You can hammer a tent peg through his head, if you want, but he's eaten at our table. I'm not going to have our names going down in the history books.'

'He forced his way into our house.'

'See to the children, Clementina.'

Jean pulled out a drawer of the bureau, dumping the contents on the floor. Then she went round the room, collecting and placing small valuables into the empty compartment.

Janet came in and clucked her tongue at the sight of the snoring Redcoat. 'What kind of a soldier gets as drunk as that in the house of an enemy? They're the same out in the barn, too.'

'Good,' said Jean. 'Help me with this. We'll collect the plate and then go across to Bohally until they've all gone.'

'Donald wants to take them prisoner.'

'And do what with them? Make them promise to stay locked up in the barn till the prince comes by?'

The two women looked at the stranger. Saliva dribbled from the corners of his open mouth, making his stubbly chin glisten in the candlelight.

'We could smash their weapons,' said Janet.

'They'd soon be back with more and wouldn't bother being polite next time.'

The two women manoeuvred the drawer downstairs, where they filled it with plate. Donald strapped the valuables to a sledge and within minutes the household was ready. Their plaids tightly wrapped against the keen wind, the little band hurried across the river meadow in the lea of a wall, where the snow was thin. A gibbous moon, reflecting off the white cover, lit their way to the ferry.

At Bohally, the absent laird's home was little different from the other dwellings in the township, but his housekeeper had built up the fire, and there were feather mattresses in the box-beds. While the children slept, the others talked far into the night, until the tension of the evening drained away.

The next morning, as soon as the township began to stir, Jean emerged through the low doorway and was shyly greeted by the women, who were filling pots at the hamlet's well.

During the night, a rise in temperature had brought rain from the south-west. Already the snow had been washed from the branches of trees and the top of the dykes. A quarter of a mile away across the river, the back of the mansion was visible through the thin mist. A few Redcoats were moving up the hill from the mains.

Jean shivered and pulled her plaid tighter about her. She was returning to the cottage, when a distant crackle of musket-fire came from behind her. She turned on her heel.

A ragged cloud of powder-smoke erupted above the roof of the mansion and, snatched by a gust of wind, was dashed into the trees of the orchard. Shots came again, bringing the people of the township out of their cottages to stare across the river.

A few minutes later a file of Redcoats marched round the side of the house down the track towards the road.

'I counted twenty-three, Donald,' said Jean.

'And I,' confirmed Clementina, beside her.

'That's them all, then,' said Donald. 'They must have hard heads, these Englishmen. It was not a fine whisky that I sold to them.'

'Have they set the house on fire?' asked Janet, her old eyes squinting to see.

'I don't think so,' said Donald. 'That was just the smoke of their guns. What were they firing at?'

'When they're well away we'll go and look,' said Jean.

38

Occupation

In the middle of the afternoon a week after the Redcoats' visit, soldiers returned. In anticipation of such an event Jean had ordered the livestock driven up the burn to Pitkerril, where the animals should have been safe from marauding government troops. At the same time, a few sacks of meal were loaded onto sledges and hidden in a cave behind Schiehallion.

At first, when the sound of bagpipes was heard, Jean thought it must be David, and the household broke across the yard and up the knoll.

Half a mile away, files of Highlanders, perhaps as many as a hundred, marched towards them. Jean was about to run down the track to greet them, when Donald, puffing up the knoll behind the others, laid a restraining hand on his mistress's arm.

'Are you sure they're ours?'

Jean hesitated. 'They're Highlanders,' she said.

'Plenty of Highlanders are fighting for King George. Listen!' Donald gave a grim shake of the head. 'That's a Campbell rant. It's the Argyll Militia.'

'Sweet Jesus,' said Clementina, blanching. 'Thank goodness Mother's up at Pitkerril.'

'Remember Glencoe,' cautioned Donald. 'We must fly to the hills.'

'No,' said Jean.

'We must. Athollmen've been fighting Campbells for hundreds of years.'

'I'm not an Athollman, Donald. I'm an Athollwoman. And I knew plenty of Campbells in Edinburgh. I certainly haven't been fighting them. Besides, they're part of King George's army, not cattle raiders from two centuries ago.'

Utterly resolute, Jean strode back down the knoll.

'Thank heaven the valuables are buried at Bohally,' said Clementina, hurrying along in Jean's wake.

Upstairs in the darkened parlour, John was playing by one of the shattered windows. The Redcoats had shot out every pane in the house, and now only the shutters kept out the weather.

'We have only a minute,' Jean told Clementina. 'Take everyone to the kitchen. If there's any trouble, get over to Bohally.'

'Come along, Johnnie,' said Clementina. She took the boy's hand.

The fierce music of the pipes now filled the house. In the hall with Donald, Jean waited for Mary Dewar to scamper past with Euphemia.

Once the kitchen door had shut, Jean squared her shoulders.

'All right, Donald, open up. Let's make our guests welcome.'

The Campbells, smart in their dark government tartan, had just marched into the yard and come to a ragged halt behind their commander. For one moment, as their piper's rant ended in a wheeze, the men stood in their ranks. Then, suddenly, they scattered and swarmed through the barns, kicking down doors and grabbing at scrawny hens that exploded into the yard. Their officers bawled for order.

As Jean and Donald stared, more in amazement than apprehension, the door behind them burst open, and soldiers erupted into the hall. Pushing Jean and Donald aside, they pounded past them into the dining-room, into the east room, and up the stairs. Their shouts, the clatter of their brogue-shod feet, the crash as they swung or dropped the butts of their muskets – they all made for terrifying pandemonium.

'The children!' Jean shouted, and she fought her way through a mass of surprised Campbells. 'Clemmie! Mary!'

The young women cowered behind the kitchen table, the children invisible, clinging to them. A Campbell, scarcely more than a boy, stood with a drawn sword. Jean burst in, beheld the scene, and for one moment her gaze was held by the boy's bonnet and its clan badge of a sprig of myrtle, a yellow St Andrew's Cross, and the black cockade of the Hanoverians.

She felt an icy hand clutch at her heart. Then fury swamped her fear. Her home was being violated, and her children threatened. 'Put that away at once,' she ordered. 'How dare you threaten the little ones!'

The sword wavered, and the shame-faced boy lowered the blade. An older man, rummaging through the cupboards, saw the boy's discomfiture.

'Don't let the papist rebel bitch talk to you like that,' he encouraged the lad. 'But for the likes of her, we would be at our own hearths in Argyll tonight.'

The boy flushed. 'I . . . I don't fight women.'

'You don't fuck them yet either!' the man said, roaring at his own sally. 'But even I wouldn't want that one. She'd freeze a man's balls off.'

Re-sheathing his sword, the boy took off his bonnet. 'Lady, I'm sorry for his words. You would be safely out of the way behind the table with the rest of your family.'

'I go where I please in my own house, young man. Who's in charge of you?' demanded Jean.

'Archie Campbell of Knockbuy, you cow,' shouted the older soldier.

Just then a gnarled little man barged in from the yard, closely followed by a flame-haired girl. The two, father and daughter, were carrying an assortment of pots.

'Our supper's already cooking, Hamish,' the older soldier said, pointing to a simmering cauldron that hung over the fire. 'Maybe your Agnes should keep an eye on it.'

Jean hesitated, torn between her urgent desire to speak to the militia's commander and a wish to comfort John, whose white face peered at her through the protective bars of his aunt's arms.

'I'm going to see Knockbuy,' she announced. 'You dare harm these children meanwhile!'

'Don't worry, lady,' The little cook was quick to assure her. 'They'll be all right with us here.'

At that, Jean shot him a grateful look and turned on her heel. In the hall she passed Donald, who crabbed out of his haven beneath the stairs to follow in her wake, and she pushed her way through the hubbub up to the parlour. There, a small group of officers, their coats almost as long as the hems of their kilts, stood poring over a crude map.

'Which of you is Knockbuy?'

The oldest of the men looked up. 'I am Archibald Campbell of Knockbuy.'

The commander looked somewhat harassed by his responsibilities. He was in his fifties, sallow and flabby-cheeked.

'You must be Lady Kynachan.' His tone was neutral.

'I am, and I demand you and your men get out of my house at once.'

'In good time, madam. First I must ask if there are any rebels hereabouts.'

'No,' said Jean.

Knockbuy turned to Donald for confirmation.

'No,' said Donald from behind her. 'They'd have to be very

stupid with half the Campbells in Argyll coming to call.'

'Show more respect,' growled one of the men.

Knockbuy silenced his officer with an irritable wave of the hand. 'On your life, man, are there any arms here or in the townships?'

'Not now.'

'And who is resident in this house?'

Jean answered. 'My three children, my sister-in-law, and her mother, although she is not here at present.'

Knockbuy pulled at his lip. 'She would be the widow of John Stewart, the son of Patrick of Ballechin? No family in Atholl has been more vigorous in waging war against the children of Mac Chailein Mor over so many generations.'

'I must protest!' exclaimed Jean.

'Your protest is noted, madam.' Knockbuy turned his back on her to warm his hands at the fire. 'I command His Majesty's forces in this part of Atholl. This house is requisitioned. My orders are to seize all rebel arms and goods hereabouts. I shall make prisoner any traitor to be found in this country.'

'Sir . . .'

'As this estate belongs to an infamous Jacobite, all your goods and chattels are forfeit.' He paused and turned to face Jean. 'For the sake of common humanity I shall allow you and your family to occupy the small room downstairs and I shall supply you enough meal to sustain your lives.'

'Sir . . .'

'For your own safety, madam, I advise you to keep to your room. Plenty of my clansmen hold bitter memories of your husband's family.'

The other Campbells stared down the length of the room – at their enemy rather than at a woman.

Jean's face was as bleak as theirs. 'Let us hope, Captain Campbell, that your behaviour in this country does not fuel the hatred of another generation of my people against yours.'

'Well said, my lady,' murmured Donald.

'You,' snapped Knockbuy, pointing at the steward. 'Get out of here. Set foot in this house again, and I'll have you shot.'

Donald looked at his mistress.

'Do as he says, Donald.'

'As your ladyship pleases.'

'You may go, too, Mistress Stewart.'

'I should like to take my Bible and my bedding.'

For the first time, Knockbuy seemed discomfited. 'Of course, madam. Colin, help Mistress Stewart take her things out of here . . .'

'Thank you,' said Jean.

'. . . and keep the blasted woman out of my sight.'

Gradually over the next weeks a way of living evolved.

The family established themselves in the east room below the parlour. Janet stayed away at Pitkerril. Morag, Mary Dewar, and Donald lay low at the mains.

In the ground-floor room, with all peats reserved for the militia, Jean and Clementina were forbidden a fire. The first week was bitterly cold. During the day, when the shutters were opened to let in light, the room was icy. At night, the wind moaned down the chimney and whistled between the rags stuffed in crannies round the shutters. Cold and hungry, the children cried themselves to sleep.

Across the hall in the dining-room slept the Campbell officers, tacksmen with their own small tails of cottagers and sub-tenants. On the top floor, the little mid-room and the nursery were used as barracks by twenty soldiers. Wrapped in plaids they lay in neat rows on the floor like enormous bricks of peat. Other soldiers slept in the barns.

Among the townships, the militia considered Daloist the most desirable billet. As well as being far from the officers at the mansion house, it had other advantages. John Forbes was sympathetic to the Whiggish Campbells. Moreover, when her father's back was turned, Isobel could be generous to a lonely soldier with a few pennies in his sporran.

In the house, Knockbuy watched over the ammunition and the chest containing a month's pay for his command. He had a hundred troops spread across Kynachan and charge of smaller garrisons throughout Strathtummel and Glen Errochty. The captain began filling his days with whisky.

Initially, the militia maintained a high state of alertness and reciprocated the instinctive hostility of the people in the townships. As the days dragged on, however, the country remained peaceful. The Jacobite army was well beyond contact many miles across the blizzard-swept passes to Badenoch. Only in the wilds of Rannoch, where the writ of King George was no more potent in the face of local banditry than that of Prince Charles, were there any clashes between the militia and local people.

By the second week of the occupation, Knockbuy was bored.

In consequence, he took his horse and a couple of his men over the pass to the head of Loch Tay, where he was able to sample the cellar and table of his fellow clansman, Lord Breadalbane. As a gift, Knockbuy presented his host with David's well-trained setters.

The captain left the garrison in command of one of his lieutenants, and the regime relaxed. With Hamish's tacit approval, Agnes, feeling sorry for the children, invited the family into the kitchen to keep warm during the day. A cheerful freckle-faced fourteen-year-old, who was adored by Jessie, Agnes soon contrived to augment the family's meagre rations by re-routing food from the officers' table.

From Hamish, Jean learned that his daughter had survived an attack of diphtheria that had killed her mother and two sisters some half-dozen years before. Rather than rely on the charity of neighbours in their home clachan, Agnes had chosen to follow her father, who was cook, bonesetter, and drummer to the company.

The snow melted. The river flooded, creating a pond on the meadows below the mains. When the cold returned, the water there froze. Clementina and Jean strapped iron skates to the soles of their boots and swooped across the ice, towing the squealing children on sledges. The Campbells, coming from the mild west coast, had never seen such a wonder. They stood by and stared.

Early in March a fever ran through the militia, and the nursery was turned into a sick-room. Just as the epidemic had run its course, Agnes became ill, and Jean and Clementina took turns nursing her in the upstairs room.

There was no news of the Jacobite army – not until the early hours of the seventeenth of that month.

39

The Atholl Raid

At first Jean was not sure what had woken her. The night was wild, and rain lashed against the shutters. Jessie and John were asleep beside her, their breathing even and undisturbed. Then she heard an insistent tapping from outside.

Carefully, Jean left the bed. Without a fire, and the shutters closed against the storm, there was no hint of grey in the darkness. She tapped back.

Silence.

'Who's there?' came a man's gruff voice from the other side.

'Who's there yourself?' Jean replied, a tremor in her own.

'It is I, Bohally.'

For a moment, Jean closed her eyes in silent prayer. Then she put her mouth close to the gap between the shutters. 'It's Jean.'

'Thank heaven. Open up.'

Carefully lifting the bar, she opened the shutters, grateful for the roaring wind that swamped the scrape of the wood against the stone window sill. Dimly against the ragged cloud she could make out the shape of Bohally's chest and head.

Bohally's hand, cold and hard, came through the window and briefly clasped hers.

'Wake everyone up and send them through to me,' he whispered.

Jean crossed the room to the other bed. She put a hand over her sister-in-law's mouth. Clementina woke immediately.

'Don't make a sound,' said Jean. 'Your Charlie's outside the window.' She waited for a second or two. 'Are you going to be quiet?' Clementina nodded under Jean's hand. 'Quickly, then! Pass Euphemia through to him.'

Jean bundled John into a plaid. Still asleep, the little boy was unresisting as Jean poked him feet-first through the window, where invisible hands plucked him from her grasp. Jessie was next, then Euphemia. Once outside, Clementina and Jean were led through the yard, which was filled with silent Highlanders.

'Stay in here until it's all clear,' said an unseen figure when they were safely in the shelter of the stable.

'What's going on? Who are all these men?' asked Clementina.

Under their feet was the dried bracken that had been slept on by half a dozen of the militia.

'I don't think they're Athollmen,' said Jean, 'but they're part of our army. I saw boxwood on their bonnets as well as the white cockade.'

'Boxwood,' said Clementina. 'They'll be Macphersons.'

'We'll find out soon enough.'

All at once the sounds of the storm were blotted out. A set of pipes blared, and up went a great cheer, with shouts of *'Craig dubh Clan Chattan!'* and a rattle of swords against targets.

'Campbells!' bellowed a stentorian voice. 'The house is surrounded. Surrender or we will bar the doors and burn it down around your ears.'

'Burn it down?' said Clementina. 'Do they know what house this is?'

The voice bellowed again. 'Come out of the front door without your weapons. You have a count of ten. One . . . two . . . three—'

A sudden babble of voices in the yard was punctuated by a musket shot.

The detonation woke Jessie. Disoriented, she began a peevish cry.

'It's all right, my angel,' said Jean, groping towards her and stroking her back to sleep. 'It's just those nasty men being kicked out of the house.'

After a minute or two of confused shouting the door to the stable opened, and a grinning Bohally entered with a flaming torch. Clementina ran forward, and they embraced. Bohally gave her a jubilant kiss.

'They've surrendered. All of them. Are you all right? Have they mistreated you?'

'We're fine, Charlie,' said Jean. 'Is Davie here? What's going on?'

'Davie's occupying Castle Grant with the rest of the lads from the battalion. We heard you were plagued by Campbells, so we've come down from Inverness to do something about it. I've got Cluny's men with me. It's safe to go back to the house now.'

The three children were sound asleep on the bracken. Jean decided to leave them there until the excitement died down.

The yard was now garishly lit by torches that projected dramatic shadows through the rain on the façade of the house. In one corner, guarded by half a dozen of the raiding party with drawn swords, stood a large group of disconsolate Argyll Militia, many with their plaids drawn over their heads.

A Macpherson, an officer to judge by the tatty wig he wore beneath his bonnet, came over to them.

'Bohally,' he said. 'A great success. Not a scratch to any of my lads.'

'Congratulations, sir,' said Jean. 'A notable feat of arms.'

'A mere skirmish, madam,' said the officer, but it was clear that the compliment delighted him.

'This is Captain Macpherson of Strathmashie,' said Bohally. 'Strathmashie, let me introduce Lady Kynachan and her sister-in-law, Clementina.'

'An honour, ma'am, Miss Stewart.' Strathmashie bowed. 'The girl is even lovelier than you said, Bohally. No wonder you talked of little else on the march south.'

'Enough of that, Strathmashie,' said Bohally, embarrassed.

'There are militia at the mill,' said Jean.

'We'll've taken enough of them prisoner by now,' said Bohally. 'Every house and barn in Atholl occupied by the Campbells is being attacked tonight. Those at Daloist can escape over the pass to put the fear of God into the garrison at Castle Menzies.'

'But surely that will give them warning of your approach?'

'No, my dear,' said Strathmashie. 'We're not on our way back down to London. Lord George Murray is simply a little homesick. He wants to capture Blair Castle.'

'I see. And then what?'

'We'll probably return north.'

'North? So then we'll have the Campbells back.'

'I doubt it,' said Strathmashie, full of cheer. 'We'll be taking them away with us.'

They were in the house now. Donald had arrived from the mains with Mary Dewar, who was sent to the stable to stay with the children. Again, as when the estate had been overrun by the Campbells, strange men swarmed the building.

'Bring candles, Donald,' said Jean. 'Light up all the rooms. Then find whisky and boil up some broth for our visitors.'

'We've had militia here for a month,' the steward said. 'Where do you expect me to find whisky?'

'There're the jugs you hid down the well, or the barrel you secretly buried in the floor of the byre, or . . .'

'All right, you don't have to tell the world.'

Jean led Bohally and his companions up to the parlour. The place was in chaos. Of the room's half dozen chairs only two were left. A couple of legs propped by the fireplace hinted at the fate of others. Sheets and blankets, some of them torn, lay crumpled on the floor. Many had been used to clean mud from clothes and equipment – or worse. The air stank of unwashed humanity.

Bohally wrinkled his nose. 'Campbells!'

Jean indicated a chest by the fireplace. 'Knockbuy kept his papers there.'

'Archie Campbell of Knockbuy?' said Strathmashie. 'Was he in command? I know him, but I didn't see him in the yard.'

'He hasn't been here this past fortnight.'

'That doesn't surprise me.' Strathmashie laughed. 'He was never much of a soldier. Mind you, if Knockbuy's out, every Campbell in Argyll must be with the enemy.'

Clementina came up from the kitchen with a handful of tallow candles. She and Bohally touched hands as she passed.

'They must have burnt all but the private correspondence, but we'll take what there is to Blair,' said Bohally.

One of the Macphersons clattered up the stairs and announced that all was secure.

'Good, Willie,' said his commander. 'What casualties had the enemy?'

'None – save the lassie who was shot.' The soldier jerked his thumb behind him.

'What's this?' asked Jean in alarm.

From the table, where he was studying the documents, Bohally said, 'There was a wee lass in the nursery. It was a mistake. One of the lads thought she was a Campbell aiming a musket from the window. She was killed instantly.'

'Oh, Jean,' said Clementina, stricken. 'That must be Agnes.'

Shock, then tears, were in Jean's voice. 'Where's her father?'

'There's a sad little man with her,' volunteered Willie Macpherson. 'I left him there. He's not doing any harm.'

'I must go to him,' said Jean.

Clementina hesitated and looked towards Bohally before following Jean across the landing.

A couple of soldiers were in the mid-room, rifling the paraphernalia left by the militiamen. The Macphersons' coarse remarks and contemptuous laughter made them sound as alien to Jean as the Campbells they had supplanted. The door to the nursery was closed.

Turning the handle, Jean entered. A single candle flickered wildly in the draught from the open window. The rain had stopped, but a chill wind carried the voices of the men in the yard below. The little drummer sat on the floor, cross-legged, his plaid over his head, rocking slowly backwards and forwards. His daughter's slight body was face up in front of him.

Her legs were slightly apart, arms by her sides, palms towards the ceiling. The small buds that would have become her breasts lifted the thin material of her flimsy nightshirt. She had fallen at an angle from the window, thrown back in the line that the musket ball had been travelling.

The bullet had struck the centre of her face and removed the back of her skull. Her brains and strands of her flame-red hair were splattered across the wall. In the candlelight the blood looked black, and its coppery stench lay cold and heavy in the air.

'Oh, God!' whispered Jean, putting her handkerchief to her mouth. Behind her, Clementina retched.

The drummer stopped his rocking. 'She was all I had.'

With the edge of his plaid, he wiped a gobbet of blood that had run down her cheek from the dreadful hole where her nose had been.

'I always said her curiosity would be the death of her. But I didn't mean it . . . I really didn't mean it.'

He was silent for a few moments, then took hold of one of his daughter's hands.

'She looked just like her mother.'

Hamish Campbell began to rock again. At the edge of his breath, he was keening a prayer or a lullaby. Clementina left the room to be sick on the landing.

The soldiers next door saw her distress, and the cheer in their voices changed to solicitude.

'Och, yes,' said one. 'It's a terrible shame. Just a wee lassie.'

'I suppose we'd better bring along the poor Campbell mannie,' said another.

The door to the nursery was flung wide, and the torches still carried by the soldiers illuminated the grim scene.

'Let's go. You can't sit here singing for ever.'

The soldier gave his musket to his companion and, taking hold of the drummer's crossbelt, pulled him easily to his feet. 'Come on away, my poor wee man.'

'Where's the sense in it?' said the drummer.

Jean spread a napkin over the shattered face. The blood had clotted, leaving the snowy-white linen unchanged.

'Mr Campbell,' she said. 'I will send for the minister to bury her. We will put her with our own people and say prayers for her soul and for peace. We will not forget her. When the war is over you can come back to see where she lies.'

The drummer looked at Jean's tear-streaked face, his own eyes dry. 'Oh, my lady. Where's the sense in it?'

40

A Funeral and a Siege

At first light, less than four hours after their arrival, the Macphersons were gone. During the night, the thirty outposts occupied by the Argyll Militia in Atholl had been attacked. Each laird led the assault on his own estate, and, without a casualty to the Jacobites and only one or two amongst the occupiers, all were taken. Three hundred or more captured Campbells were herded north into Badenoch. At the same time, Lord George invested Blair Castle.

In the following days, the Duke of Cumberland gathered his forces at Dunkeld and posted Hessian mercenaries there and at Castle Menzies, but the folk of Kynachan were left undisturbed. The folk from the mains were ploughing, and at the mansion, the women began to remove all traces of the Campbells. The rug on the nursery floor was taken out and burnt. Then the bed, the linen press, and the chairs – all splashed by the girl's blood – were carried into the yard to be washed. Morag and Mary Dewar had balked at re-entering the room, afraid of the dead girl's ghost.

Jean and Janet scrubbed down the nursery but stains still marked the oak floor and plastered walls.

'This house was built by Davie,' said Jean, scouring a groove between the floorboards, 'and we filled it with laughter and joy and music and love.'

'It was a happy house – till last summer,' agreed Janet. 'But it'll be a happy place again.'

'Nobody had been seriously ill here, not even the children. Now we have been defiled. Agnes Campbell was a lovely little girl. She would no more like to haunt this room than we would.'

Janet found the bullet in the wall. The misshapen lump of lead was embedded in the plaster. She picked at it, but the ball was immovable.

'I wish this war were over,' said Jean.

'I'm sure it won't be long now. There may be one more battle, then they'll all come home.'

'If I tell you something, do you promise never to tell Davie?'
Janet nodded.

'I don't mind who is king any more. I was happy under King George and as far as I could see so was everyone else on Kynachan. We all talked about how much we wanted King James, but I doubt Scotland would be much better for it. For me, it's not been worth the past months of worry, and it certainly wasn't worth Agnes dying. Her father was right. It makes no sense.'

Her mother-in-law sighed. 'Last time, I didn't see Davie's father for more than a year. I know life sometimes separates us from those we love, but thirty years ago our being apart seemed pointless, although I wouldn't've hurt John by telling him so. Today it feels no different.'

Agnes Campbell's body, wrapped in a linen shroud, was placed in a coffin in the dining-room, until the minister rode over from Dull to bury her.

The Stewarts of Kynachan were Episcopalians, and so the Reverend Duncan McLea, of the established church, had never been to the mansion house. John Forbes, an elder of the kirk, and Donald escorted the coffin. It was strapped to the minister's pony and carried across the moor to the burial ground by the long-ruined church at Foss. Stung by wind-whipped sleet, his black gown flapping round his legs, the fierce old man mumbled the words of the funeral service.

Afterwards he came back and sat in the dining-room beneath the dark stain in the ceiling, where the blood had leaked from Agnes's shattered head. Clementina tuned her father's viola da gamba, Donald put a fiddle beneath his chin, and they made music. Curbing his desire to inveigh against this nest of malignants, the minister and Janet spoke of their health and of the old days at the turn of the century, when their world had been young and full of promise.

In the morning, Jean went to the parlour. The room was cold, so she decided to rake the fire before putting on more peats. At the back of the hearth, buried where the soft white ash lay deep, she found a leather pouch. She gingerly picked it up and carried it to the window, where she allowed the wind to blow away the worst of the dust. Then she undid its strap. The wallet contained several documents. Swiftly she scanned them.

Donald and Janet were in the kitchen when she burst through the door.

'Look what I've found,' she called, waving the papers at

them. 'They were hidden at the back of the fire – details of ammunition, pay receipts, and that sort of thing. But look at this one.'

Jean pointed at a line and read: '*It is His Royal Highness's orders that you give them no quarter.*' She looked up at them. 'You know what this means, don't you? The militia were told to kill our men even if they surrendered.'

'The dogs!' exclaimed Donald.

'That's why the Campbells hid it. They were afraid of what our men would do when they saw it,' said Jean. 'I must take this to Blair at once.'

'You?' said Janet. She grinned. 'Of course. Davie might be there.'

'If you go, I'm coming too,' said Donald.

The few ponies left on the estate could not be spared from ploughing, so the two set out on foot. During their three-hour journey across the hill they found the countryside silent and the few townships all but deserted. By Loch Bhac they met a runner bearing the *crois-tàra*. He was one of a team scouring the country for any able-bodied men who had still managed to escape being pressed into the Jacobite army.

The bearer of the fiery cross was one of the duke's fowlers from Glen Tilt, and he was glad to pause for a sip of whisky and to pass on news. The Jacobite army in Atholl was now a thousand strong, he said, but he hadn't seen Kynachan. He had heard that Lord Nairne's battalion was marching the Campbell prisoners to Inverness.

'What're you looking so sour about?' asked Jean after the runner departed.

'Damn cheek,' grumbled Donald. 'I could outmarch and outfight half that mob in the prince's service, and that man never considered me as a recruit.'

Hitching her bundle onto her shoulder, Jean gave him a sardonic look. 'You could always join up when we get to Blair.'

'No, my lady, much as I'd like to, I know my duty. Kynachan charged me to look after his family.'

As they breasted the hill the pair looked down on the sweep of the flood plain and the patchwork swirl of plough rigs above of the Garry. From here the travellers could hear an intermittent boom of cannon echoing off the hillsides. A couple of miles away across the river, rose the great grey castle of Blair, set in the midst of the only significant woodland in the strath.

The *crois-tàra* seemed to be doing its work. The Garry ferry was busy shuttling Highlanders across to join the Jacobite forces. Many of these men, in Duke William's battalion during the march to England, had deserted on the retreat from Stirling and spent the last few weeks in the hills, avoiding the Argyll Militia. Now they told Jean they were pleased to come out of hiding, hoping an advancing army would offer them further opportunity for plunder.

On the other side of the river, the high road from Dalnacardoch to Dunkeld curved away behind the castle and old ruined kirk. Jean and Donald trudged up the hill, where a smithy and a few stone cottages straggled towards Lord George's headquarters in McGlashan's inn. The gunfire was coming from the ground below the church, where at intervals two small cannon banged away without discernible effect at the roof of the castle, three hundred yards away. Each gun had a lackadaisical bunch of attendants. So did a furnace erected by the blacksmith in the churchyard, from where red-hot shot was being gingerly ferried to the battery.

Seated amid the gravestones, a hundred or so Highlanders provided a critical audience for the efforts of the gunners. Suddenly from their midst came a shout of 'Bean Daibhidh Choimeachdan!', and Jean saw that the men were Lord George's own battalion of the Atholl Brigade, the 2nd, many of whom were from Glen Errochty. But look as hard as she could, she failed to recognize any Tummelsiders.

Half a dozen men came forward to greet her.

'Is Kynachan with you?' she asked.

'He's in Badenoch, my lady, droving the Campbells to Inverness,' said one.

'And Lord George?'

The Highlander turned to his companion. 'Have you seen his lordship about, Jimmy?'

'Aye, there's his horse by the inn, but you'd better be quick. He's quartering the country like an eagle.'

Donald led Jean into the two-storey building, and she handed Knockbuy's wallet to an aide, who took it upstairs to the general. In the little parlour half a dozen officers sat comfortably by the fire, smoking their pipes and chatting. She recognized Shian Menzies, Blairfetty, and a couple of his Robertson neighbours. Shian spotted her first and jumped to his feet.

'So this is what Davie means when he talks of the tribulations of warfare,' said Jean.

The men laughed.

'You don't know the half of it, Lady Kynachan,' said Blairfetty. 'The greatest hero of this assault is Molly.' He gestured towards a young and curvaceous serving girl, who gave Jean a dazzling smile.

'Do join us for a glass of claret,' continued Blairfetty. 'Campbell claret – which makes it all the sweeter.'

Soon Jean was being regaled with an account of the week-long siege. The castle's commander, Sir Andrew Agnew, an old covenanting loon, according to Shian, had an explosive temper. None of the rebels dared approach the castle to request surrender, since its defenders had been ordered to fire at any Highlander who came within range. So Molly, well-known to many of the besieged officers – very well-known, added Shian, winking – was persuaded to sashay up and deliver the appropriate note. The mirth of the young officers who received the message was dissipated by roars of outrage from Sir Andrew, whereupon Molly had picked up her skirts and fled for her life.

Lacking adequate artillery, the besiegers could do little but cut off supplies to the castle and wait. They were trying heated shot, Jean was told, but they had learned that Sir Andrew had set up tubs of urine to douse any flames. A waggish Redcoat officer, Blairfetty said, had placed an effigy of his commander in one of the windows of the tower, apparently surveying the countryside through a spyglass. The Highlanders enthusiastically blazed away at this target, attracting the attention of Sir Andrew himself. He was not amused – nor was the man who had set it up, for Sir Andrew made him brave the rebel musketry to dismantle the dummy.

'So how much longer do you expect the siege to last?' asked Jean.

She had listened to the farcical account with a smile on her lips but inside she could not help but contrast it with the melancholy which pervaded Kynachan.

'It depends what rations they have left,' Blairfetty said with a shrug.

'Will my husband be coming here?'

'I fear not, madam,' came a voice from the foot of the stairway.

Although she had never met him, Jean had no doubt that the tall kilted figure before her was Lord George Murray. His brother, Duke James, and his cousin, Lord Nairne, were stiff, deliberate men, but Lord George, although past the meridian of life, was quick in his movements and his brown eyes were alert and quizzical.

'I understand why my good friend is known as Daibhidh Choimeachdan,' he said, bending to kiss her hand. 'I shall have pleasure in telling him of the service you have performed.'

'Eh? What's this?' asked Shian.

Lord George turned towards his officers, his face now grim. 'Evidence that the Argyll Militia were under orders to give no quarter to any of our men who resisted. I have just had word that we've captured a Hessian dragoon. I'm tempted to stir up his vitals with a dirk to show that two can play that game.'

'Please not,' said Jean. 'There's killing enough.'

Molly looked up from the fireplace. Jean realized that little escaped the girl's attention and wondered how soon the Redcoats and Duke James would hear of all that transpired here, including her own presence.

'I agree. Most of the enemy are honourable men,' said Shian. 'They would no more obey such an order than I.'

'Lady Kynachan may be right,' said Lord George. 'There will be killing enough.'

Catching his change of tense, Jean felt a shiver.

A few days later, when the dragoons made their morning patrols, they found the Highlanders gone from Atholl. Lord George had received orders from the prince to lift the siege and return north. Once again, Sir Andrew Agnew commanded the whole country from Dunkeld to Badenoch.

At Kynachan, a dozen Hessians arrived. They were mercenaries, employed by the British army on the Continent, who had been shipped over to help quell the rising. Blue-coated, blond, bearded, phlegmatic, courteous, speaking incomprehensible German, they smiled as they searched the house and buildings.

Their officer and Jean communicated through a mixture of French and Latin. He was there to guard the bridge and had no quarrel with women or civilians. Having known many Highland soldiers of fortune in the European wars, he had great regard for their people. He would like to station his men in the barns and at the mains and would try to keep out of her way. In the nature of things, however, they would inconvenience her. He would pay for any food they might require. He would be most obliged for any information concerning movement of the rebels that she might give him. He gave a polite salute and retired back down the hill.

The next day, Clementina, Morag, and a couple of girls from the mains took the last of the linen down to the burn. They tied their skirts high between their legs and face to face, with hands on each other's shoulders, each couple trod the dirt of the Campbells from the sheets and tablecloths. In the chill water their bare legs turned scarlet.

Attracted by their singing, four of the Hessians marching back from their shift at the bridge stopped to enjoy the sight. When one of the girls kicked a napkin into the current, a soldier handed his musket to a comrade and plunged into the water to recover the linen. His boots scraping for purchase on the slippery rocks, he waded upstream to hand over his prize and earn himself a giggled kiss from the girl and envious jeers from his fellows.

April came, with its promise of spring. The weather grew mild, and primroses flowered along the banks of the burns. A flush of green appeared on the pastures; the hungry cattle sniffed fresh grass in the air, and lowed their impatience for summer. Whenever the weather allowed, the heavy wooden ploughs worked the land, manoeuvred along the field ridges by gangs of grandfathers, women, children, and the few remaining ponies. It was time for sowing, men's work again, but the men were still soldiering.

It turned colder. The sullen sky spat snow. And a whisper came on the wind that there had been a battle.

41

Drummossie Moor

During the previous few weeks, the Jacobite army had made its
headquarters at Inverness. On the twelfth of April, government
forces, under the Duke of Cumberland, crossed the river Spey
and moved to Nairn, some fifteen miles from the rebels, ready
for the next stage of his campaign.

Colonel O'Sullivan, Adjutant-General of the Jacobite army,
reconnoitred the ground between the two armies and selected
a stretch of flat moorland called Drummossie, near Culloden
House, as a suitable place to give battle.

The Jacobite army had been drawn up on the moor the
day before, but Cumberland had stayed away. Many of
the Highland officers were relieved. In their opinion, the
moor was an unsuitable battlefield for their men, whose
strength lay in their speed and agility and in the shock
of their charge. Theirs was not an army to string across a
flat expanse of open country to await the arrival of highly
disciplined infantry, supported by artillery and cavalry. That
was warfare for professionals on the Continent. But should the
Highland army deploy on ground more suited to them, like that
which lay on the south bank of the river Nairn, a few hundred
yards from the moor, the Jacobites ran the risk that Cumberland
would march straight past them to Inverness and capture what
little remained of the dispirited rebels' stores and equipment.
Hunger had become a potent weapon for the government,
and a considerable number of the Highlanders had absented
themselves to forage for themselves and their comrades.

To exploit the strengths of the rebels, Lord George Murray
had persuaded the prince to try a night march on Cumberland's
camp to launch a surprise attack while it was still dark. It
was also hoped that the enemy would be largely drunk after
celebrating their royal commander's twenty-fifth birthday.

Along with the rest of the army, the seven hundred men of the Atholl Brigade had walked most of the night, stumbling in fog and total darkness across bogs and heather tussocks. The Jacobites had been split into two columns – with Lord George and his Athollmen leading the first, but they had been unable to link up before they heard the bugle that alerted the enemy camp.

In the council of war that had followed, O'Sullivan urged a futile attack by the leading column upon the alerted government forces, even though the approaching dawn would allow their artillery full play. David had supported Shian, who contemptuously told O'Sullivan that he'd prefer to be killed in plain day, when he could see how his neighbours fought.

Lord George had ordered a retreat, and the exhausted and hungry Highlanders had straggled back towards Drummossie to sleep in barns, or, wrapped in their plaids, in the lea of walls – scattered across miles of countryside.

David had left the other senior officers, who were snatching some rest in Culloden House, and had joined the men of Kynachan in a hollow in the park. They were aroused by cannon-fire, pipes, and drums. Only four miles away, Cumberland's army was on the march.

The Atholl Brigade had been fortunate to manage about three hours' sleep. Meal should have been sent out from Inverness, but the commissariat had failed, and the men had been virtually without food for twenty-four hours.

It was full daylight – cold, wet, and windy. Bohally joined David a few yards off from the rest of their men, a number of whom were still huddled bundles being prodded awake by sleep-doped comrades.

'What do you think, Davie? Battle today?'

'I fear so,' replied David. Like the rest of the Highlanders, he was unshaven, hollow-eyed, and his clothes were torn and muddy. 'Have the men any food left?'

'Some of the Balnarn lads have a little meal, and George Cairney has enough whisky for a good tot a man.'

'Is that all?'

'They're lucky,' said Bohally. He nodded towards another group of stirring Highlanders. 'Garth's company has had nothing for a day. I've told George to hold his whisky till we've taken our positions.' He paused. 'Another thing, Davie – I've decided I'd like to fight with the Appin Regiment today.'

'Are you sure?'

'Aye. The men of Kynachan are your people. My forebears are Stewarts of Appin, not of Atholl, and today I might be joining them. This battle has a bad smell about it.'

'You do as you think best, old friend.' David looked round to ensure his words could not be overheard. 'And should I be killed today, keep an eye on Jean and the family for me.'

Bohally clapped him on the back. 'Ach, it's me that's feart. Remember, Kynachan lads never get a scratch.'

The Highlanders were now on their feet. From the direction of Culloden House, Lord George Murray and his cousin, Lord Nairne, came cantering over the edge of the hollow where the Atholl Brigade had slept.

'Damned shambles, Kynachan,' shouted Lord George. 'The army's all over the place. Get your lads out to the moor and take up position on the right. I'll have the rest of them up there with you as soon as possible.' Without waiting for an acknowledgement, he spurred his horse, trotting out of sight over the crest.

In front of the Camerons, the Athollmen marched across the park through a gap in the moss-covered stone walls and climbed between straggling birches to the ridge where lay the open moor. They were the first of the army to move out onto the battlefield.

In spite of the alarm that had been raised, there was no sign of the enemy. Two miles behind, the men could see the white-flecked, grey waters of the Moray Firth, where a naval sloop rode at anchor. Ahead in the drizzly distance stretched the empty heather moor and a ridge of low black hills.

A few mounted figures were moving slowly over the ground. One of them came across to direct the Atholl Brigade – which now incorporated the clan regiments of Robertson and Menzies – along a rough track through the heather to their position. In front of the men of Kynachan marched thirty tenants from Killiechassie, an estate just down river from Taybridge.

On the far side of the moor, alongside a dry-stone dyke, the brigade came to a halt. Beyond the wall, the ground fell towards the river Nairn, three-quarters of a mile away. The Highlanders lined up in ranks six deep – files two yards apart, so that a man could wield his broadsword.

In front of each company stood the laird or his deputy. Immediately behind were his tenants, behind them the sub-tenants and cottars, and, at the rear, the most humble of the landless clansmen. Down the line, through the regiments of the Camerons, the Stewarts of Appin, the Frasers, the McIntoshes, the McLeans, the Farquharsons, and the Macdonalds, father stood by son, brother by brother, cousin by cousin, neighbour by neighbour, and friend by friend.

By mid-morning, the bulk of the army was deployed across the moor, about a mile west of the positions they had held the day before. The front line, seven hundred yards long, consisted entirely of the clan regiments. The 1st Battalion of the Atholl Brigade occupied the coveted position on the right. A hundred yards back, on the right of the second line, were the Lowlanders of Ogilvy's Regiment. The same distance behind them stood the handful of cavalry that still had their horses.

The prince had come on to the moor with the Camerons, next in line to the Athollmen, and had ridden the ranks, lifting the spirits of the clansmen before he retired to the rear of the army.

The Jacobites waited. The scream of dozens of sets of warpipes was snatched away by a chill, rain-bearing wind, which snapped standards, probed the coverings of musket flashpans, and hurled flurries of sleet into the Highlanders' faces. A battery of three small cannon was dragged in position by the dyke to the right of the Strathtummel men. Killiechassie's company closed with Kynachan's to give the gunners room and a field of fire. Lord George Murray and Lord Nairne rode over to offer advice to the inexperienced artillerymen.

A runner skipped across the heather, bringing news that Clan Donald had taken umbrage because they were not on the right wing, the position promised to them in perpetuity by Robert Bruce after the battle of Bannockburn, more than four centuries earlier. Lord George rode off to soothe ruffled feelings.

Concern arose over the nature of the ground on the right. This terrain had not been reconnoitred, and, beyond the stone wall, the field fell away out of sight down to the river, from where the enemy could approach unseen. O'Sullivan arrived to give his opinion that there was no danger, since the wall would give protection to their flank. Experience had taught David that advice from that source was invariably wrong, and he told the adjutant-general that he would prefer the dyke knocked down, as it would provide an excellent firing position for the enemy. The returning Lord George supported him.

The government army came into sight – three slow-moving columns of red-coated infantry, their white gaiters flickering as they marched. Amongst them were dragoons on their heavy horses, artillery, and a substantial number of Highlanders – companies from Lord Loudon's and Lord John Murray's Highlanders and hundreds of Campbells of the Argyll Militia.

David walked back to the ranks of his men. In spite of the stinging sleet and rain in their faces, many leaned half asleep on their broadswords.

'We'll soon be at them now, lads. The Redcoats haven't stood our charge for a hundred years, and they won't this time.'

In the fourth rank, Angus Ferguson, putative father of Isobel Forbes's child, stood alongside his sixteen-year-old brother, Robert. The boy swayed on his feet, his smooth cheeks grey with cold, hunger, and exhaustion. David tested the edge of Robert's broadsword and gave him an encouraging pat on the shoulder.

'They ran from us at Gladsmuir, boy. They ran at Falkirk, and they'll run now. Keep your powder dry, take their bayonets on your target, and we'll all see Schiehallion again.'

The government troops, twice as numerous as the Jacobites, were now advancing onto the moor. Even over the rough terrain they marched in step to the distant tap of the drum. They formed three lines, five hundred yards in front of the waiting Highlanders, and, in a neat parade-ground manoeuvre, turned to face their enemy.

Lord George, watching carefully from the vantage point of his horse, stood in his stirrups to point to the left, where one of a battery of enemy cannon had become bogged down and a swarm of men worked to free it. Such soft ground was impossible for the dragoons, but it could also prove troublesome for the charging Highlanders.

A hiatus ensued for a few minutes, and the two armies stared at each other across the heather. Then a single horseman trotted from the midst of the government lines, riding coolly across the moor to inspect the Jacobites from a distance of a hundred yards. The weary Highlanders raised a great cheer of defiance and waved their bonnets. The government side barked a hoarse answering 'Huzza!'

To the right of the Atholl Brigade, the battery of little guns crashed into action. The smoke from their discharge was carried back by the strong wind. Immediately the other Jacobite field pieces opened fire and were answered by the government's far more formidable ordnance.

Lacking trained artillerymen, the Jacobite guns on the left soon became silent, but the little battery alongside the men of Kynachan and Killiechassie continued to bang out against the continuous thunder of the government cannon.

A ball removed the head of the commander of the battery, an officer in the French Service, and his pumping heart jetted blood six feet into the air, before his body slumped into the heather. His guns continued to fire into the bank of powder smoke that drifted across from the government lines. The music of the pipes was now punctuated by the dreadful thud of iron shot smashing flesh as it skittled through the ranks, scattering the broken, screaming bodies of the Highlanders.

David, a dozen yards in front of the Kynachan men, shouted across to Lord Nairne, whose horse had its ears back, chewing at its bit.

'We must charge! We can't take this much longer.'

As he spoke, the side of the animal exploded when a ball passed through its body, stringing its steaming entrails across the heather, and cut down a man at the rear of Killiechassie's company. Cursing, Nairne hauled himself up. Lord George came over to check on his welfare.

'We must charge!' repeated David. 'The enemy won't. They have no need. They're killing us where we stand.'

Lord George gave a helpless shrug. 'We must await the order.'

David walked back to his men.

'There'll be nobody left alive if we don't move soon,' shouted George Cairney, who stood on the right of the company's front line. The ball that killed the man from Killiechassie had passed within an inch or two of him, flicking him with the horse's blood.

'Don't fret,' replied David, raising his voice over the pipes so that all his men could hear. 'Kynachan lads never get killed. If you've any whisky, George, I think now's the time you passed it round.'

The resulting cheer, when Lord George turned in surprise, nearly brought him from the saddle.

From beyond the dyke on the right, a scout arrived bearing the news that David had feared. The Campbell militia and some dragoons had broken through into the enclosure over the ridge and were moving to outflank the Jacobites. Lord George cantered back through the front line to direct a battalion of infantry and a handful of cavalry to the wall in order to defend an attack on the rear.

Meantime, cannonballs continued to come whirring through the smoke, and they smeared bloody stripes through the heather. Miraculously, the men of Kynachan were left untouched.

Suddenly there was movement.

The McIntoshes could stand the pounding of the cannon no longer, and they had broken into a charge. Unless the entire front line charged with them, the battle would be lost. Lord George raised his sword. The pipes reached a crescendo, and the music cut off as the pipers stuffed their instruments in their pouches and unslung their muskets.

David pulled his bonnet low over his head and risked a glance behind him at the set faces of the men amongst whom he had passed his life. When he turned back to face the enemy, he found himself thinking of Jean.

Lord George brought down his sword, and the Atholl Brigade surged forward. Excitement cancelled fatigue as the men bounded over the heather, intent on smashing through the Redcoat lines and silencing the murderous guns.

It took two minutes for the Athollmen to reach the enemy. Within the first, the dyke to their right suddenly sprouted a line of black-cockaded Campbells, who poured fire into the flank. The men of Killiechassie flinched to their left, pushing the whole battalion towards the centre of the field, a movement compounded by a bulge in the wall.

In the middle of the moor, the McIntoshes, ahead of the Jacobite left wing, drew the cannon-fire of half the government army. The clansmen shied to the right, round the soft ground where the enemy guns had mired when they were dragged into position.

A minute and a half into the charge, the Atholl Brigade had passed by the militia, but their front had been constricted. The invisible cannon were now firing grape and canister shot, which tore into the Highlanders as they charged through the reeking powder fumes.

A hundred yards out, the enemy infantry came into sight – a ribbon of white leggings below the smoke. So congested was the line that many Highlanders were unable to discharge their muskets for fear of hitting their own comrades. Dropping the useless firearms, they scrambled the final few yards over the bodies of the fallen.

On the left wing of the government lines, a regular regiment had been drawn up *en potence* – at right angles to and slightly ahead of the rest of the army. The cannon were joined by regular volleys of musketry that punched into the clansmen from front and side.

The charge drove home.

The two Redcoat regiments on the left of the government army crumpled as the screaming, slashing mob of Highlanders carved their way through the gap between the formations, capturing the pair of cannon placed there and crunching into the second line. But the second line held, and the impetus of the attack died.

Seeing that the intitial charge had failed, Lord George, now hatless, wigless, and horseless, managed to fight his way out of the midst of the enemy and temporarily retire, intending to bring the second Jacobite line into the battle.

But the battalions of the Atholl Brigade, the Camerons, the Stewarts of Appin, and the McIntoshes had ceased to exist. Those Highlanders not straggling in dazed retreat across five hundred yards of body-strewn moor were dying beneath the bayonets of the infantry.

On the left wing, the clans' attack had scarcely started. The Duke of Perth managed to persuade the sullen Farquharsons and Macdonalds to march within musket shot of the enemy and discharge their weapons, but having done so they retreated. Determined to salvage their clans' honour, their officers charged unsupported and many were killed. At other points along the line, the charge had withered and died. Survivors stood impotent, shaking their broadswords and throwing stones at the immaculate ranks of Redcoats. From behind bristling bayonets, they continued their musket drill, plying their trade of killing their enemies.

The Jacobite army began an orderly retreat, but much of its right wing was left lying in the heather.

Part III

THE AFTERMATH

42

Naught but Whispers

The whisper came on the wind that there had been a battle. Jean may have heard it first. As she was returning from the shed with an armful of peats, a sudden gust hissed through the bare black branches of the great oak on the knoll.

Head to one side, she listened, gazing due north at the hillside above Bohally. It was as if the fairy warriors of Fingal were flying before the wind and the breath of their passing had touched her. After a few moments, she shivered and hurried back indoors. Removing her pattens in the kitchen, she went up to the parlour.

'I just had the oddest feeling,' she said.

Janet raised her head from her Bible. 'What kind of feeling?'

'As if something had happened. As if something had suddenly changed, and the world had become an utterly different place. It was eerie.'

'Wind in your bowels, I expect,' said Donald, who was clearing the winter's accumulation of ash from the fireplace. 'In a minute I'll bring you a bowl of broth. That'll help.'

'It was a message from the other world. About the future,' said Clementina.

'Och, no,' said Janet. 'The second sight almost always foretells death. That gives the seer a bad feeling, not just a queer one.'

'Charlie once told me he saw a washer the night before he was to fight a duel,' said Clementina. 'It was the wraith-like shape of an old woman by the burn, dipping a sheet of linen into the water.'

'That'd be his shroud,' said Janet. 'You see the washer before you die.'

'Charlie's still alive,' said Jean.

'Aye, but when did he say he saw it?' asked Janet.

'Quite a while ago,' replied Clementina. 'Years and years.'

'Well, then. He's going to die sometime. He was just given early notification.'

'Poor little Agnes didn't see a washer,' said Clementina sadly.

'There aren't as many such things about as there used to be. Besides, Agnes never went down to the burn, so perhaps the washing was done without her being there to see it.'

A few days later, on Sunday afternoon, Catherine Stewart from Drumnakyle was ushered into the parlour, where the family was occupied in ways suitable to the Sabbath. Her news was ominous.

'They were talking about it after church,' she told them. 'A rider from Logierait brought word to the garrison at Castle Menzies this morning. There's been a battle.'

'What kind of battle?' asked Jean, a chill touching her heart. 'And whereabouts?'

'Up north. They say our army attacked theirs on Tuesday night, but no-one knows who won.'

'That's all?' said Clementina.

Mrs Stewart nodded.

'That's good news,' said Janet. 'We must have beaten them. Anything less and the Redcoats would be trumpeting a victory.'

'Do you think so?' said Jean dully.

'I know so. We'll hear all about it in a day or two.'

'Men die in victories just as they do in defeats,' Jean said.

'But not our men, Lady Kynachan,' said Mrs Stewart. 'Not everyone in Atholl was as keen as the laird to fight, true enough, but it's been the making of my Ian and many of the other lads. Men seem to have to fight a war before they amount to anything.'

'So long as they do not die,' said Jean.

Next morning, Jean was in the kitchen early. Most days, by the time the maid had swept the hearth and drawn water from the well, a couple of Hessians were stamping their feet outside, expecting a bowl of soup from the simmering cauldron. This time Jean was at the door waiting for them.

'*Bonjour,*' she called as two large young men with wispy blond moustaches and beards trudged up the track past the barns.

'*Bonjour, mademoiselle. Vous parlez francais?*'

'*Un peu.*'

'*Moi aussi. C'est rare, ici en Ecosse.*' The soldier shot her a smile of complicity.

'*Voulez-vous soupe?*'

The soldier's face brightened. '*Jawohl, soupe. Potage?*'

'Yes,' said Jean, nodding. '*Potage.*'

The two soldiers entered the kitchen, the iron studs on the soles of their boots scraping on the flagstones, and unslung their muskets before sitting at the kitchen table.

'*J'ai entendu dire,*' said Jean carefully, '*qu'il y avait une bataille la semaine dernière.*'

'*Ja, c'est vrai. J'espère que tout va bien avec vos amis. On dit que c'est une grande victoire.*'

'*Victoire?*'

'*Ja, pour le Duc de Cumberland.*'

The last word was so mangled by the Hessian's accent that it took some moments before Jean understood.

'*Le potage est excellent, mademoiselle. Merci.*'

'*Merci. Excusez-moi.*'

Leaving the soldiers to their soup, Jean went up to the shuttered gloom of the parlour and sat by the fire. At some point Janet entered.

'Cumberland won the battle,' came Jean's lifeless voice.

'Oh, Jean,' said Janet, startled. 'I didn't see you there. Cumberland – are you sure?'

'It's word from one of the Hessians.'

'Och, that's just rumour. If I had a penny for every rumour there's been since the prince landed, I could buy out the Duke of Atholl. All we can do is wait for proper news. There's no point in brooding.'

'I know,' said Jean, but her voice was bleak.

Wednesday, one week after the battle, was a fine warm day, and the first swallows of the year circled high above the strath. Donald called Jean down to the kitchen, where a pedlar lounged over a tot of whisky outside the back door. His pack lay on the top of the garden wall, overhanging it a yard on either side.

'This man has just come from Blair, my lady. He has information on the battle.'

'That's right, lady.'

The packman was powerfully built. He wore breeches and heavy wooden-soled shoes, and a broad indented stripe crossed his forehead.

'The rising is finished. The prince's army was routed, and himself is being hunted throughout the country. The slaughter was terrible.'

The packman was proud of his dramatic news.

'Who told you this?'

Disturbed by the coldness of Jean's voice, the pedlar felt the need to justify himself.

'Who told me? Who *told* me? Everybody told me.' He waved his arms. 'The hills told me. The Redcoats told me. The Macpherson near Dalnacardoch told me. Cluny's men missed the battle but they've disbanded, he said. The MacGregor regiment told me. They were marching to Balquhidder before they disperse. A man from Strathardle told me. He had a sabre cut on his arm. He said the Atholl Brigade was in the thick of it. He saw the corpse of Mercer of Aldie, the duke's own cousin, on the field, surrounded by a garland of dead heroes.'

'You speak the truth?'

'Aye, lady, I speak the truth. I left from Perth eight days ago to sell as far as Inverness. Not now, though, not with Redcoats chasing rebels through every glen. The country is too dangerous. I am going back to the Lowlands.'

Jean remained silent for a moment or two, considering his information.

'This man from Strathardle. Did he say he was with the Atholl Brigade?'

'No, he grew afraid. Only a fool would admit to fighting in an army that's just been routed, he said.' The packman jerked a thumb west. 'The Hessians at the bridge are on the lookout for fugitives. There's a Campbell with them, asking the questions.'

With practised accuracy, the pedlar spat a gobbet of tobacco juice onto a rat-run by the door. Jean thanked the man. Tossing down his dram, he squatted, his back to the wall, and shouldered the pack, adjusting the strap about his forehead as he straightened up. Then, bowed forward to counterbalance the weight on his back, he trudged off down the track.

When the man disappeared, Jean asked Donald whether the packman's word could be trusted.

'He'll be telling the truth as he sees and hears it, my lady. His wares – even his life – might be forfeit if he ventured where it was unsafe. And wherever he goes, his welcome depends as much on the reliability of his news as on what he trades. I would say there has certainly been a battle, and I doubt the outcome has been in our favour.'

'Why is there no word of our men?'

'It's well known that Kynachan is one of the prince's most prominent supporters,' said Donald. 'The soldiers'll soon be keeping an eye on this house – if they aren't already. No-one will dare come here.'

'How will we hear, then?'

'There'll be word.'

Late that evening, the children in bed and their elders about to follow, the day's events were being reviewed in the parlour.

'The estate'll be forfeit, mark my words,' prophesied Janet. 'It wouldn't surprise me if Davie's already on a ship for the Continent. That's where he'll be if he's any sense. The Highlands won't be a good place for a Jacobite for a while.'

'I'm a Jacobite,' said Clementina. 'And the Highlands are good enough for me. I'll wager Davie and Charlie are still with the prince and Lord George. They'll've marched into the hills, and it won't be long before we hear they've attacked somewhere else. They'll be like Montrose, striking the enemy where they least expect it.'

'I wish we had news,' said Jean.

'Don't fret,' said Janet. 'We will.'

From downstairs came sudden sounds of an altercation. The women heard Donald's stentorian shouts, punctuated by a scream. Rushing into the kitchen, they found a Highlander of the Argyll Militia arguing with the steward, who was in his nightshirt. By his side, one of the Hessians had tight hold of a sobbing girl.

'What's this?' shouted Jean.

'Ah,' exclaimed Donald, swinging round to her in relief. 'This Campbell's trying to take away my wife.'

'Your wife!' said Clementina.

'She's a spy,' roared the Campbell. 'She was sneaking in here, hoping not to be spotted.'

'You're a silly man,' Donald retorted. 'I sent her out a minute ago to see what the noise was. It must've been you we heard.' He shouted over to the girl. 'You get back into bed now, woman, d'you hear?'

The Campbell, dragging the girl to the glow of the fire, pulled back her shawl to reveal a head of flaxen hair and sharp elfin features.

'This lassie's still a bairn,' he said.

'She's older than she looks,' grunted Donald, more in hope than conviction.

The soldier ran a rough hand across the girl's chest. 'Look, she's still to grow her tits. She's too young to be anyone's wife.'

Twisting free of the soldier's grasp, the girl threw herself at Donald's feet and in one quick motion pulled up his nightshirt.

'Bairn!' she spat, grasping the steward's genitals and brandishing them at the intruders. 'I'm no bairn. What bairn can put fire in these old balls?'

'Mercy,' said Janet into the shocked silence.

Donald's dismay became a scowl of embarrassment. He gingerly disengaged himself from her hand and hauled down his shirt.

'Get to your bed, wife,' he growled.

Following his pointed finger, the girl went to his bracken-filled mattress on its shelf by the fire and crawled under the grimy blanket.

A couple of drams later, the door slammed shut behind the soldiers. The girl poked her head out of the covers, saw it was safe, and jumped out of the bed.

'I'm sorry, missus,' she said, addressing Janet. 'I didn't mean to lay hand on your husband like that.'

Clementina hooted with delight.

'Heavens, lassie,' said the scandalized steward. 'That's not my wife. That's Kynachan's mother.'

'Who is this child, Donald?' asked Jean.

'I've never seen her before,' said Donald. 'Truly,' he added, reacting to the scepticism on his mistress's face. 'I opened the door, and in she came. And in came the soldiers after her.'

'I'm Lizzie Reid,' said the girl. 'My father's Drumchaldane.'

'Och, yes, I know you,' said Donald. 'Although I can't imagine where you dreamed up that wee trick. Her father's Alexander Reid, my lady, ensign in Duntanlich's company. He's brother to Hugh Reid, in Balnarn.'

'We had a message. My father and a couple of others are hiding in the wood west of the bridge. One of them was wounded in the battle.'

'What others?' asked Jean.

'We don't know.'

'It might be David,' said Jean. 'I must go to him at once.'

'No,' said the child. 'They say the prince is skulking in Atholl. There's thirty thousand pounds on his head, and the soldiers are everywhere tonight. In the middle of the day someone must go to the Wood of Kynachan, to the place where the burn of the Fairies crosses the track.'

'You're a very brave girl,' said Janet.

'Yes,' said Jean. 'We thank you.'

'I am my father's daughter, kin to Struan.'

'Take some meal and cheese for your mother, Lizzie.'

'Thank you, my lady. God knows we need it. I'd best be off now.'

'But what if they come back looking for you?' said Donald. 'You're meant to be my wife.'

The child gave a wicked smile. 'Tell them I ran away with a soldier. I'm the sort of wife who'd run, and you're the sort of husband who couldn't hold me.'

43

Fugitives

Shortly before noon the following day, a barefoot stooped figure in a ragged plaid slowly herded a couple of cattle along the high road towards the bridge. Although their shaggy black coats concealed jutting bones, the little cows tottered, weak from blood-letting and poor winter fodder.

Coming the other way, two old men greeted the cowgirl respectfully and forbore to enquire why the Lady of Kynachan should be walking alone in the drizzle, masquerading as her poorest farm servant.

On the north side of the bridge, a knot of soldiers was questioning two Highlanders with a pack pony. One of the Hessians spared Jean a cursory glance. A couple of scraggy cattle driven by a solitary woman was not worth challenging.

Passing the huddle of bothies and the inn, Jean branched off the military road onto a path between the river and the long north ridge of Craig Kynachan. As soon as the oaks and birches screened her from sight, she stopped to put on the shoes concealed along with a heavy bundle in the folds of her plaid.

Half a mile from the bridge, the burn of the Fairies, marking the boundary between Kynachan and the neighbouring estate of Crossmount, crossed the track. The cattle halted and began to graze on the flush of grass of a miniature water meadow. Jean looked anxiously about her.

Farther up the hill, where the burn carved a passage through the trees, a piece of white material briefly showed above a rock. A glance behind confirmed that nobody had followed her. She left the track and scrambled up through the heather alongside the tumbling water.

A voice came from behind the rock. 'That grass'll upset the cows, Lady Kynachan. It'll go straight through them.'

'Who's there?'

'Alexander Reid, Drumchaldane.'

The man came out. He was trying to re-bandage his right arm with the scrap of bloody material he had waved at her.

She pushed his hand away and examined the injury – a long shallow slash that was beginning to heal.

'Your Lizzie came to the house. You've a lass to be proud of there. Bathe that in water before you put the bandage back on. Who else is here?'

'Garth, Bohally, and a couple of Camerons.'

'Kynachan?'

'No, I'm sorry. I haven't seen him since the battle.'

Jean's face expressed the pain of dashed hope. For a moment she sagged back against the damp moss on the boulder. She gave herself a little shake and rallied.

'Are you the one who's hurt?'

He gave a short laugh. 'I've had worse than this from a bramble bush. It's Bohally.'

'Charlie? Where is he?'

Reid led the way up through the trees. A dirk and a dragoon's pistol were thrust in his belt. His kilt and plaid were torn and stained. Jean saw that his bonnet lacked its white cockade.

A quarter of a mile up the burn, he struck off by an ancient oak whose leaves were still tight in bud. A hundred yards on, an outcrop of rock – apparently no different from others that studded the bosky hillside – created a clearing amid the trees.

Reid headed for the spot, where he disappeared into a narrow cleft. Jean followed. The passage ran a dozen paces and opened into a dank cave, its muddy floor strewn with trampled heather. Three men sat there. Bohally lay wrapped in his plaid.

'Lady Kynachan,' exclaimed one of the men.

Jean recognized William Stewart of Garth, a laird from the other end of Glen Goulandie. She did not know the other two.

Bohally struggled to his elbow. 'Is that you, Jean? You shouldn't've risked coming here yourself.'

Jean began unpacking her bundle – fresh bandages, a bottle of laudanum, and medicinal herbs; whisky, meal, cheese, and half a leg of smoked mutton.

'I'm doing most of the doctoring on the estate now,' she said, her tone light. 'I was best for the job. Where are you hurt?'

'It's my leg.' He looked apologetic. 'But I was stitched by a surgeon, and I'm fine now.'

The others fell on the food. Bohally asked for whisky. His hair lay matted and tangled on his skull, and, in spite of the cave's chill, sweat beaded his forehead. Jean drew back the plaid. A red-stained rag bound his thigh. She felt the fever radiating from his body.

'What happened?' she asked as she unravelled his bandage.

'We lost,' said Bohally.

'Have you any news of Davie – or of the rest of the men from the estate? We've heard nothing. Are they still with the army?'

Bohally broke an uncomfortable silence. 'There is no army, Jean – except Cumberland's. Most of our lads are in hiding.'

'Those we didn't leave to the mercy of Cumberland and his butchers,' said Garth, his mouth full, his dirk hacking at the mutton.

'I fought with the Appin regiment,' continued Bohally. 'The gun-smoke was so thick I could see nothing of the Athollmen.'

'That was how it was,' confirmed Garth. 'And the noise – the roar of the guns and the cries of the wounded. I'd never heard the like.'

'Sandy Stewart from Glen Lyon came across me on the field and carried me off on a horse he'd found in the hills,' said Bohally. 'I owe him my life – him and those lads' – he nodded towards the unidentified Highlanders – 'Camerons from Rannoch. They helped bring me south.'

'Blood – you'd never believe a man could have so much in him,' said one Cameron, a look of contentment on his face as the whisky hit his belly.

'Bohally's a big man,' said his companion. 'The bigger the man, the more blood he carries.'

'My brother would have been right behind Kynachan,' said Reid, who was keeping watch at the mouth of the cave. 'They'll be together somewhere with the rest of their lads.'

Listening and sifting their words, Jean worked over Bohally, pictures of the battlefield seething in her head, *the smoke, darkness like the cave*, the sword had sliced deep into the muscle, *guns thundering, warpipes screaming*, the wound had been stitched but was red and swollen, *the groans of the wounded, and Davie – in the midst of it all was Davie*. She laid comfrey leaves over the injury, after that a layer of dry sphagnum moss, and then bound the thigh with a fresh bandage.

'You were lucky, Charlie,' she said, her voice tightly controlled in an effort to cut off the visions.

Bohally thanked her.

'It'll take you a week or two before you're right in yourself, and longer before you'll be much use in a reel,' she said, grateful for her sudden levity.

Jean reported the local news and told him about Clementina. 'She would fight by your side in the next campaign.'

Bohally grunted his amusement. 'So long as the prince was by her other elbow.'

'You do her injustice. For you she's stronger than the finest Ferrara blade.'

'My sword broke on Drummossie Moor,' Bohally said gloomily.

'She'd die for you, too, and with all the Redcoats around she may yet have to.'

'You're right,' said a chastened Bohally. 'It's a woman's war now. We rely on you to keep us alive.'

'That you do, Charlie. I doubt I'll be able to keep Clemmie away tomorrow.'

At the cave entrance, Jean turned to Garth. 'Does your wife know you're safe?'

He was shamefaced.

'Then I'll get word to her.' Jean looked to the Camerons. 'Have you families?'

'Aye. They know we live.'

Alexander Reid escorted her as far as the rock and then returned to the cave.

'No news,' whispered Jean to the unresponsive cows, 'no news of Davie.'

Amid the kindly ranks of gnarled oaks and birches she released her misery, and the grey sky wept in sympathy.

44

In Shackles

The aching days crept by. In his cave, Bohally's bear-like constitution threw off the infection, and his flesh knitted, leaving a puckered red scar. He complained that it itched abominably.

The Redcoats patrolled without respite, each eager to claim the fortune that awaited the man who caught the prince. Some returning Jacobites were captured and thrown into prison. Others skulked in the woods and hills, awaiting the sea-change that would allow them home.

David was high on the list of wanted men. Notorious as one of Atholl's most fanatic Jacobites, he was at the same time known to all the officers captured at Prestonpans and was further believed to have commanded the raid on Kynachan that had humiliated the Campbell militia. Daily the troops searched the house. Daily they ferreted the townships. The incessant drizzle seeping through the cottage roofs dissolved the soot on the undersides of the thatch and spotted their scarlet tunics with tar.

One day a small boy was at the back door of the mansion. Would the Lady of Kynachan come to Daloist at once? John Forbes wanted to see her. And the lad darted off before he could be questioned further.

Forbes met Jean's pony at the mill. He said nothing but looked both ways along the empty high road before beckoning her into the adjacent smithy.

'What is it?' she asked.

'Speak to him,' said Forbes, nodding to the smith.

Duncan Kennedy, a somewhat unctuous man in his sixties, stood by the forge. He dry-washed his hands as he greeted her.

'You know that the penalty of death applies to anyone who gives help to a rebel?' he said.

'What of it?' asked Jean, already impatient.

'Now the rebellion's over, it behoves a man to take particular care not to fall foul of the authorities for a cause that is lost.'

'I did not trail this way to listen to this.'

'It's Angus Ferguson,' said Forbes. 'The lad betrothed to Isobel.'

'Get to the point. He's with the army.'

'No longer.' Forbes turned to a dark corner behind the massive bellows. 'Come out, Angus.'

The young man, wearing only a ragged shirt and the remnants of a kilt, emerged from the shadows. Iron cuffs linked by a heavy chain encircled his wrists.

'He was taken by the Redcoats and escaped,' said Kennedy.

'Heavens above!' exclaimed Jean. 'Get those things off the poor lad.'

'That's my point, my lady.' The smith ducked forward, rubbing his hands like a housefly. 'Striking the shackles, you see, would be construed as aiding a rebel. I would hate to be the one to bring down the wrath of the authorities upon our community.'

'Don't be absurd,' said Jean. 'He's one of our own. Get them off him immediately.'

'If you just cut the chain, Duncan, you wouldn't be actually striking off the shackles,' said Forbes.

The smith's face brightened. 'That'd do it. Lady Kynachan ordered me, and I didn't actually take off the shackles.'

He prodded the boy to the anvil on which he laid the chain.

'I'll pay you when I can,' said Angus.

The smith shot a furtive glance at Jean. 'There'll be no charge, Angus.'

With a few accurate blows, Angus was free of the chain. He still wore the iron bracelets, but that did not seem to detract from his relief. He thanked the blacksmith and said he would tell everybody how kind Kennedy had been to him. Jean moved restlessly, irritated by the smith's fears.

'No, no, boy,' Kennedy said, waving his hammer in alarm. 'We'll keep it a little secret between us.'

'Angus, where have you been?'

'Inverness, my lady. I escaped a week ago.'

'When were you taken prisoner?'

'After the battle.'

Jean's heart gave a lurch. 'Were you in the charge?'

'Of course, my lady. I was taken in the midst of the enemy. I was stunned.'

In the dim light of the smithy, it was just possible to see that his cheek and temple were stippled by black specks, grains of powder tattooed into his skin by the shot that had disabled him.

'Then you must have news,' said Forbes.

'What sort or news? I've been travelling in the hills for a week. No, not much news.'

'You booby!' shouted Forbes. 'News of the Kynachan men. You're the first one home. Do you know where the rest are?'

'Yes,' he said, almost surprised by the question, for the answer was obvious to him. 'They're still at Drummossie. The charge, you see – we made it farthest in the charge. They're dead.'

The ensuing silence was broken only by the sound of the pony cropping the grass outside. When Jean spoke, her voice was gentle.

'Dead? All dead?' she said. 'How many Angus? Who? Who did you see?'

Angus stared into the glowing charcoal of the forge. 'I saw Willie Kennedy fall, and Balnarn. Drumnakyle was in front of me. I saw him die – he and his son.'

His audience was aghast.

'I saw George Cairney take a bayonet in his chest. He dragged three of them down. And we ran through the gap this made in their line. Our lads fought like lions.'

'What of my husband, Angus?' asked Jean. 'Did you see Kynachan die?'

In the ruddy light, Angus's face was wet with tears.

'No, my lady, I did not see him die. I saw my brother struck down beside him. When I last saw Kynachan he was wounded but still alive.'

Jean's face was chalk-white, her voice almost cooing. 'Wounded, you say. How so?'

'I would have said he was hurt in the arm, my lady . . . when I saw him.'

'In the arm,' she whispered. 'That doesn't sound a killing wound.' She raised her voice. 'Is that all?'

'Yes, my lady. His sword was broken, but when I saw him he still lived.'

A tiny change of tone in his voice made her persist. He was reluctant to meet her unblinking eyes.

'Angus, look at me. You have something more. What is it?'

He hung his head and kicked at a worn ox-shoe half-buried in the dirt floor. He was like a small boy caught out in a lie.

'It's just stories I heard in Inverness.'

'What stories?'

'We can't be sure, you see – not really sure.'

'Tell me.'

'I heard that some of our worst wounded had been carried to a bothy. I heard that Kynachan was there – Shian, too. The Redcoats burned it down. All inside perished.' Angus stole a glance up from the floor. 'I'm sorry, my lady. I was told by a man who saw the dead. He said it happened as I say.'

Forbes and Kennedy glanced fearfully at Jean. Her face revealed nothing but her concentration on Angus and his words. None of the three saw the blood seep between her fingers from the cuts made by her nails in her palms.

'But you do not know for certain Kynachan was amongst those who died there?'

'All I know is what I have heard.'

For a few moments Jean was silent, her eyes empty and far away.

'How many of the men from Kynachan do you believe still live?' she asked.

Angus lifted his head. Tears had cut pale rivulets through the dirt on his face.

'None lives, my lady. None save myself.'

Jean left the smithy and let the pony have its head back across the moor. She had told Forbes to give Angus money so that he and Isobel could flee south to the Lowlands. She would reimburse the man.

The pony veered away from the house and followed a path to the woods. The animal halted on the ridge at the edge of the trees above the little bothy where she and David had spent those blessed hours of their wedding night. As Jean sat in the saddle, overlooking the strath, sunshine pierced the heavy clouds. The light glinted off the river and turned the tumbling burns on the opposite hillside to silver.

She dismounted by a gnarled rowan, its branches shaggy with lichen, and leaned against its mossy trunk. Only then did her grief burst from her. In a monstrous act of birth, it left her helpless, her body racked with sobs.

Carried by small running boys with frightened faces, the word flashed round the townships. Donald broke the news to Janet and Clementina. Later that day, when he saw the old grey pony grazing loose in the paddock, he left the grieving household and followed the path past the walled garden.

He found his mistress amid the damp dead bracken. She was curled in a shivering ball, still pressed against the trunk of the rowan. Removing his plaid, Donald wrapped it round her and lifted her to her feet. Jean rose without resistance, but her eyes were dull, and she did not look at his face.

'Poor lassie,' he murmured, gently moving the damp hair from her cheek. 'You'd be better off at home. You come away with me.'

Suddenly her eyes focused on his, and once again tears were spilling down her pale cheeks.

'He's dead,' she whispered.

'I heard, my lady.'

'They burned him, Donald.' Her voice rose to a crescendo. 'They burned my darling man. They burned my heart and my life. *They – burned – my – life.*'

Her cry rang through the wood, putting a clattering pigeon to flight. She stumbled back, hands clutching her head. A storm of weeping shook her frame, and Donald gently drew her into his arms, stroking her hair, hushing her, comforting her, as he would a child or a distressed animal.

Gradually, she quietened.

'Nothing is real,' she whispered. 'Nothing is real but this terrible thing inside me.'

The pain was one she could not bear. She wanted to spew it out but knew that nothing in this life could ever, ever make the suffering go away.

The intensity of her grief made Donald's heart desolate.

'We need your strength,' he said.

'I'm not strong.' Still her voice was very low. 'But I must be – for his children and his people.'

'Blessed are they that mourn, for they shall be comforted,' Donald said, and he felt his own tears. 'Davie, now. He's the lucky one. He has fulfilled God's purpose. The Lord is still testing us who are left.'

'I never knew you had such religion in you.'

'It has its place, my lady.'

'But what can God want of me?'

'That's not for us to know. We each do what must be done. Time alone will tell us what that's to be. Come along, lass.'

He led her gently back along the path to the house. There she was folded into the bosom of her mother-in-law.

45

Bissett Advises

Even as the people of Kynachan closed their doors on their grief, the soldiers stepped up patrols in the search for rebels, weapons, and any remaining flickers of Jacobite resistance. Many clans had remained loyal to the government during the Rising, and now the garrison guarding Tummel bridge was augmented by a company of McLeods. Led by a Whig son of the laird of Glen Lyon, they went on the rampage, looting and burning towards Rannoch and the west. They hit the lands of Struan in particular, forcing the old chief to fly for his life. He took refuge at Carie, on the south side of the loch, and his beloved Hermitage was burned to the ground.

From farther north, rumours of the terror unleashed by Cumberland on the people of the Highlands filtered down to Atholl. It was said that the Redcoats were raping and murdering their way through the glens, uncaring about connections between their victims and the Rising. In their search for anything worth stealing, troops were even digging the dead from their graves to rob them of their shrouds. Drovers attending the sales in May at Kinloch Rannoch, when Jean sold her cattle and goats to meet debts, told tales of wild auctions in Perth, where soldiers disposed of goods that they had looted from all over the Highlands, and of gaols in the south crammed full of suspected traitors.

Within days of the battle, the Scottish Episcopalian church was singled out as a fountainhead of Jacobitism, and its places of worship were closed. Soldiers stripped the chapel at Fortingall of bibles, prayer books, and furniture, and burned them before the shocked people. It was made illegal for more than five persons to meet in an act of worship outside the form of the established church. For a second offence, the officiating clergyman faced transportation for life.

So long as the community's culture survived, the authorities knew that the Highlands would remain a continuing source of instability to the realm. Over the succeeding months,

Parliament passed acts forbidding the possession of arms and the wearing of the kilt or tartan. The Gaelic language was suppressed, and the power of the chiefs was broken for ever by the abolition of Heritable Jurisdictions, which transferred the administration of law from the lairds and chiefs to professional sheriffs and magistrates.

In Atholl, in order to preserve the estates of his master, Commissary Bissett brought all his skills of diplomacy into play. Duke James had always supported the government, but many members of his family had played a prominent part in the Rising, and many of his vassals and tenants had joined them. As a consequence, the authorities were reluctant to accept Bissett's protestations of loyalty and repentance on Atholl's behalf.

When Bissett rode up the track to the mansion house of Kynachan in June, with four Hessians as his escort, he was the first civilian visitor since the battle. Taking the commissary's cloak and hat, Donald ushered him into the dining-room. Janet greeted him, bedecked in the full mourning she had worn on the death of her husband a decade earlier.

'Mr Bissett. A glass of whisky? I'm afraid we have no claret.'

'Madam. I am sorry that we should have to meet in such unhappy circumstances.'

The commissary shook his head sadly, and the tight curls of his full-bottomed wig trembled along with his jowls.

'I came to see how you were,' he said. 'I hear melancholy reports of losses during the recent unpleasantness.'

'The men of Kynachan are dead,' said Janet, pointing him to a chair. 'My son and all who went with him – save one lad.'

Bissett clicked his tongue in sympathy as he sat down. 'Such tragedy, but I have heard that the authorities suspect your son may still be alive and in hiding. They believe the report of his death may be mistaken – or a device to deflect the search for him.'

His shrewd eyes scanned Janet's face, ready to weigh the truth of what she said.

'They are wrong. He is dead.'

'I see.' Bissett's glance roved the room, noting the shattered windows, the deep scores in the mahogany table made by careless soldiers, and the blood stain across the ceiling beneath the nursery. 'My deepest sympathies. However, my immediate priority is to foster a good relationship between the people of Atholl and the soldiers.'

'I won't quarrel with that,' said Janet.

'Good. We must put past divisions behind us. From His Grace down to the most humble, we all wish life to return to normal as soon as possible.'

Janet's politeness fractured. 'Return to normal!' she cried. 'How can life ever be normal again? Did you not hear me, man? *They're all dead!* Just one half-daft laddie came back.'

'Yes . . . yes.' Bissett's jowls shook the more, and he trumpeted into his handkerchief to cover his confusion at her distress. 'Understand me, madam. I am here purely to offer my assistance. It is both my duty, since your son is – was – His Grace's vassal, and my own desire, because of the kinship and mutual regard between our families.'

'I note your words,' said Janet.

'All arms have been ordered to be surrendered to the authorities. Unfortunately, innocent people are being killed by some of the king's troops when they attempt to hand in weapons, so I am organising the collection myself.'

Jean had come downstairs and she stood in the doorway.

'We have no arms, Mr Bissett,' she said. 'The men on Kynachan handed in their arms on Drummossie Moor.'

'Madam.' Scrambling to his feet, Bissett took in her widow's weeds and her gaunt face, which was etched with lines of strain and grief. 'I . . . I'm most distressed to hear your news. Allow me to express my sympathy and to offer any help that is within my power.'

Jean inclined her head in acknowledgement.

'The soldiers,' prompted Janet.

'Yes, the soldiers are troublesome,' said Jean. 'They frequently burst into this house and ransack it from top to bottom without so much as a by your leave.'

'Mm . . . yes. I'm afraid the whole country is under military law, and the troops are charged with arresting all those who were lately in rebellion. I believe that many such men are skulking in the hills.'

'Indeed,' said Jean, her face expressionless under his scrutiny.

'Perhaps you had not heard,' said Bissett, but his tone revealed a degree of scepticism. 'Although I have no direct control of the king's troops, I shall be placing meal and fodder near the bridge to supply them. I trust this will forestall any need on their part to . . . to live off the land.'

'I hope your trust is not misplaced. Perhaps those who harried Struan's estate were merely bandits?'

Bissett gave a nervous laugh and fluttered his hands in embarrassment. When he went on, he asked if the people had food and whether the crops had been sown.

'God willing, the season will be bountiful,' said Jean.

'Excellent. And last year's harvest was good? There is meal still in store?'

Jean cast him a cool look. 'Alas, no. The contributions of the tenantry to his Royal Highness's cause were such that nothing was left.'

'And February's feu duty for His Grace?'

'You will have to take the clothes from our backs, sir.'

Bissett's hands were fluttering again. One fell upon the whisky glass, and he took a restorative sip. 'Never, madam. But the disruption over the past months has led to inordinate costs for His Grace, not to mention non-payment of his rents.'

'I sympathize with the troubles of His Grace. I hear he has recently fallen into the hands of his enemies.'

'The duke?' For a moment Bissett was puzzled, then he frowned in irritation. 'You are mistaken, madam. His Grace is at court. His brother William, one-time Marquis of Tullibardine, has lately been justly apprehended and will stand trial as a traitor. It is unwise to confuse the two.'

'Unwise? Should I take lectures from you on matters of wisdom?'

Bissett gave a heavy sigh. 'Madam, if it is true that my cousin is dead, I regret it. He was a fine man and a fine husband. But he brought about his own destruction. Whether he has brought about that of his family as well, remains to be seen.'

Indignant, hot words began to spill from Janet's mouth, but Jean hushed her.

'Let us hear what Mr Bissett has to say,' she said. 'We have little to lose.'

'There lies the trouble, Lady Kynachan,' Bissett said. 'I fear you have much still to lose. After the Rising thirty years ago, participants were attainted with high treason, and their estates forfeit. I should be surprised if the same course was not followed on this occasion. Your late husband' – he nodded towards Janet – 'was successful in regaining his lands, but this time it may very well be different.'

Jean had drifted over to the window and rested her hand on the sill. She watched a clutch of freshly-hatched chicks scramble over the midden and behind her she could hear her mother-in-law softly weeping. Jean stretched her fingers as she felt the warmth of the sun on her skin. On the stone sill beside her hand, her wedding band cast a pale yellow reflection. Eventually she spoke.

'David is dead. Is that not punishment enough for him and for us?'

'Who knows? It is my strong advice, madam, that you seek allies in the world as it is now and as it shall remain – for the sake of your son, if not of your husband. Jacobitism is dead. You must renounce it.'

Jean turned away from the window and looked at the commissary. 'What you say may be right, sir, and kindly meant, because I believe you when you say you have a regard for us.'

'Yes, indeed, madam.'

'But to do as you recommend would be to betray the memory of my husband. You must know that cannot be.'

Unhappy, Bissett puffed his cheeks.

'David was never less than honourable. He never did less than his duty to his king, his people, and to God. It is my duty to him and to all he believed to do no less. I am no Vicar of Bray. I am wife and mother of Kynachan.'

Bissett struggled to his feet. 'I admire your spirit, if not your nous, my dear lady. I'll do what I can for you.' He paused. 'I note the absence of your sister-in-law, Clementina. I trust she is in good health?'

Jean inclined her head. 'She is, sir.'

'Good, good.' Bissett gnawed his lip. 'I believe she and Bohally had a . . . an understanding?'

'You are well informed, Mr Bissett.'

'Yes – well, he and many others sought for rebellion are yet to be accounted for. The government will show no mercy on those suspected of harbouring or assisting traitors.'

Bissett averted his gaze from the contempt on Jean's face.

'Have no fear, Commissary. I shall betray Bohally to your butchers the moment the opportunity should arise.'

Bissett looked at her with sadness. 'My dear, I hope you learn to temper your tongue. Otherwise . . .'

46

On the Hill

Life always overwhelms Death. One is a great roaring cataract, unstoppable, impelled by Time; the other is still.

The days grew longer. The stock moved up the flanks of Schiehallion, following the growth of grass as the last crevices of snow disappeared from its rocky summit. Naked children splashed in the icy burns and ran to their mothers, teeth chattering, their hands clasping tickled trout. Soldiers marched to and fro along the high road, but otherwise Kynachan seemed cut off from the rest of the world.

On estates where the laird had been less of a Jacobite, many tenants had paid to avoid joining the army. But not on Kynachan. There, women might have had some justification for blaming their late master for their current misfortunes and for transferring their resentment to his family. But Jean shared their plight. Moreover, the romantic story of her wedding and metamorphosis of their dashing laird into Doting Davie had amused and warmed hearts beyond the confines of Atholl. The other widows knew what Jean had lost, and none felt less than pity.

Over the months that followed, the little cave in the midst of Kynachan wood sheltered a variety of fugitives – amongst them, John Stewart, son of the Laird of Foss; Woodsheal, commander of Struan's men at Culloden; the nephew of Stewart of Tempar; and Allan Stewart of Innerhadden, who whiled away his time writing songs and verse. They spent much of the summer surviving as parasites on the Kynachan cattle that grazed the woodland.

After some days, grumpy Garth had had enough of Bohally's company and left the cave. He climbed over the hill and took shelter on his own estate in the chasm of the Keltney burn, beneath the ruin of the Wolf of Badenoch's castle. The Camerons departed to join the caterans of Rannoch, and Bohally rebuilt his strength and chafed against the inactivity. The guard on Tummel bridge slowly relaxed; the level of patrols diminished. It seemed that the authorities believed Atholl to be pacified, and its people gave thanks.

At Pitkerril, George Cairney's widow sat in front of her cottage, chatting to a neighbour. Both were spinning flax in the warmth of the August sun. Before them stretched the great flank of Craig Kynachan and the burn that ran down the glen to the distant meandering river and the sparkling blue patch of Loch Tummel. The older woman was talking about her grandson, shepherding that morning in the hills.

'It's not easy for a fatherless lad,' said the neighbour, another Culloden widow, who was carrying a seven-month foetus and had two little girls by her feet.

'Aye,' said the boy's grandmother. 'He's still very wee.'

'I haven't seen Kynachan's lad about much.'

'He'll be missing his father.'

'So's yon.' The young widow nodded in the direction of the hillside. 'Kynachan's boy shouldn't be in that house all the time. He'll grow soft and prone to weakness and agues.'

'But he'll be company for his poor mother,' said Mrs Cairney.

She made an adjustment to her thread. After a moment, the two wheels were clicking again in soporific rhythm.

'They say her face is set like stone these days,' said the neighbour.

'Och, it's a shame. Losing her mother and sister so recently, too. D'you mind when she and Kynachan kissed the day the men went down to England?'

'Aye, but she's not the only one without her man.'

'She's a lady, not as used to hardship as we are.'

'She's better off than us.'

'Aye,' said Mrs Cairney, although neither woman seemed that sure.

Then they went silent, each lost in memories.

High on the west shoulder of Schiehallion that golden morning, Mrs Cairney's grandson sat lazily watching his sheep. Round him the purple heather was drowsy with the murmur of bees working to pack the townships' skeps with the sweet distillation of summer. Suddenly, he jumped to his feet. Out of the corner of his eye he had spotted movement far below. Scattering one or two sheep, he ran to the vantage point of an outcrop.

Towards him along Strath Fionan – the bright strath –

between the mountain and Craig Kynachan, a band of soldiers was loping past a reedy lochan dotted with waterfowl. They travelled along the track from the direction of Rannoch, scattering packs of whirring grouse. As the boy watched, part of the troop branched right, up a path over the shoulder of Schiehallion that led towards the shielings behind the mountain in Glen Mor. The main body continued into Kynachan. Then the young shepherd launched himself down the hill, leaping from boulder to boulder, to warn his grandmother.

Mrs Cairney paused in her conversation with her neighbour and listened indulgently to the child's breathless report.

'Well done, Jamie, you're a clever lad. Soldiers? Highland soldiers?'

The little boy gave a vigorous nod.

'A company of the Black Watch, no doubt. They'd not be above taking a sheep for their dinner. You'd better get back to them.'

Her grandson scampered off up the hill. Round the quern stones, by a cottage door, a brisk argument broke out amongst the sparrows. A battered black tomcat asleep on the turf wall of the adjacent kaleyard opened a yellow eye, yawned mightily, and twisted round to expose its other flank to the sun.

'Look there!' said the neighbour, puzzled.

Not a hundred yards away by the burn, half a dozen Highlanders were loping purposefully through a skimpy crop of ripening oats.

'What are they up to?' wondered Mrs Cairney aloud. 'The Redcoats were here just a few days ago.'

'They could be bandits from Rannoch,' suggested the younger woman.

'Nonsense. Even if they were outlaws, they wouldn't dare harm us with all the soldiers about.'

'I'm not trusting anyone, Mrs Cairney – not these days.' The young woman ushered her children into her cottage, came back for her wheel, and shut the door behind her.

Save for Mrs Cairney, the township was empty, the running men out of sight behind the trees that fringed the burn.

Then the little boy was rushing towards her.

'Campbells! They're Campbells! It's the Argyll Militia!'

47

The Raiders

The Campbells came down the glen, fifty of them, driving the livestock they had already taken from the shielings. Penning the animals in the miller's field at Daloist, they split up – some going to Drumnakyle, others to Balnarn and Foss. A group of fifteen continued down the high road towards the mansion of Kynachan.

The harvest had begun in the river meadows. From the shade of a willow, Janet supervised the tiny children, who played in the burn near where it joined the Tummel. Out in the heat of the sun, a line of women from Bohally and the mains, their sickles swinging in time to their song, were bent over the rigs. In their wake – swallows and martins darting through the swarms of disturbed insects – the young gathered the sheaves and stooked them to dry.

Straightening her back, a girl from Bohally looked over her shoulder and stared puzzled at a column of smoke rising behind Craig Kynachan. Then she gave a cry, pointing her sickle towards the track. Like a wolf pack, dark-tartaned Campbells were flitting between the trees.

The singing broke off. The women stood frozen. Jean dropped her sickle and ran towards the track, her skirts and hair streaming behind her.

Two of the militia, their muskets carried at the trail, detached themselves from the others and jumped over the wall to intercept her. She easily evaded them, and they found themselves surrounded by a dozen sickle-wielding women screaming abuse. Jean raced up the hill just behind the rest of the Campbells.

The back door was open. Donald was slumped, dazed, in a corner of the kitchen, his head bloodied. Upstairs, the house resounded with thundering feet. Jean knelt by his side for a moment, then a crash and a bellow of laughter brought her running through to the hall and up the stairs.

The long-case clock was lying on its face across the parlour floor. A musket butt had been driven through the slope of her writing desk, smashing the ink pot inside. Its contents had splashed her papers, and, to the amusement of his two comrades, the face of the musket wielder.

'Get out of this house!' shouted Jean, enraged.

The Campbell nearest the door wheeled in surprise and grabbed her wrist, twisting it hard so that she was forced against the wall.

'Ho! Look here.' He dropped his musket, his free hand groping the thin material of her skirts. 'A rebel bitch needing to be tamed.'

Thrusting his hand between her legs, he grasped the top of her thigh and swung her off her feet. He then crossed the room in a few strides and threw her onto a heap of blankets that had been torn from the bed.

Jean half rolled as he flung himself on top of her and she fought to get clear of the suffocating filth of his plaid. Cursing, the man tried to claw his way through the layers of material still separating them.

'Where's the plate, woman?' shouted one of the others, who was tipping the contents of the bureau to the floor and smashing the empty drawers against the wall.

Jean's head came clear and she saw a brass candlestick on the floor by her head.

As she stretched for it, a boot pressed cruelly down on her wrist, and the blade of a broadsword flicked the candlestick out of her reach. The boot lifted and was launched in a great kick at her would-be rapist, which sent him sprawling across the floor.

'You're a pig and you've always been a pig,' said the owner of the boot, an officer who had just come into the room.

Jean sat up, pulling her torn bodice across her breasts, as the young officer's pale eyes looked on dispassionately.

'If you must debauch yourself with rebels, you might choose one with a bit more flesh,' he said to his men. 'This one's as scrawny as a kain hen.'

Jean flinched as his sword stirred the hem of her gown.

He chuckled. 'I'd also prefer one a bit younger myself.'

The hatred in her eyes killed his mirth.

'And one with a sweeter disposition,' he added. 'I am Hector McNeil of Ardmainish, woman, Lieutenant of the Argyll Militia. How dare you interrupt the king's troops about their lawful business of punishing rebels?'

'Punishing rebels!' she spat. 'One old manservant, his head cracked open, and a handful of women. King's troops, indeed. You're beneath contempt – Campbell cowards, thieving because you know our menfolk are away.'

'Away? Dead, I heard,' the officer said, curling his lip. 'Exterminated – as traitors deserve. Who are you?'

'I am the wife of Kynachan.'

'The devil's own whore! Perhaps a whipping might teach you respect.'

The other two soldiers had paused in their destruction of the room to enjoy the discomfiture of their comrade, who was picking himself off the floor. Now one stepped forward, his face troubled.

'Perhaps we should let her be,' he said.

The Campbell officer was surprised. 'What's with you, Archie?'

'I heard from Knockbuy's drummer about her, Ardmainish. She promised a decent burial to his daughter, the lass who was shot.'

'With the blood of that innocent on her hands, she dares accuse us of making war on women,' sneered Ardmainish.

'Slit the bitch's throat,' growled the man who had attacked her.

The other soldier doggedly continued. 'Hamish of the Drum gave her his blessing,' he said.

'Knockbuy's drummer!' snorted the officer. 'Why should I care?'

'He knows the old ways, Ardmainish,' the soldier said, uncomfortable. 'For her charity, Hamish of the Drum put Lady Kynachan under the protection of a spell. That's what I heard. Hamish was crossed once by my mother's cousin. The milk dried in all our kinsman's cows, and within two years he was dead of the pox.'

Ardmainish took a step back.

'And remember the wee lassie was a Campbell. This woman treated her with respect and honour.'

Ardmainish thrust his sword into its sheath. 'The creature is lucky. Do her no harm. Shut her in the stable, then we'll finish here.'

'Finish? What do you mean finish?' demanded Jean, as she was dragged to her feet.

The lieutenant of the militia gave her a mocking bow. 'My dear lady, your husband and that brigand Bohally treacherously attacked our comrades here in the spring. It is our duty – nay, our pleasure – to punish rebels and confiscate their goods. It's fortunate for you that we may wish to garrison this house. Otherwise we'd put it to the torch.'

For an hour Jean remained locked up, straining for every sound as the militia ransacked the mansion. At some point, the wooden bar across the door was drawn back, daylight flooded in, and Clementina was hurled to the floor. The Campbells were rounding up the livestock, she told Jean, and were beating any who dared interfere. The ferry had taken Janet and the children to hide on an island in the river.

Then the raiders moved on, and the two women were left in silence, their arms round each other for comfort. Once they heard a distant scream and a bellow of anguish from a cow, another time three faraway musket shots. Shortly after, Jean tore a hole in the thatch and Clementina climbed through to unbar the stable door.

Torn bedding and broken furniture littered the yard. The two women went into the house through the front door, which was askew, prised from its hinges. The interior had been wrecked and anything worth stealing had been taken. The kitchen was empty, a puddle of blood showing where Donald had lain.

They hurried down the track to the mains. Two cottages and a barn were on fire. Fuelled by the dry thatch and roof timbers, smoke and flames towered into the sky. From the other townships, more columns of smoke rose above the strath.

Clementina joined the loose chain of women and children shuttling buckets across the hundred yards of stubble from the burn, but their task was hopeless. Already one roof had fallen in, and nothing would quench either fire until each ran out of fuel, leaving smoking stone shells.

Sitting on the field-wall opposite one of the blazes sat the slumped, dejected woman whose home it had been. Two small children wept by her feet. Her twelve-year-old son, his face smoke-blackened and tear-streaked, stood by her, a protective arm round her shoulders. The possessions they had rescued from the flames were at their feet – a few scraps of blanket, a stool, a couple of wooden bowls, and horn spoons. The cooking pot would be recovered undamaged when the fire died down.

'Have many been hurt?' shouted Jean above the roar and crackle of the flames.

'I don't think so, my lady,' the boy answered. 'Donald had a knock on the head but he's down by the river with your children.'

'Oh, thank God,' exclaimed Jean. She looked more closely at the boy. One side of his face was swollen, an eye half shut. 'Are you all right yourself, Malcolm?'

'Aye.'

'What happened to you?'

The boy swallowed a sob. 'They took our goat and the geese. I tried to stop them but I had no arms. A Campbell hit me with the hilt of his sword. It doesn't hurt. They scattered the peat from the fire onto the bedding.'

'You're a brave lad, Malcolm. Your father would be proud of you.'

'I'm the man now, my lady.'

That day, the militia visited every settlement on Kynachan and neighbouring Foss. There, the elderly laird had carefully avoided committing himself to either side, although one of his sons had joined the Atholl Brigade along with a dozen tenants. None of this made any difference to the Campbells. They stripped both estates of livestock. They looted and smashed the smithy, the mill, and every cottage, burning the homes of any who dared show resistance. Stolen chattels weighed down stolen ponies. Driving scores of cattle, sheep, and goats before them, the raiders withdrew towards Rannoch and Argyll.

Protestations to the military authorities at Blair and Castle Menzies were met with indifference. They were still looking for rebels along the Tummel, particularly Stewart of Kynachan. In their opinion, to relieve his estate of some of its movables was almost laudable, the more so when carried out by Campbells, who had been so badly served in the Atholl raid.

Meanwhile, the people shared the little that remained. The harvest had barely started when the raiders struck, so the corn at least was safe, along with the few beasts overlooked in the woods and corries at the time of the attack. Then, too, Lady Kynachan could afford to waive rents, as she had had the foresight – or so people saw it – to restore her credit by selling much of her stock in May. In instances of real hardship, should the winter not be too long, she could supply sufficient meal to sustain life.

Ten days after the Campbell raid, the alarm was raised that Redcoats were approaching the bridge from the north. The people melted into the heather. An army of over a thousand soldiers, in four regiments, marched through the estate, heading for the pass and Strathtay.

A little later, Rob Ban Robertson of Invervack, the white-haired old man who had brought Struan home in General Cope's coach, tricked a group of eight Redcoats a mile or two north of Tummel bridge. He leapt out from a clump of bushes, brandishing his illegal broadsword as they lay resting, their muskets propped against a boulder. Threatening them with a dozen imaginery companions at his back, he took their weapons and disappeared. The people exulted.

As the country became peaceful, patrols and searches grew perfunctory. Those still skulking in the hills found it safe to return to their homes, where they lived quietly, ready at the first warning to flee back into the woods.

Then, one day, a visitor came to call upon the house of Kynachan.

48

A Visit From Kinnaird

On an October afternoon, when the birches were turning to
gold, Alexander Stewart of Kinnaird picked his way delicately
down the track to Kynachan. Behind his glossy chestnut mare,
a valet led two pack ponies. A few yards to the rear marched a
couple of Redcoats hired from the regiment at Crieff to protect the laird from the desperadoes who, he was convinced,
were swarming the countryside.

In the yard, Kinnaird dismounted, and the soldiers accepted
a few coppers from the valet. By the time Donald came
to the door the Redcoats had begun their march back to
barracks.

'Oh, disaster!' Kinnaird declaimed.

He was examining the façade of the house, the gaping
windows, the bullet-pitted rendering, the crudely repaired door.
Peeling off his doeskin gloves, the music master put them in his
hat. His wig was long, and the well-cut blue coat beneath his
cloak flattered his narrow frame.

'Aye,' said Donald, admiring the lace cuffs of the visitor's
shirt, his buckskin riding breeches, and shiny black boots.
Kinnaird had obviously continued to prosper during the past
year.

'What happened? Rebels?'

'Mostly Campbells. A wee bit Redcoats. It's been quite busy
round here.'

'It has been a hard time for us all.'

'Aye. For some more than others,' said Donald, earning
a sharp glance. 'Her ladyship's in the garden. Wait in the
dining-room. You'll find a chair in there. I'll tell her you're
here.'

A single dining chair remained intact, its leather seat slashed
and carefully stitched. One of the table's legs had been replaced
by a rough plank, and an iron strap held together the broken
top. Set either side were two crude benches. Oddly unscathed,
the portrait of John Stewart still stared out imperiously from

the wall by the fireplace, and, directly opposite, one of William Mercer, more enigmatic, stared back.

Jean entered, dressed in black, with Donald in tow.

'Alexander,' she said, giving him a warm smile as he bent to kiss her hand, no longer soft-skinned and pale but calloused and at the moment stained by juice from the blackberries she had been picking. 'How kind of you to come to see us.'

'Jean, so it is true.'

'What?'

He gestured to her black gown. 'David. In Edinburgh he is thought to be still alive.'

'Here at Kynachan we lost him six months ago.'

'Alas' – Kinnaird pulled a lace-edged handkerchief from his sleeve and dabbed his eyes – 'such a dear, dear friend.'

'He was that. Are you fatigued after your journey? I apologize, but our hospitality is not what it was. Still, I trust you will be with us for a few days.

'Just for the night, I fear,' said Kinnaird. 'As well as with you, I have business at Blair and at my estate. Then I must return to town.'

'I am sorry to hear that. We shall see if we can find a fatted calf for you tonight.'

'My dear Jean, I trust you don't think of me as a returning prodigal – least of all, as your son.'

'The prodigal son was destitute, Alexander. He would not have had fine silver buttons on his coat.'

Kinnaird gave a small pleased smile. 'In spite of these straitened times, one tries to maintain standards.'

'One does,' said Jean. 'If you would excuse me now, Alexander, I have work to do. You will be in the mid-room. Donald can take care of you and your man's needs, and we shall meet this evening.'

'Good. I must change from my riding clothes and I have some papers to study – and by the way, Donald, there's a bottle or two of claret in my bags. Be careful when you take them upstairs.'

That evening, Kinnaird emerged from his room to join the ladies in the parlour and tell them of his travails.

'We've had a dreadful time of it in Edinburgh. When David was there last autumn the castle garrison actually fired on the town. An acquaintance of mine, a silversmith, was killed.'

Kinnaird gave a deprecating little laugh. 'But you would know all that. David must have told you.'

'I'm pleased to see you've come through all right yourself,' said Janet.

'With difficulty. So much disruption everywhere! It's been difficult to get supplies from the south. An estate like this provides all one needs. You're so lucky.'

'Aye,' said Jean. 'And you must miss Barbara?'

'Oh, yes, such a grievous loss. I am still most upset. But the end was peaceful, as it was for your mother. Your aunt Meg was by their sides, and I am comforted that they have been received into the bosom of our Maker.'

In the candlelight, the three ladies of Kynachan were spinning or sewing. The children were in the nursery, having earlier been paraded before the visitor for his tentative inspection. Furnishings in the rest of the house had been sacrificed to supply the parlour with some semblance of normality, and the dim light hid the worst of the darns and repairs.

'Of course, I have no idea what condition my own estate is in. I hope the tenantry have prospered, as I've had no rents for a year. I believe, though, that those who did not fight for the rebels were forced to pay for those who did.'

'Your neighbour in Wester Kinnaird, young Gilbert Stewart, died at Culloden,' said Clementina.

'No!'

'As did Tempar, Foss's son, Young Inchgarth, Balnacree, and many others.'

'How dreadful. I had no idea so many had fallen.'

'Every man but one from Kynachan was killed.'

'So Donald mentioned. Such tragedy,' sighed Kinnaird. 'But is there news of Bohally? Did he die with the rest of them?'

'Oh, no,' said Clementina. 'Charlie was wounded but he's fine now. He'll be over for supper; in fact, he should be here any minute.'

Kinnaird nearly spilled his claret on his blue satin breeches.

'Here?' he gasped. 'But if he's not dead, he must be a fugitive. We lay ourselves open to arrest if we have anything to do with him.'

'Is that so?' said Janet. 'In that case, Clementina deserves to be drawn and quartered. She kisses the brute.'

'Mother!'

'This is most upsetting,' said Kinnaird. 'What if I am discovered here with him?'

'If soldiers come, we will have warning,' said Jean. 'We have learned to be absent when the servants of King George call by. We now keep watch day and night. The Campbells will not take us unawares again. But I doubt they'll be back. They know we have nothing left worth stealing.'

'Although it is known that I am no Jacobite, I cannot afford to become suspect,' said Kinnaird. 'That is why David trusted his business affairs to me.'

'You won't be suspect,' said Jean in an attempt to soothe him. 'I assure you that we'll know if any danger threatens.'

Kinnaird remained unassured. 'Humph!' he grunted. 'I was prepared for some risk from bandits but not from the king's soldiers.'

The door opened, and Bohally strode into the room.

'Kinnaird, you old shirker! I heard you'd come creeping over the pass on your fine mare. With a brace of tame Redcoats, too.'

As Bohally greeted the ladies – Clementina meriting a swift peck on her cheek – Kinnaird scowled at him. Bohally's frame carried less weight than it had the previous summer, and he walked with a limp. But he still seemed larger, and louder, than life.

'Charles, I can't say I was expecting to see you.'

Bohally's eye lit on Kinnaird's glass. 'Claret! A hint of returning civilization. And what a pretty man you are, Alexander. Better to wave the bow of a fiddle than a broadsword when there's powder-smoke about, eh?'

'The only sensible course, wasn't it, Bohally? And as to my new tailor' – Kinnaird smoothed a tiny wrinkle from his silver-embroidered white satin waistcoat – 'he made a cloak which was presented to His Royal Highness, the Duke of Cumberland, by some Edinburgh admirers.'

'I was told your escort is at the inn at Coshieville, where they'll be dead drunk by now. Their colonel's not going to be pleased with you when you get back to Crieff.'

'Hang the man,' said Kinnaird dismissively. 'I shall be returning by Dunkeld.'

'Chasing rents on your estate?'

'Yes. And I am not quite clear about my brother's activities during the last year.'

'No-one is. Slippery fellow, your sibling. When we marched north in February, he just faded away. One moment he was there, the next he'd gone. No-one's seen him since.'

'I did expect John to keep out of trouble,' said Kinnaird.

'He tried. Heavens, how he tried.'

'Good, and if only others had been as prudent. So many wasted dead. Such foolishness.' He raised his glass in a toast. 'Absent friends.'

Jean broke the short awkward silence.

'Alexander,' she said, 'I should explain that none of us has any doubt that the path we followed since the landing of the prince was right. We may have lost a battle and more – much more – but our cause was not foolishness. Davie has joined the company of martyrs in heaven.'

'Well said, Jeannie,' said Bohally, a tear spilling down his cheek as he filled a tankard from Kinnaird's bottle.

Kinnaird, too, was moved. 'My dear Jean, you make me ashamed of my worldliness. So many young widows and orphans – life is a cruel taskmaster.'

'Cruel indeed,' intoned Donald from the doorway. 'Your supper's ready. Green broth, boiled pike, and roast moor fowl. And there's claret, if he keeps it coming.'

And Kinnaird did keep it coming. He also did his best to drink his share before Bohally's thirst dried up the supply. Janet and Clementina drank their modicum from horn beakers, but Jean took little. Kinnaird passed on the Edinburgh gossip, telling of romances and scandals and of the authorities' irritation at the fashion for tartan amongst ladies of quality.

At the other end of the table, Bohally and Clementina had their heads close together. In the light of the candles, her face shone with joy and love, her eyes fixed on the half-smile on his lips in anticipation of his growled, whispered words. Occasionally they laughed, awaking melancholy echoes in the hearts of the other two women.

Even Kinnaird noticed. He reached down the table to pull the claret bottle to him. 'When are you going to marry the girl, Bohally?'

'Would you advise her to marry an unrepentant Jacobite?'

'Certainly not, but she's obviously used to you, else I can't think why such a pretty girl would want such a hairy ruffian.'

'Mr Stewart, he's not a ruffian. He's handsome and kind.' Clementina put her hand over Bohally's.

Embarrassed, Bohally fiddled with his spoon. 'I was waiting until an amnesty,' he said. 'Being chased across the hills by Redcoats is no qualification for a husband.'

Kinnaird raised his glass.

'To the future prosperity of you both.'

49

A Proposition

In the parlour after dinner, blankets had been draped over the windows, and a well-banked fire of peat supplemented the light from the two candles. Clementina took up her harp and sang a soft Gaelic song of love and loss. On a cushion by her side, Bohally sat on the floor. From time to time, he absently massaged his thigh as he gazed into the hearth through the blurred spokes of Janet's softly clicking wheel.

Opposite, Kinnaird had Jean's ear, but her face was turned towards the fire, shielded from his eyes by her hair.

'I admire your courage, Jean, especially since I can understand your grief. When I lost your dear sister, I thought my heart would break.' He took a sip from his glass. 'She was very like you, you know.'

'I always felt she was a kinder, gentler soul.'

'But not so beautiful.' He gave a slight frown. 'I don't mean, of course, that I agree with your estimation of your character, my dear.'

Jean lifted her head with a small smile. 'I wish no gallants, Alexander.'

'But you're still young,' protested Kinnaird. 'David would not have wanted you to become a nun.'

'My life is now dedicated to preserving the estate, so that David's line will continue here.'

'Ah, that brings me to the nub of the problem. If I may speak bluntly, David's affairs are in some disarray. He made me executor of his will, and he has considerable debts. At the moment, his creditors must hang fire, since the authorities consider him merely missing.'

'But he is dead. He was burned alive after the battle.'

Kinnaird shook his head. 'But he's not legally dead. That's what's important.'

'Is it, indeed?' said Jean, her voice cold. 'Commissary Bissett suggested that David might be attainted of high treason and the estate confiscated.'

299

Kinnaird clicked his tongue to show his doubt. 'That is still possible. The list of the most prominent traitors, those who hold estates from the Crown, has already been published, but a secondary list is being prepared and it may well name David.'

Jean gave a weary sigh. 'Where does all this leave us?' she asked, looking into the shadows, where Clementina continued to sing for her spellbound lover. 'These machinations seem childish games compared to the business of avoiding Redcoats and finding food to stay alive.'

'You must take your predicament seriously,' said Kinnaird. 'Very seriously indeed. Even if David is not attainted, your difficulties are far from over. Your son is heir to Kynachan, and he is a minor. Under the law, the revenues of this estate would be enjoyed by the duke until young John reaches the age of twenty-one. Without those revenues, you will have no way of paying the annual rents on your debts.'

Jean was further dismayed. 'You mean that whatever happens the law will take Kynachan from us?'

'Yes,' said Kinnaird. 'Without forethought, your difficulties will overwhelm you.'

She studied the fire in stricken silence.

'I could not bear for the family to end up in rooms in some teeming tenement in Perth or Edinburgh,' she said after a few moments. 'You imply there is a way through this maze of obstacles. Do you see hope for our future?'

Kinnaird leaned his head closer. 'I do, my dear. As you know, until my grandfather lost this estate it had been in my family for generations. David was soft with the tenantry and kept rents too low, which is one reason for the extent of his debts. Now, most of those tenants are dead, and you'll never get decent rents from widows. Kynachan needs new blood.'

'Charlie and William Stewart of Garth are to be Johnny's guardians. Neither they nor I would dispossess folk whose loyalty to Davie has cost them so dear.'

Kinnaird patted her hand. 'A couple of skulking rebels are unlikely to prove satisfactory protectors for your son. But your concern for the welfare of the tenantry is thoroughly admirable and yet another indication of the virtue of your character, my dear.'

'You should be a courtier, Alexander,' said Jean, withdrawing her hand.

'Do not dismiss me lightly. I can secure your future and the future of your dear children.' He nodded across the room.

'And, of course, that of your mother-in-law and Clemmie. I have decided to offer you my hand in marriage.'

'*What?*'

At her cry of astonishment, Bohally momentarily looked up, but almost immediately the soft beauty of Clementina's song recaptured his attention and he returned to his visions within the glowing peats.

Kinnaird gave a complacent chuckle.

'I know it's a surprise to you, but I have thought about it carefully,' he said. He paused deliberately to look across at the swell of her breasts and her skin, which reflected the golden glow of firelight above the dark silk of her gown. 'You are still a beautiful woman, Jean, with much to offer a man. And by marrying you, my family would be back on our ancestral lands.'

For some seconds, Jean studied him, her face expressionless. Then her gaze returned to the fire.

'Well? What do you say?'

'I . . . I'm speechless.'

'I can understand that,' said Kinnaird. 'You must have thought the future bleak with a mountain of debt and no husband to protect you.'

'Bleak certainly describes my life without David, but I still have that part of our uncle's legacy that is not ensnared in the courts.'

'That sum is not enough. I know, because I enjoy the portion bequeathed to Barbara.' He leaned closer, so that he could whisper into her ear. 'It was you I always wanted, Jean.'

She cast him a sidelong glance. 'Do you not remember? You asked me to marry you once before but you withdrew your suit.'

'That was before you had a tocher. Then David came and swept you off your feet with his talk of fate and spectres. A mere Edinburgh music master could not match the gallant laird.' Kinnaird's tone was bitter. 'David had you and Kynachan – the two things I most wanted. I married your sister, but she was second best. And she gave me no heir.'

'Poor Barbara,' whispered Jean. 'She truly loved you.'

'Aye. Then she died. But I always knew David's Jacobite opinions could be his downfall, so I stayed close to him, involving myself in his affairs and biding my time. Now my opportunity has come.'

Jean sat there, frozen.

'I have bought up more of the bills in which David pledged Kynachan as security. When the estate reverts to the duke, he will be liable to pay me. Were we to wed, Bissett would undoubtedly advise His Grace to save cash by granting the charter of Kynachan to me. Since I am a known supporter of the government, he would welcome me as a vassal. Marry me, and the future of you and your family is secure. If we have a son, he would be heir to Kynachan. If not, I shall bequeath the estate to John on my death.'

For a further long moment Jean was silent, her face averted. Then she spoke.

'You astonish me, Alexander. I have known you for many years and would never have thought such a stew of schemes bubbled away inside your head.'

'A dish with as tasty morsel as you at its heart, my dear, is worth such time and trouble.'

'A distasteful comparison, but when do you expect your stew to be ready for consumption?'

Kinnaird's lips twisted in a grimace. 'If the estate is not confiscated, nothing can happen until David is declared legally dead. How long it may take the government to concede that he has faced a higher authority than theirs, I cannot say. If Donald's account of David's death is true, it is a cursed nuisance that the body was burned beyond recognition.'

Jean shuddered. 'You should choose your words with more care, sir.'

The music master was instantly contrite. 'That was thoughtless of me. I apologize.' He moved his head close to hers again, so close that his breath stirred the fine hairs on her neck. 'I take it that you agree to my proposition?'

It had grown late. Clementina and Bohally mumbled their excuses and disappeared. Janet was finishing work at her wheel.

'I . . . I shall need time to consider,' said Jean.

'Of course.' Kinnaird pulled back. 'I have presented you with a great deal to think about but I am a patient man.'

'What if I say no?'

He made to get to his feet.

'Of the two things I want, I would obtain only one – Kynachan. You and your family would be expelled from here and would sink into poverty and obscurity, just another broken family.'

Jean rose and kissed her mother-in-law goodnight at the parlour door, then stood waiting for Kinnaird to cross the landing to his own room.

'You have a rare way of wooing, Alexander,' she said.

A wry smile flitted over his lips.

'You are an intelligent woman,' he said. 'I would not insult you by assuming you could feel love for me so soon after David's death. You will marry for love – but love of your children, not for me. That you will come to feel later.'

50

A Woman's Weapon

The following morning, Kinnaird left for Blair. Through the open shutter of the dairy, where she and Janet were at work scouring utensils before the next milking, Jean could follow his progress for some twenty minutes as the music master's little caravan climbed the track above Bohally.

One time when she raised her head, she saw him rein his horse and turn to look back. From there, high on the hillside, she knew that Kynachan was laid out before his eyes from the bank of the Tummel to the peak of Schiehallion.

Janet followed the direction of her troubled gaze.

'I saw him whispering away in your ear last night. You mustn't mind Kinnaird. He's a sneaky wee man but he was always a good friend to Davie.'

All at once, unwanted and unexpected tears spilled down Jean's cheeks.

'Och. Don't fret, my dear.' Sympathetic moisture welled in Janet's eyes.

'I'm sorry,' said Jean, running the back of her hand over her face. 'This usually happens only when I am alone.'

'I know, I know,' said Janet. 'We all miss him.'

'In the night, when I stretch out to touch him and he isn't there, I know hell can have no torture for me that can compare to my desolation.'

'Oh, Jean.' Janet crossed the floor and put her arms round her daughter-in-law. 'Davie would be proud of you, just as I am proud of you.'

When Jean disengaged herself, once more in control, she picked up a wooden bowl and dipped it into a trough of cold water.

'Kinnaird reckons he is in position to take Kynachan, whether or not the estate is confiscated.'

'The devil!' exclaimed Janet.

Jean explained the situation. Janet was aghast.

'We can all stay here,' Jean told her, 'but only if I consent to become his wife.'

'And what did you say to him?

'I didn't have to say anything. He assumed my consent.'

'And do you?'

'I would die rather than betray Davie with any man, let alone one such as Kinnaird. He disgusts me.' Jean's voice was scathing.

Janet put down the horn spoons she had just scrubbed. At the open door she glared up at the tiny horseman, who still looked down from the hill, and shook her fist. The movement must have caught Kinnaird's eye. He flourished his hat before disappearing behind a rocky ridge.

'The man's a salacious rogue – sniffing round you, subtle as a billy goat. The world is in his favour these days, but you'd think such a parlour warrior would have a greater understanding of a woman's heart.'

'Was I wrong to refuse him?'

'Of course not. But it'll be dreadful to have to leave here.'

'Do you not think I know that?' cried Jean. Once more she began to weep, this time silently, and her tears fell into the trough. She took up a bowl, rinsed it, and placed it on the shelf above.

Without warning, the shelf gave way. The heavy plank and the basins it carried crashed down into the trough. A wall of icy water surged over the rim and slapped against Jean's belly. She shrieked and staggered back.

'God damn!'

She turned a shocked gaze towards her mother-in-law, her hand flying to her mouth.

Janet's lips quivered, her shoulders heaved, and she let out a guffaw. Suddenly the two women were helpless, and the small shed reverberated with laughter.

After half a minute, Jean wiped her eyes with the sodden corner of her apron. 'That will teach me to give way to self-pity.'

'I can't recall the last time I laughed like that,' said Janet, gasping.

'I have been behaving as if Davie was going to come home and magic our troubles away. But it is now up to us.'

'In that case, you'd better get out of that gown before you catch your death.'

Janet moved to gather the fallen basins, but Jean caught her arm.

'No, wait a moment,' she said, the glimmer of an idea in her eye. 'Our problems begin when Davie is declared dead and we lose the Kynachan rents. The authorities believe he still lives. What if we were to pander to their belief and started a whisper that he wasn't killed but had fled overseas? We might keep him alive for a year or more – and Kinnaird out of my bed.'

'It would certainly buy us time,' said Janet. 'Time changes circumstances.'

'Kinnaird fights with the law, but the law can be a woman's weapon too. I can use it to protect us. Let me think on it.'

The following day, a boy was sent round the townships to summon the leading tenants to the mansion. John Forbes and Duncan Kennedy arrived from Daloist, Catherine Stewart from Drumnakyle, Christina Reid from Balnarn, and Janet Cairney from Pitkerril. Donald led them into the dining-room, offered them whisky, and went to fetch her mistress.

The women sat uneasily on the benches. The two men lounged against the fireplace.

'Does anyone know what this is about?' asked Mrs Stewart.

'No,' answered Mrs Cairney, 'but when a laird asks to see the tenants it's not usually good news.'

'There's precious little of that about,' said Catherine Stewart, sipping her whisky.

'A year ago, in this very room, Kynachan went against my advice and ordered us to raise the fighting men,' said Forbes. He shook his head. 'A sad, sad day.'

'Aye, but our men were heroes,' Mrs Cairney said.

'Dead heroes are two a penny on Kynachan,' said the miller. 'We could've done with some cowards, who'd be here to put in a day's work.'

Nobody round the table ventured to disagree. Forbes helped himself from the whisky jug.

'I can tell you one thing,' he continued. 'Even if the Redcoats stay away it'll be a tight winter. Those damned Campbells.'

The door opened, and Donald ushered in Jean. She had changed out of her workaday shift into a black hooped gown. The women rose; Forbes and Kennedy gave small bows.

Jean greeted them and got straight down to business.

'All of us here know how parlous is our state,' she said. 'But

I want to discuss with you the gravest of our concerns and see how we can help one another.'

'It's the bairns,' said Christina Reid. 'They're the ones who suffer most. Two mothers on Balnarn have lost their milk, and we've nothing left but a single nanny goat.'

'It'd be a great help, my lady, if you would waive payment of the rents that were due at Martinmas,' said Duncan Kennedy.

There was a murmur of agreement.

'Aye,' said Mrs Cairney. 'And we're bound to provide two men and two ponies to bring down the peat for you. We've no ponies and no men.'

'I know,' said Jean. 'I shall be asking for no more than anyone can give. I was doubtful about telling you of the peculiar difficulties I face but I feel it is your right. Especially as it affects you.'

The tenants exchanged uneasy glances.

'One way or another, the estate faces confiscation. It looks as though this family will lose Kynachan.'

'What will become of us?' asked Mrs Cairney in horror.

'I doubt it'll make much difference,' said Forbes. 'I regret your predicament, my lady, but a change of laird will matter little to the people.'

'How can you say that,' cried Catherine Stewart. 'Doting Davie was like a father to us.'

'He's dead,' said Forbes. 'The world moves on. Is there any indication who the new laird might be?'

'Stewart of Kinnaird,' said Donald, and spat into the fireplace.

'The Waddling Laird? Yon who rode through yesterday with a couple of soldiers at his heels?' said Kennedy.

'The same,' Jean confirmed.

'His race had Kynachan before. He will respect our ways,' one of the women said.

'That was half a century ago,' said Mrs Cairney. 'And he's a man of the city. I hear he's a harsh landlord to the folk on his estate.'

'He says my husband was too soft with his people,' said Jean. 'He is also of the opinion that women are not so productive and so should not hold tenancies. He will wish to maximize rents.'

'Who does he think does all the work?' said Mrs Cairney, indignant. 'All men are good for is drinking, sitting on their arses, and fighting.'

'And dying,' said Jean.

'Aye – and dying.'

'He'll still need a miller,' said Forbes.

'That he will,' growled Donald, 'because he'll find you dead in a ditch.'

'With your throat slit,' added Duncan Kennedy.

Forbes threw the smith an angry look. He was used to the man's support.

'Stop this!' snapped Jean, obtaining instant silence. 'Times have changed. We can no longer defend ourselves with weapons of war – that we all know. We must now use our wits, and I can use mine as well as any man.'

Forbes frowned. 'What can you do against the Redcoats? They're sure to be back.'

'I can use the law. None of us here took up arms against the German lairdie. Therefore we have as much right to protection under the law as any Edinburgh clerk or London alderman.'

She paused and looked from face to face.

'For a start, I propose we join together to take out a legal process against the officer of the Campbell militia who led the raid last month and sue him for the losses we suffered.'

'They'd never allow that,' exclaimed Forbes.

'Even if we do not win, we shall have enmeshed the man in the law. More fortunes have been frittered away in the courts than on the gaming tables, and he will know it. No licensed freebooter would dare set foot on Kynachan again.'

'That's not a bad idea,' said Kennedy, looking at Jean with new respect.

'It's a very good one,' said Jean. 'I shall start the action. Those who wish to claim for loss may join me. If we are united, it will be the better for us.'

Kennedy offered his immediate support; Mrs Cairney and Catherine Stewart followed suit. A look from them to Christina Reid ensured her participation. That left Forbes.

'Think of yon ditch,' said Donald ominously.

The miller gave in.

51

Bohally Takes the Plunge

That winter the Highlands were again ransacked by Redcoats. Folk retreated to the remote high haunts of the ptarmigan, where, blasted by blizzards, they eked out a grim existence relatively safe in caves and shieling huts. The soldiers' passage through the glens was marked by burnt clachans, whose black ugliness was softened beneath coverings of snow.

Thanks to the efforts of Commissary Bissett, who toiled to maintain a structure of civilian authority as a buffer between country people and the military, the core of Atholl was spared the worst of the depredations, although twice Redcoats swept through the land in search of rebels.

On each occasion, news of their approach flushed Bohally and other wanted Jacobites, who returned to the woods and corries. Old Struan Robertson was carried on the willing backs of his clansmen into the secret depths of the Black Wood of Rannoch.

On their second visitation, following the stabbing of a soldier in an alehouse quarrel at Bunrannoch, the troops torched every surviving township and mansion house between Tummel bridge and Loch Rannoch. Impotent, their owners could but watch from the crags above.

When word spread through Atholl that Hector McNeil of Ardmainish had been summoned before the Lords of Session to answer Jean's process, the military became wary. Kynachan was a legal quicksand best avoided, and the Redcoats who replaced the Hessians on the bridge were warned to take care when they searched the estate for its elusive laird.

The second summer after Culloden, the weather was kind, and the quality, if not the quantity, of crops good. In the south of England, thousands of cattle died of plague, which raised the price of the few carefully husbanded beasts from the Highlands.

In June 1747, the government declared an amnesty for most of those who had taken part in the rising – with the exception of notorious Jacobites such as Bohally and, of course, David. Two months later, the bill was enacted banning the Highland garb. Jacobite supporters or not, anyone wearing tartan coats, plaids, kilt, or trews was liable to six months' imprisonment for the first offence and seven years' transportation for the second. Thus deprived of the distinctive dress worn by their ancestors from time immemorial, Highlanders were bitterly angered and immensely distressed. Into the dye tubs of every township went the subtle tartans and kilts were stitched up the middle to create a pastiche of breeches for the shamefaced men.

From the remnants of Lochiel's regiment, destroyed alongside the Atholl Brigade at Culloden, emerged Duncan Cameron, who had been Episcopal priest at Fortingall before the rebellion. His chapel had been laid waste, its contents burnt by the soldiers, but he came to the house of Kynachan each Sunday morning to hold a service in the parlour. Under the law, no more than four other people could be in the room, so he preached from a window to a small congregation in the courtyard below.

In early autumn, a company of soldiers marched into Kynachan. At this same time, high on a hillside north of the river, Bohally was supervising the cutting of a millstone from a granite outcrop to replace the old one at Daloist. He had seen the Redcoats on the high road. When a boy brought news that the soldiers had made camp on the haugh land a few hundred yards east of the bridge, where drovers had traditionally pastured their cattle, the big laird had collected a few handfuls of meal and taken to the heather to wait for the troops to go.

But they stayed. They repaired and enlarged a bothy by the river, and cut timber from the Wood of Kynachan, squandering it on their fires. They posted four men at the inn to strengthen the guard on the bridge and strolled about the townships, where their English dialect met astonished, suspicious Gaelic. Folk were unused to English Redcoats who offered money instead of stealing. But soon their presence was taken for granted and even appreciated. A permanent company by Tummel bridge removed any lingering fears of forays by other troops, as well as enriching the estate's economy.

The situation did not suit Bohally. Instead of the comforts of home, he was back in the chasms and corries, lashed by wind and rain, while the new soldiers saluted their way politely round Kynachan.

By the end of the first week a handful of scraggy cattle, calves at foot, were once more wending their way from the mains each day to Bohally's old hiding place in the cave. There he would wrest milk from the reluctant teats of the cows while his disgruntled foot held back the bawling calves. Sometimes Clementina would drive them, but – particularly when the weather was poor – the beasts were in the charge of a lad.

The lieutenant and ensign commanding the detachment quickly seized upon the mansion house as an oasis of civilization in a desert of Gaelic barbarism. So they took to dropping by for tea in the afternoon.

Clementina was to blame. When the soldiers first arrived to investigate the nest of the most notorious local Jacobite, she had just returned from playing milkmaid in the wood. Upon flinging open the newly repaired front door – cheeks flushed, her smile sunny – she instantly captivated both young officers.

The lieutenant, a vicar's son from Devon, could only stare; his more polished junior, the seventeen-year-old sprig of a Shropshire squire, with a freshly purchased commission, took off his hat and abased himself in a worshipping bow. Before the outraged Donald could prevent her from asking them in, Clementina had the two stammering in the parlour, tea cups balanced on their knees. In the row that followed the officers' departure, Clementina argued and won her case. Good relations with the military, which she had just initiated, could not but benefit everyone on the estate.

So, in mid-afternoon twice a week, the two officers found that their duties permitted them to ride out to the house. They would deposit their hats and swords in the hall and partake of tea in the parlour while the women did their spinning.

The younger man, Ensign Arkwright, had four sisters at home. Even Jean warmed to him when he would crawl about the floor with little Jessie bouncing excitedly on his back and using his wig to belabour his rump.

On one such afternoon, the lieutenant was discussing matters of sport, when Donald interrupted to announce to Clementina that she was wanted in the kitchen.

'Can't you deal with it?' she complained.

'It involves Tearlach Mor,' said Donald, speaking Gaelic.

'Can I be of any assistance?' asked the lieutenant.

'No,' said Donald, rounding on him. 'If I'd wanted you, I'd've asked. But I can think of no reason why I ever would. So shut your mouth and drink your tea.'

'I say!' said the startled lieutenant.

'Donald, that's impolite,' said Jean.

'Aye, my lady,' answered the steward.

'I can't think why you put up with him,' said the ensign after Clementina and Donald had gone. 'We certainly wouldn't tolerate that sort of behaviour from a servant at home.'

'Donald would die for us,' said Jean.

'Yes,' drawled the youthful officer. 'I can see that might be in his favour.'

In the kitchen, two new girls from the mains – a scullery maid and a kitchen maid, both thirteen – stood by the fire. They nudged each other knowingly when Clementina entered.

'What about Charlie, then?' she demanded.

'Hush!' said Donald, gesturing towards the back door.

'What's wrong?'

'Yon Redcoats in the parlour brought a man. He's in the stable with their horses and some whisky. We don't want him to hear.'

To Clemmie's increasing exasperation, Donald put his fingers to his lips and crossed to the open window, which overlooked the walled garden. Cupping his hand to his mouth, he produced an odd wail.

Bohally's head popped above the level of the window sill.

'Charlie!' cried Clementina in astonishment.

'Hush,' said Donald and Bohally in unison, provoking an outburst of giggles from the girls.

'What was that dreadful noise about, Donald?' said Bohally, heaving himself up.

'It was the cry of the curlew,' replied the steward proudly.

Clementina strode to the window. 'Charles, are you mad? What are you doing away from the wood? You know the Redcoats are in the parlour having tea.'

Bohally was now inside, grinning hugely and giving her a proprietory pat on the bottom.

A cocked hat appeared at the window above the features of the priest, Duncan Cameron. Donald hauled him into the room. He frowned at the two servant girls, whose mirth was threatening to spiral out of control.

'Mr Cameron,' said Clementina. 'What on earth are you doing here?'

'Oh, for heaven's sake, Bohally. You drag me over the hills from Fortingall, and the lassie doesn't even know we're here to marry her?'

'What!' exclaimed Clementina. 'Marry me? Now? Here?'

'Hush,' said Bohally, taking her by the hand.

'I'm the groomsman,' said Donald. 'And that little pair' – he gestured at the girls – 'will have to do as your attendants.'

'But . . . but . . . '

'I thought we'd better do it now rather than later,' said Bohally cheerfully. 'With all these Redcoats scurrying about shooting off their muskets, a man must set his house in order. If I get killed, I want you to be able to live at Bohally and have all the rights of my widow.'

'What a horrid idea!'

'Marrying me?' He laughed, taking her hand and patting it. 'Anyway, it's high time you and I were wed. I need an heir, and you're not getting any younger.'

The priest lifted his eyes to the ceiling.

Clementina snatched her hand away. 'Damn you, Charlie Stewart!'

'Hush,' said Donald with a chuckle. 'He's jealous of yon Redcoat boys making eyes at you.'

The best man ducked to avoid the groom's blow.

'See,' said Donald, full of glee. 'The man's pea-green.'

'Stop it, you two,' said Clementina, stamping her foot.

'Thank you,' said the priest. 'Can we please proceed?'

'No,' said Clementina. 'Quite apart from calling me an old crone, he hasn't bothered to ask if I'll marry him.'

'Of course I have. You said yes last year.'

'That was then. This is now.'

'Enough, girl,' interrupted the priest. 'You want to wed him, he wants to wed you, and that's why I'm here. And any minute one of those Redcoats is going to come through the door asking for a drop scone. Bohally, take off your bonnet.'

The priest drew a prayer book from his pocket and asked for the ring.

'I gave it to you,' said Bohally.

'Oh, so you did.' Cameron fumbled in the pocket of his waistcoat, eventually producing the gold band.

'I want it,' demanded Donald. 'I'm the groomsman.'

He took the ring and bit it, giving a grunt of approval at whatever he thought had been revealed.

'It's not how I imagined it would be,' sniffed Clementina.

'Och, but it's lovely, Miss Clementina,' said one of the bridesmaids.

'Aye,' said the other. 'He's risking his life to marry you. It's like a story.'

The priest cleared his throat and indicated that the couple

should kneel. He opened the prayer book and read out the English words.

'Dearly beloved, we are gathered here in the sight of God, and in the face of this Congregation, to join together this man and this woman in holy Matrimony . . .'

The bridesmaids, having only the Gaelic, understood not a syllable, although the priest's chanted cadences and sonorous delivery held their attention, as did the romantic scene before their eyes.

The marriage service continued. Suddenly the door burst open, and there was panic. Priest and bridegroom dived for the illegal dirks in their belts. It was Jessie.

'Mama was wondering where you were, Aunt Clemmie.' The child ran into the room and came to a faltering halt, looking round her with interest. 'Why are you and Uncle Charlie kneeling on the floor? You'll get all dirty. And what's he doing here? The Redcoats'll have him.'

'Not if nobody tells them,' said Donald, taking her hand. 'You can stand by me and be maid of honour.'

'Before we have Cumberland turning up to act as witness, can we please finish this business?' pleaded the priest. He held his book up again and ran a finger down the page. Then he went on to read the final words. 'Those whom God hath joined together let no man put asunder. Thank Christ we're done.'

Snapping shut his prayer book, Cameron slipped it into his pocket and reverted to Gaelic. 'You may now kiss the bride, Bohally, and Donald can find us a dram to toast the pair of you.'

Bohally began kissing the bride with enthusiasm. Donald was quick to produce a jug.

'I got a very nice drop of whisky from Jimmy the Still,' he told Cameron.

'Up Rannoch? I didn't know Jimmy was in business again.'

'Aye, he's selling it to the soldiers.'

Easing the bung from the jug, the groomsman nodded at the newlyweds, who were still kissing.

'Before we have to chuck a bucket of water over them, I'd better propose the toast.'

'Wait,' said Clementina, tearing herself away from her husband. 'Give the girls a drink.'

'I want some,' said Jessie.

'You're too wee,' said Clementina.

Jessie's bottom lip trembled and she burst into a wail.

Before anyone could stop her, she had run from the room and slammed the door behind her.

'She'll have the whole house in here,' said the priest. He drained his quaich, threw it on the table, and was out of the window.

'Away with you, Charlie!' Clementina pushed her new spouse after the priest.

For a few moments Clementina stood by the window, looking after the two men. Just before they scuttled behind the half-finished garden wall, Bohally turned to blow her a kiss.

'Quick, Donald, follow me upstairs with some biscuits.'

In the dim hall, Clementina checked herself in the mirror and removed a birch leaf that had transferred to her hair from Bohally's coat. As she did so, she caught her own reflection grinning back at her.

When Clementina entered the parlour, she was the immediate focus of the appraising eyes of her mother and sister-in-law. Jessie's head was buried in Jean's lap, where she was sobbing out an incoherent tale of black ministers, Uncle Charlie, and whisky – all fortunately in Gaelic.

Clementina moved unobtrusively to her chair and pressed the pedal on her spinning wheel.

'What's wrong with the child?' asked the lieutenant.

Jessie lifted her sullen face. 'I wasn't allowed any whisky.'

'By God, ma'am. They start their tippling young in this country. Crying for her grog like a gouty old general.'

'Aye,' said Jean, casting her sister-in-law a cool look of enquiry.

'I hear your husband kept a fine strain of fighting cocks,' said the lieutenant, returning the conversation to the point where it had been broken off.

'He did. The Campbells ate them.'

'Barbarians!' gasped the ensign.

There was a thump at the door, and Donald swept in with a plate held high on his tray. Ignoring Jean, he marched straight to Clementina.

'Your biscuits, Lady Bohally,' he said.

'Clemmie,' cried Jean. 'Charlie's gone and done it?'

'Don't weep, Jeannie,' said Clementina, jumping up and throwing her arms round her sister-in-law.'

'I'm so happy for you,' sobbed Jean.

Janet began to sniff, and tears welled in Clementina's own eyes. Donald beamed. Wriggling out from between her mother

315

and aunt, Jessie stumped indignantly over to the two Redcoats.

The lieutenant looked bewildered.

'They're a bit dribbly,' Jessie explained.

'Yes,' said the ensign with sympathy. 'My sisters leak some-times too.'

52

A Visit to Perth

The symbolic end of the old order came fifteen months later, in the spring of 1749, when in its eightieth year the turbulent life of the chief of Clan Donnachaidh came to a peaceful close at Carie. Turning out in their thousands, the men of Rannoch and Atholl marched fourteen miles behind his coffin. The cortège wound its way through the ancient Robertson lands in Glen Errochty, long since held by the dukes of Atholl, and ended at the churchyard at Struan.

Soldiers still maintained the peace, pursuing ever smaller bands of fugitives, who lived in the hills on the proceeds of cattle theft and banditry. Some of these desperadoes had been in hiding since Culloden, some had refused to give up their arms or submit to the restrictions on dress, but the line between honourable reivers and common outlaws had become increasingly hard to determine.

The secondary list of traitors, which included Bohally and David, was never promulgated, and Clementina and Charles were able to live openly at Bohally. At Kynachan, Jean's little family flourished. John, the only one old enough to remember his father and to have been touched by the events following Culloden, became a familiar sight round all the estate's townships. At the same age, David had already been sent to school in Perth, but Janet was in charge of young John's education, Greek and Latin being supplied by Duncan Cameron.

Harvests were good, livestock fattened, prices remained high, and the soldiers bought the extra butter, eggs, cheese, sheep, and goats. Cash, previously a rare commodity in the Highlands, became more and more common, especially since demand remained strong for the linen spun by every woman in every township.

The smith, Duncan Kennedy, had raised money from his fellow tenants to match the sum provided by Jean, and Ardmainish was sucked ever deeper into the mire of the law. When exposed, the treatment meted out on Highland folk by Cumberland's troops caused revulsion throughout the nation, and this kept the case alive. But the authorities could not allow so dangerous a precedent to be created, for the way would have been paved for other innocent victims to lodge a host of claims against the military. Eventually the process snagged on the rocks of bureaucratic opposition.

Kinnaird paid an occasional call on Kynachan, but Jean gave him no answer to his marriage proposal. She spent months poring over her father's old law books and had cooked up a scheme to counter the music master. Now she bided her time. Since David's affairs were in limbo until the legal declaration of his death, the estate's revenues were still free to pay annual rents on his debts.

Then, at the end of 1750, Kinnaird set in motion the registration of David's will, which, once proved, would make official the laird's death at the battle of Culloden. Immediately, Jean left Atholl for the first time since that fateful day. Accompanied by her son and Jamie Kennedy, the offspring of David's old gillie, she rode to Perth to consult her lawyers.

Almost four years after her husband's death, the Lady of Kynachan showed little of the suffering she had endured in the intervening period. Yet the naïve Edinburgh girl was no longer. Jean's face had gained in strength and resolution, which added to rather than detracted from her beauty. A faint tracery of lines about the eyes only served to highlight her fine bone structure, and sadness had bestowed on her a certain stillness. This gave her an air of mystery

The little party was welcomed into the old Mercer townhouse by Meg, who flung her arms round her visitors.

'My darlings,' she exclaimed. 'John, you're so tall – and Jean, you look as lovely as the last time I clapped eyes on you.'

'You too, Meg,' replied Jean.

Meg laughed. She was ten years older than Jean and had burgeoned into ample middle age, a fact not concealed by the wide hoops and large red and yellow checks of her gown. Releasing Jean, she buried John's head in her massive bosom, causing him to twitch like a nervous deer.

'You monstrous liar!' boomed Meg. 'I'm as broad as a heifer these days. My heart bleeds for any horse that has to carry me.'

An arm still round John's neck, she led them into the oak-panelled parlour, where a coal fire blazed against the evening chill. Ordering tea from the latest of her line of handsome young footmen, Meg immediately banished the fatigue of Jean's journey by sweeping her into a cyclone of gossip and laughter.

When tea was over, the footman was delegated to take the boys on a tour of the city. After bundling them off with blazing torches, Meg sat Jean beside a jug of mulled claret and settled herself opposite.

'You're still missing him,' said Meg. It was a statement, not a question. 'Aye, if he'd been mine, I'd still miss him too. And all I ever had from him was a kiss.'

She laughed.

'The rogue,' said Jean. 'He never told me.'

'He wouldn't tell you he'd been kissing your maiden aunt. Back in the days when you were in the schoolroom, Davie kissed half the girls in Scotland, and I all their brothers. A wee minister once denounced me from the pulpit of the Canongate Kirk.'

'Meg, that's not something to be proud of.'

'Maybe not, but it's something to be remembered,' Meg replied comfortably. 'By the way, I saw Kinnaird in Edinburgh some weeks ago. He had a smirk all over his face and kept dropping hints I refused to pick up. What's his game?'

'You wouldn't believe the man. He thinks I might marry him in exchange for his financial support.'

Meg shook with laughter. 'And will you?'

'I shall never marry again.'

'Och, don't be so sure. There's a lot of living in you yet.'

'I'd sooner wed a donkey than Kinnaird.'

'Well, choose a pretty one.'

'Don't be indelicate, Meg. For me to marry again would be akin to eating a stale herring when you were replete with caviar.'

'Perhaps, but a body gets hungry.'

'Not this one. I have never felt the slightest hunger for anyone but Davie.'

'Poor Jean.'

'Don't pity me. I would have it no other way. Davie will fill my heart until the day I die.'

For a moment, Meg's lip trembled, then she briskly returned to business.

'You're here to see your lawyers, then,' she said.

'Yes. The moment David's will has been proved, John inherits. As he is a minor, however, the duke will take the rents of Kynachan, which will bankrupt us, and Kinnaird will take the estate.'

'So that's what the scallywag was after – Davie's lands as well as his bed. What are you planning to do?'

'Outwit him.'

'A slippery salmon like Kinnaird?' Meg looked sceptical. 'Thomas Bissett's no simpleton either.'

'Ah, but my campaign's been a long time a-planning, Meg. Remember, I first unsheathed my legal sword in the process against the militia.'

'And certainly dealt a telling wound to Ardmainish. I'm told he's for ever whingeing round Edinburgh, claiming to have been a simple soldier pilloried for doing his duty. He gets short shrift from society. But His Mightiness of Atholl may not prove such easy prey. He will have whole regiments of lawyers to defend him.'

'My plan's quite simple, really. The rents are transferred to the duke once John inherits Kynachan. But before that happens I sue for debt.'

'John or the duke?'

'John. When I was widowed, my marriage contract stated that the estate must pay me one thousand pounds Scots annually, a sum which has been accumulating since Davie's death.'

'But you can't possibly sue your own son!'

'Yes, I can,' said Jean. 'Johnnie will be unable to pay, and his trustees, Garth and Bohally, will renounce the estate to me. I am no minor, I keep the rents, and they continue to pay interest on our debts. Naturally, when Johnnie comes of age I transfer the estate back to him.'

'By God – but will it work?'

'I have examined the matter from every angle. There is nothing that can prevent it.'

Meg began to chuckle. Soon her ample body heaved with delighted laughter, and she had to dab her eyes with a handkerchief. 'You sly devil, it was a lucky day for Davie when he saw yon *tamhasg*. Kinnaird will have a seizure!'

Jean's week was busy with both lawyers and Meg's mantua maker. It was time, Meg had told her, that the Laird of Kynachan was better clothed than a country tinker. Evenings were spent socializing. Jean's now almost legendary romance with David, the tragedy of her young widowhood, and the cod-Jacobitism now fashionable made her a plum, and during her visit hostesses vied for her company.

On the evening before her return to Kynachan, Jean and Meg attended a reception at the town-house of the Murrays of Ochtertyre. After a light supper, the younger members of the party had begun dancing in one room, when Kinnaird appeared in the doorway of another, where Jean and Meg sat conversing on a settee.

Meg dug her niece in the ribs.

'It's time you mucked out that byre, my girl,' she said, and called out to Kinnaird.

'Curse you,' came a hiss from Jean.

Meg clicked her tongue. 'Temper, temper!'

As the music master approached, Meg rose with a creak of stays, patted Jean on the arm, and glided away. Kinnaird bowed. As usual he was immaculate.

'You are looking well, Alexander,' Jean told him.

'And you, my dear Jean. Your mother-in-law is in good health – and the children?'

'Yes, thank you. Even Euphemia is in the schoolroom now.'

'I am pleased to hear it,' said Kinnaird. 'You have heard about David's will?'

'Yes.'

There was an awkward pause. Kinnaird took a pinch of snuff. Trying to appear casual, Jean twirled her fan.

He said: 'In that case, I . . . I would be interested to know whether you have come to a decision concerning our nuptials.'

She said: 'Yes, much as I respect you and shall always be grateful to you, I shall never marry again.'

Her fan fluttered; his snuff spilled.

'But . . .' began Kinnaird.

'I have decided that it would be best if John renounced his inheritance to me. I am taking over Kynachan and its debts myself.'

Kinnaird's eyes bulged, his jaw dropped open.

'Naturally, I shall repay our bills to you, with full interest, as soon as possible. But I should be grateful if you did not press me.'

Kinnaird turned red. 'But, but, but . . . you're a woman!'

Then the full implications of her move dawned on him. He turned apoplectic.

'And you're not a minor! Damn you, Jean!'

Snapping shut her fan, Jean bestowed on him her sweetest smile.

'You are always welcome at Kynachan, Alexander,' she purred, rising to her feet. 'After all, you're part of our family. Now, why don't you join me in a reel? I have not felt like dancing since Davie died.'

53

Horse Thieves

The mills of the law grind slowly. It would take several months before the process came to fruition. As if resigned to the failure of his schemes, Kinnaird stayed away from Kynachan, particularly after brusque Black William of Garth met him at the cattle tryst in Crieff and threatened to give the music master a whipping for his conduct to Jean. From the legal regiments of His Grace of Atholl came not a word.

Spring led to summer, and throughout Atholl and Rannoch the talk was of a band of freebooters led by the Big Sergeant, one John Dhu Cameron. The Big Sergeant liked to think of himself as an honourable reiver, one of the last who fought for the old Highland way of life against the Redcoats, but times had changed, and many Athollmen now considered him little more than a common thief.

Down river from Kynachan, the glen of Fincastle stretched a finger of fertile land into the rampart of hills between the strath of the Tummel and the blair of Atholl. The young Laird of Fincastle had been a captain in David's battalion at Culloden and, along with Bohally and Garth, had been nourished by the Kynachan cows.

When six horses belonging to Fincastle's tenants were stolen in the night by the Big Sergeant's band, folk along the length of the Tummel were angered. The incident was more than the lifting of an odd sheep or goat, and the theft became the subject of heated discussion.

Jean had recently employed a grieve to manage the day-to-day workings of the mains. Like many Athollmen, his name was Alexander Stewart, and – like all Alexander Stewarts – he was known by his nickname. In his case it was the Bailie, a sobriquet he had earned many years before, when he was a follower of Rob Roy MacGregor, and people used to swear oaths of secrecy before him. Later, in the ranks of the Black Watch, the Bailie had been wounded at the battle of Fontenoy. In the aftermath of the rebellion, he had returned with his regiment to Castle Menzies, from where the Highland soldiers patrolled Strathtay. But chasing fellow Athollmen about the hills had not been to the Bailie's taste and as soon as he was able he had resigned from the Black Watch.

Late one midsummer afternoon, only three weeks before Jean would journey to Perth for the hearing of her case against John, the Bailie and Bohally were out on the slopes of Craig Kynachan, accompanied by beaters and a couple of deerhounds. The two companions were hunting mountain hares. Hunting the hunters, progenitors of the autumn's swarms of midges rose from the vegetation surrounding the peaty pools, which were half hidden amid tussocks of coarse grass and heather. A mile below, the whitewashed mansion of Kynachan was lit by the low sun, and distant Loch Tummel reflected the blue sky.

'The man's no more than a thief, Bohally, and no better than the villainous scum they put in the king's uniform nowadays. Yet he claims to be a man of honour.'

'You're quite right,' said Bohally.

The Laird of Bohally, who wore a pair of mustard-yellow breeches of nankeen cotton, looked far removed from the wild Highland fighting man of a few years before. Since his marriage he had grown somewhat stout.

The men sat on a large rock beneath a frowning granite spur, the Bailie holding the two hounds by their collars. The job of the beaters – young Kynachan and a couple of his contemporaries – was to flush hares and drive them towards the hounds.

'The Big Sergeant didn't come all the way from Rannoch by chance,' continued Bohally. 'What concerns me is that he must still be getting help from someone in the strath. Somebody had to tell him that Fincastle's tenants had horses worth stealing.'

'He won't find it easy to locate a buyer,' the Bailie predicted. 'They'll be on the lookout for those beasts all the way from Crieff to the Great Glen.

'Wake up, Bailie!'

A hare, its ears flat along its back, jinked across the hillside towards them. At the sight of Bohally's yellow breeches, it turned and ran up the hill. The Bailie released the collars of the hounds, and they flowed over the budding heather, hot on the heels of their quarry.

'We'll not be seeing those beasts again for a bit,' said Bohally.

'Och, yes. I can whistle them in any time. I trained them myself.'

About fifty yards away, half a dozen red-deer hinds came into sight round the hill. Like the hare, they balked at the startling colour of Bohally's breeches and turned down the slope.

'Why don't you whistle?' asked Bohally, watching the bobbing white rumps of the little herd vanish. 'You could send the hounds after them.'

Placing his thumb and forefinger in his mouth, the Bailie produced a loud summons. The sound echoed from the crag above. When nothing happened he whistled again. A meadow pipit dashed by, a merlin in close pursuit. Both men watched for the kill, but the birds too vanished over the hill. Another couple of hares went past, following the hounds' path through the heather. The Bailie made a final effort, then sat down and fished out a flask of whisky. Filling a short clay pipe, Bohally pulled out his tinderbox and was soon contentedly puffing tobacco smoke at the midges.

'Did you see the deer?' shouted John, as he and his companions came scampering towards them. 'Are the hounds after them?'

'They were fairy deer,' said the Bailie. 'A mist came down and swallowed them up. The hounds whimpered like fretful bairns and refused to follow them.'

'No!' exclaimed John.

'Aye. The hounds took off up the hill as if Auld Nick himself was on their tails. Isn't that right, Bohally?'

Bohally took his pipe from his mouth. 'Now they won't come back to the Bailie's whistle – and he says he trained them himself.'

'It's true!' exclaimed John. 'And it was the Bailie who trained the great hounds of Rob Roy.'

'Did he now?' said Bohally, looking askance at the Bailie. 'Rob's great hounds?'

'He'd got rid of his pack by the time you knew him,' said the Bailie, returning the whisky to a pocket and rising to his feet. 'Anyway, it's time I was getting back. I've a beast coming down from the shielings. She's due to calve and she's never easy. She went with that great bull from Drumnakyle.'

'She'll be fine on the hill,' said Bohally.

'I want to protect her byre against witchcraft,' said the Bailie. 'I think that may have been her trouble before, and she wouldn't be safe in the hills tonight, eh, Johnnie?'

'Not on midsummer's eve on Schiehallion,' said John. 'All the fairies are about.'

Returning home through Kynachan, Bohally found Jean and the two girls knitting beneath the oak tree on the knoll by the house. A gentle breeze tempered the sultry heat of the evening, and summer thunder grumbled over the mountains to the north.

'Did you catch anything?' Jean asked.

'No,' said John excitedly, 'but we saw some fairy deer!'

'Good evening, Charlie. Are Clemmie and the baby well?'

'Clemmie's fine. The brat pukes and shits and smells like them all.'

'Oh, Charlie!'

Jean put her knitting into a linen bag and stood up. They began walking down the knoll towards the mains.

'Is there any news about the stolen horses?' Jean asked. 'We must put a stop to that sort of thing.'

'It's a job for the soldiers.'

'But it's our folk who're suffering. I think you should put the word round that Tearlach Mor Bohally will punish anyone in the strath giving help to the thieves.'

Bohally laughed. 'Like everyone else, Tearlach Mor Bohally has turned his sword into a ploughshare.'

'You've still got a reputation, though,' said Jean. 'And at every ceilidh the whisky helps it grow. It would cost you nothing to use your fame.'

The little township was empty save for a small girl in charge of a flock of geese. The burned cottages had been rebuilt, and all external scars inflicted by the militia had healed. Jean and Bohally strolled as far as the wicket gate that barred the path to the ferry.

'It may be worth trying, Jeannie,' Bohally said. 'But it won't worry the Big Sergeant. I'll put the word about just the same and say Garth's in with me on this. He's ill-tempered enough these days to frighten anyone.'

One morning a fortnight later, a dozen Redcoats marched through Kynachan. Small boys had been reporting their movements from the hillsides ever since they left Blair. A few hours later, the young heir to Garth panted into the house of Kynachan with startling news. His father had been arrested, accused of entertaining bands of robbers from Rannoch, and now the soldiers were coming for Bohally. The shackled prisoner would be coming over the pass within the hour.

'What on earth can they be up to?' said Jean.

Donald, with John and the small messenger, had burst into the parlour, where Jean was talking business with the Bailie.

'A traitor laid information against him,' said young Garth. 'Alexander Stewart in Drumachuine.'

Jean turned to the Bailie. 'Do you know that man?'

'I think so. It'll be Alister Breck – a man of little account.'

The name struck a chord in Jean's memory.

Donald grunted. 'You remember yon bull that was stolen from Foss all those years ago?'

'Of course, Alister Breck!' exclaimed Jean. 'But I remember Davie saying he'd had him hanged in Edinburgh.'

'He was reprieved,' said Donald. 'They were that desperate for men. Of course, he deserted.'

Jean turned to the young messenger. 'Were any other names mentioned, Rob?'

'Oh, yes, my lady,' said the boy. 'Commissary Bissett and Mr Stewart of Kinnaird. They went with Alister Breck to get the arrest order.'

'The commissary and Kinnaird?' said the Bailie. 'Two careful men there.'

'Because they're careful, there must be something behind these arrests,' said Jean. 'Mr Bissett's a just man.'

'I wager Alister Breck is the Big Sergeant's informer. Having heard Bohally and Garth's threats, he'd be only too willing to lay false information.'

'Maybe, but why was his tale believed?' said Jean. Then her face cleared. 'Of course! What villainy! Garth and Charlie are Johnnie's guardians. Were they out of the way, they could not attend the court next week and Kynachan could not be conveyed to me.'

'By God, you may be right,' said Donald.

Jean turned to the Bailie. 'Get over to Bohally and inform Charlie what is happening. Tell him I think he ought to pay Alister Breck an immediate visit and persuade him to withdraw his accusations. Go with him yourself.'

'Can I go too?' asked John.

'Certainly not. It might be dangerous,' said Jean.

'Let the lad come, my lady,' said the Bailie. 'He's old enough, and I'll make sure he stays out of harm.'

'Oh, please,' John implored. 'Tell her I can go, Donald.'

'He'll be fine,' Donald agreed. 'The Bailie'll look after

him.' And he shot the Bailie a dark look that said he'd better.

Jean relented. 'But you must do exactly what Uncle Charlie tells you, Johnnie.'

An hour later, the soldiers knocked politely at the door of the Bohallys' cottage. Garth sat waiting on his pony in shackles. After asking around to no avail, the Redcoats squatted by the side of the track and drank the ale they bought from one of the tenants.

From higher up the hill, Bohally, the Bailie, and the boy looked down on the township.

'It's all right,' said Bohally. 'The soldiers aren't going to make trouble. Let's be off. The sooner we find Alister Breck, the sooner we're home.'

54

The Road to Blair

At ten o'clock that night, when the three companions looked down on Drumachuine from a small copse of Scots pine, the summer sky was still light. Below them, the township's eight cottages huddled by the empty high road. In the still air, a calf bawled for its mother. There was no other sound of life.

'Is Alister Breck at home?' asked Bohally.

The Bailie pointed to a cottage set slightly apart from the others. Smoke seeped through its thatch, and behind it a stone paddock held three ponies.

'They'll be the stolen horses!' John said, excited.

'Not necessarily,' said the Bailie.

'He may have arms, even a pistol,' warned Bohally.

'I suggest we sneak up and catch him unawares,' the Bailie said.

'I've never sneaked up on anyone in my life,' snorted Bohally. 'You check that he has no henchmen about. I'll go in the front.'

'There'll be no henchmen,' said the Bailie. 'Alister Breck works alone.'

'Check all the same. Johnnie, you watch the back of the cottage from up here. If he breaks, it is vital we know where he goes.'

The boy nodded. Bohally hefted his sword. It was a sabre he had taken from a dragoon on Drummossie Moor, the blade now rusted from idle years in his thatch. Then the big laird was off, leaping down through the heather. At the unnatural sight of a pair of yellow breeches covering the backside of a charging Highlander, the Bailie shook his head in disgust before plunging down the hill in pursuit.

The two men crossed the road and flitted stealthily between the small buildings. Bohally was within a yard or two of his destination when an emaciated mongrel let out an indignant yap. But, a wild charge already launched, his momentum burst him through the cottage's door of plaited heather.

A woman was ministering to a pot that hung over the fire. By the time Bohally's eyes adjusted to the smoky gloom, she was crouched in a corner, cowering on a bed of heather. The Bailie was seconds behind him.

'Where's Alister Breck?' demanded Bohally. His sword prodded the heather round her. 'Where is the wretch?'

'He's not here,' said the woman sullenly. Then she noticed the second man. 'Bailie!' she exclaimed.

'By God, it's Molly!' said the Bailie. 'What are you doing here?'

'You know her?' asked Bohally.

'So do you,' said the Bailie. 'She used to work from the inn at Blair. It was she who asked the castle to surrender when none of the rest of you had the stomach for the job.'

'Heavens, yes. Sweet Molly. The years haven't been that kind to you.'

'I could say the same about you too,' said the woman. 'You've grown fat, Tearlach Mor.'

'A good wife and comfy living,' said Bohally complacently. 'Where's Alister Breck?'

'If you're going to kill him, kill him slow. But he's not here.' Molly lifted her skirts to show an angry burn on her leg. 'He did this to me.'

'Where is he?' asked the Bailie.

'He'll be in an alehouse.'

'At Trinafour?' asked Bohally.

'It could be Bunrannoch. He should be back by dawn. They'll put him on his pony and let it take him home.'

Bohally thought for a few seconds. 'We've no choice, Bailie. We'll sleep on the hill and snatch him when he returns.'

'Why don't we tarry here?' said the Bailie.

Bohally considered. At the same moment his eye took in the pot, and his nose sniffed the air.

'Aye, there's plenty in there for the two of you,' said Molly.

'It's three,' said the big man, and he put down his sword. 'Bailie, call down the lad.'

By morning, after they told her why they were in pursuit of her paramour (and after the Bailie had hinted at the loneliness of his bothy), Molly had agreed to accompany them to Blair, where, they had said, they hoped to wring a confession of perjury from the man they hunted. That would not be necessary, Molly had told them. She herself would be pleased to testify to his villainy.

At around six o'clock, John spied Alister Breck's dapple-grey pony ambling down the highway towards them. Still half a mile away, the beast clopped sleepily along from the direction of Trinafour. Its rider was loosely trussed to the animal's back, and the man's head was buried in the pony's mane.

John was sent to collect the three other mounts from the paddock round the back. Bohally climbed onto the first one, John and Molly doubled up on the next, and the Bailie rode the third. Just as they were about to set off, John called attention to the others' naked swords. Without a word, the two men leaned over and buried their blades deep in the heather thatch of Alister Breck's cottage. John handed his cudgel to Bohally, and the caravan set out to meet the on-coming dapple-grey.

Out on the road, as they passed the drunken man's pony, the Bailie simply bent over, appropriated the club that dangled from the saddle, and gathered the animal's reins. With a snort of resignation, the dapple-grey wheeled round and fell in at the rear of the procession.

By seven, they had branched off onto a track through Glen Errochty and were almost in sight of the kirk at Struan. The Bailie's horn flask had gone up and down the caravan several times. Despite the serenade mixing cows, lost love, and misty mountains that Bohally had been regaling them with at the top of his lungs, the prisoner remained unconscious. At some point, Molly had chimed in with Bohally, harmonizing soft and sweet, her head against John's chest. At some point, the boy's hands had crept to her compliant breasts. Then, without warning, a ball fizzed over their heads, followed by the boom of a musket. A hundred yards ahead of them, powder-smoke jetted from a gully.

'Jesus!' said Bohally, reining in. 'Quick. Back we go. It must be the Big Sergeant.'

'It's Redcoats,' cried John. 'They're behind us, too.'

Two soldiers blocked the track to the rear. From the gully, four others came running towards them.

'We'll charge down the two at our backs,' said the Bailie, releasing the reins of the dapple-grey. 'Keep behind me, John.'

'Use your head, Bailie. We can't fight them.' Bohally raised his hands. 'We have no weapons,' he called out to the soldiers.

Muskets levelled, the Redcoats panted up to them.

'What do you think you're doing?' yelled Bohally. 'We might have been killed. I'll have you flogged for this.'

'Oh, yes?' The corporal in command of the party, a burly man with a missing ear and a great scar on one cheek, was unmoved by the threat. 'You're Bohally, aren't you?'

'Ha! You recognize me. You know my reputation.'

'I recognize those yellow breeches. We were on our way to arrest their owner for horse theft.'

Bohally ground his teeth. 'I am Tearlach Mor Bohally, the finest swordsman in Scotland.'

'That's not worth a bucket of piss these days,' said the corporal. Resting the butt of his musket on the ground he removed his hat and took out a plug of tobacco. He put it in his mouth and began to chew. Then he strolled from pony to pony, inspecting them and their riders.

'Morning, Molly.' He gave her a nod. 'Miserable little outfit you're with today – one stout braggart . . .'

Bohally's hand went to his cudgel but was stopped by the *tock* of a musket being cocked a couple of feet behind his back.

'. . . one snoring drunk, one beardless brat with his hands on your tits – a bit young for you, isn't he? – and him.' The corporal paused by the scowling Bailie and peered into his face. 'Do I know you?'

'Don't ask me. I can't remember the face of every English-man whose ear I've cut off.'

The Redcoat gave a whoop of laughter. 'Why, you nasty, nasty Highland man.' He stopped. 'Of course! You're the Highlander. A Frenchman sheathed his bayonet in your shoulder at Fontenoy.'

'Eh?' The Bailie's expression softened. 'I'm damned if I know you, Redcoat.'

'In the church afterwards. We were side by side, waiting for the surgeon.'

'And that damned woman stole our boots! You were the Redcoat with the bandaged head. Well, well, so you didn't die?'

'No.'

'Neither did I. It's good to see an old comrade-in-arms again.' The Bailie turned to Bohally. 'This man and I lay wounded together after the battle of Fontenoy.'

'I gathered that,' said Bohally.

'I'm sorry to see you mixed up with horse thieves,' said the corporal.

'We're not horse thieves.'

'Oh, aye? Your own horses, then, are they?'

'Yes,' said Bohally.

332

'No,' said the Bailie.

'Aha, yes and no. Now we're getting somewhere.'

'They're his,' said Bohally. He pointed to Alister Breck.

The corporal spat a stream of tobacco juice into the dust and moved to the drunken figure. Grasping him by the hair, he lifted his head. 'Are these your ponies? If they are, say so.'

The corporal let go. The head flopped back.

'No, he doesn't seem to think they're his.'

'They're telling the truth,' said Molly.

'Is that right, Molly? But truth is a variable commodity to a girl of your profession.'

'I didn't say I was telling the truth. I said they were telling the truth.'

'I trust the word of the Highland man. He says he didn't die at Fontenoy, and I believe him. I also believe he has whisky.'

'Not true,' said the Bailie, and he gave the proof by up-ending his flask. 'There is no whisky.'

The corporal broke into a wide grin. 'You see? Again his truth is evident. But I think this is one occasion when we should make him a liar.'

'Agreed,' said Bohally, who fumbled in his purse for a coin.

While a soldier repaired to Struan for a jug of whisky, everyone else moved to the shade of a copse, where all but Alister Breck sat on the grass to wait.

Later that morning, a bizarre caravan entered Blair. On the lead pony was a boy wearing a Redcoat's hat and carrying a musket. He held the reins of a burdened dapple-grey, which followed behind. Next, on a third pony, came a corporal and a woman, alongside whom – a hand on her knee – strolled the one unmounted civilian of the group. The last horse carried a big man in yellow breeches. Whirling a borrowed sword above his head, he was in the midst of some tale of derring-do. Round him, five dishevelled soldiers hung on his words.

Drawing level with the inn, the boy's arm shot up and in a piping treble he called for a halt.

Two startled faces appeared at a first-floor window. One belonged to a military officer, the other to Commissary Bissett.

'They've captured Bohally,' said Bissett.

'Bring them up here,' called the Redcoat, a major.

The room upstairs, a long, low-ceilinged chamber doubled as office and living quarters. Strewn with crumpled napkins, a dining table bore the remains of a meal from the night before. Bohally, Molly, the Bailie, and the corporal stood before the Redcoat officer.

'You've been drinking, Bohally,' said Bissett.

'Ain't we all,' drawled the officer.

'I'm glad you're here, Bissett,' growled Bohally. 'We've brought Alister Breck to clear up this pack of lies about me and Garth.'

'Lies?' said Bissett.

'Yes, this woman will confirm our innocence. She will swear that Alister Breck was the horse thief, not us.'

At a desk, a foppish lieutenant toying with a quill looked up.

'Molly,' he cried, 'you're back!'

Bohally began his tale, which was confirmed by the other two. As the story unfolded, Bissett became increasingly uncomfortable. By the time Bohally finished, the commissary was red-faced with shame.

'You see,' Bohally concluded, 'Alister Breck wanted to damage us because I'd passed word that anyone in Atholl helping the thieves would be answerable to me.'

'That was setting yourself above the law,' said Bissett.

'Stuff and nonsense,' said Bohally. 'That was upholding the law, which is the duty of every loyal subject of His Majesty. Or would you say otherwise?' He turned to the nearest Redcoat. 'Mark his answer well, general.'

'Major, actually.'

'You, Commissary, and that caitiff Kinnaird, chose to believe that miscreant' – Bohally pointed vaguely to the window – 'against two of the most honourable gentlemen in Atholl.'

'Honourable, eh?' The major suddenly took an interest. 'How dreadful, besmirching a gentleman's honour. You must challenge him.'

'What?' asked Bohally, irritated by the interruption.

'You know – challenge Mr Bissett to a duel. As the wronged party, you have choice of weapons.'

'What a frightfully good idea, sir,' said the lieutenant.

'Here . . .' Bissett was alarmed.

'Bohally's one of the finest swordsmen in Scotland,' said the Bailie.

'The finest,' corrected Bohally.

'Oh, good,' said the lieutenant. 'We've nothing on this afternoon, have we, sir?'

'No,' said the major.

'Capital! His Grace's gardens have some fine classical statuary. It would be a fitting place to settle an affair of honour.'

'You can't mean I fight Bissett!' exclaimed Bohally. 'It'd be no harder than slaughtering a pig. Besides, who'd look after Atholl when he was dead?'

'He should've thought of that before he dishonoured you,' said the lieutenant.

'For heaven's sake!' said Bissett. 'I'm not going to fight with this gentleman.'

The major was astonished. 'But you must. Otherwise you have to apologize.'

'But of course I must apologize,' said Bissett. 'By allowing the interests of His Grace to colour my judgement, I have done these gentlemen a great wrong.'

'If you apologize, you show yourself to be a coward,' said the lieutenant.

'Really?' said Bissett. 'So Bohally must fight me? He would kill me. People would say he had murdered me. I would be dead, Bohally and Garth would probably hang, and Alister Breck would escape. It all sounds a very poor idea. Atholl would be plunged into turmoil.'

'You're absolutely right,' agreed Bohally.

'Haven't the belly for it, I suppose,' said the major.

'Nowadays in the Highlands, captain, we don't consider such murder very civilized.' Bohally turned back to Bissett. 'But you've made a right arse of yourself, haven't you? You've blackened our names all over our country in an attempt to get rid of us and further your villainous schemes.'

The commissary paced to and fro. 'This is all most unfortunate, but I can assure you I acted in good faith. I'm afraid I have also written to His Grace to inform him of your alleged involvement in banditry.'

'He's not going to be pleased to hear it's a lie.'

'I don't quite understand how the duke is involved in this affair,' said the major.

'He isn't,' said Bissett.

'But he is,' contradicted Bohally. 'With Garth and me out of the way, he would have been free to steal land from an innocent widow.'

Bissett flapped his hands. 'I really cannot allow that. The error is entirely my own. His Grace has been nowhere involved. I can't tell you how much I regret this misunderstanding.'

'What, then, do you propose to do?' Bohally asked.

'There is only one course open to me. I shall register a written apology before the Court of Session.'

The Bailie nodded gravely. 'That ought to do the trick, don't you think Bohally?'

'You'll swear you wronged Garth and me before the Lords in Council in Edinburgh?' asked Bohally.

'It's the least I can do,' said Bissett. 'But I fear you'll meanwhile need a safe conduct to get home.' He gestured towards the writing table. 'I think you'd better give them an immunity to the arrest order, major.'

'I'm not sure I can,' said the major. 'It wasn't my arrest order, you see. I certainly passed on your information, Mr Bissett, but the order came from my superior officer. Until he countermands it, Bohally and his friend are still fugitive cattle thieves, and, like all such scum, are liable to be shot on sight.'

The lieutenant let out a snicker.

'That's an insult to my honour, general,' said Bohally. 'I challenge you to a duel with broadswords – here and now.'

'Oh, well said,' murmured Bissett.

The major spared the commissary an icy stare.

'Ten pounds on Bohally, at five to one on,' said the Bailie.

'Pounds sterling or Scots?' asked Bissett.

'Sterling,' said the Bailie.

'Done,' said the lieutenant.

The corporal removed his hand from Molly's bottom to ask if he could lay five shillings on Bohally.

'Now, now, don't let's be over hasty,' said the major. 'Lieutenant, I'd be obliged if you'd draw up a letter of safe conduct for these gentlemen.'

55

Strike

A fortnight later, Jean's case came to court. She and John's trustees, Garth and Bohally, went to Perth. In the same court-room, only a day earlier, the Big Sergeant was sentenced to be hanged; Alister Breck, who had informed on the cateran, was to dangle from his own gibbet at Kinloch Rannoch in the autumn.

On the morning of Jean's appearance, a small army of litigants, lawyers, and clerks packed the chamber. Meg beamed from the front row, and a number of her friends fought for space to sit. The day was breathless, and bluebottles droned above the sweating spectators. When Jean's case was called and the plaintiff took her place, the sheriff shook himself awake and, taking a sip of claret, blinked his appreciation.

The entire proceedings were matter of fact. For one moment, when he understood that the petitioner was suing her own son, the sheriff lifted an eyebrow. Ten minutes later he issued the judgement in Jean's favour. The triumph seemed complete.

Meg Mercer, insisting that Jean should stay on in Perth another few days, plunged her niece into a dizzy round of celebrations. Wherever she went, Jean received congratulations. Even the few Whigs who had always cut the Laird of Kynachan and his lady for their politics now came round to the Mercer apartments to pay their respects. But even as Jean accepted these plaudits, more than anything else her feelings were of relief and hope for the future.

On her way back to Strathtummel, she called at Castle Menzies. The warmth of Sir Robert and Lady Mary, and their delight at her news, touched Jean greatly. Less delighted was Commissary Bissett, who arrived at the castle just as Jean was leaving and requested a short interview with her.

'Have you come to acknowledge your defeat, Mr Bissett?' asked Jean, when they were alone in the library. She was pleased to see he seemed uncomfortable.

He gave a wan smile. 'I have nothing but admiration for the battle you have so far waged to retain your lands for your son, my dear lady.'

'So far? What do you mean so far?' She laughed. 'Our war is over. I have won. I am Laird of Kynachan.'

Still Bissett avoided meeting her eye. 'His Grace is displeased at the prospect of losing the revenues of the estate.'

'Och, the poor man. My heart bleeds for him,' said Jean.

'I advised the duke to accept you as his vassal the moment the court found in your favour. I now regret to tell you that His Grace has chosen to reject my counsel.'

'Pah! Your duke is powerless in this matter. He can do me no further harm.'

Jean glared at the commissary, daring him to contradict her. He did, although Jean saw that it gave him no satisfaction.

'I wish it were so, my dear,' he said. 'But you cannot beat a man like the duke – not in the real world.'

'The real world!' spat Jean. 'I'll tell you whose world is real. The one in which my husband was killed, my people harried, and my children face destitution. A pox on your duke and his machinations!'

Bissett's face expressed pain at the lash of her fury. 'His Grace has the ear of the king and the government. He will never confirm the transfer of Kynachan to you. Since he refuses to sign the Charter, the estate can never be yours.'

Jean suddenly realized that Bissett was not upset because she had beaten him. He could have put this news in a letter, but had chosen to break it himself through sympathy for her. She knew he told the truth and she felt her anger drain away, leaving an empty desolation which was all too familiar to her.

'But he must,' she said desperately. 'Under the law, his signature is a mere formality.'

'A must for the likes of us is not a must for the Duke of Atholl. His Grace has determined that Kinnaird should hold your estate.'

'Why does he persecute me so?' Jean said, her voice on the edge of tears.

'Is the reason not plain?' Bissett's voice was infinitely sad. 'He considers your family traitors. Your husband was his enemy, a rebel always strong in support of his elder brother. His Grace knows you yourself were at Blair during the siege. He will never rest until he has driven you and the last of David's seed from Atholl.'

Bissett tried to offer a few words of comfort, but Jean hardly heard. After he had left, she spent some moments by the window in a daze. The switch between triumph and disaster had been too sudden. All she wanted now was to return to Kynachan. When she had composed herself, she sought out her host and bade him farewell.

The countryside was still and sunlit as Jean rode over to Strathtummel. Cattle were spread across the hillsides, and from the small clachan near the top of the pass women's voices were raised in sweet song as they harvested a patch of tall flax. But her new despair isolated her from the tranquillity of the scene.

She reached home to find that the folk of the estate had gathered to welcome her and celebrate her success. As she rode into the yard, fiddles struck up and a torch was thrust into a bonfire at the foot of the knoll. Young John and his sisters, prettily decked out, darted and fizzed amongst the throng. The yard seethed. Bohally, the Bailie, and Donald were in charge of the whisky cask, taking a tithe of every dram they poured. After dark, she could take no more and withdrew indoors.

A short while later, concerned for her daughter-in-law, Janet went to find her. Jean was in the parlour. Slumped in a chair, she was bathed in the eerie, dancing light that came through the window from the flames of the bonfire. Hearing the older woman enter, Jean's eyes opened. What Janet saw there struck fear in her heart. Wordless, the old lady sank into the chair opposite.

In a barely audible monotone, Jean told of what had transpired at the castle. When Jean fell silent, Janet too was vanquished. As the fiddle music flooded the room, jaunty and exalting, some satanic alchemy transformed the strains into a mockery of the two women's wretchedness.

'And the others?' asked Janet eventually. 'When shall we tell them?'

'Tomorrow,' said Jean. 'We'll tell them then.'

A week later, a message arrived from Bissett. Eschewing comment, it stated three facts. The duke no longer trusted the commissary to handle the eviction of Jean and her family; His Grace had decided to keep his own counsel and handle the affair himself; and in thirty days, accompanied by a dozen retainers and a body of troops, Kinnaird would be despatched to take possession of Kynachan.

Even before Bissett's letter had been delivered, the duke's intentions had become the talk of Atholl. At once, the economy of the estate began to falter. Because tenants might be scattered to the wind by a new laird, pedlars refused to give credit in the townships. By the same token, one or two farmers refused to give credit to drovers who came round to buy cattle.

Folk looked to the Lady of Kynachan for a lead, but they soon believed that she had lost her wits and that misery had driven the *tamhasg* from her body once more to haunt the estate. The wraith-like figure ignored them as it flitted through the woods, and people averted their eyes, making the sign to ward off evil when they saw her.

Beside herself, Jean wandered the long summer evenings. Each stone, each tree, each clump of heather held David. Each had been trodden by his foot or touched by his hand. He had charged her to look after Kynachan and pass it on to their son, and she had failed. For hours, she roamed the whiskery heights and shadowed tumbling burns. In her head was singing silence. As once the living David had been snatched from her on the field of battle, now the David of her memories was about to be torn away. The last time they had loved, she had not known he would be violated in blood and fire at Culloden. This time there was foreknowledge. It was a new kind of bereavement – perhaps more terrible than before.

At night, Jean often crept from the silent house to sit alone on the knoll. With her back to the great oak, she listened to the hoot of owls, the squeak of hunting bats, and the occasional bellow of a cow from the direction of the looming mass of Craig Kynachan and the vast protecting mountain behind.

One such night, some seven days after her return from Perth, her desolate abstraction was suddenly broken. On high, the starlit sky was slashed by the silent fire of a great meteorite, and the darkness seemed to come alive with mystery. Across the waiting moors and heather, as if issuing from the heart of the fairy mountain, came the mighty roar of a stag. Clear and clarion, its blast thrilled Jean to her depths. She knew no mortal stag would roar in summer.

It was as if Schiehallion had spoken, and once again she felt the presence of David's gentle shade giving her hope, giving her strength. And she knew her war was not yet over.

56

Counterstrike

Jean revealed to no-one the means of her epiphany, but her family and people were quickened by her new-found resolution. Overnight, the Mistress of Kynachan had regained her old determination.

The Bailie and Bohally had begun arranging for the sale of stock from the mains. At the same time, Clementina had been orchestrating the preparation of a cottage across the river for the evicted family, and kitchen girls shuttled back and forth shifting the contents of the larder and storage barns. Jean interfered with none of this.

In the midst of the activity, Duncan Kennedy came over from the smithy with an announcement. Conscious of the valiant way Jean had led them during and after the Rising and of the way her larder had been open to them in times of need, the tenants of Kynachan had collected more than three hundred and fifteen pounds Scots for her as a token of their regard. It would have been more, he said, but folk were uncertain of their own futures. The interest they would charge was almost an afterthought.

Then, with only a vague word of explanation to her mother-in-law, Jean absented herself for three days and returned to Perth.

'What are you doing here, Jeannie?' exclaimed Meg, scrutinizing her niece closely. She was delighted to see Jean again so soon and further delighted to establish that she had not lost her wits, as reports stated.

'I'd heard you'd given up,' Meg said.

'Not quite. I see my lawyers tomorrow.'

Jean was exhausted, and Meg made her rest before dinner, but her peace was suddenly broken by her aunt's bellows of laughter echoing through from the parlour. When Jean rejoined her, Meg was bursting with news.

'I've just heard about Kinnaird,' she cried.

'Don't tell me,' said Jean. 'I would dearly like never to hear about Kinnaird again.'

'You'll like to hear this, my dear.'

'Have you been up to something wicked?' asked Jean, a gleam of anticipation kindling in her eyes.

'Poor man,' sighed Meg. 'I'm told urchins dog his footsteps, jeering at him.'

'All right,' said Jean. 'Let me hear.'

'I knew you'd want to,' said Meg, pouring them each a glass of wine. 'I wrote a letter last week to a friend who's a sergeant in the Edinburgh Town Guard. Have you ever met him? Robert Stewart, an Athollman, kin to Bonskeid, I believe, and uncle—'

'Come to the point, Meg,' begged Jean.

'Well, I happened to mention your fresh troubles with your brother-in-law, and guess what? Just now while you were resting, I learned that he was making his way home from a tavern the day before yesterday, when – by pure coincidence, mind – he was kidnapped by unknown ruffians.'

'Kidnapped? Kinnaird?'

'Kinnaird kidnapped.'

'Was he hurt?'

'Och, no. He didn't get a scratch.'

'What happened to him?'

'Nothing. He turned up safe and sound the following morning – bound and gagged, with his breeches down to his ankles and his arse in the air.'

'What!' Jean began to laugh.

'Shocking, isn't it? On his backside, I'm told, was a depiction of His Grace of Atholl's crest.'

'I don't believe you,' Jean gasped. 'Where was he found?'

'It gets better,' said Meg, now grinning broadly. 'You know the statue in Parliament Square of King Charles on his horse?'

Jean nodded.

'It seems the statue is hollow, and there's a wee opening in the top of His Majesty's head. Over the years the whole thing had been filling with rainwater. Kinnaird was on the plinth. Somebody had bored a hole in the horse's pizzle, and it was pissing on his arse.'

Jean was now helpless with laughter, and Meg herself was heaving like an Indiaman in a typhoon.

'There's a wee bit more,' she told Jean, pulling out a

342

handkerchief and dabbing her eyes. 'On his way to court, Lord Dundas saw the spectacle and forbade Kinnaird's release until all the other judges had seen. He was there much of the morning – and so were half the citizens of Edinburgh!'

On the road back to Atholl, Jean was regaled with the story of Kinnaird's humiliation at every township south of Glen Goulandie. So sweet was the tale that repetition did nothing to dull pleasure. She managed to outstrip the news over the pass.

Janet was in the parlour, and Jean immediately told her the story of the music master's downfall. They sat in the same places they had occupied on the night of the bonfire. This time, instead of being plunged in gloom, the two women made the room ring with mirth.

Hearing their laughter, Donald came rushing up from the kitchen, and Jean had to tell the tale again. Soon his guffaws were shaking the windows in their frames.

After the others had recovered their senses, Janet demanded to know the reason for Jean's sudden visit to Perth.

'I was preparing a little surprise of my own – for the duke,' Jean explained, her eyes still dancing with glee. 'He's not going to like it.'

'Might this tale go down better with a drop of brandy?' said Donald. His mistress did not seem to mind that he poured himself the largest measure and settled himself comfortably in an armchair.

'When the government ended the chiefs' rule over the people . . .' Jean began.

'The Abolition of Heritable Jurisdictions,' said Donald carefully.

'That's right. The duke received a fortune in compensation, but . . .'

'Typical of him to profit from the Rising,' said Janet.

'Will you two please stop interrupting!'

'Aye,' agreed Donald who glared reprovingly at Janet as his mistress took a sip from her glass.

'Well, carry on then, dear,' said the old woman.

'It doesn't seem to have dawned on anyone that as well as no longer making the law, the duke is now subject to it.'

'So?' said Janet.

'So – I have just put His Grace to the horn.'

343

In the stunned silence that followed, Donald groped for the bottle.

'You can't!' Janet said to her daughter-in-law. 'It's inconceivable for people like us to horn the duke.'

'No man, let alone a woman, has ever dared do such a thing before,' said Donald. 'It won't work.'

'Maybe not, but try to imagine it,' Jean said, and she laid out the scene for them.

One day the following week, with the Edinburgh drizzle sparkling on the clothes of the bustling citizens, one James Thomson, an official of the court, marches solemnly down the crowded High Street, past the High Kirk of St Giles, to the Mercat Cross.

They're horning the duke, the word goes round, they're horning the duke.

A horning. A subject's last resort when a judgement in his favour recorded by the Lords of Council and Session is ignored.

On this day, a mighty potentate of Scotland is to be shamed by one of his vassals – a mere woman. A ripple runs through the onlookers. This may not be a hanging but on this grey September morning it is no mean substitute. The proud Duke of Atholl, should he not bend to her wishes, will be declared a traitor.

Thomson pauses. In spite of the fine rain, he takes off his hat and holds it across his breast. Squaring his shoulders, he looks round. The crowd is the largest he has seen at a horning. He clears his throat, takes a stiff parchment, one of several carried by an attendant, unrolls it, and declaims:

In His Majesty's name, I command and charge, James, Duke of Atholl, to confirm Jean Mercer, widow of David Stewart, in the lands of Kynachan herein mentioned. Under pain of rebellion against the Crown.

A second assistant opens a way through the crowd, and Thomson marches over to Parliament House, where he fixes one of the parchments to the wall. The crowd presses in to see. The attendant holds people back, and the official proceeds to attach another copy of the letters of horning a few yards farther along. Satisfied with his work, he and his two helpers set off for Leith, where the same solemn proceeding will be repeated on the Pier and at the Shore. In a short time, all Scotland will hear of it.

Back in the parlour at the mansion house there was a thrilled silence when Jean had finished.

'Duke James accused of rebellion!' Janet breathed. 'By God, that word alone will shrivel his miserable soul.'

When she looked into the exultant face of her son's widow, Janet found her own eyes full of tears.

'Ah, my lady,' said Donald dreamily, cradling the empty brandy bottle on his lap. 'It's a fine, fine story you tell. The equal of any bard's in Atholl.'

'It's a masterpiece,' said Jean, hugging herself with delight. 'Whatever the outcome, I, Jeannie Mercer, will have publicly branded the Duke of Atholl rebel and traitor. Is not the irony beautiful?'

On 30 September 1751, James, Duke of Atholl, Lord of Man and the Isles, Marquess of Tullibardine, Earl of Strathtay and Strathardle, Viscount of Balquhidder, Glenalmond and Glenlyon, Baron Strange, Lord Murray, Balvenie and Gask, Lord Keeper of the Privy Seal of Scotland, signed the charter. And Jean Mercer, relict of the deceased David Stewart, was confirmed Laird of Kynachan.

Envoy

A couple of hundred yards from where the charge of the Atholl Brigade was halted on Drummossie Moor on 16 April 1746 stood the cluster of stone buildings of the farmstead named Leanach.

On that day, after the government army moved off the field in pursuit of the retreating Jacobite army, some of the rebel wounded were helped or carried to the shelter of one of the outbuildings by their more lightly wounded comrades or by the compassionate amongst the beggars who had come onto the field to loot the dead.

The only names recorded amongst these twenty or so wounded were Archibald Menzies of Shian, David Stewart of Kynachan, and Colonel O'Reilly, an officer in the French service attached to Ogilvy's Regiment.

Shortly after the battle, Cumberland posted guards round the moor and forbade anyone on or off the field. The wounded lay neglected in the open. Forty-eight hours later, government troops were despatched over the battlefield to bayonet anyone who still lived.

At the approach of these soldiers, about a dozen beggars took refuge with those inside the Leanach barn. The troops barred the door and set the building alight, killing all within. Later, spectators came from Inverness to view the charred corpses.

Adjacent to the Visitor Centre at Culloden, the National Trust for Scotland has rebuilt Old Leanach farmhouse. A plaque on the ground marks the site of the barn where David Stewart died.

THE END

MARIANA
by Susanna Kearsley

As soon as Julia Beckett saw Greywethers, a handsome sixteenth-century farmhouse in a small Wiltshire village, she had a strange feeling that she was destined to live in it one day. But when, many years later, it became her home, she found that the house's turbulent past began to intrude upon the present.

While becoming friendly with the residents of the village, including Geoffrey de Mornay, the handsome young squire, Iain, a local farmer, and Vivien, the village pub landlady, Julia found herself being transported back in time as Mariana, who lived at Greywethers during the great plague of 1665. She experienced, as Mariana, all the terrors and hardships of that grim time, and the dangers of the Civil War's aftermath, as well as falling in love with Richard de Mornay, the forebear of the present squire. As her present-day relationships prospered, Julia increasingly felt that her other life as Mariana was threatening to overwhelm her. She found that she had to play out the ancient drama and exorcise the past before she could find love and happiness in the present.

Mariana is the second winner of the Catherine Cookson Prize which was set up in 1992 to celebrate the achievement of Dame Catherine Cookson.

0 552 14262 X

LEGACY OF LOVE
by Caroline Harvey

Charlotte was the first – wildly beautiful, wildly frustrated – who married her soldier husband solely to escape from the claustrophobic respectability of Victorian life in Richmond. When she reached the British lines in Kabul she was bewitched and fascinated by the exotic world of Afghanistan – and by Alexander Bewick, the scandalous adventurer who aroused an instant response in Charlotte's rebellious heart. As the city of Kabul turned into a hell of bloodshed and misery, Charlotte was forced to choose between her devoted husband, and her reckless lover.

Alexandra lived – always – in the shadow of her legendary grandmother, Charlotte. Reared in a gloomy Scottish castle by a mother who resented her, she finally had to reach out and try to create a life of her own.

Cara had inherited the wildness, the passion, and also the selfishness of her great-grandmother Charlotte. Smouldering with resentment because she had to help care for her crippled mother when her friends were all joining up at the outbreak of the Second World War, she finally found, as the tragedies of the war began to erode her life, that she also had the courage of Charlotte – a courage that was eventually to bring her happiness.

Caroline Harvey is the pseudonym of the award-winning writer Joanna Trollope.

0 552 13872 X

ZADRUGA
by Margaret Pemberton

In Belgrade, in the balmy spring of 1914, neither of the royally related Karageorgevich sisters had the slightest presentiment of disaster. Seventeen-year-old Natalie was enjoying the danger and secrecy of friendship with young nationalists, eager to free their lands from Habsburg domination. Katerina, her less volatile sister, was deeply and secretly in love with Julian Fielding, a young English diplomat.

Then, when accompanying their father on an official visit to Sarajevo, Natalie inadvertently plunged their lives into chaos as she found herself caught up in the assassination of Franz Ferdinand. As the Austrians demanded her extradition Natalie had no choice but to flee the homeland she so passionately loved. She chose to leave in a manner that was to prove catastrophic – as the bride of Julian Fielding, the man her sister loved.

0 552 13987 4

THE HUNGRY TIDE
by Valerie Wood

In the slums of Hull, at the turn of the eighteenth century, lived Will and Maria Foster, constantly fighting a war against poverty, disease, and crime. Will was a whaler, wedded to the sea, and when tragedy struck, crippling him for life, it was John Rayner, nephew of the owner of the whaling fleet, who was to rescue the family. Will had saved the boy's life on an arctic voyage and they were offered work and a home on the headlands of Holderness, on the estate owned by the wealthy Rayner family. And there, Will's third child was born – Sarah, a bright and beautiful girl who was to prove the strength of the family.

As John Rayner, heir to the family lands and ships, watched Sarah grow into a serene and lovely woman, he became increasingly aware of his love for her, a love that was hopeless, for the gulf of wealth and social standing between them made marriage impossible.

Against the background of the sea, the wide skies of Holderness, and the frightening crumbling of the land that meant so much to them, their love story was played out to its final climax.

The Hungry Tide is the first winner of the Catherine Cookson Prize which was set up in 1992 to celebrate the achievement of Dame Catherine Cookson.

0 552 14118 6

THE LAND OF NIGHTINGALES
by Sally Stewart

1919 – when Phoebe Maynard – after her mother had died – found the old journal in the attic it reminded her of several things – of her early childhood growing up in Spain, of her father's distress whenever she spoke of that country, and of her mother's long years of fretful ill-health once they had returned to their Oxfordshire manor house. Phoebe, and her sister, Lydia, had never understood why the 'land of nightingales' was such an emotive subject within the family, but when their father died it suddenly became clear. His will revealed that Phoebe and Lydia had a Spanish half-brother – Juan Rodriguez.

It seemed that Juan was as shocked as they were by his foreign connections and was determined to have nothing to do with his English relatives – but the blood-tie was there.

As Phoebe and Lydia finally found a happiness of their own in England, the past constantly intruded on their tranquil lives. It was when young Holly, Phoebe's orphaned niece-by-marriage, came onto the scene that the two worlds met and exploded into an emotional turmoil that was to be made even more violent as Holly and Juan found themselves caught up in the turbulence of the Spanish Civil War.

'A marvellous panoramic book . . . I feel very impressed indeed'
Susan Sallis

0 552 14296 4

A SELECTED LIST OF FINE NOVELS
AVAILABLE FROM CORGI BOOKS

THE PRICES SHOWN BELOW WERE CORRECT AT THE TIME
OF GOING TO PRESS. HOWEVER TRANSWORLD PUBLISHERS
RESERVE THE RIGHT TO SHOW NEW RETAIL PRICES ON
COVERS WHICH MAY DIFFER FROM THOSE PREVIOUSLY
ADVERTISED IN THE TEXT OR ELSEWHERE.

☐	14058 9	**MIST OVER THE MERSEY**	*Lyn Andrews*	£4.99
☐	14049 X	**THE JERICHO YEARS**	*Aileen Armitage*	£4.99
☐	13992 0	**LIGHT ME THE MOON**	*Angela Arney*	£4.99
☐	14044 9	**STARLIGHT**	*Louise Brindley*	£4.99
☐	13952 1	**A DURABLE FIRE**	*Brenda Clarke*	£4.99
☐	13255 1	**GARDEN OF LIES**	*Eileen Goudge*	£5.99
☐	13686 7	**THE SHOEMAKER'S DAUGHTER**	*Iris Gower*	£4.99
☐	13688 3	**THE OYSTER CATCHERS**	*Iris Gower*	£4.99
☐	13977 7	**SPINNING JENNY**	*Ruth Hamilton*	£4.99
☐	14139 9	**THE SEPTEMBER STARLINGS**	*Ruth Hamilton*	£4.99
☐	13872 X	**LEGACY OF LOVE**	*Caroline Harvey*	£4.99
☐	13917 3	**A SECOND LEGACY**	*Caroline Harvey*	£4.99
☐	14138 0	**PROUD HARVEST**	*Janet Haslam*	£4.99
☐	14262 X	**MARIANA**	*Susanna Kearsley*	£4.99
☐	14045 7	**THE SUGAR PAVILION**	*Rosalind Laker*	£5.99
☐	14002 3	**FOOL'S CURTAIN**	*Claire Lorrimer*	£4.99
☐	13737 5	**EMERALD**	*Elisabeth Luard*	£5.99
☐	13910 6	**BLUEBIRDS**	*Margaret Mayhew*	£4.99
☐	13904 1	**VOICES OF SUMMER**	*Diane Pearson*	£5.99
☐	10375 6	**CSARDAS**	*Diane Pearson*	£4.99
☐	13987 4	**ZADRUGA**	*Margaret Pemberton*	£4.99
☐	13636 0	**CARA'S LAND**	*Elvi Rhodes*	£4.99
☐	13870 3	**THE RAINBOW THROUGH THE RAIN**	*Elvi Rhodes*	£4.99
☐	13545 3	**BY SUN AND CANDLELIGHT**	*Susan Sallis*	£4.99
☐	14162 3	**SWEETER THAN WINE**	*Susan Sallis*	£4.99
☐	13845 2	**RISING SUMMER**	*Mary Jane Staples*	£3.99
☐	13299 3	**DOWN LAMBETH WAY**	*Mary Jane Staples*	£4.99
☐	14296 4	**THE LAND OF NIGHTINGALES**	*Sally Stewart*	£4.99
☐	14118 6	**THE HUNGRY TIDE**	*Valerie Wood*	£4.99
☐	14263 8	**ANNIE**	*Valerie Wood*	£4.99